Pollen

Also by Jeff Noon

Vurt

Pollen

Jeff
Noon

Crown Publishers, Inc./New York

Published by Crown Publishers, Inc., 201 East 50th Street,
New York, New York, 10022.
Member of the Crown Publishing Group.

Random House, Inc. New York, Toronto, London, Sydney, Auckland

Originally published in Great Britain by Ringpull Press in 1995

CROWN is a trademark of Crown Publishers, Inc.

Printed in the U.S.A.

Design by Jennifer Harper

Library of Congress Cataloging-in-Publication Data

Noon, Jeff.
Pollen / Jeff Noon.
1. Hay fever—Patients—England—Manchester—Fiction. I. Title
PR6064.045P65 1996
823′.914—dc20   95-34551
ISBN 0-517-59990-2

10 9 8 7 6 5 4 3 2 1

First American Edition

For Julie

John Barleycorn

There were three men came out of the west
Their fortune for to try
And these three men made a solemn vow
John Barleycorn must die.
They've ploughed, they've sown, they've harrowed him in
Threw clods upon his head
And these three men made a solemn vow
John Barleycorn was dead.
They've let him lie for a very long time
Till the rains from heaven did fall
And little Sir John sprung up his head
And so amazed them all.
They've hired men with the scythes so sharp
To cut him off at the knee
They've hired men with the sharp pitchforks
Serving him most barbarously.
They've hired men with the flailing sticks
To cut him skin from bone
And the miller he has served him worse than that
For he's ground him between two stones.
And little Sir John in the nut brown beer
And the whisky in the glass
And little Sir John in the nut brown beer
Proved the strongest man at last.

Anon.

The Sneeze

May 7th

Sunday, 6.19 a.m.

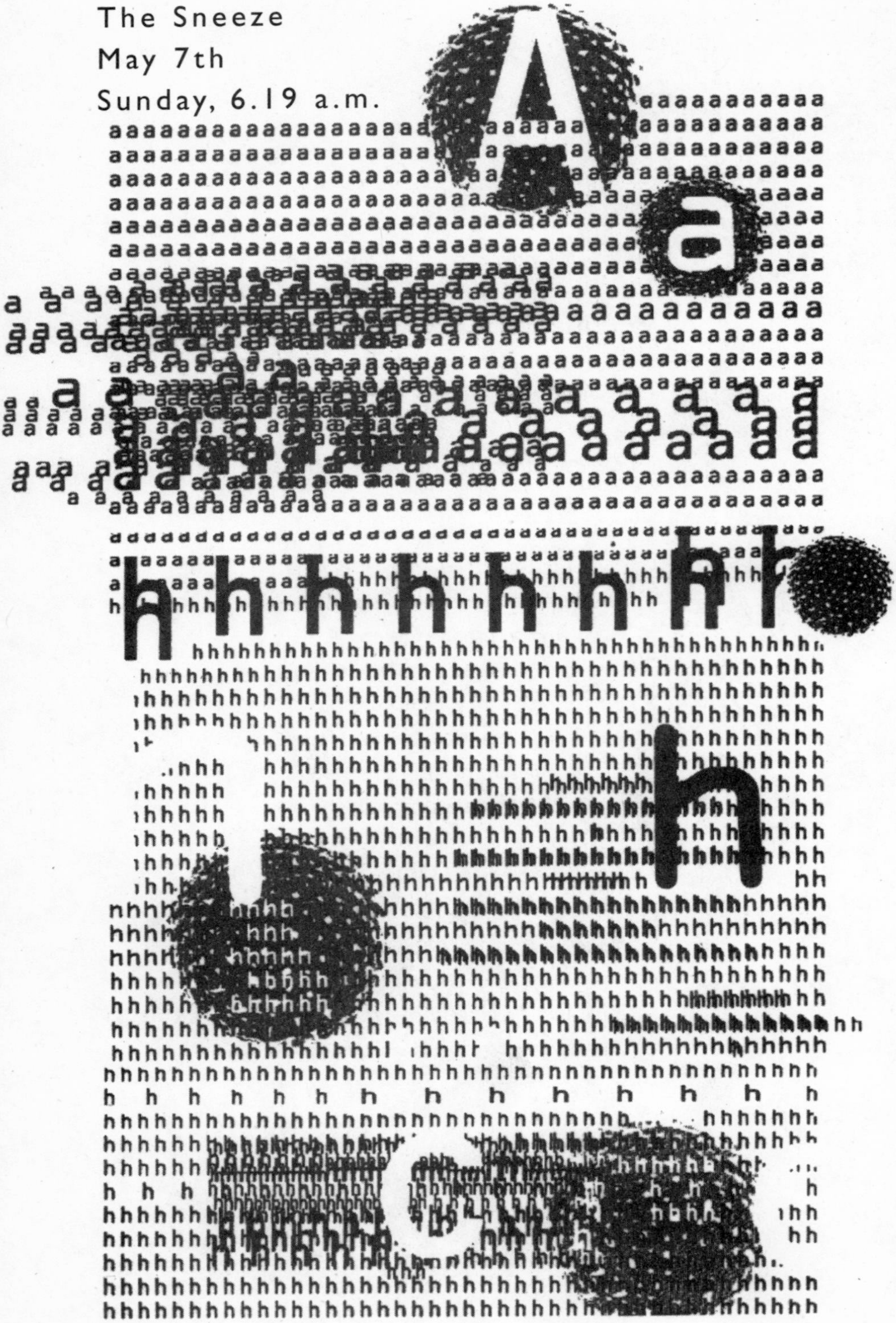

Extracted from *The Looking Glass Wars*
by R. B. Tshimosa

There is now little doubt that one of the most important discoveries of the last century was the ability to record dreams onto a replayable medium, a bio-magnetic tape coated with *Phantasm* liquid. This liberation of the psyche, in its most advanced form, became known as Vurt. Through the gates of Vurt the people could re-visit their own dreams, or, more dangerously, visit another person's dream, a stranger's dream.

It is generally accepted that this 'doorway between reality and dream' was first opened by the amorphologist 'Miss Hobart,' but the actual origins of the Vurt and the method by which human beings travelled there (via 'dream-feathers' which were placed into the mouth) will always be shrouded in mystery.

Much of this frustrating lack of knowledge stems from the nature of the Vurt itself, because the 'world of dreams' very quickly achieved a life of its own. The early people of Earth were, in the main, ignorant of this aspect of the invention. It was this 'self-dreaming' attribute of the Vurt world that eventually led to that series of battles we now call the Looking Glass Wars. This book will attempt a dispassionate overview of the terrible wars between the dream and reality, a conflict in which both parties would suffer terrible losses before an eventual victor was declared.

All the great theories of warfare can be reduced to a manifestation of greed. Thus it was that the creatures of the dream, as they grew more powerful, started to despise and look down upon the original dreamers, whom they called the mere 'storytellers' of planet Earth. Indeed, the creatures of the dream now saw their fantastic realm as a separate world, Planet Vurt. The 'Vurtuals' longed for independence.

One particularly weak point in the barrier between dream and reality existed in the psychic air that surrounded Manchester, a rain-drenched city to the north-west of Singland (which was known in those primitive days by the name 'England'). It was in this fabled city that the incident now called the *Pollination* took place. This is generally believed to be one of the earliest skirmishes in the Looking Glass Wars . . .

Monday
1 May

My father told me that I would live as many years as the grains of dust I could hold in one hand. Consequently I have lived to such an advanced age that now, when my body is ravaged by time, and powerless, all I have left to me is this voice, this shadow, this urge to tell.

My name is Jones. A simple gift made uncommon by the Christian name my father gave to me—Sibyl. Sibyl Jones. I was born with the curse of the *Unbeknownst,* which meant that I was never able to dream. Imagine, a life of unpopulated sleep, in the days when the whole world was addicted to Vurt feathers, the shared dream. The state of *Unbeknowing* is a genetic lack; six per cent of the populace would always suffer from this inability. The ones who could dream called us the *Dodos,* the flightless birds. Often, in my youth, I would envision the Dodo part of my body as a river of dark, sterile liquid in my veins. At other times, a black, hungry beetle seemed to be alive in my stomach, gorging himself on my just-born dreams.

This was my curse. The gates to Wonderland were locked.

My salvation was the gift of the Shadow, which allowed me access to other people's thoughts. I was a head-tripper, a mind-reader, living my life at one remove. One hundred and fifty-two years I have lived in this state, and the dust gets everywhere. Every orifice is clogged with it. The folded map of the brain becomes a drifting garden of powder.

It was not always so.

Once I was young and juicy, constantly wet—whether with blood, or love, or drink—well, it matters little. Take it as read: I was making recompense for the lack of a dream. I was a willing

participant in the flood of ripeness, a willing victim of biology. But
oh, the dust came to me, earlier than most, so that I got old before
my time—my husband left me because of this, my daughter left me
—until all that remained was the urge towards a non-specific justice.
I became a Shadowcop in the employ of the Manchester Police,
lending my telepathy to their interrogations. And all things in those
days were neat and deftly placed; my life became a long crusade
against crime and betrayal, and, beneath that, a river of alcohol and
smoke and loneliness was roaring. My life was at home with this
pattern of denial.

It was all soon to go astray.

I want to tell you this story, my daughter, this story of fragments gathered from Manchester: flowers and dogs and dreams and
the broken maps of love. I think it's time. Soon she will die, this
mother of yours, this woman of dust that I have become. Please
listen closely. This is my story, your story; my shadow, your shadow;
my life of drifting air, my book, my Sibylline book . . .

Coyote is the best black-cab driver of all time. He's taken more
people more miles, to stranger places, in stranger times, with less
hassle, less shit on the windscreen, with slicker twists of the wheel,
deeper moves on the map, with fewer accidents, fewer wrong turn-
ings, fewer complaints, fewer refunds, along more shortcuts and
outlawed roads, and with more *gravitas,* for less money, and with
more wounds to show for it all than any other driver could even
imagine.

Two minutes to four in the morning, May 1, the world is
fluttering all around him; dark birds, wings of soot, black fields and
a blinded moon. Also, it's just about to start to rain. Badly. This
matters little; Coyote is a top dog driver and now his jaws are
slobbering at the thought of some rich meat, some golden fare,
some big juicy muscle of money.

Meat and money: twin dreams, a way to pay back the debts.

God knows Coyote has enough of them. Debts to the banker, debts to the court, debts to the little girl who lives down the lane. This is what he calls his daughter, a sweet kid he sees now and again, and whose mother—Coyote's ex-wife—is constantly asking for more support payments. Coyote doesn't mind paying, in fact he likes paying; it's just that he doesn't have much money at the moment.

Everybody, everywhere—they all want money.

So does Coyote. Not too much, mind. Just enough would be fine. Just enough to pay off his debts and then some for himself. He has the idea that maybe he will head on down to sunny Pleasureville one day. Set up a little cab service there, sit in an office, watching the fares flood into his system. Live the life of a pedigree for a change. For the first time in years, Coyote has started thinking about the future again. If he can just get some capital together, some buried *bones* together. He'd vowed he'd never return to Limbo, but this is a lean period for good rides.

Now Coyote is waiting on this big meaty trip, booked two days ago, time and place specified to the last digit; fare to be paid at the drop-off point. He knows that most of the regular drivers insist upon money up front, but Coyote is old-fashioned. That's why he drives a black cab. He even has the original fare-meter up and working. Modified to his own specifications of course, but still— nobody does that any more. Coyote is *unique,* and so proud of it. It's just that unique gets kind of lonely after a while.

The time on his dashboard clock blinks back at him. It's 4.02 in the morning. The fare is late. Thick-bellied clouds are gathering over the moorland track where he's parked, looking like the first stirrings of a wet dream, and still no sign of the passenger. Coyote is getting nervous. Not about the threat of rain; Coyote has driven fares through hurricanes. Nor about the dark world all around him. In fact he likes the darkness. These days most of the rides he takes are highly illegal, and the darker the better is the rule. It's getting close to the daylight and, if the passenger doesn't turn up soon, he is going to call the whole trip off, and that is that. Time is Coyote's main enemy. Time is where the daylight lives, and there the cops live too; sitting fat and desperate, waiting for some outsider-dog like Coyote to speed along, breaking the rules. He's broken the rules before—Coyote lives to break the rules, that's his job in life—but one careless day he had been caught for it, and was still paying off the fine. He wants to pay off the fine—that's the human in him. But still, this isn't something he wants to repeat. Trouble is, he just can't stop breaking the rules. That's the Dalmatian in him.

Coyote is a half-and-half creature.

He stubs his Napalm cigarette in the dashboard ashtray, grabs another pack from the glove compartment, gets out of the cab, breaks the airtight plastic wrap open with his claws, lights up another cig, leans against the cab, watches the clouds dancing for a while. Through the gloom the dark moors seem to be moving. Coyote is feeling nervous; he's the only dogman for miles around, and the Zombies are gathering around him in the fields of the night. He knows that the moors of Limbo belong to these half-dead monsters, but this is where the big fares live. Is the top dog driver going to give up on that chance? Some jumping flea-jitters shiver through his skin, and suddenly these dead fields are too much to take; he needs some human company, some voices. He reaches into the cab to turn the ignition, and then strokes the radio. As usual he's tuned into FM Dog National. Those sanitized howlings from the Dog Jockeys and all those records they play, sugar-coated bones sung by sweet young bitchgirls, are not right for his current mood. He wants something more human, something to appeal to the *human* side of his soul. Leaning in through the open cab window he retunes the radio until he reaches Radio YaYa. The fading moments of a long-ago song transform into a voice deep and slow and as parched as the earth Coyote is standing on . . .

'And that was *John Barleycorn Must Die* by The Traffic, a mighty folk-rock paean to the regenerative spirit of Mother Earth coming to us from nineteen sixty-nine. Sure was a fine year, and a lovely touch of flute in there—you catching me, people? This is the good Gumbo himself starting the new day, May the first, the day of fertility, with a wish that John Barleycorn keeps on rising. As long as he keeps his polleny fingers out of this old hippy's nose. The time is four minutes past four, and the pollen count for today is coming in at 49 grains per cubic metre and steady. This is day one of the sneezing season, so Gumbo YaYa says to all his listeners, keep a clean and sweet pair of nostrils about you. Coming up in the next hour the official news from Wanita-Wanita, plus all the stuff the Authorities don't want you knowing about. You know that's why you love the Gumbo so much. And now a hot twist from sixty-six, *Are You Experienced* by the Jimi Hendrix Experience. Play some loving guitar for me, Jimi . . . Ya Ya!'

This will do. This ragged noise makes Coyote want to howl. Gumbo YaYa is a pirate DJ broadcasting a diet of 1960s classics along with classified information stolen from the cop-banks. All of which comes floating from some unknown location in Manchester. Gumbo YaYa is an anarchist trickster figure, strictly anti-authoritarian and this appeals to Coyote's psyche. Coyote leaves the radio to play and then turns on the cab's headlights. They cut two dying, yellow paths through the air, illuminating a huge but withered oak tree. Coyote drags deep on the cig, looking at the new pack for its message; SMOKING MAKES YOU LOOK COOL —HIS MAJESTY'S IMAGE CONSULTANT. He manages a small grin, just to keep the fear at bay, and then looks back at the clouds.

Coyote loves the rain. It makes him think of the streets of Manchester. And he loves his Napalms. But best of all he loves his black cab.

You just can't get hold of these cabs any more, not since Xcabs appeared on the scene. Xcabs! With their computerized, super-slick vehicles, all armour-plated yellow-and-black paint jobs.

Designed by accountants, driven by retards. Xcabs were latter-day
self-styled Knights of the Road, and there were a thousand rumours
surrounding them. Coyote's street-smarts told him that most of the
rumours were true. For example, that the drivers were drained of
all previous life-knowledge, fixed up with robo implants and a complex knowledge of the streets. That the overall system was run by
some nebulous cab-creature calling himself Columbus. That the cabs
had guns mounted on the front, just next to the headlights. That
the drivers were in some way prescient, they knew you wanted a
taxi even before you knew it yourself. Nowadays you called a cab,
Xcabs turned up within less than a minute, guaranteed.

But not Coyote. He's a real antique-scenario. Oh God, how
he hates those Xcabbers.

He grinds his cigarette into the dirt road. Lights up another
immediately, because suddenly he is thinking about Boda. Boda is
one of the Xcab drivers, and she and Coyote have met up a few
times at late-night cafes, and got to talking. Coyote had had to water
down his image of Xcabbers—Boda came out shining in Coyote's
eyes. She was the genuine diamond, the one he had always been
looking for. Coyote was dazzled by her presence, especially when
she made up a song for him, just sitting there in that late-night cafe,
the smokiness of her voice erecting his fur in tingles of joy. They
had chatted until the street lamps went off, and it seemed to Coyote
that the Xcabber was getting right inside his mind, speaking to him
direct. It was like he had no secrets left. This made him think maybe
she was one of the Shadowgirls, but he didn't like to ask. Because
weren't Dogs and Shadows sworn enemies? And anyway, weren't
the drivers supposed to just live for the Xcab Hive and that was it?
So why was this glamorous specimen talking to him then? And why
the traces of Shadow reaching into Coyote's mind? Surely Xcabs
would have removed those wayward features. But he could see the
fear in her eyes as she talked to him, like she was sinning against
some kind of hidden code. So Coyote had kept his jaws closed on

that score, regaling her, instead, with tales of his black-cab adventures. Boda had seemed to love all this; she had promised to pass some business his way, stuff that was too illegal for Xcabs. Xcabs couldn't operate beyond the city's boundaries.

This is the reason Coyote's standing here, in the fading darkness, waiting for a pick-up miles from anywhere. Boda had given him the number to ring and a dark-tongued voice had answered his call: *Proceed to The Floating Pig, carry on past it, taking the dirt track second on the left. Proceed three hundred yards down the track to the withered tree. Wait just there, four o'clock in the morning. Wait for fifteen minutes. If nobody turns up, leave. You catch that?*

He caught it. Now here he is, standing around and waiting, the morning coming on strong in a mini-dress of orange. Why was Boda being so good to him? Coyote couldn't answer. It had been ages since goodness had lapped at his bowl. Why now? All he could do was thank her with a kiss, and then proceed to his destination. But that kiss had sparked something within him, a recognition of the good times long gone, and those yet to come, like the mileage on a black cab's clock; roads taken and untaken.

There is a noise to the right of him, out beyond where his headlights fade. He turns to look, but can see nothing, only the parched grass moving in slow waves like thickened tongues in the night. He goes for a deep sniff, letting the whole of the landscape into his nostrils. He catches the ozone bass of the rain clouds, and the tart mid-range sterility of the grass and earth, and some high, treble note he can't place. But nothing dangerous, nothing human or half-human. Not yet.

He leans against the driver's door, cig in mouth, listening to Gumbo YaYa introducing the next record, watching the clouds getting heavier, and thinking about his daughter, and about driver Boda, and the time, and how it is all running out, for him and for everybody else, all his big-money-grabbing so-called friends, *unless this fucking fare turns up!*

He drags the Napalm down to the filter, throws it away. It glows for a moment, lighting up a small patch of earth. The earth was one step away from death around here, since the Bad Blood had fallen. Thanatos, the big papers had called it. The cheaper ones called it Limp, or Gaga or Mothballer. Christ! Did it matter what they called it? The world beyond the cities was a desert of dreams. It rained about once every six months this far out from the towns, and they say there are some *holes* in the world in these parts. Trust Coyote to get the job of driving through it all, on the dark roads, with maybe some bad passenger on board. If they ever make an entrance, that is. It was now 4.10 and still no sign. Sometimes Coyote thought that Manchester was the last wet place on earth, and it was this that made him long for its dampened streets. He curses the fact that he is out here, maybe waiting on nothing, just some crazy rumour that Boda has heard. Maybe there isn't a fare. The only legal transport that works the Limbo is the big monster trucks of Vaz International as they smooth their way from city to city. He had passed one on the way to the pick-up point: a massive juggernaut filled with firepower and floodlights, a screaming steel banshee in the night that had almost caused Coyote to total his black cab into the darkness. This road isn't even on any of the official maps. Of course Coyote doesn't hold with official maps. He has the world inside his head. Like a dog urinating on lamp posts, Coyote marks out his territory as he comes to it.

Coyote is a map.

He lifts his snout to the wind, sniffing out the odours of storm, and then glances down at his watch.

4.12.

The sun is making a pink glimmer at the edges of his world. The day is fast approaching, and unless he delivers this fare within the next hour Coyote could well find himself out on a fragment, driving in Limboland, giving free rides to Zombies and other undesirables. It just wasn't on. Didn't they realise that time was death? *If you got the seconds wrong . . .*

Something screamed in the distance: a terrible keening, a high, scratching sound, like grit inside an eyeball.

Coyote fires up a replacement Napalm, sucks deep of the smoke and then looks out over the moors, watching for the parasites. Mostly they were called Zombies, sometimes Ghosts, sometimes the Half-alivers. Like most things these days they had many names. And Limbo was where they lived, but not from choice. Strict regulations kept them out of the towns and the cities. So this dried-up expanse of wind-beaten rock and earth had become a nesting place. But they couldn't resist the warmth of human companionship, and the few passing cars were the perfect chance to hitch an illegal ride back home. Coyote isn't too worried. He has a lot of dog in him, and a Dog can beat a Zombie, on a good day. Still, best to keep an eye and a nostril open.

He looks at his watch again. 4.15. The sun is definitely up and running along the edges of the night. Maybe it is time to call this ride off? Didn't they say wait until 4.15 and then get out of there? Now it's raining. Just his luck. It rains twice a year, Coyote catches a shower. But it wasn't a Manchester kind of rain, more of a viscous flood of thick liquid; looks like being a real drenching session. Another scream from the darkness. There are only so many terrifying screams in the night that a young dogboy can take. Coyote places his paw on the cab's doorhandle, turning it to open . . .

But listen . . . listen and smell. Just now, just on the edge of a new day . . . he catches the scent of flowers.

Flowers! In this part of the world? On the moorlands? It just doesn't make sense. Nothing can grow in such germ-ridden, festering soil. Bad Blood has rained on these lands.

So what exactly is this aroma?

Petunia. Jasmine. Rosemary. Primrose. Several other scents in there as well, intermingling—his usually all-knowing nose unable to distinguish the various elements. The smell is making him want to sneeze. Coyote suffers from hayfever, every year, no exceptions. Was this going to be a bad season?

Leaves shiver on the oak tree. Something dark nudges into Coyote's vision. Shit, there weren't any leaves on that tree, Coyote was certain of this. What, exactly, was shivering?

Two people appear out of the mist. A man and a child. The man is carrying a large sack. They don't smell like Zombies; this is Coyote's first reaction. They smell like a garden, an unruly rain-sodden wilderness.

The child is hiding under an extra-long anorak, hood up, draw-string pulled tight, so that you can't see anything of her, only the eyes. Eyes of bright emerald shining out from the darkness of her hood.

Coyote knows that the child is female, maybe ten or eleven, right on the edge of puberty. He can tell this from the smell, the smell of young girl. The scent is sweet and high, in relief against the smell of the rain, which is acrid and sour. The rain is making a sleek mess of Coyote's fur. Coyote has the uncomfortable feeling that these people are bringing the rain with them. He can smell the flowers real strong now. His nostrils are being invaded. Coyote is sneezing. He squashes his cig underfoot, into the soft mud that is forming there, opens the cab door, gets in, turns off the good Gumbo.

Coyote knows his place.

The girl climbs into the back of the cab, plumping herself down on the leatherette seats. The man is banging on the boot with one hand, demanding it be opened. Coyote activates the boot-switch, and he feels the cab groan slightly under the new load of the sack. The man comes round to Coyote's window. He has a face made out of soot. 'She's got the fare,' he says. His voice is like mud being stirred up on a rainy day. 'You know where she's going?'

Coyote doesn't even nod, he's too busy spreading *Sneeza Freeza* on his nostrils. With his unjuiced other hand he activates the meter, the flag fall. This was what the old boys called the initial fare. It comes from way back, when a green flag had dropped down from the mechanism, indicating that the cab was chosen. Coyote still calls it that, even though the green flag has long vanished; that's the kind of guy he is. The meter comes up all green and shiny: 3.80. Standard fare, one passenger. He hits the extras button for the sack-luggage. It comes up with a 0.60 for the weight. Then he pressed the button marked L for Limbo, and the meter lights up a cool 400.20, which is what he charges for a pick-up outside the cities. Limbo-driving is very dangerous, and Coyote reckons he's worth every penny.

'Alexandra Park, Manchester,' the man says. 'You got that?'

Coyote ignores him.

Black cab sure is a beauty; just listen to that old engine ticking! Coyote feels the power coming on. The Knowledge. That's what the drivers call it—the Knowledge of all the streets: where they all lie, how dangerous they are, what lies in wait in all the dark shadows. Coyote is running it already.

The back wheels spin up a cloud of mud as he moves off. The man is hanging on to the door. Maybe he gets some friction burns that day.

Like who the fuck cares?

4.22.

The day is already up, soon to be light; now it will be even more difficult to steal past the City Guards on duty, they will be checking all incoming vehicles for Zombies. Coyote is going to have to play this neat, maybe take a hidden door through Frontier Town. There can't be many city dwellers with Coyote's knowledge of the hidden roads into and out of Limbo. Time back he used to take some Vurt feathers to help him drive. But he came to know that his edge was crumbling. Nowadays, Coyote drives naked, featherless. The cab's headlights pick up images of dead trees and the burnt out carcasses of cars. He is driving like a Zombie himself, totally at one with the knowledge of the real and its shadow.

Zombies were the curse of every driver's life. Coyote had heard tales in the all-night cafes about cars found lodged in some

slimy ditch somewhere down a back street of Manchester, the
drivers' bodies jammed in the seat, hands still clenched on the
steering wheel. There were various stories about the state of
the bodies. That all of their teeth had been removed. That their
heads had been severed, and placed on the front of the hood like
some Rolls-Royce Spirit of Ecstasy. That their genitals were found
inside the petrol tank. Coyote doesn't know what to believe. All he
wants, all that he can do, his only skill, is to drive people from
address to address, whether they be in Manchester, or in Limbo.
And now here he is doing it, his favourite game: driving some
strange fare towards Manchester, accelerating towards the thin gap
that leads to a small country road that leads back towards the heat.
Maybe this time the dream will happen, and Pleasureville will be
lying in wait just around the next turning. If he could just deliver this
fare.

  4.41.

The dashboard clock is shining a bright green. It reminds him
of the passenger's eyes. So very pure. He bends around a little, to
speak through the wire grille, 'What want Manchester, miss?' The
question comes out like a low growl, because the Coyote is a
halfdog and this is how he speaks, making human words out of a
dog's tongue.

The young girl doesn't answer.

Coyote tries again. 'You got ID?'

No answer. No matter; Coyote knew this was an illegal run
anyway.

'Strapped up proper?'

Again, no answer. But by twisting around Coyote can see that
the safety straps are in place around that young body. 'Weather
bad,' he tries. 'Time of year?'

The young girl in the back pulls her anorak hood tighter
around her face.

Okay, so she's not a talker. She will just have to live with
Coyote's voice, that is all. Coyote likes to talk to his passengers.

'What name, kid?' he asks.

Maybe she's not going to answer. There's a full ten seconds or so, and then, finally, she says, 'You can call me Persephone.' Her voice is sweet and sticky. Like a dollop of honey.

'Persephone. Name is nice,' Coyote tells her.

No response.

Just the soft whispering of black trees on either side of the road. Now and again, the moon peeping out, a mute face from the clouds. But the sun is coming up, and Coyote's driving down towards it. Maybe he's free of the Zombies this run; those half-alivers hated the daylight. The noise of rain against the windscreen. The smell of flowers coming from the back of the cab. The air is cloying. Coyote feels a real big sneeze coming on. *This hayfever is going to be the death of me.*

Straining with his doggy eyes to steer a good clean path through the torrent of rain, he gets a sudden picture of Boda's sweet face in his mind. He lets that vision draw him forth, back towards his Fallowfield flat. Then he gets the tingle; the fur on the back of his neck sticking up straight. Something's about to go wrong, he knows it. Coyote's looking all around, left to right, for trouble. Sees nothing. Then a loud, pulpy thud from the back of the cab, and the young girl starts screaming.

Coyote checks the mirror, just sees darkness, the girl moving away from the left side window. He turns his head, his nose taking in bad smells. He can't see what it is. 'What happening?' he calls out. The girl just screams some more. Coyote turns his head right round to see, and the car hits something in the road. *What the fuck was that?* Coyote spins his snout back to the front, only to see the hedge coming up close. He switches to hyper-dog mode, makes a cool swing on the wheel, turning the cab around to where the Catseyes are winking. Something hits the windscreen.

Jesus!

The face of a Zombie, squashed against the glass.

Now he's got two of them, one on the back, one on the front, and the stench of half-life is making him retch. The one on the front is staring in at him. Its face is cracked and ragged, wet with rain, with bits of skin hanging off in black flags. Red eyes look at him, full of a terrible need for sustenance. The girl is making some kind of noise from the back seat. Dog driver just yells at her to keep away from the window, but already the front rider has got a finger's grip on the door handle.

Should've taken that Vurt, mad dogger!

The only way forward is forward, so Coyote presses his foot all the way down, turning the world into a dark blur. The rider is still hanging on though. Now its other hand is banging on the driver's side window. Wouldn't be so bad except it has some kind of rock in there. Coyote swerves the cab to the left and then a fast right again, driving on all fours now, like a true dog. But this Zombie is a seasoned hitcher. The rock comes down with a hard blow, making a web of cracks in the window. Another blow, and the window smashes. A shard of glass embeds itself in the taxi-dog's cheeks. No pain, not yet, just the overwhelming sense of pride being punctured. *That's my cab window, Limbo-fucker! Get your filth off my life!*—Coyote works the lock and then knocks open the cab door—hard!—so that it flies back on a well-greased hinge, taking the Zombie with it. The thing is smashed against the body of the cab, and then the door swings around again. Coyote knocks it back again, but those hard-riding fingers are still gripping the door handle. Coyote pulls the door shut. The Zombie is pressing his broken face against the smashed-up window. Meanwhile Coyote is scrabbling about with one hand in the glove compartment. *Where the hell did I put that thing?* The Zombie's head is reaching in to take a bite. Another blow, from the back this time, as the other Zombie makes a crack in the back left window. The girl is screaming.

The front rider's teeth are dripping with juice, and its savage hand reaches in; long, years-uncut fingernails madly scratching at dog-flesh, drawing blood. Coyote finds what he's looking for, and then raises his free hand towards the Zombie's face. He stares deep into a pair of monstrous eyes for a tiny moment and then pulls the trigger. The pocket gun makes a sweet discharge; small fire from a taxi-dog's fingers. A rich and hot splatter of Zombie flesh sizzles on Coyote's face as he drops the gun to the cab floor, only to let the smoke clear on a broken nose and one clear and dripping eye looking back at him. The other eye is a messed-up pulp of blood and gelatine. The rider is still clinging, hanging on to the door frame with crooked fingers, screaming out messages of hate, its burning face still reaching in for the dogman.

Coyote does the only thing he can, bringing his jaws down hard—

Christ! I'll need a bath after this!

—around what's left of the Zombie's sorry face. He has the satisfying feel of meat in the mouth, even if it is the taste of death he is rending from the bone. Coyote is total dog for just about two seconds as he bites clean through the blood and the flesh and the pain and the time and the bad smell of a bad day in a bad life, until the screech of a bullhorn calls out to his submerged self. A glimpse ahead blinds him with headlights and fear, but everything's working now, the game is his. He opens his jaws to let the Zombie struggle free, works the wheel, turning the whole world to the left to let the oncoming behemoth of a Vaz truck squeeze past, a splinter's breath, wrong side of the road, and then jabs a good elbow into the rider's face, just the right moment, sending it flying loose from the cab. It splats against the steel-plated sides of the truck. *Way to go, Zombie-breath.*

He checks the mirror. A pale white arm is wrapped around the girl's throat. Her anorak hood is protecting her somewhat, but hardly enough, and Coyote can see that she's suffering. Maybe he should stop the cab, open the door, get out and confront the Zombie with his flame gun and his world-famous bite. Maybe give him the same message that his partner got: a faceful of pain. But can he stop the cab? Maybe there are other Zombies waiting for a free ride? And can he afford the time anyway? The sun is rising, and how is he going to get back into Manchester, in the daylight, with an illegal immigrant on board?

What kind of bad game is this, exactly?

But then a wailing comes from the back seat, and Coyote thinks he has lost his fare, which kills his soul; Coyote has never lost a passenger before. He glimpses the young girl in the mirror, and she's smiling from under the hood. The Zombie is clinging to her body, but its face looks a mess, like the girl did something to it. Coyote can't work out what has happened, only that the scent of flowers is smothering him. He can't stop sneezing, and then he thinks, *what a time to be sneezing.*

'Done well, kid,' he says to her, receiving no answer, only the restful swishing of the windscreen wipers.

'Okay back there?' he asks. Meaning—*if you want to push that Zombie out the window, go right ahead, but you'll be doing it yourself. This road is just too dangerous.*

Silence from the passenger, so Coyote glances at the clock, 5.30 it reads, and then he adds some more extras to the meter to take account of the cost of two broken windows and the pain of struggling with Zombies. Standard fare now reads 18.40. Extras now reads 1275.60. Zombies cost money. Coyote didn't enjoy struggling with them, but if he had to, and if he turned out the winner, well then, he was grateful for the cash; the dream trip was coming up close. In the mirror he can see the passenger stroking the Zombie's head, like it's some kind of pet. *Jesus! Can you believe this girl? What the hell am I carrying? And what did she do to the Zombie? Why is life so difficult for a top dog driver? And why am I feeling so completely sexy, all of a sudden?*

Indeed the dog driver has an almighty erection. He can feel it nudging the bottom of the steering wheel, and it feels so good that Coyote thinks he can drive that cab no-handed. It must be something to do with the smell she's giving off, stroking that dead Zombie like a well-fucked lover; the whole cab feels like a garden in the springtime, heavy with a fog of pollen. Coyote is sneezing with a hard-on, which is like coming from both ends. It tastes like summer is in his mouth and in his pants, and the night is turning into the golden flower of morning as he slides the cab down the throat of the hills towards the drop-off, twelve miles to go before the seeding point . . .

Frontier Town North.

The clingers to the centre have absolutely zero idea of what the boundaries are like. They imagine giant, electrified fences encircling the limits of the Manchester map. They imagine heavily armed City Guards patrolling the circumference. Of course, at the four gates, the north, east, south and west gates, this was more or less true. But all the spaces in between are populated with chancers eager for extra cash. The further you went from the centre, the trickier the company. Frontier Town, they called it, this circular conglomeration of shanties and gypsy-dog camps. Edge-walkers. The people of the limits. Outlaws and roustabouts. Coyote pays an Asian dog-girl two black Vurt feathers to let him through her hidden road. Some small trouble then, with a couple of cop-cars patrolling the frontier. But the map and the road come together. The journey is foreplay, and he handles it with aplomb. He has to stop off a few times to let some more patrollers go by, and just to collect his fear and his bearing, but mostly he makes the driving easy, bringing the cab into a smooth entry.

Manchester was his lover.

Cruising home.

At one point, riding the Oxford Road, just past the University, an Xcab passes them, heading back towards Manchester Centre. With a sweet rush of blood to his head and yet more to his groin, Coyote recognises Boda behind the wheel of the rival cab. He raises a wet paw to her wave, and he can hear her talking to him, in his mind; she's saying something like *Imperial driving, dogboy,* like she can send these messages out, loud and clear. Like she has the Shadow. Maybe she *was* a Shadow. Maybe she was. He sends back the message, *Got young Persephone girl on board.* Just thinking it, and, sure enough, Boda comes back with, *Good Limbo tripping, Coy.* Maybe they could really get something together, Coyote and Xcabber. Definitely. He would go find her in the taxi-rank later, once this fare is dropped.

'Good Limbo tripping, Coy,' the passenger repeats, like she too has been spoken to by Shadows.

The fare meter, all added up, thanks to the sorry little cop chase, now reads a very healthy 1597.20. Big money! Coyote's ticket out of trouble. But listen to him sneeze. Also, the almighty hard-on. 'Perfume heavy, flower-girl,' he says.

'Thank you,' the passenger answers. 'Are we there yet?'

'Nearly there,' he replies. 'Alexandra Park, you want?'

'Take me to the grass.'

It was an easy ride. Driving towards the curried flavours of Rusholme, and then a right on to Claremont Road. The park was shimmering by, a brooding expanse of trees and shadows.

'Just here, on the left, please,' the passenger calls.

Coyote stops the cab by the park gate. 6.14. Spots of rain are hitting the windscreen. The dogman feels at home. 'You okay, passenger?' he asks. 'No cab-lag?' This is what some of the weaker travellers feel when pushed through bad fare-zones. One glimpse tells him that all is sweet with the young girl. He looks at the fare meter. 'That will be one thousand, five hundred and ninety-nine pounds and forty pence, please.'

When it comes to asking for a fare, Coyote speaks pure English.

'Got it right here.' She pulls a flower, a black pansy, out of her anorak pocket.

'What this?'

Persephone passes the flower through the grille, so that Coyote can hold it in his paws. The eyes of a poor dog captivated by petals of night. But still, will this pay for Pleasureville?

'Some joke, passenger-girl?' Coyote asks.

'Try it,' the young girl says. 'Why don't you?'

So Coyote feeds the flower into the credit slot on the meter. At 6.16 a.m. precisely the green light of the fare turns to a yellow 1599.40, and the words PAID IN FULL appear on the screen, and Coyote is amazed at the sight. The money has flooded into his system.

At that precise moment—Monday I May, 6.16 a.m.—a boy named Brian Swallow vanished from his feathery bed in Wilmslow. The parents, John and Mavis Swallow, didn't notice their son's disappearance until they awoke at 7.30. Brian's room was empty, his blankets ruffled as though by a violent struggle. His window was locked, from the inside, as were all other windows and doors. They called the police. An Inspector Tom Dove came to see them. The parents told Tom Dove that they'd kissed their loving son before he went to sleep at 10.15 the night before, and then gone to bed themselves, locking all the doors behind them. The detective had looked around the boy's bedroom, sniffed at the bed sheets, and then at the air. He had experienced this atmosphere too many times before not to know what it meant. Somebody, somewhere, was being exchanged for something from the Vurt. That wouldn't make it any easier to explain to Mr and Mrs Swallow. Tom Dove sighed, and then broke the news to the distraught parents.

Coyote feels light-headed. The money is getting to him. He feels like an insider all of a sudden.

'You like?' Persephone asks.

'I like. I do like. Good ride.' He gazes at the paid-in-full sign for a while, before opening his door. He curses at the broken window,

and at the pain in his right cheek, where the glass was digging in.
Never mind all that. This fare was worth it. He moves around to
the back door of the cab. The girl undoes her straps, pushing the
now weightless body of the Zombie on to the cab floor. Coyote
realizes that he'll have to dump that sad and drained creature somewhere. Then the young girl gets out of the cab. She steps up close
to Coyote. Her perfume is caressing his nostrils. He wants to
sneeze, but manages to hold it back.

'Thanks for getting me here,' she says.

'No problems,' he answers.

Just a cold, rainy morning on the moors, a bad trip through Limbo,
two crazy Zombies, one of them lying dead in the cab, some glass in the
cheek, some half-dead flesh in the mouth, a big mother of a Vaz truck
almost flattening me, a small loss of blood, a maze-game with the City
Guards, a ride with the scent of flowers exploding my nose.

'Let me pay you,' Persephone says.

'Already done.'

'More than that.' Persephone pulls down her hood.

Coyote looks at the young girl. Her face is very beautiful. He
feels like a bee, drawn to that sight, that perfume. So tempting. He
doesn't know where to look. He looks over to the trees of Alexandra Park. Does no good. He has to look back. Those sparkling eyes
of green, they look just like two flowers staring deep into him. The
girl's young and full lips, like two trembling petals. 'Kiss me,' she
says. This girl must be eleven years old at the most, but Coyote's
lips cannot help but descend to hers, tasting the pollen. He can feel
her tongue pushing deep into his throat . . .

Jesus, nobody can have a tongue that long.

He is thinking about his unknown father, his dead mother, and
his rarely seen daughter. And about his angry ex-wife, and about
Boda's sweet and tempting song. Some last feelings.

And then his mind explodes with blackness and colours.

. . . oh my God! The flowers are dancing . . . dancing . . .

One minute twenty-five seconds later, Coyote was dead.

* * *

My boss was called Kracker: Chief of Police, Jakob Kracker. The only man named—by his parents—after a certain brand of thin, dry wafer. All the cops called him the Biscuit Boy behind his back. It was Kracker's voice, coming over my bedside telephone, that started me on this trip. It was early morning, 1 May of the year in question. His words took a hard journey towards my parched, wine-heavy brain: 'Sibyl Jones... I've got a case for you.' A body had been found, just outside the gates of Alexandra Park. I was to get over there immediately. This was a strange one, Kracker had said, but would say no more. What did I care? Death was my speciality. So I had dressed quickly and then made my usual detour into the second bedroom, where my love, my Jewel, lay sleeping. I had lifted the lid to his cot, blown him a kiss. Then I left the house and stepped into the Ford Comet, riding it through the rain towards the park at Moss Side. I hated to leave Jewel alone, but a cop must work hard in bad times. I grabbed a cigarette from the dashboard pack with one hand. Napalms, of course. The message read: SMOKING MAKES YOU WRITE BETTER—HIS MAJESTY'S OFFICIAL BIOGRAPHER.

The taste of smoke in my throat. In these days of dry dust I can still remember that taste like the breath of a wicked lover on the lips and tongue.

I lived in Victoria Park in those days, as I still do; a comfortable rented flat that I had bought from the landlord after my husband left. I had married early, age of eighteen, already pregnant. Had my baby girl, Belinda Jones, seven months later. My husband left nine years after that. And four days after my husband, my daughter, Belinda, ran away. She was nine years old, and that was no age for a young girl to go wandering. But wander she did, calling me some bad names for forcing her father to leave. This was her way of seeing it. I guess she loved him more than me, despite everything. But where did she go? Where? I had searched all over for Belinda since then, but no trace of her anywhere, not even her name or her destination. This has been one of the journeys of my life.

Now that journey was nearly at an end. Towards the dream . . .

The cop system was a bellyful of messages that long-ago morning as I drove my Fiery Comet over towards Moss Side. I wasn't in the mood for official voices—all those coded tales of imminent or actual violence—so I had moved along from the police waves, until I picked up the Gumbo YaYa talking. The Manchester Cops had been searching for this hippy pirate for years, finding nothing but his voice floating down from nowhere . . .

'Dearie dearie. Good morning, or what? That was *I Can Hear the Grass Grow* by The Move, and there has been a sudden surge to the old Gumbo's nostrils. Flowers in the rain, indeed. Big jump in the grain count. I can *hear* them jumping. This old hippy is sneezing already. Ya Ya! The flowers are spurting pollen all over the Manchester map. Gumbo never seen such a giant, golden step before. Spent some seconds accessing the data-feather; last such power-surge logged in the far-off and forgotten days of Fecundity 10. Of course we are nowhere near the all-time record count yet, but still, this is worrying. Must be a freak blip. Stay cool. Keep those nostrils clean with *Sneeza Freeza*. Send off today for the Doctor Gumbo's own-brand nostril plugs. May John Barleycorn show mercy. The pollen count is 85 and rising. News just in from the street of a juicy murder. More on that when I access today's cop-feather. You know they change the code every day but the good Gumbo, he can always find a window. And now my people, listen to this beauty from Scott Mackenzie, nineteen sixty-seven. And remember, if you're going to San Francisco this year, be sure to wear something floral in your hair . . .'

Gumbo YaYa always seemed to know more about cop-cases than we did ourselves. He even had a phone-in line up and running, but whenever a cop called that number, the signal vanished into a mesh of darkness, which was the symbol of hiddenness in those days. A condom-virus was on the wave.

Through a veil of rain, I negotiated the sharp, fast left onto Wilmslow Road and then the right onto Claremont, riding the Comet towards a stranger's death. It was 6.57 a.m. Just down the road I could see the police lights flashing, making red arcs in the rain, and the half-darkness, the black trees of Alexandra Park passing by to my left, the flickering lights of robocops moving through the leaves. One more scene of crime. My life. A crowd of dog-people were hanging around. Luminous cop ribbons were strung from lamp posts and cop-cars. One vicious dogboy had his jaws clenched around the ribbon. As I pulled up next to a black cab that was parked, half on, half off the pavement, I saw sparks fluttering in the morning rain. The dogboy yelped at the shock and then fell back into the paws of a young bitchgirl. A fleshcop brandished his gun at the crowd. I got out of the car and a young robocop officer came up close, beaming on me for identification. I walked over to where a crowd of cops were pressed around a dark shape on the ground. We were just opposite the side gate to Alexandra Park, Claremont Road entrance. A big dogcop was growling at a bunch of pissed-off, rain-dampened officers, telling them to shake some flesh. One of them sneezed.

'What have we got, Clegg?' I asked.

The dogcop turned at my voice. His dirt-brown fur was greasy-slick from the downpour. 'Where's Kracker?' he asked. Clegg was the one cop who didn't call the boss the Biscuit Boy. Sometimes he even used the word *Master* when referring to the chief. Now, Kracker wasn't one for the dirty work. He usually put in a scowling appearance at the scene of crime and then rushed back to his desk. This time he hadn't even shown his face. He had a good excuse; his wife was expecting their twenty-first baby any second.

'He's looking out for his new kid,' I replied.

'That's a shame. So they send us a fucking smoke.'

Chief Inspector Z. Clegg was a fine, upstanding dogcop. His long snout and extra-rich sense of smell had sniffed out a whole batch of homicides and dogicides. He was half dog, half man, with a real hatred in his mind for anyone with the Shadow in them. Me, for instance. I am a smoking-woman, which means I have an abundance of Shadow in me, mixed in with the flesh. All creatures have got a trace of the Shadow, but some of us have direct entry. Clegg's intense dislike for the Shadow was pathological.

'The victim's got some dog in him, Zero?' I asked. I said this because of the wet, glistening look in Clegg's eyes. I'd seen it too many times on previous cases not to know what it meant.

Z. Clegg just nodded.

The Z stood for Zulu, but Clegg hated that name, so he called himself Z. I called him Zero, just to get the fur on his back erect. He really hated it. Zero was one of those dogmen who desperately tried to deny their canine side. Which was some kind of joke considering the patches of fur on his face, and the long whiskers that sprouted from each side of his cheeks. He really hated being called a dog. Maybe because the dog-people were considered the lowest of the low in society. Most citizens saw them as being only a claw-scratch above the people of Limbo, the so-called Zombies. Even a robo was seen to be of more worth than a dog. Zombies, Dogs, Robos, Shadows, Vurt and Pure; this was the scale of worth. Therefore most dogs ended up on the wrong side of the law. A dog who joined the cops was constantly under pressure. Not only from the pure cops but also from the mad dogboys on the street, who saw it as the ultimate betrayal. On top of that add Clegg's dislike of the Shadows, and the fact that he wasn't married, that he was never seen lusting after women, or men, or even dogs for that matter—and you'd find a picture of crossbreed loneliness building. I had a million theories about why Clegg acted like he did, all that twisted bitterness. None of them made our relationship any easier. But most of all Zero hated it when somebody with even a tiny bit of dog in them got killed. This was his one concession to the dog he carried around inside his mixed-up genes.

'You got a name, Zero?' I asked. 'You got a time of death?'

'Sure. The ID card in the cab calls him Coyote. Forensic clock puts the last gasp at 6.19 a.m.'

'Ever heard of him?' Zero knew all the dogs of importance, especially those on the dark side of the law.

'Get to it, Sibyl,' Zero growled. 'Make me a happy man.'

I pulled a pair of steri-gloves onto my fingers, and then knelt down next to the body; early twenties, a smooth wave of black and white fur rising from his shirt collar, forming a sleek and spotted mask all over his face. Dogboy beautiful. Dressed in black jeans and a leather blouson, the jacket decorated with fan-club badges— Manchester City Vurtball Club, Belle Vue Robohounds, Rusholme Ruffians Basketball Posse. This victim was a Manchesterophile. Some wounds on the face—teeth marks and glass shards. Despite all this, the victim had a smile. It was captured on his dead face. Inside of the smile someone—the murderer?—had stuffed a bunch of flowers. Red flowers they were, rising on tall green stalks and then drooping back over his cheeks, softly. Clusters of red petals all tightly bound into long tassels. Their sticky smell was getting to me as I lowered my face back towards the body. Beyond the mouth of flowers a thin glaze of grease was smeared across the nostrils. His fur was shining, here and there, with spots of yellow powder.

'Anybody touched the body?' I asked.

Zero Clegg sneezed before answering. 'You're the first.'

I sniffed at the grease on his nose. 'He was suffering from hayfever,' I said. 'This is *Sneeza Freeza*.'

'This is really going to help us capture the perp, Jones,' Zero answered. 'You want to do that shadow-search?' He made it sound like some kind of disease.

Maybe it is.

This is why the cops employed me. I can read the minds of the living and sometimes, if we get to them early enough, I can read the minds of the dead, their last thoughts, whilst they still linger. This is what I was now trying, letting my hands of smoke play over the corpse's face, feeling my way towards his final seconds of life.

Contact. Dying moments coming through to me, dust to dust, smoke to smoke . . .

. . . *taste is so sweet, so rich . . . can hardly breathe . . . so sweet . . . so full of the taste of honey . . . I am kissing flowers . . . her tongue is like a vine . . . and for a girl so young, so very young . . . it is the taste of . . . the taste of Eden . . . let me sleep there . . . let me sleep . . . sleep and grow . . . let me sleep and grow . . . Jesus! Nobody can have a tongue that long . . .*

And then a burst of colour that made me weep.

. . . *oh my God! The flowers are dancing . . . dancing . . .*

I was travelling inside a dead dogboy's head, drifting from a spectrum burst into a fall of emptiness . . .

. . . *think about me, Boda . . . sing that song one last time . . .*

That last line of Coyote's life drifting into silence . . . that name he called with such need. It was a sweet death.

'What did you say?' Clegg's voice.

'What?' I was still feeling the passage into darkness.

'You said it was a sweet death, Jones?'

'Did I?' I don't know what I said. Maybe I just sent the message on the Shadow-paths, mind to mind, Shadow to Dog.

'Is there such a thing, Smokey? A sweet death?'

'There's flowers in his head, Zero.'

'I noticed.'

'No, no. In his mind. Like an explosion . . . a burst of flow-ers . . . I . . .'

'What's wrong with you? All I want is a clue.'

'I can't describe it . . . an explosion of flowers . . .'

'Some fucking use you are.'

I ignored the remark, reaching instead for one of the flowers in Coyote's mouth. I made a move to pull it loose from the bunch.

'You want to tell me how he died?' Clegg asked.

'That's Skinner's province.'

'Don't get me going, Smoke. You find a name in that brain? The murderer, maybe? Is that too much to ask?'

'She was young. A girl, maybe. The name of Boda came up. That mean anything to you, Zero?'

'No it doesn't. And stop calling me Zero.'

The flower was not coming loose. Something was holding it tight inside the dogboy's mouth. I gripped both hands around the stems of the full bunch, and then gave a good tug on them. No good. It felt like the roots of the flowers were being gripped by a hand equal to mine, somewhere deep in the throat.

'Who the hell would stick a bunch of flowers into a victim's mouth?' Zero asked.

'They won't come out,' I answered, still struggling.

Zero pushed me aside. 'Here, let me . . .' He knelt down and grabbed the stalks out of my hand.

'Zero! The prints . . .'

'It just needs a good strong dog-pull . . . Jesus-Canine!'

'Told you.'

'Pissing bunch of flowers!' The dogcop made an almighty effort. There was a tearing sound, and then Zero was falling backwards to land on his hindquarters, the bunch of flowers in his two front paws. 'Bleeding flowers!' he exclaimed, and then sneezed, violently. And I saw that the liquid in his eyes wasn't just tears, not just tears of pain. 'This damned hayfever!' he snorted, desperately trying to get himself back on to two legs. 'It gets earlier every year.' He handed the flowers over to me and I made a quick examination of the ends of the stalks. They were ragged and juice laden. I put my hands deep into the dead dog's throat, feeling for something there. My fingers passed over a series of sharp needles. And when I pulled my fingers out they were smeared with sap. I looked over to Zero.

'What's going on, Smokey?' he asked.

'The flowers weren't just placed in the mouth,' I answered.

I had my fingers back down deep in the victim's throat. I could feel where the roots of the plants were embedded in his throat muscles. It was totally beyond my training.

'What are you saying, Shadowgirl?'

'I'm saying that I'm way past a girl.'

'Cool down on the politics, Jones. Spill it.'

So I told him: 'The flowers are rooted in his throat.'

'This is one bad scenario. Smells crazy-bad to the good nose. Take a look at this, Sibyl . . .' Using my first name, he was gesturing over to the cab. 'Take a look at the meter.'

I looked into the cab. The driver's window was broken, and a greasy smear was spread all over the door and the bonnet. I dabbed some onto my finger, sniffed at it. 'Zombie juice, right?' Zero said. 'Looks like he ejected a hitcher.' Then I saw the tariff, shining in luminous yellow.

'Where was he delivering from?' I asked. 'Australia?'

'Further than that, Smokey,' Zero replied, moving around to the boot. 'Dog must have been picking up from Limbo. Must have dealt with some bad Zombie. Boot-luggage was registered.'

'You tried it yet?'

He shook his head and pulled out a tube of Vaz, squeezed some into the lock, worked his cop-key until the boot lifted with a slow wave. Just emptiness in there. 'We got a call from the cops out in Frontier Town, northern sector,' Zero said. 'They traced him bringing in an immigrant. Lost him in the maze. Jesus-Dog! Sure was a mean dancer, that Coyote. Some big hero on the streets, so I'm expecting flak from this. I'm expecting another dog-riot. Kracker's going to have my hide if I don't deliver.'

The first dog-riot had taken place some years ago, fired-up by the random slaying of a young bitchgirl in Bottletown. Robo-Skinner and his team in forensics had found that the victim had been Shadow-raped. One more incident in the war between the smoke and the fur. We had tried our best to keep it from the streets but Gumbo YaYa stole the knowledge from our Wave. He then proceeded to broadcast it over his station, and the dogs had risen up in protest, demanding justice, equality and revenge. Since then the dog-people had been on a fur-trigger; exploding periodically—on some kind of canine cycle—whenever a dog was taken out. Coyote was just the latest in a long line.

Zombies, Dogs, Robos, Shadows, Vurt and Pure. The ladder of worth falling into war, rung against rung.

'You got any clues, Clegg?' I asked.

'You know what, Smokey? I'm reckoning this is a mist job. I'm thinking a Shadow did it.'

'Right . . . I see . . .'

'You got any other suspects, Smokey?'

'Every time a dog dies, you think a Shadow's done it.'

The dogcop ignored my remark. 'Let's try the back seat,' he said. The door opened and a soft wave of yellow air drifted out into the street. Zero was holding his nose against the smell . . .

'Jesus!' I breathed.

'You said it, Smokey . . . oh shit . . . not again—'

He was going to sneeze . . . it was the smell . . .

AAAAAAAHHHHHHHHHHHHHHCHOOOOOOOOSSSSHHHHH-HHHHHHHHHHHHHH!!!

'Dog-Christ!'

The smell of flowers from the back of the cab. The air inside seemed to be glowing with the scent of a thousand blossoms. Sparkles of colour floating, and something else under that, like flowers on a wound . . . the smell of death submerged.

'You ever smelt that before, Jones?' Zero was wiping his nose with a sodden rag. 'Some perfume, uh?'

'No. Never.' I looked over to the other cops. They were all sneezing now . . . soft explosions . . . cries . . . curses . . .

'You want to close that door now? Please!'

I didn't answer him. Something about that other smell, the hidden smell . . . I leaned into the passenger compartment . . .

'One question, Jones. How come we're all sneezing our guts out, and you're just walking free? How come you're not sneezing?'

Inside the cab . . .

. . . the world was a scent . . . I was climbing into it . . . changing senses . . . the sparkles of colour on the seat . . . same as on the dogboy's face . . . look closely . . . yellow . . . intense . . . tiny . . . smear one onto my finger . . . it tickles . . . head fuming . . . foggy . . . underneath that . . . the hidden . . . there . . . the seat . . . a smear of grease . . . Sneeza Freeza? . . . No . . . not that . . . too purple . . . familiar . . . fingers in it . . . burning . . . cold . . . smell it . . . death . . . half-death . . .

I climbed out of the cab, to face Zero.

'Jones?'

'Bad news.'

'Spill.'

'He brought one through. A Non-Viable Lifeform.'

'A Zombie?'

'It was still alive, Zero. There were no last thoughts in there.'

'A Zombie. Excellent. Well done, Sibyl. A Zombie killed Coyote. Couldn't be better. We've got a bona fide street-hero killed by a Non-Viable. The way Bottletown is at the moment, any other scenario, any king of *Shadow-scenario,* we could've had another dog-riot on our hands. Guess I just call up the Zombie squad, let those low-level cleaners deal with it.'

The flesh cops were sniggering and sneezing in turn. It was a joke to them now, this case. Zombies were high in the public's mind, mainly because the half-dead were invariably ugly and brutish, and the whole image of some creature born from the desperate mating of a living person and a corpse was still reviled in those days. In fact, to the cops they were classed as a nuisance more than anything, something they had to clean up, like litter on the municipal road. Zombies were weaklings away from their Limbo, especially when the light shined upon them; that was the paradox of their hitching travels.

Zero shoved a Vurt cop-feather into his mouth, so that he could talk to Chief Inspector Kracker direct. And being made the way I am, Vurtless, it was all silence to me—just the happy grimacing of Zero's face as he relayed the news to the boss, who was no doubt clinging to his wife's hand at the moment of birth.

All I could do was watch and shiver from the sidelines. Coyote's final message playing around and around in my mind, making patterns. Shadow patterns . . . that name he called out at the last . . . *think about me, Boda . . . sing that song one last time . . .*

Zero pulled the feather from his mouth, and then he was growling loud to the fleshcops, 'Let's clean up here, officers. It's a wrap.' The cops were already going through the motions, telling the tribe of dogs to clear the area, game was over.

'Is this wise, Zero?' I said.

'What's your problem, Smokey?'

'I think you're being a bit premature.'

'Try me in bed one time, then we talk about premature.'

'What about the flowers?'

'Zombie put them there. Coyote picked up a Zombie. The Zombie killed him, stuffed the flowers into his mouth.'

'That deep?'

'Shit, I don't know how these Zombies work. They learn some strange arts and crafts out there in Limbo, I guess. What else they got to do?' He was shouting at some voyeurs to get back home, ignoring me.

'What about this Boda reference?' I asked.

'Kracker's well happy with the Zombie angle. I reckon I'm with the chief on that.' He snarled at the dog-tribe beyond the ribbons.

'How about an autopsy?' I asked.

'Sure. I'll book robo-Skinner for tomorrow.'

'Tomorrow?'

'You think this is the most important death in town, Smokey? Listen, I've got a disappearance case on my hands already. The only son of the Inspector of Dripfeed got stolen by the Vurt this morning. Officer Dove's on the case. You think maybe I should refuse him back-up? Also, I've got to organise a patrol of Bottletown. Kracker's told me to clamp down on any sparks. No more riots. You hear me?' He turned to the squad. 'Okay, you officers, keep moving that shit away.'

I was a lonely figure around which a cop circus performed. I was two feet away from the body of Coyote. The ripped-out bunch of flowers was lying on the pavement. A fleshcop scooped it haphazardly into a specimen bag. One of the blooms fell free, rain washing away the petals, grains of yellow merging with the water, and some wayward thoughts flickering through my Shadow.

Thirty-six years old I was.

Days of cop-work. Days of juice and smoke, mist and flesh. Days of wondering and wandering. Days of air.

All gone now, all gone . . .

Xcab driver Boda is travelling back towards Manchester, having made a good drop in the Bottletown zone. The time is 6.01 a.m., the same day. She had had some trouble some minutes before, whilst riding Claremont Road past Alexandra Park because a cop-van had pulled in from a side street, speeding like a dose of Boomer drug to the brain. The van was iridescent purple, with one-way windows, and the cop logo painted on the side—a glistening map of Manchester bound by handcuffs. It raced alongside Boda for a spell, forcing her into a bad kerb-jump, until the Xcab had sprouted long knives. Boda knew all about how the cops and cabs were supposed to be working together for the common good these days, so she had set the blades to caress level only. The cops didn't feel a thing as the knives scratched five delicate lines in the purple paint job. Well, it would give the boys something to do when the shift was through. Boda had then asked Charrie for Boomer speed, which left the cop-van standing, and Boda was the queen of the road again.

'Nice work, Charrie,' Boda had said to her cab, and the words ALL PART OF THE SERVICE, DARLING had scrolled back across Boda's taxi-vision. Boda is her Xcab name. Short for Boadicea. Just like Charrie is short for Chariot. Drivers were obliged to give up all their possessions, all of their hair, all their memories and treasures when they joined the cab-hive. Their *pre-cabian* lives vanished into a trail of road-dust, and one of the treasures given up was the original name, the parents' name. Boda wasn't the name she was born to, but it's the only one she knows.

Boadicea's chariot riding the waves of Manchester with customized blades sliding back into recesses.

The Wilmslow Road now, back into town.

The Oxford Road.

6.05 a.m.

Which is when she sees Coyote cruising by in his beautiful black vehicle. *Imperial driving, dogboy* she had sent out to him, not even knowing if that feeling would get through. But some hazy message had come back from the dogboy's brain. Something about having a girl called Persephone on board, so Boda had sent back, *Good Limbo tripping, Coy.* The blackcabber brought out the best in Boda, he brought out the song of the road. Romantic shit, of course. But what the hell, isn't she feeling good this morning?

Columbus comes onto the taxi-waves. STOP THAT SING-ING, DRIVER BODA. And Boda did stop then, as she always did when Columbus came on line. YOU FEEL LIKE GETTING BACK TO THE ST ANN'S RANK SOMETIME TODAY, DRIVER? MAYBE PICK UP A FARE OR TWO?

'Will do, Columbus,' Boda answers.

It is 6.12 or so when Boda touches base at the St Ann's rank, and she gets landed with another journey straight off: a clean run carrying a robocrusty back home to Chadderton, after an all-night Boomer session. The way he talks about it sure makes Boda hungry for some of that sweet stuff. Maybe later on . . . with Coyote in tow?

Sure, worth a try. Boda makes that drop-off, gets flagged down on the way back, some loony hippy-dog wanting to make an early start at a Vurt Convention. She gets some crazy feelings about Coyote, just from the smell in the back; bad dog! Despite that, it was a simple journey, slick and smooth, no problems. Well, almost none. On the way back a small lump of something had lodged itself to the underside of her cab, some chancer hiker, hoping to parasite its way back into Manchester. That was the trouble with suburban fares; some of the smaller Zombies had managed to get that far. Now one of them was reckoning on an easy ride; it hadn't reckoned on Xcab's in-car monitoring system. A red warning light blinked on the dash, and the words SYSTEM VIOLATION flooded into Boda's taxi-eyes. SCENE OF VIOLATION . . . THE MANIFOLD. CAUSE OF VIOLATION . . . UNIDENTIFIED HALF-DEAD BEING. DO YOU WANT TO TERMINATE, DRIVER? Boda thought that yes, yes she did want to terminate. 'Do it good, Charrie, babe.' TERMI-NATION SEQUENCE COMMENCING. 'Going through some tur-bulence, passenger,' Boda said aloud. Her voice was picked up by the in-car system, transmitted to the hermetically sealed executive suite in back. 'No need to panic.' TERMINATION ACTIVATED. The Xcab shone fiery red for a moment, as the current flowed towards the manifold. One thousand volts of anger. Boda had tuned into the down-side camera. She saw something shit-coloured screaming, its pathetic claws burned to a crisp. Must have been some stray Ghost Cat clinging on for dear furry life. And then the lump of stuff falling off into suburban nothingness, bouncing like a sponge ball on the tarmac. 'Chew on that, Zombie fucker!' SYSTEM CLEAN, DRIVER. 'You bet! Let's ride.'

So they ride the grey roads together, Boda and Charrie, rider and chariot, joined into one being. She's keeping her eyes on the traffic, her ears on the radio, but really Charrie is driving alone; Boda is too busy thinking about Coyote. The blackcabber had come into her life three weeks ago at the Nightingales cafe, where all the cabbers hung out when off-duty. Coyote didn't visit there that much, because the Xcabbers looked on him with suspicion, but this night he had, and he and Boda had got to talking. In fact they had got to beyond talking, but just sly looks from eye to eye, you know? Boda can't be sure as yet, but she was certain that something good was developing between them. Something that Xcabs didn't allow, especially not with a rogue black-cab driver. Xcabbers were supposed to marry only with other Xcabbers. This was their way of keeping the cab-genes pure. Columbus had come on super-strong, saying to Boda that she was a breath away from termination. Boda hadn't listened. How could she listen? The road was getting too wild, especially when Coyote had told her he had actually visited Columbus a few times. None of the drivers had any clue as to where Columbus was, or even what he looked like so Boda was curious to know more. Coyote had only hinted at deeper secrets but the fact that he had more *freedom* than her had really heated Boda's desire. She had met up with Coyote four more times, and on the second time she had felt her thoughts drifting away from her mind into his, like she had the Shadow, or something, *Cab-Christ! What is happening to me?* Boda's thoughts in the presence of dogboy flesh. It really was too much to bear. Coyote had responded to her secret whisperings, as though her mind was being shared. And on their last meeting, two nights ago, she had given him the clue to a Limbo fare. Xcabs were banned from driving over the boundaries. The internal map stopped at the edges of the expanded city, and all the Knowledge faded away there, Frontier Town, so that no Xcabber could venture forth. And on that passing of a fare, they had kissed over two half-empty cups of Chrism juice, and it was very juicy that kiss, full of potential. Boda had not been able to sleep that night, just from thinking about it. Maybe this taxi-dog was going to take her somewhere beautiful.

Boda is eighteen years old, a few boyfriends here and there, nothing special as yet; she's just about prepared for something good.

She lights up a Napalm with the in-car lighter. The pack message reads SMOKING IS GREAT AFTER SEX—HIS MAJESTY'S OFFI-CIAL MISTRESS.

7.04 a.m.

Boda takes another fare, easy fodder, and on the way back towards Manchester she tunes in the pirate wave...

'Massive jump to the hippy-nostrils, unprecedented. Gumbo YaYa is sneezing already. I raise my flowers to the wind to smell the future... the future is a nose explosion. Grab your Good Gumbo fever masks, my children; this is going to be a harsh ride through the clouds of pollen. Not since the days of Fecundity 10 has such fieriness been felt, when the drifting seeds brought home a pollen count of 862, the highest ever for Manchester. Gumbo YaYa reck-ons this is going to beat that record. May John Barleycorn find you desireless. And remember, don't believe the authorities; only the Gumbo has the true reckoning. Pollen count, 125 and rising...'

Now Boda's waiting on a new job. 7.29 a.m., St Ann's rank, tenth in the column, some fifteen minutes or so from the next ride. She gets out of the cab and walks up to the third in line.

Boda—the way you walk, long and loose-limbed, like an angel with wings of smoke. And the way you look: hair shorn to the skull, skull laser-tattooed with twisting streets in black and white. A walking A–Z of bliss you are, all dressed in denim and felt, lace and polyvinyl chloride. Vazboot trainers on your feet and a cummerbund of velvet around your waist. A corduroy bag slung easy over one shoulder, holding all of your world; your antique Manchester map and your woollen hat, and your money, your cab-licence and your smokes.

The third-in-line driver's name is Roberman. Roberman is a sleek and shiny robodog, a Doberman Pinscher by birth, but all the guys in the rank call him Roberman, because that is what he is. Not a trace of human in him, just a mess of dog-flesh and info, all mixed up in a tight bundle of muscle and plastic. This mixture was called *hardwere* by the gene-mechanics. There was no human trace in Roberman, but sometimes dogs can be more human than humans. Xcab employs him because of his dog-knowledge of the dark streets. Most of the guys in the rank don't talk to Boda, because they think her too much of a loner, too distant, too twisted to bother with. Roberman is different. He makes a long series of low growls, none of which Boda understands, but the tears in his eyes tell a tale. She places her left hand on the door of his cab; this is all it takes for you to be inside of the cab system. Each Xcab comes complete with an in-car sound system. Roberman's voice comes over the speakers, his keening yowls changed by the translator into English, all for the benefit of nervous passengers. This option is necessary if the driver and the passenger are of different races. 'You heard the bad news, Boda?' the voice-box announces.

'I just got back. What's happening?'

'They killed a driver.'

'Oh shit. Which one?'

There is a real street-cool value in taking the life of an Xcab driver, just because they are so protected. And because possession of an Xcab is a prize worth killing for.

'Not one of ours, Boda,' Roberman says, choking on it.

'Not an Xcabber?'

'Runner-dog.'

'A dog driver?'

'The black-and-whiter.'

'Coyote?'

'Made a bad Alexandra Park drop.'

'Coyote . . . oh Jesus . . .' Now Boda is looking up and down the street, looking for comfort. Can't find anything. Nothing good.

Only the wind and the rain . . .

'You okay, Boda?' Roberman asks.

'Yeah . . . yeah, sure . . . I'm . . . who did it, Rober?'

'Cops smell neg-shit.' Which means that the cops don't know

shit, but she's not listening any more. Sure, one hand kept tight to the cab, but the other hand is rubbing at her face for some reason.

'You sure you're okay, Boda?' Roberman is asking.

'Boda's fine,' she replies, making her voice work somehow. But inside, all she can think about is that blackcabber dogman. Just the last of his kind. Just the beauty of his life gone to nothing. Just the next best thing to a good lover that she's met in a long while. And she hadn't even . . .

'The dogs are gonna fight against this. Gonna be trouble.' Roberman's voice speaking to her, and the rain falling down in lines of dull pain. Boda, you have no answer to give. Just the glistening bulk of St Ann's Church in your eyes, and the vision of Coyote's last wave, all the way from the window of that sweet black cab.

The sound of the Roberman sneezing violently, like he has the world plugged up his nostrils. The love song of a taxi dying in Boda's heart, and the rain falling on her Manchester City Vurtball Official Supporters' Club blouson jacket. Coyote had invited her to a game, presented her with a ticket for the semi-final, four days' time.

She will miss that game now.

'Roberman, we gave Coyote that fare.'

'Don't tell me about it.'

'Roberman, we're to blame. He picked up a girl called Persephone from Limbo. Delivered her to Alex Park. Maybe the fare killed him.'

'Please, Boda. I really don't want to know.' Roberman looks scared as he says this.

At that precise moment, 7.34 a.m., Columbus the Xcab King was listening in to the cab-wave. He hears driver-Boda mentioning the name Persephone to driver-Roberman.

CAB-SHIT!

Columbus was scared suddenly. His one per cent of humanity comes into play, overriding the Vurt-logic. Driver-Boda must have spoken to the blackcabber Coyote about the ride. Boda knows about the visitor. She knows that Coyote delivered Persephone to the drop-off at Alexandra Park.

What could he do about this new situation? He needed to take Boda out of the equation. Columbus considered his options for less than a moment and then made a secret call. He then returned to the cab-wave . . .

Columbus comes onto the cab-line, interrupting the flow between Boda and Roberman. DRIVER-BODA, A WORD PLEASE, he says.

'Switch?' Boda can hardly even manage the boss's call-sign through the tears.

GOT A FARE FOR YOU.

'Switch, I'm feeling . . .'

ASKED FOR YOU BY NAME. I THINK YOU'VE GOT AN ADMIRER OUT THERE, A MR DEVILLE. YOU KNOW HIM?

'No, I . . .'

PICK-UP AT HYDE ROAD, ARDWICK. DROP-OFF AT DUKINFIELD. BE CAREFUL DOWN ARDWICK. IT'S KIND OF BLEAK, THIS TIME OF THE DAY.

'I don't think I can make it . . .'

YOU'RE AN XCABBER.

'I just got some bad news, Switch.' Boda's voice is parched. She can't get her head around the loss.

MAY I REFER YOU TO CLAUSE 7.2 IN THE DRIVER'S CONTRACT? WHICH STATES QUITE FIRMLY THAT ALL DRIVERS MUST—

'I know what it states, okay?'

WHAT'S WRONG WITH YOU, BOADICEA? YOU LOSING THE EDGE?

'I'm going. Okay? I'm there already.' Boda climbs back into Charrie and starts him up, her hands slipping on the controls.

GLAD TO HAVE YOU ON LINE, DRIVER.

Columbus disengages himself, and Charrie's voice comes scrolling up to replace him as the ride starts. WHERE WE GOING, BODA?

'Hyde Road.'

IS SOMETHING THE MATTER?

'Just fucking drive, will you!'

Charrie falls silent. The cab moves with sadness.

Boda just wanted to drive; she wanted to drive away from the whole world . . .

Instead she makes it as far as Ardwick, where the rising sun casts a glimmering sheen on the waste ground around a bunch of abandoned factories. A man is waiting at the designated pick-up point. He's the only person in sight, and he's so thin Boda has to look twice before she sees him. An unknown figure, she's never driven him before. She brings Charrie to a halt, speaks through the cab's system: 'Deville?'

The man nods. He looks edgy for some reason.

'Get in.'

The passenger settles his bony shape into the back seat. Boda sees the Vurtball ticket that Coyote had given her, resting on the dashboard. She starts up the cab. Charrie hardly responds, just a slow chug-chug along the road.

'Charrie, what's wrong?'

I DON'T KNOW, BODA. I FEEL A LITTLE SICK.

'What?'

I FEEL LIKE I'M LOSING STRENGTH . . .

'Oh, come on.'

Belinda hears the passenger window sliding open.

'Here will do nicely,' says the passenger.

'I'm not in the mood for games.' Boda turns around to see the window opening between her and the passenger. He's smiling at her. Belinda presses at the window button, receiving a no-response answer. The window is now fully open. Boda turns back again.

A gun is levelled at her head. The passenger motions at her to stop the cab. Boda refuses, turning back to the dash, calling up the Switch . . .

WHAT IS IT?

'I've got a loony on board, Columbus.'

OH DEAR.

'Did you check this guy?'

YOU KNOW THE PROCEDURE, DRIVER. ACTIVATE DEFENCE MECHANISMS.

Boda presses at Charrie's Shock Button, aiming the juice into the passenger compartment. Nothing happens. The passenger is just sitting there, smiling, the gun held straight and true. 'What's happening, Charrie?'

I CAN'T HELP IT, BODA, the cab says.

'What?'

COLUMBUS IS HINDERING ME.

Charrie's voice fades into darkness. The passenger presses the gun against the back of her neck. 'Why are you doing this?' she asks, trying to get her voice under control.

'Keep quiet!'

'Columbus, what's happening here?' Columbus doesn't answer. For the very first time, Columbus doesn't answer. Boda's eyes are resting on the Vurtball ticket, like it was some ticket out of trouble. She reaches for it. It feels like she's reaching for Coyote.

Boda grabs hold of the ticket, just as . . .

Just as the passenger presses down on the trigger. Boda's head is slightly awry because of her move towards the ticket. The bullet drives a road into the side of her head, grazing the tattooed map. The bullet travels from there, a deflected line to the windscreen of the cab. The glass splinters into a web of containment. Emergency procedures. Charrie bursts into a sudden motion. The passenger and Boda are thrown back by the acceleration. Charrie drives himself forwards, makes a vicious U-turn. The passenger's head collides with the passenger window, the gun falls from his hands.

'Charrie? What's happening?'

WE'RE GETTING OUT OF HERE! HANG ON, the cab replies.

The passenger window slides shut as the cab speeds back down Hyde Road, a left onto Brunswick, the passenger being thrown around in the back, locked in the cab-space. Boda gets her hands back on the wheel. Columbus coming on strong: BOADICEA, WHAT ARE YOU DOING?

'What the fuck are *you* doing?'

THERE'S BEEN SOME MISUNDERSTANDING.

'You bet there has.'

DRIVER-BODA. PLEASE EXPLAIN.

I'm on a new fare, Columbus.'

NEGATIVE. NO FARE REGISTERED. PLEASE EXPLAIN.

'I'm making a pick-up.'

NO PICK-UP CALL REGISTERED. EXPLAIN.

'Fuck you.'

THERE IS NO FARE, BODA. DO YOU REGISTER ME?

No choice.

No choice for the driver or the map.

The passenger called Deville is flailing around in the sealed compartment when a fast right on to Upper Brook Street sends him flying again, the cab speeding dangerously along the street as Charrie comes scrolling up: BODA, LET ME GO, PLEASE. STOP MESSING ABOUT UNDER MY DASHBOARD. TAKE YOUR HANDS OFF THE SIXTEEN PLUGS UNDER MY DASHBOARD.

'What?'

UNDER MY DASHBOARD, THE SIXTEEN PLUGS. PLEASE DON'T PULL THEM OUT.

'I'm not touching you.' Her eyes on the road ahead, every few seconds a glance back to see how the passenger is getting on. He looks like a dying goldfish behind the glass.

YOU'D BETTER NOT PULL THOSE SIXTEEN PLUGS LOOSE, BODA, BECAUSE THAT'S WHERE THE SWITCH IS

CONNECTED TO YOU. YOU WOULDN'T WANT TO LOSE COLUMBUS, WOULD YOU NOW?

'What will that do to you?'

DON'T WORRY ABOUT ME.

Columbus comes on line, his words burning into the system. WHAT THE FUCK ARE YOU DOING, XCAB CHARIOT? YOU FANCY THE SCRAPYARD ALREADY?

I'M DOING ALL I CAN, COLUMBUS. EVERYTHING I POSSIBLY CAN.

Boda smiles. 'I'm on the case, Charrie.'

Boda reaches down, under the dashboard, to where the system wires are plugged into the cab. She pulls the first one loose. Charrie screams then, and Boda moves her hands away from the board.

GOOD DRIVER, says Columbus. LET US NOT BE FOOLISH. But there is a waver in his voice that gets to Boda. Her hands reach back under the dash, to pull out the second plug, looking towards a manual overdrive. Chariot is calling out to her, over the diminishing waves, his voice growing darker and darker, the letters fading from Boda's taxi-vision . . . DON'T WORRY ABOUT ME . . . BODA . . . DON'T YOU WORRY ABOUT . . . BODA . . . DON'T YOU . . . DON'T YOU WORRY . . . DON'T YOU . . .

Ignoring the fading voice, even though it kills her to be doing so, Boda's fingers are pulling on the ninth socket when Columbus kicks back.

OKAY, BODA. LET'S TAKE THIS EASY. THIS CHARIOT BELONGS TO ME.

'We'll see.'

The thirteenth plug . . .

YOU LEAVE ME NO CHOICE.

'Is that so?' The fourteenth plug . . .

BOADICEA JONES, YOU ARE HEREWITH TERMINATED FROM THE EXTRAORDINARY PRIVATE PERSONNEL TRANS-

PORTATION COMPANY. ALL OUTSTANDING SALARIES WILL NOW BE IMPORTED INTO YOUR SYSTEM.

Boda sees her credit meter glow to a sad and blue 227.60.

The fifteenth plug...

GOODBYE, DRIVER-BODA. NICE WORKING WITH YOU.

Columbus's final words echoed by the faint voice of Charrie...

GOODBYE... BODA... NICE WORKING... WITH...

MAYBE ONE LAST SHOCK BEFORE I VANISH?

Boda works the Shocking switch to the passenger compartment. Stunning volts. The cab gleaming. The passenger screaming from the back as he takes the lightning, and then falling, fading...

NICE WORKING WITH YOU... WORKING WITH YOU ...NICE...

Chariot drifting to a standstill. The splintered windscreen blinded by rain. The Mancunian Way layered above her on concrete stalks. Cars speeding by. Boda pulls out the sixteenth and last plug.

This cab is Boda's now. Alone.

The time was now 7.42 a.m. and something very strange was happening to the Manchester map. All the roads were twisting and turning in the Xcab system, breaking their connections with each other and then joining up into new shapes. There were 2000 cabs in the Xcab system all connected, each to each. There were now 1999 broken connections. The removal of a single cab from the Hive had caused this mutation, because the part was the whole. Gestalt system. Xcabbers city-wide thought they were taking fares to the correct drop-off, only to receive abuse and refusals to pay when the cab pulled up outside the wrong destination. Columbus went crazy with the strangeness; he didn't know what to do. He felt ill. Like a virus had come into his body. That bitching Boda had removed herself from the Hive. Nobody had done that before. Columbus was at a loss for some few minutes whilst he felt some ninety-seven complaints come flooding in. Xcabs never got complaints! Jesus-cab! Columbus was overloaded for a while then, and he felt himself to blame for the mishap. If only he hadn't tried to take Boda out. If only he hadn't let his one per cent of humanity rule his feelings. Despite all these misgivings, he managed to get some semblance of his former self back on line. He had a back-up map available, thank Barleycorn, but it would take a while to access it. He started that process, at the same time answering all the complaints personally. It took just under fifteen minutes for the new map to load. It was an early copy, a remnant from the first years of Xcab life and it would be full of gaps and omissions. It would have to do for now.

Once that replacement map was up and running he put a call out to all the cabs and told them to ride easy with the passengers, and then he declared that today would be a fare-free bonanza; anybody could travel gratis to any destination. Another first. No payments to be made. This was damage limitation in the Switch's manual. And once all that was in place he then called up all of his empty cabs and told them to find that rogue driver. Columbus wasn't that worried about Boda, it was the vehicle he wanted back. That cab called Chariot was part of his system, a vital organ of the body Xcab. The new map he had planned would be useless unless he was complete.

SHIT! WHY DID I LET THAT BITCH . . .

Columbus hated getting angry, it was too much like human behaviour. The situation wasn't over yet. He had only six days until the new map came through from Vurt. Persephone was a short-flowering bloom. Six days in which to find his lost cab, and silence Boda.

Once and forever.

FUCK THAT IMBECILE PASSENGER! CAB-JESUS! HE WAS SUPPOSED TO KILL THE DRIVER, NOT MAKE HER ESCAPE THE MAP.

Columbus also had this problem: now that the Chariot was

lost from the Xcab system, it was just another car on the streets. The Switch could trace the car through the city, but he couldn't talk to it. He couldn't direct it. Chariot was now a free radical. A maverick. Of course he had the location of the cab: the junction of Upper Brook Street and the Mancunian Way. Columbus sent four cabs toward that position. And he had the home address of Boda still in the banks: Dudley Road, Whalley Range. He sent another two cabs to stake out that place. Another three cabs to Alexandra Park, just in case Boda headed over to the blackcabber's last fare-drop.

All points covered, and Boda being run down, but deep in his intersections Columbus felt the loss eating away at his road-soul.

Boda drags the passenger's shocked-up and dormant form from the compartment, and then climbs back into Charrie. She works the controls until she manages to get him moving again. The road is sluggish, and the cab feels sick under her fingers, and it's only after she's driven some fifty yards or so that Boda realises she doesn't know where she is.

A stranger newly arrived in her home town, Boda's Xcab mind-map is dead and buried. For the first time in nine years she is lost. A lost girl. The feeling makes her hands tremble on the wheel. She turns the cab into a side street and then parks. The street is called Cloak Street. Boda racks her brain for what this could mean, but can find no knowledge there. No clues. Her head-map is aching from where the bullet grazed her, and she rubs at the damaged roads there. Her fingers wet with blood. A faint light shines along the windscreen, and a voice of trembling words: WELCOME BACK, BODA, HA, HA, HA.

'Charrie! It's you.'

YOU DON'T GET RID OF ME THAT EASILY. LET'S DRIVE, BABY.

She gets a tight smile on her face; Xcabs will also be lost without her cab in the Hive. For sure Columbus will bring up some

back-up copy, but until then Boda is free to roam. It may only be a
few minutes, but that is all she needs. Ignoring her pained skull,
Boda reaches over for her shoulder bag on the dash and pulls out a
tattered, antique copy of the Manchester A–Z. She looks up Cloak
Street in the index, locates her position, and then scans the first
pages with their overall coverage of Manchester. Her eyes come to
rest on a place called Whalley Range. That makes a connection. Her
home. Her little bedsit with its posters of Kid Bliss and its broken
Boomer bottles. Fifteen seconds later she's turning the cab around
into the adjacent land, driving back along the Mancunian Way towards Whalley Range. She doesn't know how to get from A–B,
never mind A–Z, but with the map propped up on the dash, Boda
is going to make a good road of it. Charrie's voice in her mind, how
can that be? WE CAN DO THIS, BODA.

'I hope so.'

TOUCHY, TOUCHY.

Charrie is now driving free, along the way, turning and turning.

There is something in the air, something Boda can't quite work
out, some kind of heavy presence along with her pain. Chorlton
Road, the sight of four Xcabs chasing after her in the mirror. Boda
is working the wheel like a natural, but her nose is starting to itch,
tears forming in her eyes. The scent of flowers penetrating her
nostrils. She wants to sneeze. It feels like gunpowder up there,
packed into her nose . . .

Now it is going to . . .

But then the feeling passes, and Boda is left with only a sense
of emptiness and a headful of frustrated desires, and a wondering
about what the next note will bring.

She does a handbrake turn onto Stretford Road. The first
Xcab overshoots the junction, but the other three make the curve
quite easily. From Stretford she makes Henrietta. Straight on towards St John's the trio of Xcabs following; the father, the son, and
the Holy Ghost of her past life. Boda's eyes are darting from the

road to the mirror, from the mirror to the A–Z. The leading Xcab is nudging her rear bumper as she drives onto Russell Road, and then a right onto Dudley, where she lives. The smell of flowers coming from a nearby garden.

Once again Boda tries to sneeze.

The moment . . . the moment . . .

Flowers in the rain.

She is going to . . .

Sneeze!

Sneeze!!!

Come on, you bastard! Blow it out! Do it!

No. Not happening. Absolutely no good, no sneezing to be done.

This is not fair.

Boda is feeling like some kind of unexploded bomb.

She rides the curve of Dudley Road until her house is in view. Two Xcabs are parked outside her garden. Boda presses her foot down to the cab-floor. The cab streaks between the two vehicles, licking yellow and black paint off the sides of each one. She watches in the mirror as the two Xcabs try for a U-turn, getting caught up in the three cabs that were following. Two of the cabs smash into each other. Boda makes a left onto College Road. A right onto Withington. She hits the speed-till-you-die button, checking the mirror. Two cabs following her. Left onto Wilbraham Road. It's a fast route, Wilbraham; Boda burns the tarmac to escape the pursuers. The truth is, she hasn't a clue where she is, or where to go. This girl is just driving. Another Xcab pulls out of Wilmslow Road, heading straight for her. Columbus is all over the system, tracking her every route. How can she possibly escape his gaze? Boda makes a hair's-breadth adjustment to the steering wheel. Her cab peels by the intrusion, clipping the wing of the Xcab. And as the Xcab crumples under her impact, she can see the other cabs wandering lost for a second as the hive-map adjusts to the loss. Now she's turning

onto Kingsway, wherever that is; her A–Z has fallen from the dash
with the turning. Boda Jones is lost in a village called Burnage, two
Xcabs still desperate to catch up with her. She turns into a side
street called Kingsway Crescent, stops the cab, activates the old
Boadicea wheel-blades. The Xcabs are dancing their way into her
rear-view vision. She reverses her cab at high speed into the front
of the first Xcab. A satisfying crunch of steel on steel, as she pushes
the follower backwards, bumper-locked, until she can make the new
right back onto Kingsway. Boda takes two wheels to the pavement,
shaves some paint off a parked car, rips two long slashes in the
Xcabbers tyres at the same time. The second Xcab drifts loose as
the first Xcabber breaks down. Boda's radio comes on. Boda is
sailing. Back down Kingsway. Home free. No idea where home
should be any more.

The scar on her head runs down a tattooed Kingsway, and the
road she is travelling is equally wounded, a phalanx of crashed
cars and burning houses. Her mind settles at last onto Columbus's
betrayal of her. *What the fuck was that bastard up to? The boss had
tried to have her killed! What was happening to the world?*

'Thank you, Wanita, for that rendering of the latest news.
Your sweet voice can make poetry out of death, even, and isn't that
bad news about the taxi-dog? Coyote is down, people. The Gumbo
has travelled in that fine black cab many the time when the Magic
Bus was off-road. Call me old-fashioned but this hippy has always
had a soft spot for the rugged individual, the rebel, the outsider.
Coyote was a hero to me.'

'And to me,' Boda says.

'His ride was so much more of a *journey* than the super-clean
and efficient Xcabs. Who, by the way, are having a little trouble
today with their ever-so-big metamap.'

'You bet, Gumbo.'

'I'll be tapping into the map later to find out just what's going
wrong there. And the secret cop-news for today? Zero results, as

per usual. Oh yes, some splendid creature meets an ignoble end at the hand of yet another dog-voider, and what are the cops up to? Absolutely nothing. When a dog gets killed, the cops go to sleep. Ya Ya! Coyote was a fine specimen, and his murder will make waves in the canine kingdom. Meanwhile, back in the garden, pollen count is coming on strong. 195 and rising. This next record is for the memory of Coyote. May he find a big bone in doggy heaven. *A Day in the Life* by The Beatles. I read the wave today, oh man. About a lucky dog who made the grave. He blew his mind out in a blacker-than-black cab. Mr Lennon, as usual, on the total case. Take it away, boys . . .'

The sound, then, of the Beatles making music out of death, and Boda listening with tears as she drives down Kingsway. Charrie comes into her mind again, SAVE THE TEARS, HONEY, he tells her. LET'S GET HIDDEN.

'Like where?'

The blood from her scar flows south from Kingsway, down her neck into the dark realms of her clothing.

THERE'S ONLY ONE SAFE PLACE, DRIVER.

Tuesday
2 May

The first slice with the scanner knife cut a deep trench down the left cheek, from the edge of the lip, towards the neck muscles. And then came the second cut, the same, but on the other side, the right side. The cop-doctor's name was robo-Skinner, and he had fitted job to name quite perfectly. I watched him peel back the twin slices of skin until I was looking deep into the inner reaches of the victim's mouth. I had his throat muscles on view, a violent abstraction on the screen, and I could see the broken stalks of the flowers nesting there. His throat had been pierced by them. Skinner made the third cut straight across the skin of the throat, left to right, and then another, lower down, searching for the source.

Those feelers went deep inside, suckers to the root.

Skinner opened up Coyote's black and white chest with the video gun. Cracked some ribs, pulled them loose, reaching into the body with both lenses, fondled the stalks, followed them with camera fingers, all the way down into dark flesh, the flesh and blood map of the body. I was watching all of this on the monitors from the observation room, the same time replaying Coyote's last thoughts in my head . . .

let me sleep there . . . sleep and grow.

Some more deep, deep cuts, before Skinner found the roots. They were imbedded in Coyote's lung walls, a hard fist of growth like a plant cancer.

. . . Jesus! Nobody can have a tongue that long!

Zero Clegg, dogcop, was just standing around, dancing paw to paw, bumping into exhibits. I'd never seen him like this before.

Usually he took to autopsies like a dog to a butcher's counter. 'Dog-Christ!' he snarled. 'Will you look at that root, Jones!' Then he smiled a little bit, like the smell of death was getting to him, but wasn't he fighting it?

'Anything on the flowers yet?' I asked.

Clegg lets go of his armour, sneezes, violently . . . and then comes up for clean air, grimacing.

. . . the flowers are dancing . . . dancing . . .

The smell of death, the scent of flowers—an intimate link.

'Sibyl, we've got botanists working overtime.' My real name being used, again, telling me that Clegg really was out of his depth, reeling from the impact of Skinner's digging.

'And?'

'Listen to this.' Zero plugs in a tape. A fruity voice responding from the speakers . . .

'Report on floral sample 267/54, by Jay Ligule, Department of Botany, University of Manchester. May 2nd, 8.04 a.m. Initial findings: A variant of *Amaranthus Caudatus*. Petals of a deep red colour arranged in a spiral formation, making up long tassels. Nineteen inches at the apex. The flower responds eagerly to testing. Secondary findings, spreading the petals: triple stamen. Clusters of pollen on anther pod. Brightest yellow ever seen. 75 microns. Too large for the species. Should be in the range 20–40. Pollen clinging in groups of six. They seem to be moving. Tertiary findings: pollen grains respond to electric stimuli. They shift away from pain and death. Carbon molecules found there. Some kind of flesh-life? Unknown variant. Notes: is this a joke being played? Never seen anything like it. Request sample sent to Kirkpatrick, Professor of Cytology, University of Glasgow. Shit! Pollen grains have escaped the micro-slide! Where are they? Shit! Pollen is dancing. Other notes: cannot stop sneezing. This is one powerful flower. Never seen anything . . . shit! Unless my eyes are mistaken, pollen is moving towards me. Jesus! Why do I get all the shit jobs?'

The track ended with the sound of violent sneezing.

Skinner came up with his cameras full of tears and blood, and a sneeze in his metal throat. Even the robos were suffering. What kind of hayfever was this? And why wasn't I suffering? Usually, every spring was a nightmare for me. But now, whilst Dog and Robo were suffering all around, here was this Shadow woman totally immune. Maybe it wasn't the usual hayfever strain. And I couldn't stop think-ing about Boda, for some reason; a lost girl in the final dreams of a taxi-dog from the filthy streets. *Think about me, Boda . . . sing that song one last time.* Why was that final line calling out to me so strongly?

'This is no Zombie killing, Clegg,' I said.

'What is this, Justice for Zombies Society?' Zero had pulled in his nerves.

'We need to let Kracker know,' I continued. 'Because if this isn't a Zombie killing, then what the hell is it?'

'We can't allow it to be anything else.'

'I think that's too simple, Zero. I think we should keep on looking for this Boda clue.'

'You think so?'

'Zombies don't put roots into the lungs of their victims.'

'Kracker says wind it up, before another dog-riot starts.'

'I say we keep on looking. Word from the street is that Boda was Coyote's girlfriend. You know that most murders are commit-ted by partners?'

'Is that a fact?'

'You ever had a girlfriend, Zero?'

'Kracker has released the body.'

'What?'

'The funeral's tomorrow.'

'Clegg, isn't that a little early?'

'Kracker wants the dogs happy. What would you have me do, Sibyl? Go against the boss?'

'The master's voice. Bow wow.'

Clegg gave me his best show of teeth, but I could feel the hurt over his bristling Shadow. A strain of fear.

Maybe even then I knew that this investigation was to be mine alone.

Coyote had lived in a small flat perched above a fish-and-chip shop on Ladybarn Lane, Fallowfield. The shop was called *Bingo Rex's*, and a cluster of angry dogboys bayed around the entrance as Zero and I pushed through them, Zero snarling at them with his cop-teeth. Bingo turned out to be a greasy Vaz-dripping dog-husband who led us through a damp living room where a tattered and very human wife was smiling through a bruised face, dipping pieces of fish into a tub of low-grade batter. From there a staircase ascended into darkness, and the musty stench of a high dog. Zero was holding his snout from the smell, like he didn't want to recognise this victim as one of his own.

'You okay, Zero?' I asked.

'Sure thing, Smokey,' he answered. 'Keep climbing.'

It was just gone 2.15 p.m. The papers and the daily feathers had pounced on the story.

Hero-dog Killed by Blooms?
The Killing Fields.
Death by Petals.

Headlines. Worst of all, Gumbo YaYa was on the march, mocking the cops with his easy access to the info-wave. *The Flowers of Evil,* Gumbo was calling the case.

And so, here we were, a reluctant dogcop and his Shadow, looking for clues. I couldn't help but feel sorry for Zero, torn between the good cop mode, and his loyalty for the master, Jakob Kracker. Zero had told me he was coming along just out of friendship, which I was grateful for, even if I didn't believe it.

A paw-scratched door opening onto a vista of cleanliness. A

recently hoovered carpet. A single bed freshly laundered. A shelf of books. A collection of *AirVaz* plastic models—all neatly arranged, dangling from the ceiling on pieces of string—and a big, laminated map pinned to the wall.

'Victims' rooms,' Zero said.

'What about them?' I asked.

'Always so lonely.' He was pulling drawers out from the sideboard. 'Oh yes!' he announced. 'Pornography!'

Zero had a pink feather in his paws. He pushed it into his mouth, and his eyes closed in bliss for a second. He pulled the feather loose, and then said, 'Very nice. Very human. Not a sign of a bitch in heat. This man has taste.'

'Sometimes, Zero . . .'

'What?'

'Sometimes I can't make you out.'

'Sometimes . . .' And Zero Clegg looked at me then, as though to say *Sometimes I can't make myself out. So shut the fuck up.*

I got all this bitterness over the Shadow, so I did what I was here for. 'Let's search,' I said.

The two of us going through a taxi-dog's personal belongings, hoping for a trace, finding nothing but trivia, the collected fare-droppings of a lonely life: biscuits crumbling and model aeroplanes dancing and cold tea solidifying in a china cup. Cheap crime novels folded open beside the single bed. Manchester City Vurtball programmes piled up neat in files. An official supporters' club diary lying on the dresser. I opened it up, turning to the latest pages, saw the name *Boda* there, shut the book tight. I slipped it into my pocket, not wanting Zero to see.

'What you found?' Zero asked.

'Nothing yet,' I lied, not knowing why. Except that Zero was looking for traces of a Zombie pick-up, because that would pacify the dogs of the city, or so Kracker believed. The cops were still hoping to close this case down quickly, with a Zombie at the end of it. But the Zombies were not natural-born killers, they were just desperate survivors. The world in those days was on a constant knife-edge between species. Through the tiny window above Coyote's bed, I could hear the dog-people barking, their growling voices full of hatred and fear.

'Jesus, I hate this,' Zero said. 'Searching through victims' things. It's so depressing.' He was holding up a clear plastic container.

'What's that?' I asked.

'Nano-fleas.'

'What?'

'Robo-fleas. You buy them from the pet shop. Symbiosis, Smokey. The give-and-take scenario. Keeps a doggy clean.'

I shuddered, right down to Shadow-level; the things that dog-people got up to. Now Zero was twisting off the lid, and I was scared suddenly, irrationally. *Please don't let those monsters out of the jar!* What can you do with such feelings?

'Come look at this, Clegg,' I said, hoping to distract him. My eyes were scanning the big map on the wall. 'You seeing what I'm seeing?'

Cop-dog sneezed: 'Just looks like a mess to me. What you saying?'

'I'm saying this is where he went.'

The map was pricked with pins, and scribbled over with felt-tip markings. It was a map of Manchester, and all the outlying regions. Limbo was represented by snakes creeping along dirt roads. 'You see, just here?' I said, and Zero came in close. 'This is where Coyote made the pick-up.' I was pointing to a lonely pin stuck into the map, into the Limbo out beyond Littleborough, north-east of the city, where the map went fuzzy with bad knowledge. Blackstone Edge. Just beneath the pin, written in a doggy hand, yesterday's date, May 1, and a time, 4.00 a.m. Below that, a featherphone number.

'I think you should call that number, Clegg,' I said.

Clegg breathed in loudly, and then sneezed, sending the jar of

nano-fleas flying. 'Jesus-Dung! Look what you made me do now.'
Already he was scratching at his fur.

'I'm not saying this Boda killed him,' I said. 'I'm just saying that
she might have. Are we good cops, or not?'

'You think we're good cops?' Zero was itching from the flea-
bites.

'Can you get Columbus to download a picture of Boda for
me? If Boda didn't kill Coyote, she just might know who did. We
can at least try.'

'Kracker says no, Kracker says close it down. That's it.'

I couldn't believe that Kracker and Zero Clegg were so might-
ily against searching for Boda. Surely that was the major route? Was
something secret going on, some hidden cop-story? Or else was I
just full of bad Shadows? Whatever, I was sure that I didn't want
Zero to see the taxi-dog's diary.

'Kracker's the master,' Zero was saying. 'He's the boss. And
there's more important things on his files. Xcabs are complaining
about Gumbo YaYa again, about how he keeps breaking into the
map-data. Kracker wants me on that trail.'

'You think I'm worried about some old hippy, Zero?'

'Who just happens to be breaking the law.'

'I've got some strong feelings about this case, Zero.'

'Keep them to yourself, and stop calling me Zero.' He couldn't
stop scratching at the jumping nano-fleas.

'Give me one run at it, please. Let's track down that map
number. Are you going to help me?'

'I came here with you, didn't I? Shit. It's a good job nobody
fancies you, Smokey. They'd have a hell of a time keeping up.'

I didn't answer.

Later that day, Zero drove out with me, North, to the dead places.
There were flowers growing from the tarmac as we travelled
through the city of Manchester, and tribes of dogs gathering at our

heels. The air was heavy with pollen messages. Zero was sneezing and scratching as he stuffed a blue phone-feather into his jaws. He called up the number listed on Coyote's wall-map, and then told me that only static cracklings were answering him. And then he sneezed once again, and cursed the hayfever. This journey had caused some arguments, especially when I asked for a three-car patrol: one in front, one behind. And a heavy gun presence. All of which had met with refusal. Zero was playing it strong, saying that no Zombie fucker was going to mess with him. But I could see the fear in his eyes, especially as we moved through the mutant tribes of North Manchester. 'Jesus-Dog!' he said to me. 'What's up with the world these days? Nobody's just themselves anymore. Jesus, will you look at that! You see that creature there, Smokey? What the hell is that? Fucking mutant!' This last shouted through the window.

'You know what, Zero?' I answered. 'They say that some of them have even got Dog inside them.'

'Yeah, well ... that's a cheap shot, Smokey. Dog-Christ! It makes you wonder just how bad Zombies are.'

Then we came to the northern gate of the city, outgoing, a giant shell of a building where sparks flew from lightning rods, and the monster trucks were washed down for Zombie travellers. We nudged the car into a waiting line behind an International Vaz transporter. Its back wheels loomed larger than the Fiery Comet, and City Guardsmen shone lasers under the truck's carriage for illegal goods. Behind a wire fence I could see over to the incoming door, where tankers were being sprayed with anti-Zombie juice.

The truck in front of us moved forward, and whilst Zero was feeding his cop-code to the guardian, a snarling came from the incoming side, and something banged against the wires.

Zombie hitcher sprayed down from the incoming vehicle.

Legs and arms thrashing against the wire.

Zero shouted to some dumb customs attendant, 'Jesus-Dog! Do we have to put up with this?' The incoming Zombie worked his slithering arms through the mesh until he was almost scratching at our car with his talons. Sizzling grease splashed against our windscreen. Zero pulled out his gun. 'I'm gonna take that fucker.' He wound down the window. I told him to cool down, but once the dog was up in Clegg, there was no stopping him. The guardsmen got to the Zombie first, stabbing at the creature with their lightning rods. Then, a terrible howling that even Zero backed away from, and the smell of burning half-dead flesh in the air. The Zombie was shrivelled to a crisp. It made me think about my sweet, illicit Jewel, left all alone in his bedroom back at my flat. How could I protect him?

We made our way through the checkpoint, left the main road, and then scudded along a dirt track, past crashed cars and a burnt out train carriage in the middle of the moors, miles from any railtrack.

Limboland.

A large, withered oak tree we found there, bent by the wind, its branches forming a web of connections. Beyond that a final telegraph pole was etched against the trembling sky.

Exact co-ordinates. Blackstone Edge.

There was nothing but dead grass and dry winds. Zero was sneezing crazy, his gun-hand twitching constantly at his holster as he scanned the moorlands for Zombies. 'You know there's holes out here, don't you?' he said. 'Holes from the Vurt.'

I walked further out into the moors. Off the telegraph pole a long wire dangled from one of the connectors; tuberous roots sprouting from the end of it disappeared into the wet suck of the earth.

To the south of the city, just beyond the realms of the map, before the vast moorlands of Limbo take over, there is an Xcab parked under an overhang of rock. It was safe here, no cops to deal with. The road dropped away into nothingness just beyond Alderley Edge. The driver had travelled just far enough to disengage Columbus.

It had been a lonely path out to this rock, courtesy of an A–Z

book. Boda had paid a tidy sum to a sullen perimeter-being in order
to find a hidden track. Last night she had slept in the cab, with the
brush of leaves against the windows, and the moanings of Zombies
from the outlying moors. She had activated all the defence systems,
and Charrie had promised her he would keep his eyes open, but
still her sleep had been fitful, disturbed by the heavy rumblings of
Vaz wagons as they thundered by and by the pain that travelled her
wounded road. And, more deeply, by the thoughts of Coyote. She
couldn't get rid of the thought that she'd killed him; it was her fault.
Her mind had played at this for hours in the darkness. If only
Roberman hadn't passed that Limbo fare to her. If only she hadn't
given Coyote that same fare. If only Coyote hadn't called that number. If only she'd loved him more, and earlier. If only, if only, if only
. . . there are too many *if onlys* in her life. And what was Columbus
up to now? What had she done wrong to bring on the boss's
wrath? Boda had reached into her shoulder bag then, to pull out
her address book. In it she had jotted down the number that Coyote had rung. Limbo number. She could maybe ring that number?
Find some clue that way about the killer of the taxi-dog. Does she
want to find his killer? Yes, because that would redeem her for
giving him the number. But how can she get to a phone without
going back on to the map? Eventually she had drifted into sleep,
woken up with the same problem. She's been sitting in the cab for
hours now, getting hungry and frustrated. It's the second day of her
new world, getting towards dark again, Zombie time, and the girl is
feeling scared.

There are lights playing above the horizon, deep into Limboland. She doesn't want to think about what may be out there.
She has heard so many rumours. Boda is safe here, for the moment,
caught between authority and chaos, as long as she can keep the
Zombies at bay. But the idea of stasis does not appeal. Another
Vaz wagon speeds along the Limbo road. Charrie rocks with the
vibrations. DO I HAVE TO PUT UP WITH THIS DISTURBANCE?
he says.

'What choice do we have?' Boda asks. 'And how come I'm still hearing your voice? You should be dead to my ears.'

I WOULDN'T MIND SOMETHING TO EAT, ACTUALLY.

'Eat?'

PETROL, DEAR.

'Me too,' Boda replies. 'Food, that is.' A second Vaz wagon thunders by, like an ocean liner lit by fire. Boda starts up Charrie's engine and pulls on to the road in the wake of the wagon, speeding down to where the lights are dancing in deep Limbo.

Twenty minutes later they pull on to the forecourt of an isolated petrol station and cafe. The building is bleak as a ruin, standing alone amidst the wastes of Limbo. A ramshackle neon sign reads COUNTRY JOE'S FOOD AND FUEL SALOON. TAX-FREE PETROL. LAST STOP BEFORE THE END OF THE WORLD, ROOMS VACANT. From lasers mounted on the roof of the cafe, lights are playing in the sky. Boda pays for some petrol and then asks the young dogkid on the pump if a room is available. He just gives a nod towards the illuminated sign and growls, 'Can't you read, Shadowbitch? Ask for Joanna.'

What does he mean, Shadowbitch? Is that what I am now? It throws her for a second, as she makes her way towards the swing doors of the saloon. Country and Western music can be heard from the inside, a woman's voice singing, and the sound of men joining in with ribald whoops of delight.

Boda stands outside, looking in over the top of the batwing doors . . .

Directly opposite, on a wooden stage designed to represent a hillbilly-style ranch house, the woman is singing to her own acoustic guitar accompaniment. The singer is a ravaged blond affair, done up in cowgirl clothing: Stetson, bootlace tie and a frilly gingham skirt.

'. . . As some good steer makes a run for open ground, Joe makes a loop to pull that maverick down.'

Then she goes into the chorus, something about having 'maverick tendencies' in her heart. The crowd of rough-hewn truckers join in lustily, a bellowing of cheers and a blast of sneezing. Also, a stranger noise, a kind of wet humming, comes from the farther side of the room. Dark shapes move there. The song ends and the singer makes her way over to the bar, fighting off the advances of the crowd with a firm hand and a delighted smile.

Boda steps into the room.

Silence greets her. A single throaty whistle pierces the air. Then a terrifying sneeze. About half of the truckers are wearing improvised pollen masks, coloured bandannas covering their mouths and noses. One of the truckers slaps his knee, an invitation for Boda to take a seat there.

Boda refuses, politely.

The truckers are fine—Boda can take that, having spent nine years on the road herself—but as she walks further into the bar the dark shapes in the corner start to move towards her.

Zombies! Shit!

The creatures are looking at her through a haze of smoke and sweat. The truckers are seated down one side of the room, the Zombies down the other. Between them rides a shimmering breath of thick air, like a curtain pulled across something distasteful. The singer is smiling at her from behind the bar. An impressive range of Wild West regalia is mounted on the wall, including five or six revolvers and a rifle. The truckers and the Zombies are staring at Boda's naked skull-map. Boda drags the woollen hat out of her shoulder bag, pulls it down over her head, and then asks the singer, 'You got any Boomer juice?'

Laughter from the trucker side of the room. More sneezes.

'Ain't much call for Boomer around these parts,' the singer replies. 'Got some nice Jack Daniels bourbon. That do you?'

Boda nods, pays for the fire-water, drinks half of it. Two feet away from her the trembling curtain of air separates her from a big

Zombie man, seven feet tall, who seems almost human. Sure, he's greasy and bits of his body are kind of *loose*, but compared to his drinking companions, a ragged pack of whom are now lined up against the invisible dividing wall, this lumpen guy is like some kind of Vurt star. He seems to know this. A bright yellow Stetson hat is jammed down onto his skull. The barmaid steps through the curtain of air, serves the big Zombie, and then steps back into the truckers' side.

Boda says to the barmaid, 'Are you Joanna?'

'Depends what day it is,' the big Zombie grunts.

Christ, they can speak?

'Don't mind Bonanza,' the barmaid says. 'He's just a big ox.'

'I was instructing this child,' Bonanza replies. 'I was just instructing.'

Boda ignores him, amazed at her ease. Weren't Zombies supposed to be vicious? 'You got a room for the night?' she asks the barmaid.

'You can share mine, honey,' one of the truckers shouts.

'Got plenty,' Joanna tells her. 'Comes with a meal. I can bring it up to your room. You don't want to eat with these old boys.'

'Thanks. Is there a telephone?'

'Over by the Napalm machine.'

Boda tries the number, gets back an ACCESS DENIED response. She walks back to the bar. 'That's a featherphone,' she says. 'You got a real phone? One that takes money?'

The barmaid looks deep into the new girl's eyes and then says, 'Follow me. Got one in the back room.'

They go through and the barmaid introduces herself as Joanna, the sister of Country Joe, who's out of Frontier Town just now.

'What is this place?' Boda asks. 'I didn't know there was a town out here.'

'Well then, you don't know fuck,' Joanna replies. 'It's not so much a town, more a way of mind.'

'I liked your song.'

'Why, thank you.'

'What's a maverick?'

'You don't know? Well, you should do. It's an old cowboy term. It's a cow that won't run with the herd during a cattle drive.'

They are in some kind of living room now. Mounted cow horns on the walls. Gumbo YaYa is playing, weakly, from an antique radio set. A collection of acoustic guitars is resting against the woodwork, and an ancient hand-wound telephone sits on a rickety table. 'I can't take the feathers, you see,' Joanna adds, 'I'm a Dodo. I guess you're the same, coming in here and asking for a money-phone?'

'I guess so.'

'Have you been sneezing lately?'

'Not at all. I've tried to a few times. But nothing comes out.'

'Thought not. Same here.'

'What about it?'

'The only truckers I know that aren't sneezing are also Dodos. You're not getting strange urges?'

'Like what?'

'Oh I don't know. A restlessness, I suppose. I know I am. The Dodo truckers also. You know . . . the need to escape? I'm feeling us Dodos are being called.'

What can Boda say to this? 'How come all those Zombies are in your bar? Don't they cause problems?'

'You sure are innocent, young lady. I make my living out of problems. Frontier Town is a fuzzy kingdom. You get to know the people.'

'People?'

'Sure, Zombies are people. This is the last gasp of the city before Limbo, and we have to make allowances. Country Joe's is a broad church. You saw the Wonderwall in the bar? The Wonderwall is Joe's invention.'

'Keeps the Zombies out?'

'Keeps the Zombies *separate*.'

'Would I be able to walk through it?'

'I wouldn't advise it.'

'*You* can do it?'

'I'm kind of special. What's your name?'

'Boda.'

'You're on the run, Boda, I suppose?'

'Something like that.'

'Let me see your head.'

Boda pulls off her woollen hat. Joanna whistles. 'Phew. That's one hell of a range. Oh . . . have you been hit?'

Boda's hand goes up to her wound. 'It's nothing. Just a graze.'

'Rubbish. Here . . . let me . . . oh dear. That's nasty. Let me put something on that.

'No, really. It's nothing.'

'Stay right there.'

Joanna vanishes into the kitchen, comes back carrying a cloth and a bottle of lotion. She makes Boda bend down as she applies the lotion to the scar. 'You should go to a doctor.'

'No.'

'At least let me put a bandage on it.'

'No bandages.'

'Okay.'

Boda gets up from Joanna's ministrations and pulls her address book from her shoulder bag. She looks up the number she wants— the fare-call that Roberman had given her, and that she'd passed on to Coyote. It was all that she had, no address, no names, just the number to ring. Now she's waiting for that call to be put through once more, her thoughts racing. *This has to be it. This number killed Coyote.* Something to do with the girl called Persephone. The sounds of electric passage, and then . . .

Somewhere out on the dark moors to the north of the city, a

last telegraph pole. From that pole a single line falls, bootlegged into
the fields. The line creeps through the undergrowth, turning green
as it travels, turning from wire to vegetable shoot. Now it is a
runner through clay and peat, a plant-line.

Boda is standing in Joanna's living room, listening to whispers
over the telephone. Explosions, unfoldings. Voices of darkness. Plant-
life. A subterranean storm. She is listening to the popping of seeds,
the creaking of growing roots, the slithering of worms, the cracking
of flowers.

The emptiness at the end of the line is too much for her to
bear. Her one and only clue has led to nothing, to a noise she
cannot understand. She replaces the phone in its cradle, gently,
severing the connection. No path to follow any more.

Boda climbs up to her damp room. This is what it's come to: a bed
and a chest of drawers. A small table. Nothing much.

Coyote . . .

She can't help but think about Coyote. About how he had
promised to take her to the Vurtball semi-final, second leg, this
coming Thursday evening. Manchester City. About how the point
of life is to be on the outside, not the inside. Coyote had said this
to her, four days ago in the Nightingale cafe. Was it really only four
days ago?

Xcabs was the inside. Coyote was the outside.

He died because of me. This is what she thinks.

Later, whilst eating her meal—two eggs, one sausage, hash
browns and baked beans—Boda can hear the sound of Joanna singing *Are You Lonesome Tonight?* from downstairs, and the soft whisperings of Limbo in the darkness beyond her room. A long way to
go before home, Whalley Range. If she ever gets back there. If she
ever wants to get back there. What is there to go back for? Her
head is feeling better already; a scab has formed over Kingsway.
Maybe she should just travel further, deeper into the real Limbo.

She could scrape at life out there in the darkness and the dry wind. The prospect was starting to appeal. There is a time to stay put, a time to escape. Tomorrow she would drive Charrie into the deadliest moors. She was finished with Manchester.

Boda climbs into the creaking bed. Despite her resolution, she can't help but miss the wrap-around comforts of the Xcab map. She allows herself some sleepy thoughts about those silky tendrils that were once her whole life and motion. And Roberman's instructions. That loving touch. She can remember the rides she had taken with him, age of nine and a half; when she had first joined the Xcabs. She had been his pupil for three years, sitting in the passenger seat, learning the good Knowledge from that robodog. At the age of twelve her first menstrual blood had appeared, and then Columbus had stated that it was time for her to take her own cab into the map. Boda had sailed through the initiation ceremony with no problems despite the fiery demons she had met there, and she had accepted her new name, *Boadicea,* and her new identity with supreme alacrity.

Now she can no longer trust Columbus. And if she can't trust Columbus, who can she trust?

She reaches over to turn on the room's primitive radio, her fingers moving the tuner until Gumbo YaYa's faint voice comes on, filtering over the edge of the map. A human voice. The hippy pirate is playing the song called *Blue Suede Shoes.* Boda is hoping the music will carry her into some kind of peace. But all through the song she can only think about loss. The loss of the Xcabs, the loss of Coyote, the loss of her former life. She's like a blank, a drift of snow. She had given up her whole life to the Xcabs, now she was drifting free, with no memories of her life before the cabs. She didn't even know what her real name was.

I wish I was inside you now, Charrie, she thinks. I wish I was riding the road with you. She's tired but can't sleep, and in this state of shadows she imagines a conversation with the cab.

ARE YOU OKAY, BODA? asks Charrie.

Okay as I'll ever be.
YOU NEED SOME HELP?
I'm lonely, but I guess I'll get used to it.
YOU WANT TO GO RIDING?
In the morning. Sure. Let's ride away, far away.
INTO THE SUNSET?
Into the sunrise. The sun rises in the morning.
I KNOW THAT.
And anyway, we're heading south, not east.
AWAY FROM THE CITY?
Away from everything. Are you actually talking to me?
OF COURSE I AM. I'M IN YOUR SHADOW.
That's ridiculous. A moment, and then ... *Is that what I am? Really?*
THAT'S YOUR PRE-CABIAN IDENTITY, BODA. YOU'RE TALKING TO ME OVER THE SHADOW.
And a Dodo? I can't dream?
YOU'RE LEARNING ALL THE TIME, DRIVER.

Boda smiles to herself, wrapped in a thin bed-sheet, and then whispers, 'One for the money, two for the show. Three to get ready ...'

From below her window comes the sound of Charrie's horn. Three times.

Good night, Charrie.
GOODNIGHT, BABE.

When Elvis closes his golden throat and Gumbo comes back on air, Boda gets the shock of her life ...

'Boadicea, Boadicea, Boadicea! You out there and listening, killing girl? Listeners, listen up. Boadicea, or just plain Boda, is the name of the young Xcabber who yesterday morning broke away from the Xcab circuit. This is why the map went down, and why all you passengers were left stranded. Ya Ya! Gumbo has checked the Xcab memories, and this girl was driving her cab alongside Alex Park at the time of the murder.'

Boda sits up in bed. 'What?'

'Also, she was the lover of Coyote, that beautiful taxi-dog who was killed yesterday. His funeral is tomorrow, a police rush-job. The plot thickens, listeners. So why aren't the cops after this Boda, rather than blaming some mythical Zombie for this crime? When the cops are asleep, the people must police themselves. This is Gumbo YaYa asking the listeners to look out for this wayward rider. Boda is driving a rogue cab called Chariot, and she's got a shocking map of Manchester tattooed on her head. So if you come across her, let the Gumbo know via the usual access. 7-7-7-Y-Y. You know it's a safe number. Columbus has offered four golden feathers to whoever brings that girl home. Don't give that old Cab-master the benefit. The Gumbo is offering five golden feathers! Ya Ya! Bring me that killer. Pollen count at 225 and rising. Meanwhile here's the Spencer Davis Group from nineteen sixty-five with *Keep On Running*. This is the fifty-ninth revival of the sixties that the Gumbo has witnessed. So like, huh, keep on running, taxi-girl. I'll be seeing you real soon.'

The song playing. Boda terrified. *What is this? I was at Alex Park at the time of Coyote's death? No, I wasn't. Columbus is setting me up. First he tried to kill me, now he's . . . Shit, the whole of Manchester will be after me.*

Even the people in this bar . . .

Now go, cat, go!

She jumps out of bed, gets her things together, checks the window. The nails holding it shut are deep and rusted. Charrie is still down there, patiently waiting, caressed by neon from the End-of-the-World sign. A light drizzle is falling. Beyond Charrie, a lone, bulky figure is standing in the rain. From its shape it must be that Zombie man. Bonanza, wasn't that his name? The Zombie is gazing up at her first-floor window. Boda shivers. *Keep the engine running, Charrie. We're getting out of here.*

She makes for the door as quietly as she can.

Joanna is waiting for her. The barmaid is wearing a full-length leopardskin dressing gown, furry high heels, and her blond hair is slightly awry. 'Going somewhere, lodger?' she asks.

'I've decided against the room,' Boda replies.

'You been listening to the Gumbo, girl?' Joanna says, her voice deep and shaded. 'Sure was an interesting broadcast. All about rogue riders and dog-killers. A mighty fine reward he was offering. Got no use for feathers myself, but I sure could sell them to the boys. Make me some funds, and I'm out of here.' At this Joanna steps forward, so close that Boda can see pancake makeup running to reveal bristles of black hair on the woman's cheeks. And as Joanna steps forward, she brings a gun from the folds of her leopardskin gown. She points the weapon at Boda. 'This is a genuine Colt .45 revolver, cab-girl. The gun that won the West.'

'Please, I'm innocent.'

'Like I said, honey, I could do with the money.'

'Is that Mr YaYa?'

'Do I sound like a man?'

'Is that Wanita-Wanita, then?'

'It is. What's happening?'

'Can I speak to Mr YaYa please. This is Country Joanna speaking. I have some very important news for the Gumbo. Are we on air now? Oh my God . . .'

'We are *not* on air, lady. Calm down. I suppose you've found Boadicea?'

'Actually, I have.'

'You and a thousand others, Joanna.'

Boda reaches for her pack of Napalm cigarettes. Pack message: SMOKING CAN MAKE THE NIGHT LESS LONESOME—HIS MAJESTY'S PERSONAL ELVIS. She lights one up, drags deeply, letting the smoke drift through the air between her and Joanna. Boda is sitting on a floor cushion in the living room behind Country Joe's bar. Joanna is propped against the opposite wall, gun in hand, sweating. With the other hand, she's holding the receiver of the telephone.

'Is this my last cigarette?' Boda asks.

'Shut up.' Joanna screams it in a deep voice and then turns her attention back to the phone. 'Now listen here, Miss Wanita, this is a genuine call. I have the girl here. She is sitting in front of me. I am holding a gun on her.'

'Prove it. We have access to the Xcab voice-prints. Let the girl speak.'

Joanna hesitates. She cradles the receiver in her neck as she opens the sideboard to pull out a bottle of Boomer juice.

'I thought you didn't have any call for that?' Boda says.

'I take what I want. Keep the fuck away!' Boda rises from her cushion, as Joanna drinks down two measures of Boomer. Boda knows full well the effect that Boomer can cause, having taken it many times herself. Two measures of Boomer make you blissful and careless. 'Wanita, you still there?'

'I'm still waiting, lady.'

'Okay, Boadicea is now coming to the phone. Are you ready?' Joanna gestures towards Boda. Boda takes the phone, and speaks into it . . .

'Wanita. This is Boadicea, late of the Xcabs Company. I'm being held against my—'

'Okay, okay! We've got a voice recognition. Stay right there, Boda. Gumbo, get over here. We've found the girl . . .'

'. . . Boadicea! Gumbo YaYa talking to you.'

'Gumbo, I'm innocent. Please, believe me—'

'Give me that phone!' Joanna grabs the phone off Boda. 'Gumbo YaYa, this is Joanna talking. I've got the girl, and we can make a deal.'

'Certainly . . . five golden feathers, as agreed.'

'No, more than that. Are we on air now?'

'No.'

'I want to be on air, Gumbo. I want to sing on the radio. You see, I'm a Country and Northern singer.'

'I can't just let you on air like that, Joanna. There are certain technical processes to sort out. Now if I should . . .'

'Gumbo, listen. This song is called *Maverick Tendencies*. It's my most famous number. Maybe your listeners would like it. See what you think . . .'

Joanna starts to sing then, over the phone, the song that Boda had heard her singing earlier:

> We were driving the cattle to another hick town,
> My lover blaming me for the rain coming down.
> As some good steer makes a run for open ground,
> Joe makes a loop to pull that maverick down.
>
> And I've got maverick tendencies in my heart,
> Since the night you broke me apart.
> Your love is gonna set me loose from the noose.
> I've got maverick tendencies in my heart.

Joanna's voice is crystal clear, riding the notes like the cowgirl she is singing about. Boda can't take her eyes off the show; it looks like Joanna is singing for her life. There is a desperation hidden beneath the melody and the words. This, and the story the song is telling, really get to Boda. Jesus, this woman can actually sing: every note a flame. This is a real torch song . . .

> As that good steer runs for wide open space,
> Joe standing tall in the saddle, rain on his face,
> He throws the lasso to catch the traces
> Of a prey that won't be branded or placed.

Boda picks up one of Joanna's guitars. She plucks at the simple chords of the melody. Joanna closes her eyes and actually smiles at Boda, as they go into the chorus together.

I've got maverick tendencies in my heart,
Since the day you broke me apart.
Your love has set me loose from the noose.
I've got maverick tendencies in my heart.

Boda is bewitched by the song. Or is it the singer? There is something about Joanna that reminds her of Coyote. The singer and the taxi-dog share the same place in Boda's newly born Shadow, that space reserved for the lonesome, the beauty of the remote.

The rope slips free from the horns of the steer,
That maverick beast runs on without fear
Into wide open fields. I won't shed no tears,
Come the morning, Joe, I'll be running clear.

Boda realises that she is being mesmerized. She has to pull back from the song, the situation. *Charrie, let's ride!*

Shadow riding, and suddenly Boda is *inside* Charrie, working the controls so that he starts up, and then working the cab with her Shadow, speeding towards the neon cafe sign. Boda swings the guitar over her shoulder, ready to hit Joanna with it. Joanna's eyes open, and she raises the gun, coolly, finger tight on the trigger, straight towards Boda's head. Joanna carries on singing. Final chorus . . .

I've got maverick tendencies in my heart,
I'm gonna pull this old world of mine apart.
I've a heart that won't be tamed, blamed or ashamed
I've got maverick tend—

An explosion from outside, lights at the window as Boda feels the jolt inside, as Charrie smashes into the neon sign. Joanna turns her head towards the sound. 'What the fuck was that?' Boda completes the guitar swing and then brings it forward, a glancing blow against the singer's head . . .

Echoes of a song drift through the body of the instrument, the snapped strings and the hollow bones of Joanna. The blond wig falls off, revealing an all over No. 2 crew cut. Joanna screams—a deep manly voice this time. The telephone falls. She tries to bring the gun back on target, but Boda has the advantage now. Boda grabs the gun and turns it on the singer.

'Sit down.'

'Please ... don't hurt me.' He's crying in his woman's voice now, swinging between male and female. 'Please ... no visible marks.'

'Sit down!'

Joanna sits.

'You're Country Joe, aren't you?' Boda asks. 'You're a transvestite.'

'I am not a transvestite. How dare you? I am a proper child. A child of Fecundity 10. That's all. I'm special. Very, very special. You will pay for this, girl.'

Boda picks up the telephone. 'Gumbo? You still there?'

'What's going on, Boda?' Gumbo answers.

'Get off my case, Gumbo.'

'I'm doing my public duty.'

'I am innocent. Innocent! And I will do all that I can to find out who killed Coyote. Tell that to your listeners, Mr Pirate Radio DJ. You hear?'

She slams down the phone.

'What you gonna do now, girl?' Country Joe asks.

Good question.

Boda picks up the bottle of Boomer, stuffs it into her shoulder bag. Then she spots the blond wig on the floor. This goes into the bag as well. 'Okay, Joe,' she says. 'You've got some nice clothes, I'll bet?'

Up to Joe's bedroom, gun-led. A palace of glitter, silk and sashes. More wigs, different shades. Boda chooses some of the more conservative items. 'You got the key for this room?' she asks.

Country Joe's eyes are wet with tears, mascara-smeared. He points to the key in the back of the door. 'You're not gonna hurt me, Boda, are you?'

'Well listen,' Boda replies. 'Us mavericks...we look out for each other. Right?'

'Right.'

'Because who the hell else will?'

Country Joe collapses on to his furry bed.

'You're a good man, Joe,' she says to him. 'This is just a bad day on the ranch.'

Country Joe, his voice quivering, says, 'I enjoyed singing with you, Boda. I really did...'

Locking the bedroom behind her, Boda makes her way downstairs and through to the bar area. The curtain of the Wonderwall is glimmering in the darkness, and some brute presence can be felt from the Zombie half of the room. But the door to the outside world is locked and barred, the bar is windowless. The presence behind the Wonderwall is calling to her, and when she looks deeply enough, Bonanza is there, yellow Stetson in place, his finger beckoning.

'Isn't it dangerous?' she asks.

The greasy finger beckons.

Boda walks through the curtain of air.

The air breathes around her, like skin against skin, fingers of smoke dancing over her body. She feels dizzy, almost joyous. And stepping loose from the barrier, she feels something new opening up inside her. She feels like she is walking towards another part of herself.

A feeling of strength at last.

Bonanza leads her to another door, a Zombie door that opens on to the car park. As she runs across the car park, one of Country Joe's dresses falls and is trampled into the mud. Chariot is there, entangled in the neon sign. Boda de-activates the defence systems, and then caresses the cab's skin with a tender hand. *You okay,*

Charrie? she transmits. NOTHING A TOUCH OF LOVING CARE WOULDN'T PUT RIGHT, he answers.

Bonanza is standing by her, smiling, rain dripping off his Stetson, his oily skin slick with drizzle. Boda shakes his hand. Shadow touching Zombie, girl to boy. 'Thank you,' she says.

'No trouble,' he grunts. 'Make a good journey.'

'Why are you helping me?'

'It's not you I'm helping.'

Boda climbs into Charrie. WHAT NOW, DRIVER? Charrie asks.

'Let's ride, Charrie.'

WHERE TO?

'Back to Manchester.'

Down to the root to find the killer and Boda thinks that Columbus himself would be a good place to start. Coyote himself had boasted to her about having visited Columbus but how do you go about finding such a nebulous creature, especially now that she's off-map and Coyoteless?

Bonanza is a shivering figure in the rain as Boda backs Charrie away from the busted sign and out on to the road. She can see Country Joe emerging from the Zombie door. He stoops to pick up the mud-covered dress. He goes up to Bonanza and starts to hit that creature on the chest, again and again those tiny hands coming down on half-dead flesh. The Zombie just stands there and takes it, until the singer faints into his giant arms. The two figures merge into a single being as Boda drives Charrie away from the lights of the roadside cafe.

The second body was found that night, just before the old day shaded into morning: Tuesday, 11.49 p.m. A slab of earth in Alexandra Park surrounded by a radar of flies. They were eating their fill, these insects, buzzing crazy over the smell of dead flesh. Fat creatures, hundreds of them. We had to let off a sonic bomb before we could get our hands on the burial mound.

Some dogtramp had found it, snuffling for food through patches of mist, running scared from what he had stumbled across.

Midnight. Call the cops. Call up Sibyl Jones.

I was still awake when the call came through, charged up by what I had learned from listening to Gumbo YaYa's station, and from what I had read in Coyote's diary. Outpourings of love towards Boda in every line of the last few pages, and a scrap of paper lodged there: a love poem to the taxi-dog signed in Boda's firm hand. *Will he push me again up the shaky path,* this is how it started. *Will he push me again up the shaky path I crave, and pull me down in the waving grass to drown.* The writing was familiar. Also, a ticket for next Thursday's Vurtball game at Manchester City, slipped between pages. According to the diary, Coyote had invited her to the match. Something in the diary's tale of love got to me; a sense of being desired.

I was naked from the waist up after reading it, kneeling over the cot in Belinda's old bedroom. My stomach was lodged against the cot's rim, so that my breasts were lowered toward the baby. My left nipple was being sucked at. There was no milk, of course, I was long past that juiciness. Still, my Jewel, my secret son, was feeding on something. He had started to sneeze rather badly during the night. I applied a wet flannel to his eyes and his nose. He gargled some words at me. I could only trust they were words of love, because there was no translation available. My Jewel had a dead tongue. Over the Shadow I found some scraps of love. I comforted Jewel for a while, resting his mis-shapen head in my arms, and then letting him suck once more. The telephone called me from this motherly job. Which made what we found in the park even harder to take.

The ride to Alexandra was a ride through a spring garden; tiny shoots were breaking through the tarmac of the roads, and the passing shops and houses were soft-edged with greenery. News was coming from the experts that we were heading for the worst hayfever of all time, even worse than during Fecundity 10. In the park, we found a bulbous sculpture of soil, twisted flowers rising from the earth, a fetid stench. Zombie found and accounted for. That creature had hiked his last car home; a final drop-off in unsanctified ground. A resting place in the petals. His body formed out of dirt, totally transformed.

Zero was waiting for me there. 'Know what, Smokey? It saddens me to find the perp like this. Because I had one great urge to put this Zombie down. That would really make Kracker smile. And when the master smiles, I smile. But now the bastard Zombie has gotten himself killed, and I'm left with nothing.'

'You want to put Zombies down? We used to do that to dogs.'

'Save the weeping, Smokey. Zombies aren't human.'

'They're partly human.' I knelt down beside the body.

'What the hell are you doing?'

'My job.'

'We don't need a fucking Shadow-search, Jones.'

'I'll decide that.'

'Christ, if you stepped on a cockroach, you'd Shadow-search that, wouldn't you? The case is closed. Get out of there.'

'Too late, dogcop.'

I was already dropping down into dead thoughts, with fingers of smoke drifting through to the mind of a Zombie corpse . . .

Blackness . . . no flickerings . . . no signs of life . . . half-life . . . any kind of last life . . . fruitless . . . my shadows drifting through the layers of darkness . . . deeper yet . . . the darkness growing . . . so cold . . . layers of death unfolding . . . and then enfolding me . . . the need to pull free . . . back to life . . . and then . . . a sparkle of light in the hidden depths . . . bursting . . . the world . . . bursting the world with greenness . . . too much colour to be taking . . . large sucking flowers at my shadow throat . . . fronds of love . . . flowers on fire . . . dancing . . . dancing . . .

Pull out . . .

I was fighting back to the everyday life, the living life, needing it so much.

I expected Zero to at least show some interest, but when I came back to earth, his eyes were full of disgust at my shadowy processes. With total disregard, he twisted the cop feather into his mouth, calling off the Zombie alert. 'Master Kracker, we found that monster. No more worries.' Something like that, I guess. He pulled out the feather and then shifted his wet eyes over towards me. 'One less worry, Smokey,' he said. 'Dog-killer down and nullified. Shit! *Aaaaachhhooosssshhhhh!*' He couldn't stop sneezing. 'These flowers are getting to me.'

'Okay,' I said, 'who killed the Zombie?'

'Like who the fuck cares? Jesus-Dog! Zombies don't count.'

'He was killed by the flowers, Zero. Just like Coyote. I found the same presence in both of their minds. The explosion. It's some kind of garden.'

'Kracker says that we bury the taxi-dog tomorrow. Kracker wants to announce to the press that the Zombie killed Coyote, and that we took the Zombie out with cop-fire. What do you reckon, Smokey? Is that a good business plan? Would that stop a riot?'

'And Gumbo YaYa will go along with this lie?'

'Gumbo's not running the force, Smokey.'

'Isn't he? You been listening to him, lately?' Zero nodded. 'You'll know then that he's put out an all-points bulletin on some Xcabber called Boadicea. She broke free of the ranks yesterday, some hours after the murder. She was also known as Boda. Ring any doggy-bells, Zero?'

'Canine-Jesus!' Clegg snarled. 'What is it with you and this Boda? You got the hots for her?'

'Did you lie to me, Clegg?'

'What?'

'Gumbo's claiming that Boda was caught in the cab-records. She was at Alexandra Park at 6.19 a.m., yesterday morning. The time of Coyote's murder. Did you know about this before the broadcast?'

'She was his girlfriend, Smokey, that's all.'

'Did you *know?*'

'His girlfriend! Jesus-Dog! Maybe they were fucking in the grass. Who knows? So they're doing the old dance down there in the park, the Zombie climbs out the back of the cab. They think they've killed him, right? But you know how hard it can be to kill those half-alivers. They love death, don't they? It's a mother to them.'

'Somebody killed the Zombie.'

'Maybe this Boda killed him. Good. One less Zombie. Okay, so the Zombie takes Coyote out. And what else are you going to think about in your last moments, Smokey, the state of the economy? I think not, I reckon the loverboy's name just might be on *your* final list. Or maybe you don't know that much about love?'

'Something's going on here, Zero.'

'This wouldn't be one of your Shadow-feelings, Sibyl?'

'I tried to access the Xcab records last night. I wanted to know who was delivering to the Alex Park area Monday morning. I got back Access Denied. I thought the cabs and the cops were working together. Something's going wrong, Zero, and I'm going to keep on looking, with or without you. Gumbo's claiming that Boda is somewhere down in Frontier Town South.'

'Well good luck, Smokey. Girl could be down fucking *London* by now. It's out of our jurisdiction.'

'Take a look with me, Zero. Limbo South.'

'What you on, Jones? You're taking the Gumbo too much. You think that pirate knows the truth? You're not losing your street-smarts, are you? *Aaacccchhhooooossshhhh!!!!* Shit! Pardon me. Let's get out of this weed-dump.'

'Help me, Clegg. Kracker needn't know.'

'Kracker needn't know?!'

'I'm asking for your help.'

'You're asking me to go against the boss?'

'One of these days, Zero, you're going to have to break away.'

Zero's eye went dog-bright. 'You know what, Jones?' he growled. 'Sometimes you humans really piss me off.' Never before had I heard Zero putting humans down. He understood immediately what he had said, and the dog-light clicked off in his eyes.

Fleshcops were digging at the earth, uncovering the Zombie from his burial mound of flowers. Zero shouted some instructions at them, just to take the heat off himself. The cops were sneezing like maniacs, but I was super-clean, unsuffering. Zero's big snout was dribbling with snot, as he turned back to me. 'What's wrong with you, Jones?' he said. 'Don't you like sneezing? You some kind of mutant these days?' And then his eyes filled with tears, maybe the tears of pollen, maybe not. 'I'd like to help you, Jones. I really would . . .'

'You'd like to?'

The big dogcop turned away again, striding off through the grass to plague the fleshcops. It was then that I realised that some-thing bad was really happening, something bad with the cops. And Zero was a part of it.

That canine couldn't bear to look at me.

Wednesday
3 May

His name is Dove. Thomas Dove. He rides the heads of strangers like a feather. This is what he is: bladed skater's body, orange hair cut in a wedge, a pair of cop-wings and a bloodstream full of Vurt. The dream-stream. Tom Dove is the Manchester Cops' best ever Vurt angel, and he's flying down to Rio de Bobdeniro, with a parcel of tests for the phantasms there. His cop-job is to seek out and destroy illegal dreams; to find the bootleg Vurts. Listen to his prismatic wings flapping, making colours in the smoke of the mind. Boldness. Tom Dove: a clean, human road to fantasy, so good he doesn't need to take feathers. He is mostly human, of course, except for the thick traces of the Vurt living inside his flesh.

Rio de Bobdeniro. A rich slice of the mind. A favourite feather of the sad and lonely. It allowed the Vurt traveller to enjoy the collected dreams of Mr Bobdeniro. God knows who he was; some say a psyched-up true-life villain who killed over fifteen people. Others say he was a star of cinema. (Cinema is what people did before Vurt was discovered.) Still others reckon he was a real mother's boy who couldn't even leave the family home unless it was through the door of dreams. Whatever, Bobdeniro's dreams were violent and cathartic. People loved to hook up to his vision, living inside his mind for a spell. Hatred was satisfied. Love was denied. Tom Dove the Vurtcop was flying into the sub-feather called *The Deer Hunter,* following up on a lead. There were bootleg Bobdeniros on the street, selling at a cut-rate price, spiced up with extra violence, and the estate was getting tearful at the loss of profit. Dove's other cop-job was to search out and retrieve swapped innocents. Whenever a Vurt creature made an illegal entrance into reality, something else, something random and therefore innocent, had to take its place in the dream. This was known as Hobart's Law of Exchange, because the two people or objects involved in the swap had to be of the same worth. A little give and take was allowed as long as it stayed within Hobart's Constant. Hobart was the discoverer of Vurt, and she had added this rule to the mechanism in order to maintain a balance between the dream and the real. Tom was currently searching for five different innocents who had 'vanished,' but the most intriguing was nine-year-old Brian Swallow. This was because Swallow had the most Hobartian 'worth.' Tom had sensed a heavy Vurt presence in the boy's deserted bedroom, a reading of 9.98 on Hobart's Scale. Tom himself came in at 9.99, so obviously something powerful had come through in exchange. These days the doors between the two worlds were slippery, as though the walls were going fluid. It used to be, in the old days, you got one bad exchange every five years or so. These days, it was more like one a month. It seemed that Manchester was a particularly thin membrane between the Vurt and the Real. Maybe this was because Miss Hobart had invented the Vurt feathers here. Whatever, Tom Dove had the nasty feeling that if the Manchester wall should dissolve then the whole country would follow. Dove had his work cut out searching for missing persons, but this Swallow boy was the worst yet. So far, no good clues, just a few feathery hints here and there. So this was another reason why he was seeking out Rio de Bobdeniro; sights of disturbance in the Vurt usually heralded some weak doorway.

The Deer Hunter Bobdeniro variant was set in the Vietnamese War and Tom has landed in the mind of a Viet Cong officer, urging Bobdeniro and his co-star into a no-win game of Russian Roulette. Bobdeniro has persuaded the Gooks to put three bullets in the gun. Two empty chambers have already clicked; now is the time to strike, to laugh and to grimace, and then to pull the gun away from his own head, on to the brow of the officer, which is Tom Dove, just visiting. Tom was expecting to get blasted apart any second now; the gun was moving, speed of light, according to the script, straight for his brain. But then a fluttering to his left, a *green* fluttering, a *yellow* sparkling . . .

Aaaachhhooooooosssshhhhhhh!

Bobdeniro sneezes. The shot goes wide. Tom Dove, fuelled by the game, reaches for his own pistol, shoots. Bobdeniro's head explodes. The other Gooks take out the co-star. The scene is a slow-motion drift of powder and blood. The two bodies of the famous Vurt-players lying in splatters. The Gooks don't know what to do; this outcome has never taken place before, usually they are dead by now. They feel like vapours, no life to their meanings. Tom Dove, inside the head of the chief Gook, can't believe what he's just done; he's killed Bobdeniro in the world-famous Russian Roulette scene! Vurtual sacrilege. A blow to the system. Tom's wings feel heavy.

The Gooks turn their guns on each other, in a mass feeling of redundancy. The purpose has gone from their lives, which was to die by the hand of the stars. Now all they can do is kill each other, trying to make the proper result, sneezing even whilst they fire.

Tom Dove feels a comrade's bullet entering his heart, but by now he is already pulling out, making a grab for real life. Safety. Where the rules work. His wings are heavy, heavy, so very heavy; it takes all of his Vurt-knowledge to even get off the ground, out of the closing mind of the Gook. The bullet is killing him. One last push, now . . .

Break through. Back down into the Manchester cop station, pulling the Rio de Bobdeniro Vurt from his mind, breathing badly, wheezing, tears in his eyes, back to the flesh.

Tom feels that the rules have been broken somehow, but not by bootlegs. This was more dangerous. He knows that the sneeze was a viral intruder, something not included in the original game program. And it had come from that green and yellow fluttering he had noticed in the Vurt walls of the game. There was a seepage point there, and Tom would have to investigate that hole. Cops all around him, real-life fleshcops now, they're sneezing as well, just like in the game. Flowers·are growing through tiny cracks in the station's walls. The cops are spraying the flowers with germs. Tom Dove knows all about the hayfever; about how the experts were predicting a vintage year. He knows that all the traffic cops have been complaining about the flowers breaking through the roads of the city, about all the jams caused by this.

Dear God, they have hayfever in the Vurt world now. The virus is nesting in there. What hope is left to us?

And then Tom Dove sneezes again, a real-life sneeze. *Aaaaaaaachhhhhoooooshhhhhhhh!!!*

He must go back into the Rio. He has to find that opening.

The howling of dogs in a hundred-part harmony. A sneezing, barking orison for a good guy, a canine/human mix. A pack of dogs standing on their hind legs, in rigid lines of tenderness all around the Southern Cemetery. Statues of stone dogs were standing here and there amongst the more usual tombstones.

The funeral of Coyote. A good day for it. The tombs were sun-bright, wrapped by vines sporting the most wondrous flowers. The pack of mourners was gathered from all over the city's map, because that outlaw taxi-dog was famous on the streets, dog-level and cab-level.

We were two days into the *Flowers of Evil* case. Two bodies on the files; one a half-dog and the other a Zombie. The big cops had effectively shut down the case. But I was Sibyl Jones, the Shadowcop; I could not stop from searching. On top of that, a crazy spiralling pollen count, over 500 grains per cubic metre at the morning's reckoning. The whole city was sneezing and the papers were demanding a cure.

Gumbo YaYa was calling the people to arms, against the flowers and the cops. He had turned his secret station into a cop-baiting murder hunt, making a mockery of Kracker's cheap ruse of the cops killing the Zombie. That pirate had more access than I did, and that maddened me. Despite all this, the case had faded. Kracker had asked Zero to report for a new mission. I had requested a photo of Boda to be downloaded from Columbus; this was met only with refusal. But this Flowers case was plaguing my Shadow. I was getting repeated glimpses of the green explosion gathered from Coyote's and the Zombie's minds. And the flowers that were growing over the city? Surely it must tie up? But how? And the Boda clue that the cops kept denying. Boda's name trapped in the mind of a dying taxi-dog, killed by flowers. Flowers, flowers, flowers. My Shadow was blooming with them. Was something going wrong with the flowers? What did that mean? How can flowers go wrong? I was working alone now, a surprising ally of the Gumbo's: when the cops are asleep, the people must police themselves. I was here at Coyote's funeral unofficially.

And I was scared. Scared of all those ugly runtboys and bitchgirls. Hundreds of them wailing with dignified loss at the young blackcabber's parting. My Shadow was glowing with the fear, wisps of smoke combing my skin, the dogs were sniffing at the cop-smells and the Shadow-smells with angry snouts. Every combination was there. Not many pure dog or pure human, but hundreds of crazy messed-up mutants in-between. Evil-looking creatures for the most part; bits of dog sprouting from human forms, scraps of humanity glimpsed in a furry face. Even now, from one hundred and sixteen years of distance, I can still feel traces of my distaste, my utter *fear* of dogs. Especially so many of them. Zero I had grown immune to, but I was suffocating on fur that funeral day, and my Shadows were *sweating* panic. I was scared and wishing Z. Clegg was by my side, but that dogcop had told me that the funeral was a dead clue, told me the repeated mantra: case closed.

Sure, the case *was* closed, but I had the vague idea in my Shadow that Boda just might turn up at the victim's funeral. I had given up on the idea of trawling Limbo—Zero had been right on that one—but if this Boda really loved the dogboy, maybe she would turn up at the final send-off. It was by now street-knowledge that Boda's head was adorned with a map of Manchester Central. Gumbo's five golden feathers were still up for grabs, and there would be plenty of hunters. I was one of them. Problems: if Boda did come back for the funeral she would have to be in disguise, and possibly driving another vehicle. Or maybe she was dead already, a victim of hungry life out there in Limbo. Five Xcabs were parked at the cemetery gates, so they were working on the theory of her still being around.

The hot sun burned into my Shadow. The flowers in the grave-yard were ripe and overloaded. It seemed like far too much, and way too soon; too early in the year for such abundance. Big fat blooms hung from vines that twisted tight around the stone memorials. I was sick from the perfume, drinking in the smell, lost in it. Tombstones shimmered in the heat waves. The nearest one to me read, *Brian Albion . . . beloved son . . . not dead . . . only changing*. The word *beloved* was partly obscured by sticky, fly-mapped dogshit. All around me crossbreeds were sneezing out gobs of snot from their snouts, the sunshining day rained on by dog-mucus. My best black uniform ruined by it.

Now the undertakers were pushing their way through the dog-crowd, carrying Coyote's coffin. It was strewn with orchids, and the bearers could not stop from sneezing. To give them credit, that coffin never wavered. Dogs parted like Moses was their trainer; no more barking or howling, just a collective panting from their throats. I saw the train that followed Coyote's coffin. A young woman and a puppygirl, both of them dressed in mourning.

According to my investigations, the woman was Coyote's ex-wife. Her name was Twinkle. She was purely human, and just twenty-two years old. Sixteen years old when she first met Coyote. He didn't even have a taxi at that time. He was just a strung-out wanderer of the streets, searching for something. Twinkle had a thing about dogboys. She had known a good robodog named Karli when she was small, and maybe this was the cause of her obsession. She couldn't get enough of them, and Coyote was the best she'd ever met. They had loved and laughed, and married in June. Done all the right things, given birth to a half-breed, made a home in Bottletown. And then Coyote had found his black cab and things were looking up, until he had started looking down, taking danger-ous rides, coming home with wounds to show Twinkle. Twinkle had had enough of wounds in her childhood, now she just wanted a blood-free life. Differences had led to quarrels, quarrels had led to arguments, arguments had led to divorce. Isn't that the way?

The puppygirl's name was Karletta. Four years old. She was the daughter of Twinkle and Coyote. And wasn't she beautiful? A peachy human skin sprinkled with dark spots. Karletta was holding tight of her mother's hands, keeping her steady through the slow movements of the coffin's journey. She had a dog's love for her owner, even though the only part of her that really betrayed her origins was the set of lovely whiskers that sprouted from her cheeks. She sneezed just then, and I wanted to run to her, take her in my hands of smoke, hold her close, wipe her wet nose for her. Twinkle did the wiping for her, and I was jealous. Can I really have felt such things?

Now the coffin had reached the graveside, and the dogs were panting, sneezing, even howling. Not the howling of hunger, but the howling of compassion. I put aside all discomfort caused by the sound of dogs in order to scan the crowds for Boda. Cops over by the chapel-of-rest, gun-loaded against possible dog-trouble. No sign of a map-headed girl.

The coffin was being lowered into the earth, the preacher-dog was chanting his litany . . .

Whiskers to whiskers, bone to bone...

A movement from the cops. Dogs howling from the trees next to the chapel. Something going down? I did a check on the mourners. Everything peaceful this side, but now I could see one of the cops, plain-clothed, separate himself from the group. He strode towards the trouble spot, that confident swagger...

Claws to claw...

I could see Twinkle grasping Karletta to her breast. A lovely movement. Beyond that the big cop moving through the waves of heat, his edges blurred so that they looked like fur...

Zero?

Dust to dust...

What was Zero Clegg doing here? He'd spent all morning telling me how redundant this graveyard trip was. I looked down into the grave...

Twinkle threw a single dog violet onto the top of the coffin. A blue flower with spurs of yellow. I looked up...

Zero disappeared into the haze.

Roberman Pinscher is walking back from the ceremony, over towards the gates of the graveyard where his Xcab is parked. He's worked the system so that he could be off duty for the Coyote's funeral. Some canine correspondence working. It is at this precise moment, some few steps away from the cemetery's Nell Lane entrance, that the robodog gets an unscripted thought inside his head. His name is being called up inside like a plume of smoke...

Roberman...

Roberman makes three low growls that could only be translated as something like, 'Robotic-Jesus-Dog!'

Don't be scared, Xcabber.

Roberman's looking all around to catch the talker, growling, 'What-fare-calling?' Translation: 'Who's there?' But seeing only tombstones surrounding him, each with a message of death.

It's Boda here.

Growling to himself, 'What-fare?'

I'm listening. I'm in your Shadow, Roberman.

Growling, 'Who-this?'

In your Shadow, dog-rider, talking to you. Come looking, driver. The big elm tree to the left of you. That's right. Keep searching. That's right. Just beyond that gravestone there, that's right.

Roberman walks past the gravestone, and then around the elm tree, where there is a woman waiting for him. Long blond hair, cowgirl boots, flared gingham skirt, bolero jacket. Roberman is running then, away from the vision, even as the tendrils of an intruding Shadow reach into his mind . . .

I got back to the station after the funeral only to find a message from Kracker on my desk. I was to report to his office at the soonest possible. When I got there, Zero was already in attendance. He had a pollen mask on his face.

'You bastard.' I set on him straight away, disregarding Kracker's presence.

'What?'

'What were you doing at Coyote's funeral, Clegg?'

'Sibyl . . .' His trembling voice was muted by the mask. 'I wasn't . . .'

'I saw you there. You told me it was a no-clue zone.'

'I was just trying to . . .' Zero started, a big sneeze coming out of his mouth despite the mask. Muffled.

Kracker spoke up for the dogcop. 'Officer Clegg was only trying to keep the peace, Jones. That was my initiative. I was fearful of a dog-riot, and nobody can handle the dogs like Clegg. He was there on guard duty.'

'You're keeping something back from me,' I said. 'Fuck the both of you. I want the whole story.'

Kracker brought his fingers up to a newly risen bruise on his forehead. He stroked at the wound. 'My wife hit me.' Apologetic. His tight mouth played around the tip of a thermometer. His thin, shaking body was perched on a leather chair. He told me to sit down. I said I would prefer to stand.

'You're still looking for Coyote's killer, Jones, even though we've found the Zombie who did it.'

'You know it's not a Zombie killing, sir. The Xcabber Boda is tied up in some way. You've heard what Gumbo's saying about her movements on the morning?'

'It doesn't matter what the Gumbo YaYa thinks. It doesn't matter what you think, Jones. It doesn't even matter what I think. Keeping the city in peace is more important. I've closed this case down. Clegg is now exclusively dedicated to the Gumbo search. I can't have that pirate messing up the cop-systems. As for you . . .'

Kracker turned to look at the poor dogcop. Zero sneezed again, rather loudly, and Kracker said to him, brusquely, 'I have finished with you, Clegg. You may leave.'

Zero climbed out of his chair, sneezing and crying his way to the door, and begging the Master for forgiveness. The door closed behind him. Kracker turned his dry gaze on me. 'Sit down, Sibyl. Come on, let's be friendly.'

I sat down in Zero's vacated seat. The upholstery was still warm from his body.

'So then,' Kracker started, 'Columbus has already told me that you attended Coyote's funeral this morning. Your Comet was lodged on the map at that time, that place. This is why I called you in.'

'You're very close to Columbus these days, sir?'

'You know how it is, Jones . . . the Cops and the Cabs, working together for the common good.'

'It's a very admirable slogan, sir, but may I ask—'

'May I ask what you were doing at the funeral of that dog? That was an unauthorized journey.'

'Clegg was there.'

'On my authority.'

'I was looking for driver Boadicea, sir.'

'And you found . . . ?'

'Nothing, sir.'

'Good. Very good.' Kracker's mind was distracted, I could tell that from the drifts of smoke moving through his Shadow. He was holding some deep secrets from me, and the pressure of keeping all that dark mesh in place was making his brain hurt.

In the world of fluidity the dark mesh was a solid stop sign, a blocked road on the map, a door closing on smoke; a kind of anti-Vaz that the thinker could set in place against an intruder's eye. Kracker's hands were playing with the thermometer, tapping it on the desk where a closed folder rested, and then replacing it in his mouth. He pulled it back out and gazed once more at the scale. A frown creased his thin face. 'I'm worried, Sibyl. Very worried.'

'You're catching the hayfever, sir?' I asked.

'Not yet, thank God, but I've got twelve officers down with it already. You're not feeling any pains yourself?'

'Not at all, touch wood.' I tapped at his desk.

'Good. Excellent. Clegg is suffering badly. You saw those tears? All that snivelling. Most unbecoming for a public guardian, don't you agree?'

'I'm sure he's doing his job correctly, sir. He's a good cop.'

'Quite, quite.' Kracker paused then, briefly, as though composing his thoughts. 'Can I be honest with you, Sibyl?'

'I'd prefer it.'

'Have you any idea what this position entails? Chief of Police? Can you possibly imagine the pressures I am working under? I have many people on my back. Many, many people. I don't just mean the criminal elements, I mean also the Authorities, and the public watchdogs, and the mad dogs themselves, and the robos and the Vurt-people and the Shadows. And various self-appointed guardians like that blasted Hippy Gumbo fellow. And the Xcabs of course. Sometimes I feel like the whole of the city is crouching on my shoulders. Sibyl, you must have noticed, my shoulders are very weak.'

I didn't say anything. Through the office window I could see the City shimmering in the heat haze. The roads were melting, the buildings were fuzzy with yellow growth.

'I'm pure, of course.' Kracker continued. 'You know that. No robo, no dog, no powers of the Shadow, no direct access to the Vurt. Too much Fecundity 10 in my veins of course, but apart from that . . . sometimes I feel like I'm the last real person alive in this city. Purely human. Sibyl . . . all of these hybrids look to the cops with their problems. This is why I employ people like yourself: Shadowcops, and robocops, and dogcops like Clegg, and Vurtcops like Tom Dove. But the world is getting very fluid these days. Very fluid. Dangerously so. There are doors opening between the species. Fecundity 10 is partly to blame, of course, as I know to my cost. I have twenty children, and all of them demanding upkeep.'

'Twenty-one.'

'What?'

'Twenty-one children, sir.'

'Well, never mind that. I don't want to become maudlin. These pressures are here to teach us about life, are they not? And do you know the very worst of my worries? No, no . . . it's not the rising crime rate, it's not the fever. Even the imminent dog-riot I can live with, having made a career out of quelling emotions. No. My worst pressure is the Xcabs. Yes. You looked shocked. Good. Xcabs are at my back all the time. I mean Columbus of course. But what can I do? Without the Xcab map, I cannot police this city. They are my burden. Let me tell it like it is, Sibyl . . . I'm in their pocket. We all are, all of us cops. Do you understand.'

'I'm trying to, sir.'

'Good. This is what I want. Spirit. You're a damned fine cop, Jones.'

'What exactly are you asking of me, sir?'

'Shadowcop Sibyl Jones . . . I dearly want to find this Boadicea.'

'But—'

'Please, hear me out.'

'But you wanted the Coyote case closed down?'

'It is closed. The Zombie killed Coyote. I can make the public buy that. Don't worry. Gumbo YaYa is a ton of air. Dangerous air, for sure, but I can deal with it. There are other things . . . well, let me be plain. Columbus is demanding the return of Boda and, more specifically, her cab.'

'Columbus? Christ—'

'Sibyl, please, no profanities. Xcabs are important to us. Never mind. I can understand your anger. What I'm saying is quite simple. I *have* been leading you on a lie, Jones, and that hurts me. But rather myself hurt, than your good self.'

'What are you saying?'

'Gumbo is right about Boda's whereabouts, Monday morning. She was at the park. But no, I believe Gumbo is wrong about her being the killer. I do believe she knows something about how Coyote really died.'

'So you sent Clegg on that trail? Without telling me?'

'I had to. Much to my cost. But that dog is too ill to conduct such a major case. No clues were coming home.'

'Why couldn't you send me?'

'Xcabs are ashamed of the way that Boda broke away from them, and of the damage she made to the map. Columbus is fearful of the public turning against his business. He can't afford upsets like Monday's map-chaos. The people will find alternative transport. And if Columbus can't afford it, then neither can we.'

'What's wrong with this case?'

'Sibyl, I cannot police this city without the Xcabs' map. This is why I've agreed to help Columbus get Boda's cab back on the line. He can't run the map without a complete system. Now listen closely, Sibyl Jones. I want you to find Boda's cab for Columbus.'

'Why me? Why now?'

'I believe that you have the best qualities for the job. Boda's crimes . . . theft of a vehicle, and damage to the city's map. Need I remind you, Jones, these are serious misdemeanours. Also, possible knowledge of Coyote's killer. This will be our part of the deal. Columbus gets the cab. We get Boda. This will be your case alone. No obstacles.'

'Why not earlier?'

'You have to ask?'

'Sir?'

'Your Shadow isn't strong enough for me, Jones.' He pushed the closed folder over towards me. 'Look at this,' he said. 'We downloaded it from Columbus.'

Inside the folder was a six-by-four photograph, with the words 'Xcab Driver: Boadicea' printed along the bottom, followed by a cab number. It was taken prior to the head tattoo; a sweet, innocent face even with the Xcab shave.

It only took one look, the years peeling away from a teenager's face.

And then Kracker let the black mesh away from his mind, and I saw there the thoughts he had kept from me.

'She's my daughter?' I asked.

'Because Boadicea is your daughter, Jones. Exactly. Her real name is Belinda, I believe? This is why I didn't want you on the case. Too personal. I told Clegg as much. Surely you had an inkling?'

'Jesus-Fuck!'

'Quite.'

The world was slipping away from me.

'Why should I want to arrest my own daughter? Sir?'

'Because she has broken the law, Officer Jones. Isn't that good enough for you? You will follow every order, as is your duty to the public. But there's more. And this is secret knowledge, Jones. Boda had the Shadow in her, before Xcabs took over. But you know this already, of course, you gave it to her yourself. You know what this means? We cannot afford the cost of a Shadow being involved in the killing of a dog. If the dogs should learn of your daughter's true nature, well . . . you can imagine the possible consequences, Officer Jones. She would be lynched. I want that rogue driver brought in. Maybe then we can eliminate her from our enquiries. This is a normal case, Jones. We will follow the procedures of law, but we must be discreet in the application. I will give you all the support you need, I will even give you Clegg as back-up, despite his illness. But only you can finish this case, Jones. A mother's instincts, and all that. Who else could find that miscreant?'

I stood up, accepting the mission. Taking one firm, official step closer to the edge.

The evening of that day, Roberman is working the six-till-two night shift at the rank. At 9.07 he is directed to a pick-up at the Manchester Ship Canal, Old Trafford dock. The moon is making a low play at the water, breathing ripples and junk. Roberman gets out of the Xcab, disconnecting his system. Now he's standing on the shore-yard, waiting for the shadows to lengthen. No passenger in sight, only the wind and the litter, until a far-off figure steps out from behind a rubbish dump and one of the fleeting shadows plumes itself from the jigsaw of darkness. Roberman receives the Shadow more easily this time, knowing of nowhere to run to. He's growling in his thoughts at the sight of the faraway girl, turned on, confused and angry. 'That you, Boda?' he thinks, letting the thoughts travel over the Shadow-paths, free from Columbus's prying Hive-mind. 'Really? You back, Boda? What do you want from me?'

Come closer.

Roberman walks over to where the girl is loitering against the side of a busted skip.

Boda is waiting there for him. She has Country Joe's blond wig pulled down tight over her features, and a look of desperation in her eyes. They have a conversation then, robodog and rogue driver, in perfect and human English; Boda shaping all of Roberman's growls into clear pictures, via the Shadow.

'You've got the Shadow?' Roberman asks in this newly clean voice of his.

'I'm pre-cabian, Rober. I can hear you thinking.'

'Leaving the Hive like that. It was cruel of you.'

'I was forced into leaving.'

'You think I care? Well, fuck you, traitor.'

'Columbus is the traitor. He tried to have me killed.'

'Columbus wouldn't do such a thing.'

'I need your help, Roberman.'

'Eat Shadow-shit.'

'I'm sorry for leaving you.'

'Are you? I guess you're missing the map, Boda?'

'Some.'

'So how are you getting around?'

'By fast-track.'

'Dog-Jesus! Do those rattle-buses still run? Didn't they tear the tracks up years ago?'

'I'm changing, Roberman. I liked the map, but I love the free roads more. I'm stronger now. I can't come back to Xcabs. Columbus is a bad guy.'

'You're asking for trouble, Calamity Jane.'

'That's right. I'm a gun-toting, hell-for-leather bitch from the plains who's heading for danger.' Boda pulls out the gun stolen from Country Joe. 'I need to talk to the cab-boss, pronto.'

'Cab-Jesus! Put that away!'

'It's a Colt .45, Rober. You like?'

'Put it away! Just . . . just stop pointing it at me!'

'Tell me how I can meet Columbus.'

'Nobody meets Columbus. He's not *real* enough.'

'You were my cab-teacher, Rober. I need to see Columbus

regarding the death of Coyote. I think the old boss is involved in some way. Coyote told me that Columbus could be visited, if the correct procedures were taken.' She empties the gun's chamber of all but one bullet. 'Maybe you know of a way?' She then spins the chamber.

'What are you doing?'

'Just practising.' Boda puts the gun against her temple and . . .

Roberman shouting, 'Boda!'

. . . pulls the trigger.

Click.

'Cab-Jesus on a ride to hell!' Roberman breathes at last.

'What do you reckon, Rober?' Boda says, holding the gun out to the taxi-dog. 'One bullet, six chambers.' She spins the chamber again. 'You want to take a chance with me?'

The wind blows the moon's reflection over the canal water until it covers Roberman with a silvery light. Flowers whisper against his hind legs. 'You're fucking crazy, woman!' he says.

'With Coyote dead,' Boda replies, 'I have nothing to live for, and the only thing keeping me alive is finding out who killed him. You must tell me where Columbus is hiding. And if the gun won't loosen you, then maybe this will . . .'

'Get out of my head!' Roberman screams, as a fierce pain stabs at his skull.

'You know, I'm really getting to like this Shadow power.'

'Please, Boda . . . you're hurting me . . .'

'How about this then? There, isn't that good?' A look of robo-bliss comes into the taxi-dog's eyes. 'You like having your Shadow stroked, don't you, dog driver? Sexy as hell, I'll bet. Feel me stroking. Oh, yes. Lovely. I wonder . . . if I stroked deep enough, maybe I could find some secrets. Your *pre-cabian* life, Rober? You'd like to find that, wouldn't you?'

'No. Please, no. Boda!!! Get out of me! I don't want to know that.'

'I loved Coyote,' Boda says, calmly, surfing the head-waves of Roberman for knowledge, finding none. 'I must find out who killed him. Columbus is claiming I was at the scene of the crime. He's claiming that I killed the loving dog. Can't you see that the boss is making excuses for himself? Columbus is tied up with the killing. Can't you help me find his hideout?'

'There's no way I can do that, Boda, I'm just a driver. I doubt if even the Gumbo YaYa knows where he is. Columbus is too well hidden.'

'Why didn't you tell the cops about my real whereabouts on the murder day?'

'Can I go against the map, Boda?'

'I thought we were friends?'

'Friends? How can I be friends with someone who's left the map?'

'Is Columbus stronger than friendship?' Asking this, Boda puts the gun back against her temple.

Roberman's plastic eyes close. He needs time to think about this; this is the plaguing question. He breathes in, an intaking of pollen. And then sneezes, dog-robo strong. Globs of sputum and snot speckle his Xcabber uniform. Moments of doubt, Boda against the Switch Columbus. The Switch comes out the stronger. 'Coyote was married,' he says to Boda. 'There. That's knowledge for you. Didn't you know that?'

'What?'

'Oh yes. And a kid. They had a kid. A puppygirl. She's called Karletta. It's all in the cab-wave. Columbus called it up for us.'

'He never . . .'

'They live in Bottletown. Columbus had us looking for you there. They were at the funeral. Didn't you see them?'

'I couldn't go too close. Coyote never said . . .'

'Of course he didn't. Will you let me go now?'

Boda pulls on the trigger . . .

'Please, Boda!'

...Click.

'Who told you about the Limbo fare that Coyote picked up?' Boda asks.

'Columbus...Columbus gave it to me...'

'Can't you see what's happening, Roberman? Why would Columbus do that? A fare from Limbo? It doesn't make sense.'

'I don't know...I don't know why.'

'How can I trust you?'

'You have a choice, Boda?'

Boda gives up on the Shadow, trusting more to friendship. Turnaround into softness, the Shadow dwindling. The soft realm beyond Xcabs.

'Something's going wrong, Boda,' Roberman says. 'Something's going down with Columbus.'

'Tell me about it.'

'A new operating system. The map is getting fluid. Something ...the map...he's changing it.'

'What do you mean?'

'I'm scared, Boda. I'm picking up messages. Whispers in the ranks. Nobody knows. Columbus is getting power-hungry.'

'He's going to change the map? Why should we be scared of that?'

'I don't know. I really don't know,' Roberman answers. 'But Columbus won't give up on you. Whatever he's planning, he needs all of the cabs for it.'

'Tell Columbus that I'm coming after him,' says Boda.

'I'll do that,' replies Roberman. 'Be careful...'

And Boda vanishes into the curve of a shadow that falls from the side of a rubbish skip that catches soft light from the moon that floats high and serene over the water that laps at the side of the canal that leads into the city of Manchester.

* * *

I don't know what to call you any more, daughter. Should it be Belinda or should it be Boda? I was back home in the Victoria Park flat after receiving the new mission from Kracker. All the collected notes of the Flowers case were laid out on my desk. The child Jewel was calling from his room, but I was trying to concentrate on the story of it all, hoping to make a shape out of the case. Again and again I returned to the facial image of driver Boda taken from the Xcab-banks. Was, this really my daughter? I was doing my best to shed nine years of damage from the image. I was trying to add some hair to the shaved skull. I knew that Boda was eighteen now, and that she had joined Xcabs when she was nine. And how could I forget that my daughter, Belinda, had left me at the age of nine? And that she had subsequently vanished from the data-banks?

Why, oh why? What was your motivation, my daughter? Did you hate me so much for passing on the curse of the Unbeknownst? Or was it the constant struggle towards bad love, as witnessed in the arguments of your mother and father? And after your father left, were you then cast adrift yourself, feeling unloved? I could have loved you, my child. I could've managed it, somehow, despite the dust and the doubt.

My daughter would be eighteen now. What better way to vanish than to fold yourself into the secret Xcab map of the roads? I needed to work out my feelings on the case, because I couldn't stop looking at the picture; the eyes of the cab driver were making me dizzy with half-remembered moments. I had been searching for your traces for years, daughter. Had my search for a case-clue called *Boadicea* set me on that same quest?

Jewel was still crying from his room, so I got up and went through to him. I cradled my son in my arms. My first child. Jewel Jones.

I never told you, Belinda, that you have a brother. You were both children of Fecundity 10, as was your mother. Fecundity 10 was the Authorities' answer to the black air of Thanatos, a plague of sterility that had covered England years and years before I was born. Under the influence of Fecundity 10, ten thousand babies were conceived. Desire was overheated. The pure wanted more than purity, they wanted dogs, they wanted robos, they wanted Vurt-beings. And babies were made from this. Fecundity 10 had broken down the cellular barriers between species. The Authorities banned the use of Fecundity 10. Of course, nobody listened. Fecundity 10 became a bootleg drug, liquid or feather, and already it was firmly at home in the gene pool. The Casanova of drugs, there were no limits to what you could love. Even the dead were desirable.

Our story, Belinda...

Even the dead were desirable, but the recently dead were especially so. They were shimmering waves of decay. Pures and dogs, robos and Vurts; they were all up for the pleasures of necrophilia. The chemical hands of Casanova reached deep, into the darkest genes. Babies were made from these terrible couplings: half and half creatures, expelled from dead wombs. And they were born two ways, boy or girl, ugliness or beauty. The Authorities called the boy-children *Non-Viable Lifeforms*. Zombies, Ghosts, Half-alivers, these were their given names. This was my Jewel. Their ugliness was distasteful to the Authorities; NVLs were banned from the cities. They would have to make their desperate half-life out in the bleak places, the moors, which they named Limbo, after their plight. But if the child of the grave was a girl... well then, she would have only the shadow of death upon her. That child would be very beautiful, because of this dark presence, this body of smoke she carried within her own. And because all living things carry the shadow of death within them, albeit unknowingly, shadowgirls could join their Shadow to the living. They could read the secret desires of the mind. The Authorities were fearful of the Shadow, but how could they dismiss something so nebulous? These beauties had veins of smoke. A trace of death, clinging on to life. Remember that, my sweet.

Belinda, your grandmother was a corpse when she gave birth to me.

I have never told this story to you, not completely. Its details were too gory for your beauty to take. And you never gave me the chance, leaving so soon. This is my answer.

Your grandmother was a recently deceased corpse, your grandfather was a Casanova-pumped lover of the dead. Their marriage bed was the up-turned earth of Southern Cemetery. Two months later I was born. It doesn't take long with Fecundity 10. Born to a bed of soil and flowers, with the gift of the Shadow. My life of loneliness, leading to the moment of realizing that I could not take the Vurt. Dodo feelings. The curse. My lonely life of shadows and smoke. Sleep was harsh. I could not dream. I passed this inability on to you, Belinda, and for this curse you hated me.

The tricks that I learned to play, in recompense—answering back to teachers before they had even spoken, making a dead cat in the alley jump into new life as I poured my Shadow into it, forcing words into strangers' mouths. Lonely, lonely. After the episode of Jewel's conception, I suppose I must have just *fallen* into the arms of your father. He was a very pure man, and I thought that maybe he would dilute the curse a little; the curse of not dreaming, and the curse of the dead. I had so many things to nullify. That dream was not to be. These attributes of death are passed on from mother to child, from child to child. And I know that you hated me for passing on the inability to dream, but really, it could have been worse; you could have been a boy. You were blessed with the Shadow. Wasn't that good enough for you? Of course it wasn't, but please remember that your father was plagued by his failure to make you dream. He saw it as a direct result of his lack of manhood. You were very cruel to his lack, I seem to remember, but what else could he do but leave? Was that the reason? Was it?

Coming down from memories, Victoria Park, I hugged my dying son closer to me. Jewel Jones, Jewel Jones, Jewel Jones.

My two children. One lost and already found. The other still lost.

Belinda, I will find you yet.

Many years ago, after many attempts at renewal, it was decided that the Zoological Gardens at Belle Vue were no longer a viable proposition. Their closure had been imminent, as people moved on to electronic delights, and from there to feathery Vurt pursuits. The final touch of death. Money talked. The owners sold off, or put down, all of the sad animals there. Closed the funfair, then the speedway, then the concert hall, the ballroom, the dogtrack, the restaurant, the wrestling arena. Until only loneliness remained; the wind blowing through dry grasses, through the bars on the vacated animal pens. For many years Belle Vue was a desert, set in the run-down wastes of eastern Manchester, where the only change was metal oxidizing into rust, and hope melting into poverty. Only the prostitutes found a use for those broken vistas. Belle Vue became common ground.

But then came the successful merging of dog and plastic. A proposal was put forward, passed with alacrity by the Authorities, and the dogtrack was reopened. Every Wednesday, Friday and Saturday the night air was filled with the sound and the smells of robohounds, charging the ground with their Vazzed-up claws, chasing to death some poor Zombie-rabbit. With the discovery of Fecundity 10, even stranger, wilder creatures were born. Some of them too wild, too full of curious genes to be ignored. So they opened the zoo again, filling it with the children of Casanova. Nonviables. Voyeurs dreamed of it, entrepreneurs put money into it. Oh, the thrill of seeing a hideous Zombie up close, safe behind bars. The New Belle Vue Zoo was a big success.

Wednesday, May 3. Night-time. We have placed the moment at 10.12 p.m. The dogs were running wild inside the floodlit stadium, and the zoo was closed for the night. The cages were filled with deep snufflings. Half-alive creatures sleeping. Terrible mixtures of dead women and dogs, and cats, and robos and Vurts. And the Pure. They were called monsters, those creatures, but I know that is a misnomer. I had that same flesh inside me, only my gender had saved me. Maybe one of those poor unfortunates was roused that night. Maybe it was curious about the sounds coming from the nearby flower garden. Now its eyes are adjusting to the gloom, making shapes out of the flowers. The shape of two humans, making themselves into one form, and the petals falling all over them. The floodlights from the dogtrack casting a dull yellow glow over the scene. The noise of the crazed-up robohounds pounding the track. Beneath that another sound: soft whisperings mixed with harsh commands. Maybe that creature had enough human in it to recognise the sound. Maybe it had seen this sight many times over its years in the cage: a prostitute with her client. Maybe it knew enough to realise that these urgent cries were the noises of love, a kind of love, a paid-for love. Or else it was a dumb thing, born brain-dead, living on shadows and flesh only, knowing nothing of what it saw. Maybe it sneezed just then, as the flowers moved around the young couple, and the petals fell like slow blades in the night . . .

That other figure it must have seen, drifting through the air. The screams it must have heard.

The witness came to us at 10.46 p.m., falling into the Gorton cop station like a leaf herself, her Shadows dancing with fear. It was the local sergeant himself who had called me, knowing that I was involved in the Flowers case. I was still awake by then, unable to sleep. I had been drinking instead, and smoking and thinking; shuffling through case notes, Vurtball tickets, diary entries, gazing at photographs, memories of Belinda's childhood. Looking in on Jewel in his bedroom. His sneezing and his tears were very bad, and I was fearful for his condition. I did not want to leave him, but my job was not the best one for a mother. It was 11.05 p.m. by the time I got to the Gorton station, pushing the Fiery Comet through thick packs

of slobbering dogmen. Zero was already waiting there for me. I
turned away from him.

'This is one of yours, Smokey,' he said. And then he adjusted
his new pollen mask, close-knit, as he followed me into the interro-
gation room. 'You sure you don't want a mask, Sibyl?' He kept
looking down at his wrist as he spoke. 'Jesus-Dog! There's some
heavy snot in here.' He had bought one of the new Pollen Counters,
the wristwatch model. 'Christ! 785! Sibyl, it's 785 grains in here.
789 . . . 791 . . . this bitch is rising.'

After my talk with Kracker, I had a ton of questions to ask of
Zero, but I was too busy. Too busy taking in the young woman in
the room. She was a teenage Shadowpro, shivering and crying between blasts of the most violent sneezing. She was mumbling gibber-
ish between each explosion. The room was cloudy with the scent.
'We've tried everything,' Zero said. 'Can't make head nor tail, except that she's called Miasma, and that somebody got killed. Keeps
going on about the flowers. Girl's in shock.' She had a frail Shadow;
enough to know what a man desired, but hardly enough to put it
into action. There were other cops peering in at the door, all of
them masked-up to the gills, so I just slammed the door shut on
their sneezings and then sent my smoke out to the sufferer, touching her mind with it. Our Shadows mingled, and she was so grateful
for my touch, I was almost crying with her. I didn't have to demand
much; her Shadow opened like a flower, and she told me her story
in words of smoke . . . drifting . . .

. . . *was lost in the search for money . . . the search for love and*
money . . . money . . . love . . . what's the difference? . . . a sad and sweet
roboboy he was . . . pleading for love . . . feed me, he said . . . feed me shad-
ows . . . and giving me money for love in return . . . the garden . . . feeding
him . . . flowers all over us . . . smelling so sweet . . . a good but sad boy . . .
flowers making us come together . . . would have done it for nothing . . .
little D-Frag . . . but for the flowers . . .

'That was his name? D-Frag? His street name?'

... Yes ... roboboy ... he was trying so hard to be hard, a real Vurt dealer ... but D-Frag was too soft for all that ... I liked him ... and the smell of the flowers ... he couldn't stop sneezing ... me the same ... and we were laughing then, together ... loving the nose job ... he called it that, a nose job ... I was laughing until his eyes widened and I thought it was myself, my pleasure making his eyes bloom ... but feeling the petals on my spine ... like the hand of a good lover ... I turned to follow his look, seeing the air shimmering, and the Zombies were howling in their cages ... a young girl ... a beautiful young girl ... floating in the air on petals ... a flower girl ... she had petals ...

'Tell me about the girl, Miasma. What did she look like?'

Floating ... a child ... nine or ten ... a kid she was ... kissing the both of us with petals ... eyes of green petals she had ... the scent inside me ... my Shadow wilting, and then blooming ... young girl kissing roboboy ... making him smile until he was ... until he was screaming ... I ran all the way ... I ran ...

'Tell me more about the girl. Describe her.'

... She called herself Persephone ... her name was floating ... like petals, right? Just like petals ... the girl was kissing him to death!

Miasma screamed then, along the Shadow, and sneezed at the same time, sending her mucus into my Smoke. Explosions of gold as the particles hit. I could see them dying in fire, even as I managed to pull out.

Riding the cop-car down to the zoo ...

The dogtrack was closed up for the night. All was darkness and breath. The Shadowpro led us to the bed of flowers. 'I would have done it for nothing,' she kept saying, words coming hard from her lips, eyes streaming with mucus, even with the pollen mask we had given her. 'For nothing. All for nothing ...'

'Sure thing, kid,' Zero wheezed. 'Just take us to the love nest.' He had little use for pros, less for Shadows. This combination had bitten. Miasma was just staring into an overgrown patch of the Belle Vue gardens. 'Shadowslut, you best come clean now,' demanded Zero. I was finding his mood hard to bear.

'Zero! She's scared.'

'She's scared! Shit, we're all scared. Seems like the whole of society's breaking down, running scared. It's all getting too watery, Smokey.' He was looking all around, breathing heavily through his mask, his furry brow matted with sweat, glancing every so often over to the zoo cages. 'Shit! Who the fuck would pay to see such corpses? It's not natural.'

I wanted to ask him to take a good look at his own furry face and then talk about natural, but how could I? The pro was crying, the flowers seemed to be creeping towards us through the darkness, and all I could hear from the cages was a soft slithering, like dry leaves rubbing against one another.

Zero was screaming by now. He was screaming at Miasma, at the Zombie cages, at the fleshcops, at me, at the whole world that had taken him this far. The dogcop was really suffering. He was reading off numbers from his wrist counter . . . 799 . . . 801 . . . 802. Miasma could do nothing but sneeze, even with the mask in place, and keep on pointing towards the flowers. Her Shadow was calling to me, telling me to look, to look to the flowers. *See the way the flowers are moving. See the patterns* . . .

Zero was raising his paws in the air, protesting, 'This is a strike-out, Sibyl. Let's do this pro for wasting time.'

But I was turning to the flowers now, looking into the spaces between the petals. Seeing shapes there, *seeing* the body. Miasma had been right; he was indeed a young and lovely roboboy. Fair of face, strong in his plastic bones, soft in his feelings. A fine picture of flesh and info, all wrapped up together in beauty. But none of these elements were left to us. That corpse was just a picture that the petals made, as they drifted in the breeze from the cages, making patterns of colour that corresponded to the information. There was no physical body to examine, only the edges between states. It was the moment of death captured in a floral display. A wreath of memories.

'The body is here, Zero,' I said.

'Can't see anything, Smokey.'

'You're not looking, Zero.' He went silent then, as his doggy eyes caught a glimpse of a body's shape in a certain combination of petals. 'You making a Shadow-search?' he asked, voice shaking.

'There's nothing much to search.'

But I tried it anyway. Putting my hands into the flowers. They seemed to grip, like desire. And when my mind descended into the Shadow of blooms, all I got back was the old tale of green; old in the sense that I felt by this time that I was keying into some kind of myth. The explosion of flowers I had seen in Coyote's last thoughts. The Zombie's. Now the roboboy's. I had to make a pull-out.

'Smokey?' Zero's voice came to my ears as I wilted from the greenness. 'What's going on here, Smokey?'

But I really didn't have time for him, despite the fact that Kracker had now, effectively, made *me* the dogcop's boss. Maybe this reversal of power was the source of his evident discomfort? But the way that Zero had lied about the Boda clues previously. How could I trust him? How could I trust Kracker? How could I trust anyone?

That sneezing girl needs help, Zero. I sent this message over the Shadow straight to his mind, not wanting to break the moment with speech. *And may I suggest you start digging up the drifting patch?*

'You know I hate it when you do that smoking shit, Sibyl,' Zero barked at me. 'Talk to me in words.' But I guess the message got through anyway, because the next second I could hear him screaming at those Gorton cops to bring some lights in, and to get that Shadowpro to hospital, and to start digging. 'What the fuck is up with you? Give me that spade! Shit!' He was taking his frustration out on his underlings, the human colleagues. Then he sneezed through his mask, again and again, and I knew this fever was getting bad, and going to get much, much worse. 'Jesus-Dog!' Zero's voice was crackling. 'The pollen count has reached 820, Sibyl.'

The Gorton cops found only the plastic parts of D-Frag, buried deep in the soil beneath his floating portrait. Wrapped tight by suckers they were, those plastic parts. The flesh had become flower. I learned that night that a girl of air and grass was out there in the city, name of Persephone. That our real killer was a young girl, a kid; something entirely different again. A new kind of species. I would have to issue a city-wide alert that night.

My eyes were finding dark shapes in the interior of the cages. Those Half-alivers were transformed by the flowers. The young girl ...she must have reached in to them, spreading her powers. The Zombies were dancing and blooming around the shit and the dust, flowers sprouting from their tough skins, petals falling from their mouths. It was a fine show of fauna and flora, all mixed into one being.

New species.

I could sense Zero's fear-ridden Shadow creeping up behind me. A strange blend of dog-smoke it was: fear of the Zombies, for sure, but more than that, a fear of me. A fear of the case. There were pitch-black swirls in his deepest Shadow, where all of his secrets were kept in cages. 'What you doing, Jones?' he asked.

'Zombie-watching.'

'One hell of a hobby.' He was trying his best to keep up the old Z. Clegg hard-core persona, but what a strain it was on his dribbling Shadow. 'You got anything on the Boda case yet?'

'Maybe.'

'You like to tell me about it?'

'Do you like Vurtball, Clegg?'

'Fucking hate it.'

'That's a shame. I'm taking you to tomorrow night's big match.'

'This to do with finding Boda? Shit—' Another sneeze, so loud and violent that the Zombies rushed at the bars, fluttering petal-covered limbs at us.

'Bless you, Clegg.'

'Thank you. I'm sorry for lying to you.'

'You've got a real heavy Shadow these days, dogcop.'

'I'm suffering, Sibyl. I really am. So many reasons, I can't begin
to tell you.'

'I know. You're upset about Kracker giving me the Boda job.'

'Well, yes, that hurts. I was only following orders, Sib. It really
killed me when I learnt that she was your daughter. I didn't know
what to do.'

I reached out my hand and stroked at the fur on his arm.
Stroked? Like you do to a dog? Well yes, I guess so. But Zero
seemed happy with it, for a moment. And then he pulled away from
me. His Shadow diminishing as he walked slowly through the jungle
of flowers.

Miasma died that night, the first victim of the hayfever. The
first victim not to have been killed by the killer, but by the things
the killer had left behind: the grains of pollen. I knew then that the
fever and the murderer were sisters. Flowers and death. The case
turning on that moment . . .

Everywhere I looked, new species were springing up. Maybe
the pundits were right; the world *was* becoming more fluid.

Later that night, I held Jewel close to me. Non-Viable Lifeform
No. 57,261. How I loved him. His sneezing breath, his streaming
eyes. The way he looked at me, full of longing. Jewel wanted nothing
more than life. It was the one thing that nobody could give him. Not
even I, his mother, could grant that. He would be forever on the
borderline. Totally illegal. If Kracker ever found out that I was
harbouring him, my career would explode. Zombies were not allowed inside the city's circle. Jewel was my black secret.

But this was my son and I was keeping him. Hadn't he fought
his way through Limbo to get back to me? Didn't that add up to
something? Wasn't he dying from the fever? Wasn't he on the list
of future victims?

Let them try and take Jewel away from me. Cops or flowers,
they would feel my hands of smoke upon their necks.

Thursday
4 May

The sun was heating up the pitch as the crowd waited for kick off. An evening match with no need for floodlights. The brass band was playing homage to the King. *This is the land that I love, and here I'll stay . . . until my dying day.* Golden music shimmering over the manicured grass, which was so finely genetically controlled, it was the green of ripe apples, so tangy you could taste the pitch on the roof of your mouth. Even so, flowers were growing through the grass, and the whine of the pitch-cutting machines was another song on that day, their blades clogged up with thick stems.

Supporters all around me, plying their blue-and-white feathers with Vaz, hoping for a good game. The feathers had numbers on them, each corresponding to a player.

Interactive Vurtball.

Where you can play the game inside your chosen player. The left back defender is the cheapest feather; the centre forward the dearest. But I was just Sibyl Jones, only a spectator. Not of the match but the crowd. Just a watcher. And anyway, with the hayfever growing wild, the playing feathers kept getting sneezed into the air.

The semi-final of the Vaz International Golden Feather Cup. Thursday. Second leg. Derby match, grudge match. Manchester United were the opponents, and they had won the first leg 2–1. All around the Manchester City stadium adverts for Vaz, that universal lubricator, were sliding greasily from the hoardings. Giant, inflatable red and white feathers were floating above the opposite stand. The howling of supporter-dogs coming from the Kennel Lane seats.

I was staked out at pitch level, watching the people make their way to their seats. I had with me a pair of binoculars and a walkie-talkie. Zero Clegg was in place at the entrance gate that Belinda would have to use if she came to the match. Each ticket stated upon it the entrance to be used. Clegg had protested at having to be seen with a walkie-talkie. He was used to the feathers, and anything outmoded embarrassed him. I called him up now, asked how it was looking? 'No sign as yet, Smokey Jones. I don't know what I'm looking for.'

'Keep looking.' I closed off the communication and trained my binoculars on the four vacant seats I had identified. Earlier I had spoken to the stadium's box office and they had told me that a certain Coyote Dog had purchased four adjacent seats for the match, some ten days previously. Okay, we know one was for himself—I had found it in his diary—another was for Boda/Belinda. Who were the other two for? Well, I would soon find out. But it was Belinda's ticket, of course, that I was interested in. Would she turn up? I had tried to place myself into her feelings. If she really loved the Coyote, maybe she would turn up. But I had been wrong already about the funeral. After all, what was I looking for? Imagine, my own daughter, and I didn't know what I was looking for.

A young woman makes her way into one of the seats. My fingers work the focus until I have the woman's face in my sights. Is that her? That face beneath a fringe of red hair? No, the woman passes along all four seats to sit down next to a young dogboy.

I was getting nervous. I let the binoculars range over the adjacent seats and aisles. Every young woman I see leaps into focus. I'm seeing parts of my daughter in all of them. One in particular gets my attention. The right age and bone structure. A crimson peaked cap on long brown hair. The wrong seat, of course, but who knows what Belinda has planned? I touch the zoom button. The face floating in front of my eyes now, an expression of pain upon its fragile beauty. No. The Shadow is empty in that woman. I'm moving the sight back to Coyote's seats. A woman is sitting in the one on the end right.

Zoom...

It's her. It's my daughter. Her Shadow. She's wearing a wig.
She looks like some kind of cowgirl, but it's her. The image shaking
as my hands tremble around the cool ceramic of the binoculars.

Boda's sitting tight to the seat that Coyote had bought for her, not
knowing why, and a fine spray of snot falling on her blond Country
Joe wig. Her head-map is getting sweaty under the covering, but
Boda feels at home in the new outfit. A woman's clothes. What
started out as a disguise ends up like a uniform. This is her first
partaking of femininity. She's a new being, a new road back to her
childhood. The sun is torturing. Flowers are struggling through tiny
cracks in the concrete stand, brushing against her shoes. Blue-and-
white feathers floating down. Clouds of pollen in the air. Boda can
hardly see the pitch through it all: the feathers and the golden dust
and the fanfare of snot. She has spent the night hidden in a cheap
bed-and-breakfast on the Wilmslow Road, Fallowfield. What is she
doing here?

Somebody I want you to meet.

Coyote's lost words coming back to her. The crowd pushing
in strong from all sides, songs of joy in the face of imminent defeat,
but the neighbouring seat still empty. And the one next to that as
well. And the one next to that. Three empty seats. A vacuum in the
panting. Why on earth have I come here, she is thinking. *Because
Coyote bought me the ticket, of course.* I want to find out everything
about him. Only then will I get a handle on why he was killed. But
don't I hate him for not telling me the story of his wife and puppygirl? *Don't I just?* And anyway...haven't I lost that liar for good?
And Roberman and my job and the squeezing map of Manchester,
along with him? *I've maybe totally blown my road to comfort.*

Good. Let comfort rot.

Boda is pleased with her new-found image of cowgirl strength,
but still, despite all that, here Boda is. She's waiting. Waiting for the
players. Here they come. Pollen masks pulled tight over their faces.

Their shirts sparkling with Vazverts. The sun just dripping on to the pitch. The grass is thickened with flowers. A whistle blows . . .

Kick off.

Vurtball.

The supporters screaming through their feathers, working their players towards a goal. Sneezing tactics.

Two people pushing through the crowd towards Boda. A human girl and a dog-girl.

Two people push through the crowd towards Belinda. I make an adjustment to the focus. They look like a young human girl and an even younger dog-girl. I've seen that puppygirl before. Where? Of course. Coyote's funeral. This was Coyote's daughter. Karletta was her name. The child of Twinkle and Coyote. She looks as sweet as before to my motherly eyes. And again, the stupid thought . . . Why couldn't I have had a daughter like that? So I move the viewing field back on to Belinda. She looks scared. Why is that?

The human girl has corkscrew hair that is braided here and there with brilliant feathers of blue, yellow and scarlet. Each of these feathers gives Boda a bad feeling; feathery waves coming into her Shadow. She wants to vacate her seat, the fear is so bad. But no, the decision has been made. Let us sweat this out. The two new-comers sit themselves down next to Belinda.

Somebody I want you to meet.

Is this whom Coyote meant? Is one of these girls Coyote's daughter?

Jesus!

Too much to take.

United score in the ninth minute. A collective groan from the fol-lowers. Now City need three goals to qualify. Some kind of impossi-ble task. The human girl and the bitch-child are hypnotised by the play. She's not really a bitch, that child, just some fine whiskers sprouting from her cheeks, that's all. I'm watching all this through the sights from the touchline, thinking about when I should make my move, when I should call in Zero. To make an arrest now, in the middle of that sneezing crowd, would be a real riot-maker. So then, let them play for a while. I push my Shadow into my daughter, listening over the distance . . .

Boda thinks back to what she had drawn from Roberman's mind at the canal side. Was this puppy really Coyote's kid? So who's the girl sitting next to the puppy? Maybe Coyote had another child? Christ knows what he had; Boda can't trust him any more. Even when he's dead.

City pull one back.

The crowd going wild. Feathers flying from their mouths.

The girldog has a feather lodged in her lips. The pure girl has no feather at all, but still her eyes are glazed over, like she's living inside of someone else, some smart player on the field. And then Boda's soul is shrivelling at the nearness of this girl. She wants to curl up at the very idea. Boda gets the message; this seemingly human girl is really a Vurt-girl. A juiced-up human with direct plugs to the Vurt world. This girl doesn't need feathers; she can just access the dream, no need for payment. And this is your enemy, Boda; this is your curse. The Unbeknownst cannot abide the Dreamers. Your genes are fighting a loser's battle, just like the blue-and-white team down there on the cluttered pitch. Your fear is strong, Boda, but nothing like your mother's, simply because your mother is more deeply into the clutch of death.

Believe me on this, my daughter.

Boda is shrinking back from the girl's featherness.

United score another. 4–2. No hope for the final. The bluest feathers falling into despair, and the half-time whistle blowing. Brass band playing.

Where to go from here? Boda's mind is turning.

Maybe talk to this Vurt-girl?

'You know Coyote?' Boda asks. It takes a half-time lifetime to say.

The girl just looks at her, eyes still sprinkled with passes and fouls from the first half just gone. 'Yeah, I knew him,' she answers.

'Like how?'

What do you expect from this talk, Boda? Some kind of relief?

'Crazy dogboy, Coyote,' the girl says.

'Wasn't he just?' Boda says, hoping for a come-back. Nothing does come back, so she asks of the girl, 'Are you related?'

'No, just a friend,' the reply. 'Karletta's related.' The girl is stroking the bitchgirl. 'Karletta's his daughter.'

'Really?' Boda's Shadow is a dried-up husk, from being that close to Vurtness. Is this all she has travelled into town for? A meeting with two kids, one made from feathers, the other from dog-flesh? She had expected some of Coyote's underground friends to be here, some rebel warriors who could possibly lead her towards Columbus.

'You're a Dodo, aren't you?' the girl says. 'I can feel the missing parts where the feathers should go.'

'What's your name?' Boda says, pushing down the feelings.

'Blush is my name,' the girl replies. 'I'm twelve years old. What's yours?'

'My age?'

'Name, stupid.'

'Belinda.' Boda says the first name that comes into her mind, protecting her identity.

'Belinda? Oh . . .'

'What's wrong?'

'I was expecting Boda to be here.'

Boda looks at the brass band playing upon the emerald pitch for a few seconds. 'Why did you expect that?'

'I'm going to be famous one day,' Blush says. 'Do you know that?'

'Really?'

'I'm going to be a famous Vurtress. I've got the Vurt inside me, you see? I'm in *Comatose Road* next week. Maybe you'll catch me? Just an itsy part, but I'm out to make an impression, you know? Anyway, soaps are all right, but I've got my feathers set on some bigger dreams. Like crazy dreams, you know? Well, perhaps not. Perhaps you don't know. And, maybe, after all, you won't be catching me next week.'

'Well, I could watch on television.'

'That's sad. Crazy! Who does television any more? Only a Dodo, right? Coyote talked about Boda a lot.'

'Did he?'

'Oh for sure. Like crazy, he was, for that Xcabber. He told me about how he had bought her a ticket for this match. He called her his new choice.'

His new choice. This is what Coyote called you, Boda. Isn't that strange? Strange and good?

'Why did he call her that?' she asks.

'You have to ask?' the girl says. 'Crazy Dodo.'

Well, yes. Crazy Dodo. For having to ask. For feeling your powerful Shadow shrivelling to darkness. And for having a crazy doubt in your mind.

'How come you're here, Blush?'

'Coyote bought me a ticket as well. And one for Karletta. He said I should meet this Boda girl. He said she was important. I guess that's his seat, right there . . .'

Blush is looking at the empty seat beside her, her eyes glittering with juice.

'I didn't think this Boda would turn up, not really,' Blush says, sneezing. 'Not after the death of Coyote. And not after hearing that Gumbo YaYa was after her traces. I was right, wasn't I?'

Silence, except for the crowd panting. Blasts of snot speeding through the air.

Finally . . . 'I used to be Boda.'

'Oh. What are you now?'

'I don't know. Boda was my Xcab name. I don't know my real name.'

'It's you? Crazy!'

'You said Coyote talked about me?'

'For sure. Coyote said that I'd like Boda. He said that I could tell you stuff. He said that I could explain everything. I don't know where to start.'

'Tell me about yourself.'

'I'm Blush. I'm out of Desdemona and Scribble. You've heard of Scribble?'

'No.'

'Crazy. Well anyway, Scribble was my father. I've never met him. He's lost in the Vurt just now. But, you know, I reckon he's going to be famous one day, just like me. He's going to come back to us. And Desdemona is my mum. She used to go visit Scribble in the Vurt, but lately he's not been accessible. Maybe he's working on some big scene. Like how to get back to us, you know? Well anyway, Des is only one of my mothers.'

'You've got more than one?'

'Sure. I've got two mums. Scribble made me out of two mothers. The other one's called Cinders. Cinders O'Juniper. You've heard of her?'

'No.'

'Crazy. She's a world famous Porno-Vurtress. That's where I got the feathery blood from, from Cinders. Anyway, Des is my real mum. She lives with us. We all live in Bottletown. Des and myself, and Twinkle and Karletta. It's a man-free zone. Maybe you'd like to come visit? Here, let me give you our number. And don't worry about Twinkle's reaction. She's sound. Oh, but maybe you're jealous yourself? Don't be, I beg you. Life is too short.'

How the hell would you know, young girl? This is what Boda thinks, but she doesn't say anything, she doesn't send that message over the Shadow. Boda keeps herself to herself.

'Anyway, there we all are, just waiting, you know?' Blush says. 'Waiting for a flame to come strike us. Coyote came back to our love.'

'Who's Twinkle?'

'Coyote's wife.'

'Coyote was married to Twinkle?'

'Well yes, once upon a time. Then they got divorced. But he would come round to talk to Karletta here, and to give her some toys and feathers. He can talk to her you see, the doggy tongue? None of the rest of us can manage it. Coyote was the only male we allowed in that house. So Coyote's talking to Karletta in one tongue, and he's talking to me in another. Human-like, you get the drift? And he tells me about you. He tells me crazy stuff.'

'Like what?'

'Like you're the best thing since green Heaven Feathers and Vazzed-up bread. Like you're something special. Well I hope so. You broke away from Xcabs, right? That must have been exciting?'

'Well . . .' And then considering the gleam in Blush's eyes: 'Yeah. It was exciting.'

'Crazy. The cops have still got Coyote's black cab. What do you think will happen to that?'

'I don't know. Maybe it'll go to Karletta, or to the wife. What was her name?'

'Ex-wife. Twinkle.'

'Whatever.'

The teams have come back on the pitch for the second half. The crowd raises a loud cheer. Blush pushes the blue-and-white feather marked with the number 9 back into Karletta's mouth, and then closes her eyes to feel the pitch better. Boda, you are surrounded by strong songs, but all you can think about is the meaning of Coyote's words, channelled through this young girl's mind. And the girldog herself, Coyote's daughter, sitting on the seat next to you, saying nothing, incapable of words, but speaking volumes. She's dog-girl beautiful in her silence, but with a sadness to her. You can feel it through the dog-shadow. Like Coyote was still talking to you, doggy-style. Whiskers and tongue. *This is who he wanted me to meet.* Your thoughts. He wanted to tell you all about his family, all about his child called Karletta. Get it over and done with, and then . . . maybe a new game? With yourself in the starring role?

Coyote never made it to the game.

Boda says to Blush, 'I'm innocent. I didn't kill him.'

Blush drags her eyes away from the pitch for one second. 'I know that, silly. Shush now . . . it's a penalty!'

City push in the penalty. 4–3. 'Oh yes!' Blush screams. 'Two more and we're there. We're in the final. We are going to be famous.' She turns to Boda. 'Coyote chose you, rogue driver. Kindred spirits, and all that guff. He chose well.'

'Thanks. So who wanted him dead?'

'Nobody wanted Coyote dead. He was well-loved on the streets. Except for . . . maybe . . .'

'Yes?'

'Well . . . Xcabs . . .'

'I know.'

'Xcabs would have loved that rider taken out. Your boss . . .'

'Columbus, yes.'

'So why don't you ask him about it?'

'Columbus keeps himself secret. He's slippery.'

City score another. Equaliser. The fans go sneezing wild. Vaz is dribbling from their mouths.

'Great goal,' Blush shouts. 'Did you feel that shot, Boda? Of course you didn't. Dodos, crazy! What can we do about them?'

Karletta sneezes. Blush strokes her neck, tenderly. 'Poor Karletta. What do you think about this hayfever, Boda? They say it's gonna get worse, before it gets better. You know where it's coming from, don't you, this fever?'

Boda says that she hasn't a clue.

'It's coming from a Heaven Feather.'

'What's that?'

'Crazy. You don't know? Course you don't. It's from a Heaven Feather. It's called Juniper Suction. I was travelling through Black Mercury the other day. You know about the Black Mercury feather?'

'Of course I do. But I thought Columbus destroyed all the copies years ago?'

'Of course he did. Just like you can't do Deep Throat feather any more. Listen up, lady . . . if the people want to travel, then the people will travel. And the dirtier the journey, the sweeter the route.'

'You're too old for your age, Blush.'

'Like fuck. Can I help it if the feather lives inside me, and that I was brought up in a manless home environment? I don't make the rules, I just break them.'

'Where did you find the Black Mercury?' Boda asks. 'Oh, I'm sorry. I forgot. You don't need the feathers.'

'That's right. In most cases. But some dreams are just too deep to access. They have locks on them, you know? Like condom locks? I guess Columbus himself must have sealed it.'

Black Mercury was an early version of the Xcab map that Columbus had used in the initial set-up. His hand-picked team of Vurt designers had produced it, and Columbus had then used that Vurtprint to persuade the Authorities to let him set up the real Hive-mind. A few bootleg copies had found their way onto the streets. According to Blush, Columbus had put in a sealing device that restricted direct access to the demo-map. This was to stop people like Blush, Vurt-people, from driving an illegal random cab around the map. But those bootleg feathers were available for a price, and with them anybody could ride the map, even if it was this ramshackle, early version. In the first days of Xcab life these intruders had caused havoc to the system, so Columbus had sent out a Vurtcab complete with a feather-seeker input. This feathery driver had very quickly spotted all illegal entries to the map, and had then eliminated them from the system. The users were left with useless cream feathers and a pain in the head that lasted for seven days. Black Mercury just didn't exist any more.

'Even I can't ride that one naked,' Blush is saying. 'I need the feather to do it, and Coyote very kindly gave me a copy. It was my birthday present.'

'Coyote had Black Mercury?'

'Sure he did. How else do you think he made such an easy ride out of the roads? You know what the Hive-map is, don't you?'

'I was a driver.'

'Sure. But really? It's no normal map. It's like a living map. In many ways, it's more alive than the real roads. So, anyway, I was driving through Black Mercury feather, right, just the other day? It's a vicious dream, that is. The Game Cat calls it a badass feather in his magazine, but I was just like, uh, crazy curious, you know? So I took it anyway. And I was playing the part of Mike Mercury, driving the Supercab. He's the baddest Xcabber in the Black Mercury world, but I guess you know that already? So I was trying to make this fare-drop in Demo Bottletown, without getting caught by the Fast-track Furies. I had the Hive-map up and running through my dreaming head. I had the full defences on. What could go wrong? Mike Mercury could drive his cab through the gaps between a honeymooning couple's breaths. All I had to do was deliver the passenger to Pineapple Crescent, number 666. Everything was dandy until Mike started to sneeze. Crazy, can you imagine? He sneezes so badly that the wheel starts to slip under my fingers. I zoomed into the Xcab map, and called up Demo Columbus for help. But this blinding hole was opening up at the centre of the map. There's a wall, you know, between the various worlds. It can get pretty skinny at times, especially these days. Anyway, there was all this yellow stuff coming through that hole into Black Mercury. It was like grains of stuff. I don't know. It was really getting up my

nostrils. I caught a glimpse of this other world through the hole in
the map. Juniper Suction world. Crazy shit. Read about it in the
Game Cat mag. It's a Heaven Feather. The place where the rich
people go when they die. The Outer Limits, baby. And when I got
back down to the real space, this yellow shit was still up my nose. I
was sneezing like crazy. It sure was potent. That's why I reckon the
fever's coming through from Juniper Suction, via the cab-map.' Blush
sneezes then, as though to emphasise the point, and Karletta
sneezes along with her.

Karletta . . .

That could have been my child.

Boda thinks this, and then feels so angry that the daughter of
Coyote is suffering from the fever. Boda can't escape from being so
stupid. It's irrational, it's pathetic. She understands all the things that
her mind is feeling, but still, here they are.

'My theory is that Columbus is letting the fever through on
purpose,' says Blush. 'He's making holes appear between the
worlds.'

Boda stands up.

'You going?' Blush asks. 'Didn't you like my story? I thought I
was helping you. Coyote said that I should. Don't you like being so
near a Vurt-girl? Are you afraid?'

No, it's not that. Not just that. Boda has caught a trace of
intruder-Shadow in her own. Strong and forceful. It smells like . . .

Shit!

Memories stirring. Pre-cabian . . .

The smoke of her long-ago mother. Who was my mother?

Karletta's eyes are looking at Boda, that intense gaze that only
a dog can maintain. A constant wetness.

Blush won't give up on the asking: 'You going to call that good
Gumbo, Boda? Prove your innocence to him. Maybe he can tell you
how to reach Columbus . . .'

Boda is apologizing to a blue-and-white supporter as she

squeezes past, desperate to get away from the questions and this trace of mother-Shadow.

'You'll miss the final score, Boda. Coyote wanted you here. He really loved you.' The voice of Blush following her . . .

But Boda is gone already. The time is 8.56 p.m. She's pushing through snot and feathers. Towards the turnstiles, the Maine Road exit.

I called up Zero on the walkie-talkie. I told him that my daughter was leaving right now, and that she had a 'long blond wig on her head. Bolero jacket. Gingham skirt. You can't miss her.' Then I made my way through the crowds towards the same exit.

Following, as always . . .

On the way to the exit Boda takes off her blond wig, replaces it with a black one. Another steal from Country Joe. She can feel her mother's presence still, in her Shadow. At the exit she passes a big dogman. He looks her directly in the face. Boda can feel him re-cognising her over his Shadow. He smells like bad cop-smoke. The strangest thing . . . he lets her pass on.

When I got to the outside, Zero was just standing there, looking nonplussed and feverish. Dog-lonely. 'Where is she?' I asked.

'Nobody blond came out,' he answered.

'You let her get away?'

Zero started to weep and sneeze then, and I couldn't comfort him. That dog had gone too far down for me. What was wrong with him? A black-haired girl was running through the alleyways that led away from the stadium. She disappeared into the maze-like streets of Moss Side.

Maybe she had more than one wig.

I urged Zero into the Fiery Comet.

* * *

Boda running from the mother-Shadow. She heads onto Maine Road itself, and from there to a tiny side street. This is a bad part of town and scratching dogboys are barking at her from behind dustbins. She doesn't know where she's going. Darkness is falling, slowly. The world is turning into a labyrinth of closed-up shops and derelict houses. Her black wig, her second wig, falls off. Behind her, somewhere, she can hear a car pulling up at a too-small entrance.

Just how fucking far have I got to travel?

Boda comes out onto a new street, somewhere called Broadfield Road. Without the Xcab map she's good and lost. Ahead of her a tribe of half-caste dogboys are slouching against the body of a Rasta-wagon. Hard-core dogga music is pounding from the wagon's system. Boda can feel her Shadow curling up at the presence of them. They can see the map on her head now, even though she has been letting her hair grow in these last few days. They know Boda for what she is: potential dog-voider. A white girl. Gumbo has spoken to them over the waves. They gather around her in a half-circle.

The sound of a car then, coming fast down Broadfield. It screeches to a halt and a voice from the inside, amplified: 'Okay. This is the cops. Leave her alone.'

Her mother's remembered voice and Shadow.

The dogboys make a run for it. Boda runs as well, away into the twisting alleyways. Away from her mother.

Claremont Road. Suddenly, she knows where she is. Ahead of her the overgrown paradise of Alexandra Park. Where all of this started. Across Princess Road, into the park, the cop-car following as far as the gate. Boda glances back; two cops are chasing her through the verdant flowers. Her mother and another. Shadow and Dog following. Boda falling. A tangle of roots. Her legs caught in them. The wet smell of grass as her face presses into the ground. Mother Earth.

This game is over.

* * *

Zero and I moved in on the fallen figure. Zero was sneezing badly from the over-abundance of flowers in the park. He had his gun out, but I was weaponless. This was my daughter.

I went there. Close. Reached out. Touched her.

Belinda snarled and spat. She bit me. Our Shadows clash and tangle. But I'm stronger than her, more experienced in the Smoke. I'm making her will bend to mine, even as her fingernails scratch at my cheeks. Jesus, this is like she was seven years old again, and I'm having to punish her for some naughtiness. We're both down on the ground now, crushing the flowers. A rain of petals falling. Belinda was screaming and cursing at me over the Shadow, and then I felt something cold and hard . . .

Blackout.

A blow to the back of my head.

I came to on the grass. Prone. My head alive with ache. Through slitted eyes I could see my daughter and Zero standing off from each other. Zero had his cop-gun pointed straight at her chest. Belinda's Shadow was pulsing with anger and fear. Zero's Shadow overlaid on that, bristling with flea-jumps and bad bones. All of the humanity had left him. Zero had gone total dog.

I managed some words. 'Clegg, what are you doing?'

He didn't answer. Cop-gun pointed. The sun was dropping down behind the canopy of trees, burning the flowers of the park into crimson waves. Zero's face was hidden behind the pollen mask, but I could just *feel* his righteousness. Again I asked him what he was doing.

'Following orders,' he answered.

'Kracker told you to do this?'

'The master has ordered me to kill you. The both of you.'

'You okay, Belinda?' I asked. No answer from my daughter. 'Clegg, see through this please.' I was trying to keep my voice cool, because the dogcop's Shadow was so very edgy, I feared that he might jump at any moment. 'Kracker is playing with you. He's playing

with everyone. The master has got another agenda.' The gun tight-
ened on my daughter. 'Clegg! Listen to me. Kracker is using you.'

'His master's voice, Jones. I'm being a good dog.'

Heavy pollen was rising still, from my struggle with the daughter. It couldn't find a home in us, so it settled for Zero. He sneezed
with it.

Aaaaaaaaaacccccchhhhhooooosssshhhhhh!!!!!

Zero wavered, his gun trembling. I made a move to stand up.

'Jones! Keep still. You're making me angry.'

I stopped moving.

'Please don't make me angry. I'm trying not to follow Kracker.
I really am.' Zero's brow, above the mask, was covered in sweat.
'But you know how it is, Sibyl... it's you against him. And the
master is stronger than you. He's calling to me. All I have to do is
kill you both. It's simple.'

'Won't you consider the cause of it?' I said. 'Kracker is no
longer a cop.'

'What?'

'He's aiming to break the law. I think he's tied up with the
Flowers case, Zero—'

'Stop calling me that! My name is not Zero.' Gun tightening.

'Okay . . . Zulu.'

His eyes closed for a second, and when he opened them again,
Belinda had stepped into his mind. I could feel her stepping there,
over the Shadow. She forced his hand to move, so that the gun was
pointed at me. Zero was trembling with fear, his head expanded
from the Shadow's intrusion. 'Sibyl, she's making me shoot you . . .'

And then Belinda pulled a gun out of her shoulder bag. I call it
a gun, really it was some kind of antique. A Colt .45? It looked like
a toy. Where did she get that?

A hard look in my daughter's eyes. 'Belinda, don't be silly . . .'
It sounded weak, but what could I do? Belinda looked at me, just a
tiny movement, as though the name had got through to her.

Belinda shot Zero.

I have the impression it was her very first shot of a gun.

Zero cried out. He fell down, clutching his arm. Belinda started to run into the surrounding bushes. 'Belinda, Belinda . . .' My voice following into the woods.

'Sibyl,' cried Zero. 'Please . . . please help me . . .'

I had to make a decision then, go after my daughter, or else look after the badly wounded Clegg, that stupid, master-bound victim . . .

It didn't take long, cop-rules making me weak.

I knelt down beside the dogcop, resting his head against my breasts. 'That's okay, Zero,' I whispered. 'We'll get through this.' Zero was whimpering and sneezing, telling me heartfelt excuses for his behaviour. I told him to keep quiet, rocking his warm body back and forth, back and forth under twilight branches.

The shapes in the leaves where my daughter had escaped. Not a single word had she spoken to me.

And then, some time later, Boda pushing her way through flowers which are tightly packed and bursting with primal colours, even in the gloom. All alone in Southern Cemetery. Night has covered her traces. The black wig has gone the way of all hair, but her blond hair is now safely back in place. Her bristling skull is sweaty. Had she killed that big dogcop that her mother had dragged along? Was that really her mother? It certainly smelled like her mother's long-forgotten Shadow. What was that name she called me?

Belinda?

It was too much to think about.

This place of death is too wild for people these days. Too many blooms, too much pollen in the air. The people prefer to keep themselves hidden behind doors and curtains, masks and lotions. They really think this will do some good. Boda can see the grains floating through the yellow night air of the cemetery, plant to plant, carried by the wind, or else taking a free cab-ride on the body of some insect. The bees are getting fat on nectar. Everything is accelerating, but Boda's nose is a barred gate to tiny life.

Alone with Coyote.

She comes up close to the grave. The dog-people have clubbed together to purchase a tomb statue. Unfortunately the carver didn't have a Dalmatian in stock at such short notice, so a creamed Labrador stands sentinel over Coyote's grave. The sculpture is smothered in vines and flowers. The engraved snout rising out of the blooms and the black leaves seem to form a pattern of spots over the Labrador's stone body. Coyote Dog, still trying to ride the waves.

Boda pushes her face into the flowers that cover the taxi-dog's tomb. She breathes deeply of the pollen there, hoping for some kind of reaction. Anything to get herself back onboard. Her life is getting broken.

That was my mother with her arms around me.

Nothing happens. No sneezing, no tears.

Maybe I'm dead to everything?

Only questions now, keeping only alive.

Did Columbus have Coyote killed? Was he allowing the fever to come through from the Vurt world? Were Coyote's death and the fever connected? The cops and the cabs were working together on this?

Through the overgrowth she can just about make out a carved eye, a taxi-dog's eye, looking at her through the stone. Boda takes off the blond wig, runs a hand over her skull. Bristles growing out of a map. It's her birthday in three days' time. Nineteen she'll be, and maybe getting too old for such an outlandish display. And anyway, who needs a map on their head when all they're doing is riding fast-tracks, and the combined forces of Xcabs and the cops are on their traces? Not to mention Gumbo YaYa. Or even her own mother. Boda can't even sign on for Dripfeed, because then her name and whereabouts would be in the info-banks. Her money has been squandered on fast-track fares, all of which lead to nowhere. This young woman standing in a night-fallen cemetery, before the grave of a dogboy she had written songs for, and sent love poems to, but whom she'd hardly even known, not really.

The world is on my shoulders now, forcing me down to the soil's grip. I will not give in. I will not give in to their desires.

Boda's mind is plagued by these twisting thoughts as she pulls up flowers by the root from Coyote's grave. Her fingers are bloody from the clutch of thorns, and her Shadow is dancing through the undergrowth, ridden by weeds. Coyote stands in front of her, an impassive statue, a rider of dead roads. Boda pulls loose a clump of vines from the taxi-dog's tombstone. They pull back against her effort, blossoming and turning until the stone is entangled once again.

She places a lone orchid on the grave's soil.

Friday
5 May

The road was a carpet of soft blooms that my wheels crawled through. The traffic lights at Oxford and Whitworth were entangled by vines. It was difficult to see the lights change, red to yellow to green; everything was green stems, red and yellow flowers. It didn't matter; mine was one of the few cars left on the street. The fever was taking its time with me. All I could think about was Jewel, back in the flat, suffering. I had even bought him a Gumbo YaYa pollen mask. I had smeared *Sneeza Freeza* on his nostrils. I had lined his room with *Gumbo YaYa's Very Own Protective Seal*. All for nothing; my child was dying. I knew this now. The fever had made a flourishing desert out of my city. It was a Mancunian paradise that nobody wanted, not even the dogs, who had finally run for cover from the pollen. Maybe they were just building up to a big showdown, conserving their resources. Friday morning. Here and there a few street-cops were wandering, robos in the main, but totally masked, up to the eyeballs. No one was safe. The cops weren't there to stop crime any more, they were more like protectors, keeping people off the streets, away from the pollen. Above the doors of the Palace of Vurt Theatre, a laser-sign pulsed out the following message—HIS MAJESTY'S HEALTH WARNING: THE POLLEN COUNT IS RISING. SNIFFING FLOWERS IS DEADLY. All along Oxford Street columbines, japonicas, mimosas and a thousand other varieties of flowers were growing from the cracks in the pavement, dragging at my wheels. Sixty-five per cent of the population were now suffering from severe hayfever. The number of known fatalities was now well into double figures, not including the initial murders. The towers of Manchester were being suffocated by flora. It was a jungle that I had to drive through. So many people dead, and still no clear cop-path to an answer. No leads to the flower girl called Persephone. Chief Kracker had put out an all-points bulletin on my 'miscreant behaviour' and cops city-wide were on the lookout for my traces. I had, of course, vanished myself from the station, whereabouts unknown, since yesterday's debacle with Clegg and Belinda. I was AWOL and stunted in the case, even whilst the city was growing crazy from the seeds. The pollen count had risen alarmingly in the last few hours, 1200 and growing stronger, almost as though the flowers were growing impatient. Bad times on planet Earth. The city was weeping. If Manchester went under the spell of flowers, then the whole world could suffer likewise, all the cities following, one by one. The Authorities had put blocks on the four gates in order to stop the Vaz truckers spreading the fever. Maybe it was too late. The people were blaming the cops for the danger, led on by that Gumbo YaYa's pirate voice.

I passed a street sign on the Rochdale Road that read *Welcome to Namchester.* Ahead of me the seven towers of Nam stood in silence, stark against the heated sun. Ten years ago this area had been desolated by the High-rise Wars, now the towers were home to the well-done and the well-to-do. Zero greeted me at the gates to Fortress One, which was a moist block of cement enwrapped with flowers. Zero led me up to his rooms, his face covered by the latest 'entirely newly improved' pollen mask. The wound in his shoulder had been sealed by robo-Skinner. His flat was richly appointed in all the human comforts, no hint of the Dog World. A young man was sitting on the pumped-up sofa-bed holding an armoured specimen box like it was a live rat with bad blood. He was a pure-hearted loner. His Shadow was wreathed by weakness. Zero introduced him as Jay Ligule, from the Manchester University Botany Department. Ligule had brought evidence with him, some micro-feathers.

The Alexandra Park incident had finished Zero with Kracker. Zero Clegg was a lone dog now, slipping the noose. I could feel his spirit running wild through his Shadow. He was free from the vanished master.

From now on we would be riding unofficially.

Jay Ligule was waving the micro-feather at me, like I should be able to taste those things. I told him that feathers meant nothing to me. But Zero had worked out the scenario. He'd 'borrowed' a feather-translator from the cop station. Ligule had transposed the info onto antique video. 'This is the little culprit,' Ligule said, as a moving display came up on the screen. 'Amaranthus Caudatus. Or at least, some kind of variant. A tropical plant, usually blooms in high summer, and then only in the South of England.'

'The South, you say?' Zero hated the South.

'Yes. Amaranthus . . . it comes from a Greek word. Meaning an imaginary plant, one that never fades. Commonly known as Lovelies-bleeding.'

'I reckon I've cracked this case, Smokey,' Zero said. 'I reckon we're looking for a mad botanist with a poetic streak. I reckon we catch this bugger, shove him in Strangeways Feather? What do you say?'

Strangeways Feather was where they put prisoners in those days, storing their bodies in racks whilst their dreams drifted through tiny cells in the Vurt. It was cheap and nasty, but it worked.

Jay Ligule looked up from the video screen. 'Take a look.'

. . . tiny life swimming there . . . pieces of stuff . . . minuscule monsters . . . fronds were twitching . . . knots of blackness here and there . . . moments of recognition, drifting into mystery . . .

'You see the darker spots?' Ligule said. 'These are the human element.'

'Human?' I asked.

'Basically what we have got here is a new kind of hybrid. Human and plant. Those dark spots you saw were human genes lodged inside plant cells. We have never seen anything like this before. Kirkpatrick was shocked by it.'

'Kirkpatrick?'

'Glasgow University. She's the leader of the field in plant re-production.'

'She wouldn't be a mad botanist, by any chance?' asked Zero. 'Maybe with a poetic streak?'

'She called this specimen a monster. We have a serious problem here, she said. Humans and flowers are having sex.'

Zero sneezed.

'Hayfever is caused by sex,' Ligule continued. 'You know that? It is the outcome of flowers trying to love one another. And failing. The fever is the outcome of bad plant sex.'

'Kinky,' Zero said. 'You want to explain?'

'Of course I do,' Ligule began. 'Pollen is produced by the anther of a flower, the male organ. From there it is carried by the wind or by insects, until it reaches the stigma of another plant. Or even the same plant. The stigma is the female organ. The stigma is moist and covered in fine hairs. It clutches at the pollen, making it feel at home, so that it can release its proteins. These proteins dig their way into the stigma, searching for the egg inside. This is the way of love for flowers. Sometimes a human comes in between.'

Zero: 'This causes hayfever?'

'The pollen lodges in the human's nostrils. It finds a moist and hairy place there, and thinks "this is the stigma. This is where I must bury myself." The grain releases its proteins, causing a breach in the nasal cavity. Of course the human body registers this as an attack and therefore activates its immune system. We try to expel the invader, through our nose and our eyes, with snot or tears. Hayfever is a defence mechanism.'

'You're saying that humans and plants are having sex?' Zero asked, making a sneeze from behind his latest mask. 'Jesus! You pay a week's salary for these things . . . doesn't do anything.'

Ligule joined him in the sneeze and then continued. 'The body is no longer rejecting the pollen grain. It is treating it like a lover. The immune system is trying to fight this impulse, but the reproductive system is fighting against it. And winning. The body is accepting the plant sperm. Kirkpatrick has examined some of the corpses. The pollen has made its way down to the womb. It is fusing with the human egg, as though it were a plant egg. Kirkpatrick reckons it to be the next step.'

'What step would that be?' I asked.

'The next phase of evolution, given that the country as a whole is increasingly drawn to interbreeding.'

'Jesus-Fever!' Zero was breathing deeply through his mask, making a sound like a victim. I could only feel for him, but at the same time Ligule's theories were appealing.

'Has Kirkpatrick any idea where these grains are coming from?' I asked.

'We think it goes back to Fecundity 10,' Ligule said. 'We think that Casanova has stepped into the plant kingdom.'

'What are you telling us?' Zero asked.

'Floraphilia, Kirkpatrick is calling it.'

'She means by that?' Zero again.

'We are saying that somebody has fucked a flower, and this hayfever is the baby of that union.'

'Dog-Christ!' wheezed Zero.

'We must burn all the bodies,' Ligule added. 'As a precaution. They mustn't be buried.'

'Why's that?' I asked.

'It would be like burying a seed.'

Fifteen minutes later, after telling us all he knew and gathering up his specimens, Ligule left Zero and me alone. I made to follow the botanist down the stairs but Zero grabbed a hold of me. 'Don't go, Sibyl.' I could not bear to be alone with him; memories of the park played over and over in my smoke. 'Please, Sibyl. Let me explain. Look, I'll cook you a meal. What do you say?'

I didn't say anything.

'That's a yes, then?'

We ate the food in silence. It was a fine meal. Totally human it was, that repast, no hint of raw meat in there. Green shoots, scarlet beans, thick and juicy sauce, burning chillies and golden corn. It was a hayfever meal. Zero called it his attempt to 'take this bitch on board,' and then fell silent. He kept clutching at his wounded arm whilst he was eating, as though ashamed at having been wounded by such a young girl, and when he finally spoke once more, his voice was sour. 'You know what I'm doing, Smokey? I'm trying to get well.'

'I know.'

'I'm trying my best.'

'I know.'

'So you won't help me?'

'You lied to me, Zero,' I answered. 'You were working behind my back. You were programmed to kill me. My daughter. Have you any idea how much that hurts?'

'What could I do? Kracker was the master.'

'And now?'

'The master is gone.'

'He's involved in this fever case. You know that now? He'll do everything he can to break us.'

'Yes. I know. Shall we put this behind us? I'd like that.'

'It's not that easy to forget.'

'I'll tell you everything.' Zero's eyes were staring at me through his mask's filters. He was crying, like rain against glass. 'I'll give you everything. All the clues. Sibyl, I'm trying to make amends. Won't you help me?'

I turned away from his stare. Clouds of golden pollen were moving through the air outside the high-up window.

'Sibyl . . . you're my only hope.'

I looked back at him. 'How could you do this to me?'

'I had no choice. Shit, there's too much dog in me, I guess.' This was a real confession and it made me wonder. 'Kracker con-

trolled me. You humans don't know what it's like. The dog in my
veins is a slave to love. Kracker was my owner. Please... what
more can I say?'

'Tell me.'

'You're on my side?'

'Tell me everything.'

'It might be bad for you.'

'Tell me anyway.'

'You fancy getting some air?' Zero got up from the table and
moved to the windows. He opened them up and then stepped out
onto the balcony. I followed him out there. Out on that edge, Zero
took me into a close-hold. A panic ruffled my Shadow into waves of
turbulence; there was too much *dog* around me. But his breath was
dying... dying. I could hear it drifting away through the golden air.

The two of us out on the balcony of Fortress One, floor
twenty-nine. The world of Manchester dropping away from the
barrier; a falling into zero. The yowling of the dog-people from far
below and long away; a rising tide of frustrated barking. A scent of
flowers on the breeze.

'You know what this case is, don't you, Sibyl?'

'No, I don't. It's all beyond me.'

'It's a Vurt case, Smokey.'

'What's Vurt got to do with it?'

'It's the key, Sibyl. Those that cannot dream... they are free
from the suffering.'

'Zero!'

'Okay. Keep cool...'

'Zero, all the time I'm getting lies on this case. What's going
on? You didn't feel fit to tell me this until now?'

'It was classified.'

'Classified? Jesus!'

'Kracker didn't want us to know about it. It was Tom Dove
that let me into the Dodo clue.'

'Tom Dove, Jesus! He's a Vurtcop, isn't he?'

'One of the best. The cop-banks have made an analysis. They had enough data. Shoved it all into the cop-brain; came up with this message—Dodos don't sneeze. You came up in the analysis.'

'What does this mean?'

'It means the fever's coming through from the Vurt. You never realised?'

'No . . . I . . .'

'I mean . . . not dreaming . . . not sneezing . . . you must have thought about it?'

I was closer to Zero than I wanted to admit, especially now that his breath was coming in slow wheezes and his eyes were streaming with mucus. And the fact that he had pointed a gun at me and my daughter. And failed in the attempt, slowed down. On purpose? Whatever, this is the kind of act that can force people apart, or else bring them together. Maybe he was going through pain I would never know. I was immune to things he could possibly die from. I was really feeling for the big dogcop, and that came as a shock to me.

Zero's pollen mask was turned to the sky. He moved off some way, stroked at his wounded arm, and then turned his face back to me. 'This info has already reached the street. The sufferers are turning against the immune. They're calling them the Mooners. I fear recriminations.'

'What can we do?'

'Tom Dove reckons he's found out where the fever is coming from. He's tracked it down to a particular region in the Vurt. The pollen is coming through to Manchester from a hole in the dream. This is why you're not sneezing. You can't take the Vurt. Because of this, I need your help. You Dodos may be our only chance.'

'This is crazy, Zero.'

'There's more. There was a vanishing, Jones. A swap.'

'Really?'

'Name of Brian Swallow. He disappeared some few minutes

before Coyote died.' Zero placed a photograph on the balcony's wall in front of me. He gave me a few seconds to study it before continuing. 'Nice looking kid. Nine years old. Heavily Vurt. He had the feathers inside him. A reckoning of 9.98 on Hobart's Scale. That's some weight of a dream. Tom Dove investigated. He's found out that this kid, this Brian Swallow . . . he's been swapped, you know . . . exchange rates?'

'Sure. Everything taken from Vurt . . .'

'Right . . . It has to be swapped for something of equal value from the real world. Tom Dove has found out this kid was swapped with something out of Juniper Suction. You know what that is? It's Heaven Feather.'

'Great.'

'The hayfever is infecting the Vurt as well, Sibyl. It's getting through from there. From Juniper Suction. This is the world governed by John Barleycorn. You know him? He's one of the most powerful Vurt creatures. A real demon. Tom Dove has told me the story. Juniper Suction is some kind of afterlife feather for the well-to-do. A dark story. All about Barleycorn, who was the son of Cronus, the god of time. This is an old Greek myth, right, transported into the Vurt? Juniper Suction is all about how Barleycorn kidnapped some young girl called Persephone, okay? Persephone? Shit, what do I know, but this is all fitting in, right? You found that name, didn't you, down at Belle Vue Zoo?'

'You're saying this Persephone has come through to Manchester from the Vurt?'

'I'm saying that this Persephone . . . apparently she's a goddess of flowers and fertility. All that dung. What I'm saying is that the Vurt is maybe getting angry.'

'What does that mean, angry?'

'The Vurt world is maybe wanting a way in, a way back. You know, just like the Zombies want a way back into the city? It makes a kind of sense to me. I reckon things are changing, the wall is collapsing. The dream and the real. Manchester is the focus of that wall. If Manchester goes . . . well, then . . . the whole world follows. I want to bring the Vurtcop in. I want you to work with Tom Dove—'

'No.'

Zero reached his hands up to his face, and when they came away, the pollen mask was dangling from his fingers. He threw it over the balcony.

He breathed deeply of the golden air. 'Sibyl . . . if I keep breathing this air . . . I'm going to die. Doesn't that mean anything to you?'

'No way. Absolutely. I hate the Vurt.'

'Dove is willing to go against Kracker. So am I. It means that much to us.'

'I'm not working with a Vurtcop. That's my nightmare.' My voice was full of a genetic weight. I stepped back into the room, heading for the front door.

'Sibyl?' Zero's voice from behind me. 'It's too late to be fearful, Sibyl.'

I opened the door.

A man was standing on the threshold. An orange wedge of hair. Fit and lean.

My Shadow jumped like the devil was caressing me.

We now know that the inability to dream is a genetic thing; a certain lost linkage in the double helix. And the fear of those that *are* the dream is inborn and inescapable. The reaction of an Unbeknownst to a Vurt creature is the same as that of a mouse to a cat. It operates at the same level of reality, down deep in the body's origins.

Zero's voice: 'Sibyl, meet Tom Dove.'

I was reacting to the intrusion. My smoke running in lines of fear. Tom Dove said hello to me, but my Shadow was screaming. It wanted me out of there.

'Sibyl, sit down please.' I caught Zero's words through a tremble of heat. 'I really do believe it is the solution. Imagine, Smokey: a cop who can't dream . . . paired with a cop who *is* the dream . . .'

That would be a nightmare. And I told Zero so.

'Sibyl, I am going to die soon,' he said. 'This fever will take me out. It's a fact.' This from the dogcop who had stood alone against the dog-mobs of Bottletown during the Dripfeed riots. But his voice was thick with need. 'You want to make an effort, Smokey? Look around this room. How many cops do you see? It's just us against the fever. Me, you and Tom. We lost another fifty citizens this morning. Maybe I'm the next to go.'

'No . . . I . . . Please, take him away from me.' I was waving my hands at Tom Dove, like I could fend off his Vurthood that way. Tom Dove was just standing there, his sculptured face like stone. I could almost see his Vurt wings fluttering in the apartment. Tom Dove never said a word. I tried to make a wide trip around him, towards the door.

'What the fuck do you think I am?' Zero was snarling. 'You think I like sneezing my guts out? You think I want to die of this snot? Like fuck I do! I want to die in battle, like any good dog does. Tom reckons he can send your Shadow into the dream. Don't ask me how it works. I'm just a poor, sneezing-to-death dog from nowhere. Now just make an effort, will you?'

'Zero! It's too much for me. I . . .'

'Do it!' He made an almighty sneeze then, maskless . . .
Aaaaaacccccchhhhhooooosssssshhhhhh!!!!!!!

'You've got to help me, Sibyl,' he spluttered. 'You're all I've got left . . .'

I walked out into the corridor. 'Get a new mask, Zero.' I slammed the door shut behind me, running from the flat.

That night we found the first victim of the Big Sneeze. She was a Dodo. Therefore, immune. A Mooner.

Her real name was Christina Dewberry.

She was a young woman, almost out of college, studying Bio-plastics and *Hardwere,* those twin foundations of robotic-canine life. Christina was genetically perfect, with a crystal-clear intelligence and her tutors at the University of Manchester had praised the 'objective' eye she had brought to her studies of metadogology. One of the big Metadog companies had already promised her a position upon finishing her course. During my investigations I was shown some of her final dog designs. They were indeed very power-ful: cold and distant in their intentions, but all the more startling for that.

Christina's body was found in the bushes behind St Ann's Church. The bushes had completely covered her body by the time we got there. But this was not a death by flowers. This was a human death.

At 10.34 p.m. she had left Corbiere's Winebar, too drunk to negotiate a fast-track, and had therefore decided to waste some precious grant money on an Xcab fare. She only lived in Rusholme, it wouldn't cost that much, and anyway wasn't she about to land herself a well paid job? It was the birthday of one her friends from college. Witnesses from the winebar said that Christina had felt threatened during the evening by the fact that she wasn't sneezing. The whole bar was suffering from the fever, and she had felt cold eyes all over her. A gang of rowdy robolads had started to make fun of her, calling her a Mooner. Her friends had tried to protect her, but even they, despite all their efforts, could not help feeling separate from Christina. They called her 'The Virgin.' By 10.30— the ugliness of the place, the snot flying through the air towards her, the rain of abuses—it became too much to bear. Christina had fled, towards home, towards a taxi at the St Ann's rank.

They caught up with her immediately, dragging her into the bushes behind the church. I imagine that she saw a clutch of masks descending on her as she struggled, and then one by one the masks lifting up, to reveal all the colours of the hybrids: dog and human, Shadow and robo. She had screamed out at them to stop but her open mouth was only an invite to them; the sufferers had sneezed upon her, celebrating their disease. Their leader was a big-snouted dogboy, and he had rammed his snout into her mouth and then sneezed out his anger and all his jealousy at her. Then his pack of followers had taken her in turn, each of them adding their snot-poison to his.

I had gathered all this knowledge from the Xcab drivers who had clustered around the killing zone, laughing and joking amongst themselves. Only one had tried to intervene and he was soon pushed aside. This was Roberman. Of course I had no 'official coding' for police work that day, but some of the cops were more than helpful; I think Kracker must have been stepping on tails.

I had interviewed Roberman that night, and he had told me of the distaste he had felt at the Big Sneeze. Of course I couldn't understand a growling word to begin with, even with the Shadow turned up to the maximum. There was no trace of the human in Roberman, just dog and robo, and the Shadow of a robodog is hard to catch. Reading his mind was like looking into a cellar with the lights out. Various dogcops had tried for a read-out, each of whom reported failure. Eventually Zero Clegg had appeared on the scene, called by some linkage in the dog-world. Zero had jumped on the new job with glee, easily translating Roberman's gruff howling into Pureness for me. The robodog was feeling bad, my human eyes could see that, as he gave witness to what he had seen. The Big Sneeze. This is what the sufferers called the act of murder by sneezing. Roberman described it all but could not put names to the perpetrators, no more than the other drivers could. They were lying, but this robodog was faithful to the truth. And now I saw where Roberman's grief was really coming from; where this fever-driven inhuman mutant with a plastic snout rimmed with wet snot had learned to feel for those who could not sneeze. He was close to Boda. There was a crossbreed loneliness in his Shadow that only my daughter had managed to ride through. Zero told him that I was Boda's 'mother-bitch.' After that it was quite easy. He told us about how Boda had been talking to him in the St Ann's rank, the time of the murder. Columbus had been lying about the cab-records. Boda was innocent of Coyote's murder.

Young girls drifting through loneliness; Boda and Christina, twins of the lost life, working on dreams they could never feel.

The cops dragged Christina Dewberry from her tight wrappings of church flowers, her eyes wide and staring, a dried-up river of blood on her lips. Back in the lab, robo-Skinner had pushed his sharp cameras into her mouth, and the analysis was phoned in to me at my house...

Report: victim's lung burst by bullets of snot. Death by proxy sneezing.

This was when the people's breath started to turn, from denial to acceptance. The fever taking hold. It was a fluid world and there was danger for everybody living there.

Even for those who could not dream. Myself, my daughter...

Boda cannot go home, so she has lodged herself into a down-and-dirty Fallowfield bed-and-breakfast flat for a few days. Now she's watching Blush on the room's antique television, watching that friend of Coyote's working for a living through a cheap soap called *Comatose Road*. Boda has made a drink of a kind out of the hospitality sachets. The bottle of Boomer she had stolen from Country Joe is perched on the worm-ridden dressing table. A naked bulb hangs over the bed she is lying on. That light is a temptation to the moths of Manchester; they keep batting, again and again, against its glassy surface, until their wings are frazzled. Boda watches them die with a cold eye. Let the moths, and all other creatures, die in peace. Let them reach their rightful end.

Blush is playing a newcomer to *Comatose Road,* the youngest daughter of Len Dirtyclough. Len Dirtyclough was lately married to Betty Swine, who was now calling herself Betty Dirt-Swine. Blush was playing the long lost child of Len's wild years, when he had shagged every single woman in Comatose Road, and quite gleefully, without a hint of remorse. Now he was going to pay for that stolen pleasure. Blush was a bad dream that Len Dirtyclough could not wake up from. She was his soap-nemesis.

Boda snaps out of the television world, her mind filled with Shadows. And the world that she comes back to is damp with sweat and love-juice. It's a down-towner's paradise, that room, a glistening collector of semen and despair.

Boda's money is running out.

Boda's hopes are running out.

This sad room has been her only world for the last two nights. She doesn't want to go out any more. She doesn't want to know about outside life any more. The outside life is filled with demons. Xcabs, Coyote, the cops, Gumbo, her mother, Columbus, the former Boda, the former Charrie. They all want a part of her. Meeting with her mother in that patch of park flowers had been too much. Was her mother really a cop? That would be the ultimate humiliation. Memories of her mother are crowding her mind until her mother's face seems to float over *Comatose Road*. Her mother is sitting in the lounge bar of the Sleeping Queen, which was the public house where all the *Comatose* residents drank. Her mother is drinking herself into Boda's Shadow, some-how or other.

She doesn't even know what her mother is called.

Boda gets up from the bed and turns off the television. *Comatose* vanishes into dust. She's alone again. Boda is waiting. For what? Flowers are growing over the room's windows, even though it's on the second floor. Dogs are barking from the street outside. Nature turning deadly. She reaches deep down into the Shadow, trying to find her memories. Trying to find her life before the Xcabs took it all away.

She comes up with nothing.

Darkness, darkness. Boda looks over to the bottle of Boomer on the dressing table. *Maybe it's time? Let's shut this beauty down.* She knows that Boomer can kill, if taken incorrectly.

There was a hole in your map, my daughter. You were on the edge of falling through.

Columbus had wanted her killed. Why would he want that? Because of something she knew? What the hell did Boda know? She knew nothing. Had the Cab King also killed Coyote? Was it all connected? So many questions. There's only one way to find out, and that is to get back on the map. Boda needs to talk with the Switch. She needs a confrontation.

How can she do this?

Boda turns on the radio, works the dial until she finds the pirate's station.

Gumbo talking direct to her . . .

'Boadicea, my beauty. The Gumbo has dived into the Xcab-records and come up with an anomaly. They've been changed. They've been tampered with. Yes! Listeners, listen up. Boda was nowhere near Alexandra Park at the time of Coyote's death. Somebody's setting her up, and it can only be Columbus himself. Who else would have access? Boda is innocent. The cabs are to blame, and maybe the cops also, because aren't they all tied up together? I was offering five golden feathers for the presence of Coyote's murderer. Now I'm offering six of the same for the whereabouts of his innocent lover. Pollen count is rising. 1257 grains per cubic metre. Boda, you out there? You listening? Come home to me. You know the Gumbo keeps a safe house. The cops and the cabs will never find you here. To speed your passage I'm going to play my theme tune now. That's right. *Hippy Gumbo* from 1967, by one Marcus Bolan, pre-Tyrannosaurus Rex. May his car-crashed soul rest in pieces . . .'

Music. Decision time . . .

No one else to trust.

There's a phone box just outside the Fallowfield flat. It takes coins. Boda waits for a few seconds to let her courage build up and then slips some of her last pennies into the slot.

Saturday
6 May

Belinda, our stories are creeping, closer and closer together, closer to the moment when they join.

Miles and miles and miles; waves of psychedelic light in a fogged-up cellar. Waves of music. *Strawberry Fields* is playing over the sound system as Boda falls into loving caresses. Wanita-Wanita, a funky black mistress complete with stacks and a two-foot afro, is dancing to the northern funkiness of it all. She takes hold of Boda by the waist, leads her down into the trip . . .

A dark room full of shining feathers that Boda has descended into. Colours shining from tufts that hang from the damp walls. Pieces of electrical equipment lying around here and there, their backs ripped off and wires from each to each, distending. All of the wires joining into a complex lover's knot. Some of them plugged into an old car battery, some into the household circuits, the rest leading to a wire that dangles from the overhead bulb socket. Gumbo YaYa himself is sitting inside the tangle of wires, joining a red to a white and a blue. Making sparks. Boda can feel the fire in her Shadow; impulses of knowledge dripping into smoke. Four electric office fans blow soft cross-currents of air around the cellar on which feathers of many colours float like pieces of a dream. Belinda feels nervous amidst these flights. A radiant fire erupts from a circuit board. Gumbo YaYa spits at the flame. The Beatles are so loud, the room seems to be pulsing with the rhythm. Lights are flickering here and there, like a disco constellation. Sheets of random images play over the walls, shining from old-style movie-projectors. Wanita-Wanita has let go of Boda's waist, finding no dance in her, and is now tripping out alone, her body swaying to the ragged beats, totally lost. Boda feels like a lonesome intruder. Boomer scent drifts in a purple haze.

Nothing seems real.

Gumbo YaYa is a middle-aged, creased-up wizard hiding behind a thick tangle of dirt-blond hair. He's dressed in purple loon pants and a mirrored grandad shirt. No words have been spoken. His Vaz-smeared lips are fixed to the tubing of a global bong pipe that burbles with Boomer juice. Boda can smell the sweet liquid turning to smoke on her Shadow. It makes her want to suck deep, and when Gumbo takes the tube from his mouth and offers it to her, she accepts it without hesitation.

Peace and Love to the world, coming on.

'Oh man, oh man . . . that is . . .' Gumbo's voice is trip-deep and out of here. 'That is some juice. Take two and pass.'

It's an illegal blend, a potent mixture of bliss and danger, and Boda's mind is wandering through a maze of pleasure. Gumbo says something to her, but the music and the drugs make it a riddle. Something about her past?

Swirling world. Colours and sparks, merging into a meld of love. Boomer juice working strong. Boda can no longer make out where she is. The room is slippery with light and heat and feathers.

'I don't know what I am,' she half-answers. 'I'm a mystery.'

Gumbo moves his hands through the air, a slow dance like Tai Chi, and the music grows slightly quieter. Boda can hear him now. 'Nice one . . . sure is . . . you not been downloaded, ya ya?' Gumbo's voice without his radio filters is a wavering treble, fuelled by too many drugs, too much paradise.

'I don't know what happened,' Boda replies, passing the bong pipe back to Gumbo. 'I turned off when the cab went maverick. I'm all alone now. No memories.'

'Wow, must've been one head-fuck.'

'I don't even know what my name is. Not even my second name.'

'Pre-cabian moniker? Super fine. I can tell you that.'

'Can you?'

'Sure thing, super-sugar. Hang on. Record's finishing...'
Gumbo clicks a switch on an old radio microphone and starts to
speak over the fade-out, his voice transformed into bass honey by
the handmade frequency enhancers, despite the blast of sneezing
that seizes him. Also, he dips a blue-and-silver feather into his mouth
before speaking: 'Pardon me. That was The Beatles, and this is
Gumbo YaYa with a special item. Got a mystery guest star with me
today on the wave. Gonna play the *Piper at the Gates of Dawn* album
by the Pink Floyd for you now, the whole of it, my people, whilst
the good Doctor chitter-chats to the guest. Back on the bus just as
soon as possible with the latest on the Xcabber rogue warrior.
Ooops! Did I give the game away there? I'm an old hippy teaser,
ain't that the living truth!'

Wanita-Wanita puts the needle to the groove, vinyl version.
It's a genuine 1960s player, tiny and tremulous, boosted in the bass
from a ragged box of tricks that perches on a pile of *Popular Vurt
Mechanic* magazines. Wires from the exposed back of the record
deck lead to amplifiers with Vurt feathers shoved into the various
sockets. Across the walls, waves of treble and bass are played out
in rainbows. Sitting on top of the music box is a homemade pollen
counter constructed out of feathers and valves. Readout: 1594 and
rising.

'You found your way?' Gumbo asks.

'I'm here, aren't I?'

'You should have some respect, madam,' Wanita says. 'Not
many get to visit the Palace of Gumbo.'

Boda doesn't know what to say. The music is writhing around
her in ever-tightening waves of bliss. She can't believe that the
Gumbo's famous hi-tech sound comes from such low-fi equipment,
and she tells him so. Gumbo makes no attempt to answer; his head
is already floating away into newfoundlands. He's swaying like a slow
snake.

'Gumbo likes it primitive,' Wanita tells her, dancing to the new, looser rhythms.

'What's the blue-and-silver feather do?'

'That's Cherry Stoner. One's of Gumbo's own creations. He's out of the picture, you see, twenty-four hours a day. Bless me, he's been stoned since nineteen sixty-six and he wasn't even *alive* then. Cherry Stoner allows him a moment of coolness.'

'Jesus.'

'Not what you expected, huh?'

'Can he really help me, Wanita?'

'Child, nobody comes close.'

Gumbo has been watching this exchange from his position on the floor, his eyes filled with another, gentler world. Now his fingers reach lazily for the Cherry Stoner feather. He licks it deep, and then says, 'Everything you see here, Boda, is genuine Sixties gear. All charged-up to futuristic standards, of course, but I really believe that lost decade was the best ever. You know much about that time, Cabber?'

'Not a lot.'

'It was a time of happenings and flower power. A time of changes. That's why this hayfever wave is exciting me so much, despite the danger. It's got me in two minds, this fever. The flowers are making a come-back, and the world is getting messier. The barricades are coming down. This city's so fucking *juicy* right now.'

'You can tell me about my past.'

'I can deliver. Ya Ya! *Aaaaaccchhhhoooooossshhhhh!!!!*'

'*Gesundheit,*' says Wanita-Wanita.

'Pardon me, Beautiful.' Gumbo moves his hands and the projected images change to a long list of words that write the walls with a message. Boda's history. 'I stole this from the cab-records. Good, reading, sugar...' With that the YaYa switches off once again.

Boda reads her history off the walls. Her real name: Belinda

Jones. Her attributes: Shadow and Dodo. Her date and place of birth. Her mother's name: Sibyl Jones. Her mother's occupation: Shadowcop.

'My mother's a cop.'

Gumbo has gone all wobbly again. Wanita speaks for him. 'Your mother really is a Shadowcop. And now the cop-child is on the programme. The Gumbo is loving this, believe me.'

'We used to live in Victoria Park?'

'The cab-records don't tell no lies.'

Boda looks at Wanita.

'Well . . . not often, child.'

'Does my mother still live there?'

'Easy to find out, Boda. Or should we call you Belinda?'

It only takes a moment. 'Call me Belinda.'

'Belinda, Belinda!' cries the stoned immaculate Gumbo. 'Excellent! Welcome home.' Gumbo moves his hands back through space and the Xcab history vanishes into the music from the Pink Floyd.

'Don't worry. To know him is to love him,' says Wanita. 'How do you feel about it all?'

'That's part of the trouble . . . I can't work it out. I feel like my life has been squandered on memories of nothing. I want the map back. I can't help feeling lost without it.'

'This is why you've come to us?'

'I want to find Coyote's killer. That's my job now. And I'll need to be on the map to do it.'

'What have you learned?'

'So you really don't believe that I killed him?'

'The Gumbo *knows* that you're innocent, Belinda. He made a journey into the Xcab-records. It's Gumbo-official. Columbus lied to the cops.'

'It's tied up with the pollen, you know? Coyote's death.'

'We know.'

'Also with Columbus.'

'Even better. Gumbo suspects that Kracker himself has a sticky finger in this apple pie.' A picture of Kracker appears then, on the flickering wall, projected from the Gumbo's head.

'I know this man,' Belinda says. 'He was a passenger, called himself Deville. This is Kracker?'

'Yes. The Chief of Cops.'

'Kracker tried to kill me.'

Gumbo removes the bong pipe from his lips just long enough to shout, 'Raving piglet!'

Belinda ignores him. 'Why do they want to kill me, Wanita?'

'You must know too much, Belinda.'

'I don't know anything. I'm alone.'

'Not any more. Gumbo needs you.'

'Do you always answer for the Hippy King?'

'What do you think?'

'I came here in good grace, Wanita. I expected more than this . . . this stoned-up hippy shit.'

Wanita falls silent. Gumbo gurgles from behind his bong, his face stretched and curved by the glass, and then sneezes.

'Bless you—'

'Wanita, fuck off!' This from Belinda, surprising herself. She steps over the tangle of wires to where the good Gumbo is sitting. She wrenches the pipe out of his mouth, grabs the Cherry Stoner feather from the air, her fingers crackling with fire and pain as the flights tickle her skin. No matter. 'Belinda, stop—' Wanita's voice in the colours. No matter. This feather is going somewhere. Belinda rams it into Gumbo's mouth. He starts to spit and gag, but she makes him suck.

Deep.

'Somebody told me the fever is coming through from a Vurt world called Juniper Suction. Is that right? Gumbo? Is that right?'

'My feelings exactly.' Gumbo's eyes are flooded with tears at the sudden hit of reality.

'Tell me about Juniper Suction.'

'It's a green Heaven Feather. Very rare. Gumbo hasn't seen one for years.'

'What's a Heaven Feather? Come on!'

'Fuck you.'

'Gumbo . . .'

'Stay out of this, Wanita.' Back to Gumbo. 'We helping each other, or what? Maybe I should use the Shadow on you? Hey? You want that? A Shadow-fuck?'

'No, no . . . please . . . Juniper is a place to put your mind when you die. You can live forever there, in your dreams. It's an Underworld ruled by one John Barleycorn. He lives there with his young wife, Persephone.'

'Persephone was Coyote's last passenger.'

'Bingo! That's it.'

Belinda lets go of the Gumbo. Wanita moves in to comfort him.

'It's okay, Wanita. Superfine.' The faraway look vanishes from his eyes as he turns back to Belinda. 'This is why they want you killed, driver. You knew too much about the dream-seed. The Vurt is making an invasion into our space and Persephone is the source of the fever. Columbus is the road on which the seed travels.'

'So Columbus had Coyote killed after the passenger was brought in?'

'Maybe, but what's important now is to stop the Vurt world coming through. It's deadly, like every time we sneeze another sentence is written against us.'

'Can we do anything?'

'*Aaaaaccchhhhhooooossshhhhh!!!!!* Pardon me.' Gumbo shoved the Cherry Stoner feather back into his mouth for another charge of reality juice before continuing, 'We need to get you and Columbus together.'

'Can you do that, Gumbo?' asked Belinda.

'It's possible, but it's dangerous. You willing to risk it?'

'I'm willing.'

'The first step is to get you onto the Hive-map again.'

'I'll do anything.'

Gumbo's mouth breaks into a weed-blackened grin that not even his curtains of hair can conceal. Then he looks over to a large nautical clock on the cellar wall. It reads 11.42 a.m. Gumbo works a control so that the Pink Floyd's musical patterns transform into a network of yellow and black insects that pulsate over the walls. 'This is the Xcab map,' he says.

'Jesus!'

'But first . . . the broadcast . . .'

Zero Clegg called me at 11.55 a.m., Saturday morning, asking if I'd been listening to the Gumbo lately? 'No, no, don't answer,' he said, before I could say anything. 'It's obvious you haven't, Sib, from your reaction.'

'What's he broadcasting now?' I asked. 'A list of all known Mooners?' Another half-a-dozen Mooner corpses had been uncovered during the night.

'It's worse than that.'

'Tell me.'

Zero went quiet for a moment, which was unusual. Something was wrong. I have lived one hundred and fifty-two years, and have lived through many, many strange and surprising times, but the words I heard that day over the telephone will forever be part of my deepest Shadow. Zero played me a tape recording of Gumbo YaYa's show broadcast that same morning, from 11.42 to 11.45. It started with a piece of music fading away, and then a voice coming in over the top of the last moments. Except that it wasn't Gumbo's voice, it was a woman's voice . . .

'This is Boda the maverick cabber calling the people of Manchester from the Gumbo wave. (FOUR SECONDS OF SILENCE)

My name is now Belinda Jones. That's my pre-cabian name. I never killed Coyote, and I never would have done. Xcabs are lying about my cab-whereabouts; I was never at Alex Park at that time. Columbus tried to blame me. Maybe I knew too much about his secret schemes, or maybe I just loved Coyote too much. I never got the proper chance to express it. He was taken from me early, too early. (TWO SECONDS' SILENCE) I'm determined to find out who did murder him. Coyote picked up a passenger named Persephone on his last-ever trip. Columbus set Coyote up for this ride. The Cops are helping the King Cab. Chief Kracker himself . . . Kracker tried to kill me. Keep trying, dumb-fucker cop. Persephone is a young girl, age of ten or eleven. She may be the source of the fever. Anyone with information can ring the YaYa number. He'll pass it on to me. (TWO SECONDS) Pollen Count is at 1607 and rising. (FIVE SECONDS) Gumbo is going to play *Have You Seen Your Mother, Baby (Standing in the Shadow)* by The Rolling Stones. Which is a special request going out to Sibyl Jones of the Manchester Cops. You seen any good Vurtball matches lately, Sibyl? (TWO SEC-ONDS) I'll be back at one o'clock with an update. Take it away, Mick and the boys. (THREE SECONDS) Erm . . . was that okay, Gumbo?'

And then another voice, the Gumbo's: 'That was just fine, kid. *Aaaacccchhhhhoooooosssshhhhhhh!!!* Pardon me. And more from the maverick cabber later on today. 1.00 p.m. Stay turned on now, you hear?'

And then the music started, and Zero turned off the recording and came back on line. But he didn't say anything. I could hear his wheezing, feverish breath in the darkness of my Shadow, which was trembling with closure. He sneezed over the line and then said, 'You know what this means? Gumbo has claimed your daughter.'

'What can I do, Zero? I want her back.'

'I think the fever is more important.'

'You would.'

'Stay cool, Mooner.'

'I'm her mother, Zero. I've been searching for years.'

Clegg went quiet again. I could hear him sneeze away from the mouthpiece and then his voice coming back to me: 'This is the deal, Officer Jones. I bring Tom Dove round to your flat, and then we—'

I put the phone down on his words. Give a dog a bone, and all that. Maybe one of Zero's distant relations had been a pure-bred Retriever.

I was nervous and edgy, visions of feathers floating through my mind. My son was crying from the bedroom. I went in to tend to Jewel's needs. It was more for my benefit than his. Every crack in that bedroom had been sealed, but the seed was already within him. But pretending to help my firstborn put my mind at ease, a little. His breath was softly exploding from a frail body that was covered in a hard crust of snot that I tried my best to clean away, but more just took its place, wet and slimy. I feared that he had only a few days left now. I should explain that death to a Non-Viable Lifeform was in no way similar to that of a fully living being. A mortal treats death as an enemy, fighting until the last breath. To an NVL, however, once the moment is ripe, death is more of a love affair; the long struggle between their opposing ancestors is over. Life and death in the kiss of lovers. All that matters then is to let the darker side of their nature take them to bed. The bed is the grave, the bed from which they were born. Into which they will die. How far was Jewel from that moment of acceptance? A mere breath? One more sneeze? Another jump in the pollen count? My only choice was to find a cure for him. And all this sealing was really for myself, of course, after hearing my daughter play that song for me. Have you seen your mother, baby, standing in the Shadow? A shiver ran through me, ripples of smoke. I tuned into Gumbo's wave, only to hear him boast that Belinda was staying at his secret house from now on, 'Where the cops will never find her. She'll be talking on the hour, telling Manchester the story of her extraordinary life. Exclusive to Radio YaYa, giving good tongue to the North.' And he laughed then, heartily, and it got to me, that laughter, it maddened me.

I sat down on the lounger and reached for a half bottle of red wine left over from the other night. It took me only twenty minutes to finish it off, and another fifteen to make a good start on a new bottle. During that time I must have smoked at least thirty Napalms. Tasting all of the nasty fruits, I was drifting sweetly through the caresses of Dionysus. It felt like all of my blood sugar had been changed into alcohol. My Shadow was bogged down in deep claret. The Napalm pack-message read SMOKING IS GOOD FOR THE SOUL—HIS MAJESTY'S PERSONAL JESUS.

For the first time, a Napalm failed me.

At 1.00 p.m. I tuned into Radio YaYa once again, expecting to hear Belinda telling the story of her life, my life. I must have been very desperate.

Gumbo YaYa is grinning through his layers of hair. 'Excellent broadcast, Belinda. For a beginner. Now watch. Shit, I haven't felt this good in ages.' We are travelling back to 11.46 a.m. on the morning of that same Saturday.

Gumbo and Belinda are alone now, Wanita has vanished into some deeper corridor. Gumbo is well-zonked on Cherry Stoner, and he looks *almost* normal as he points to the walls where the Xcab roads are flickering. 'This is the Hive-map up and running. The yellow dots are the cabs, the black web is the roads.' Gumbo works the controls so that the whole map tilts through 180 degrees. 'Isn't that beautiful? We can view it from any angle, any position. Keep your eyes on the road, driver.'

Now Belinda is travelling down Oxford Road just like she used to do inside of Charrie. This time at a distance. 'Where's Columbus?' she asks.

'Columbus is the whole thing taken together. That's his weakness, you see?'

'Why?' Belinda is intrigued.

'The Switch has become too powerful. He can no longer see the wood for the trees, the road for the cabs.'

'You know that he's calling up some big changes to the map?'

'It really gets to me that Columbus is doing this, you know? It's like we're both messengers, the Gumbo and the Cab King. Communication is power. We're both duty-bound to carry the message to the people and that bastard goes and abuses the power. So then, we work quickly, Belinda, yes?'

'What can you do?'

'Watch . . .' Gumbo works the switches again, so that the image focuses on one particular Xcab. 'You see that cab there, Belinda?' he asks. Belinda nods. 'That's my cab. That's the Gumbo YaYa Cab. The Magic Bus.'

'There's no such thing,' Belinda says.

'Officially, no. But that old hippy-cab is there anyway. You saw the Magic Bus outside the house, yes?'

'I saw it.'

'That's my version of the Xcab.'

'It's impossible.'

'Well, it's happening. Watch . . .' Gumbo works the controls and the hippy-cab makes a left on the map, from Oxford Street onto Whitworth.

'But who's driving it?' Belinda asks.

Gumbo laughs. 'I am. No one is. It's an imaginary cab. This is where I get my map-knowledge from. Columbus doesn't even know the magic taxi exists.'

Belinda feels like her head is exploding with this knowledge, this denial of everything she has known the map to be. 'It's unnatural,' she cries.

'Exactly. I can do the same for you and Charrie.' Gumbo looks at the clock again. 11.52 a.m. 'We'll have to move quickly,' he tells her. 'You want it, Belinda? The map, once again?'

'Yes. Yes, do it. I want it.'

Gumbo is playing at the clacking keys of an antique typewriter, from whose broken back wires lead into the lover's tangle. He reaches out to pluck a silver feather from the air, doesn't even have to look for it, despite the sneeze that ripples from him. He pushes the feather into his mouth, sucks it deep and then removes it. He pushes the wet feather into the socket of a crooked transformer. A new message scrolls over the Xcab map on the wall: WELCOME TO SLITHERING SILVER. THIS IS SHAREVURT. PLEASE BE HON-EST. PAY THE REGISTRATION FEE. 'Fuck that shit,' the Gumbo announces. 'Information should be free.' He makes some adjust-ments until the map is overlaid with a floating menu and then says to Belinda, 'At 11.59 a.m., every morning, the Xcab map gets up-dated from the Council info. This is the moment of weakness. This is the door we go through.' Gumbo's fingers are dancing over the keys. '*Aaaaaacccchhhhooooooossshhhhh!!!!!* Pardon me. Shit, this fever is killing me. Give me a new street name, please?'

'What?'

'Belinda, I'm not kidding. This window is tight. A new street please . . .'

'Shaky Path,' Belinda answers, dragging the name from dark-ness.

'Done.' Gumbo's fingers bring up an inset window on the map screen. The time is reading 11.57. Fingers dancing. In the window a new street called Shaky Path is floating over the map. In another window Gumbo has called up the Authorities' Info-bank. Their lat-est updates to the map are packed in tightly to that space. Gumbo moves the Shaky Path window over to the Council window. Then he merges the two together, with a smooth move on the keyboard. Shaky Path is then registered as a new road to be opened that day. 'Don't worry,' Gumbo says to Belinda. 'All this info has a black scrambler on it. Tell me Charrie's Xcab number, please.' Belinda tells him the number, and then Gumbo YaYa drags up an Xcab icon from the toolbar at the top of the screen. He merges the icon with the number and then places them both on the Shaky Path imaginary road. The time is now reading 11.59 a.m., and Gumbo and Belinda watch in silence as the Xcab map sucks down the Council's update. 'Okay, rogue driver,' Gumbo says. 'You're back on line.'

Belinda moves closer to the screen. Bright yellow icons are buzzing around the Hive-map. Over to the east of the city there's a new street called Shaky Path, where no street ever existed before, and her very own cab icon, Charrie, is sitting on that street, dark and waiting for a driver. Gumbo tells her that the icon is dark because the real Charrie is off-map at the moment, but as soon as she drives him over the barrier, that marker will be as bright and as lively as all the others, only in secret colours. 'I'll be able to talk to you over the system,' he says. 'Mister Big Switch won't even be listening.' Gumbo starts to laugh then. Belinda asks him how it works. 'It's easy, really: a Trojan Horse. You build a new but imaginary street into the update, put your cab on it; Columbus thinks that street is up and running, but it doesn't really exist. And your cab is riding that invisible street. It's a viral street. My Magic Bus rides a road called Strawberry Fields. That's where this house is living on the map . . . Strawberry Fields. That's why the Authorities can't find my address. The cops and the Xcabs and the Authorities, Gumbo is laughing at all of them. The map is yours again, Belinda.'

'Thank you,' Belinda says to Gumbo, her head refilling with the Knowledge. 'But I'm no closer to Columbus. You promised me a closer ride.'

'There's only one way.'

'Tell me.'

'Welcome back, my love.' Gumbo is looking over Belinda's shoulder. Belinda turns around. Wanita-Wanita is standing in the doorway, holding the hand of a child. The child is dressed in a swimming costume, and her hair is shiny with moisture. Bedraggled feathers are knotted here and there in the wet locks.

'She was in the pool, Gumbo,' Wanita says.

'Excellent. Cool as fuck.'

'Blush . . .' Belinda's voice. 'It's you?'

'It's me.'

'You know Gumbo?'

'I know everybody, Boda.'

'Belinda . . . the name's Belinda.'

'Crazy. We're all in this together.' Blush is holding a black feather in her dripping hands.

'That's Black Mercury?' Belinda asks.

'That's my beauty.'

'That's a universal beauty,' Gumbo announces.

'Through this we can reach Columbus?' Belinda asks, thinking that maybe this was the same way that Coyote had spoken to the Cab King.

'Only you can do this trip, baby,' the Gumbo replies. 'Because ain't you the good driver?'

I tuned into the Gumbo wave at 1.00 p.m., expecting my daughter's voice to come calling once again. Instead I got the hippy pirate's voice, telling me to hold tight and keep listening . . .

'People, people, people! Keep listening, and tell your friends. At two o'clock this afternoon we are going to make a trip together, over the wave. We will be descending into the Vurt, in search of the fever and its cure. Yes, indeed. Belinda Jones herself, ex of the Xcabs, will be making that journey. She wants to meet Columbus in the dream. We believe the fever is coming through Columbus from a world called Juniper Suction and Columbus is making the pick-up and the drop-off. Belinda will be driving her rogue cab towards that rancid source. Once there she will be confronting Columbus with his crimes. Stay tuned and tell everybody. This will be like a moon-trip. The first of its kind. Close all hatches. You know that only the good Gumbo can take you this far.'

I switched off the radio.

It felt like my Shadow was closing down. How on earth could Belinda travel into the Vurt? She was a Dodo, an Unbeknownst. Unless she had somebody like Tom Dove in tow, a feather-person. Would my daughter really take that risk?

All over Manchester the people are gathering towards the news. They are listening in bars and shops, in newsagents and super-markets. Even in the streets, broadcast from overhead speakers, the voice of Gumbo YaYa is talking to them, calling them forth from their daily occupations. This voyage has brought them back onto the streets. The people are feeling reckless. Here they stand in groups, masked-up and sneezing, surrounded by flowers.

At Piccadilly Fast-track Station, and at Victoria, the booming voice travels forth over the systems. Travellers postpone their jour-neys, in fear of missing the broadcast.

In Bottletown, Twinkle and Karletta are perched close to the radio. They know that Blush is involved with Gumbo, and that she would have something to do with this trip. Twinkle moves her arms around Karletta, wiping the puppygirl's nose when she sneezes.

Zero Clegg is listening to the radio from the security of For-tress One, Namchester. Tom Dove is sitting beside him on the plush sofa.

Kracker is at his home, his squalling children all around him, making a fearsome noise. He tells them all to shut the fuck up, as he listens . . .

1.15 p.m.

The radio . . .

People are lining up in Market Street and Piccadilly Gardens. Almost all of them covered by masks. The flowers entangle every building and car. The jam-parked cars fill the streets bumper to bumper with hot dazzling chrome. The Gumbo wave plays from a thousand speakers all over the city. Some have got a Gumbo feather in their mouths, but most are content to listen in public. It's a collective experience. Nobody dare move for fear of missing it.

On the wasteground in front of Gumbo's palace, a tribe of dog-crusties are gathered, perfectly still, some on two legs, some on four. Ragamuffin tepees billow softly in a slight breeze. A fire burns. Over the flames a pig-size lump of meat is roasting. Spindly iron sculptures raised to some mutant canine goddess leer through a glaze of sunlight. Old vans and a blistered ambulance are parked in a circle leading to a multicoloured transit decorated with the words Magic Bus. This is Gumbo's own transport, and these dog-people are his disciples and protectors. Thick, germ-ridden droid-locks hang halfway down their backs. None are speaking. Most of the tribe are wearing pollen masks, and their pattern of upturned goggles reflects the sun, time and time again. All of them are listening to a loudspeaker fixed to the side of Gumbo's Palace.

Inside the Palace, Wanita-Wanita is leading Belinda by the hand towards a room on the second storey of the Palace. A door opening onto darkness.

Gumbo's music playing from the interior, over speakers, softly, softly . . .

Belinda's eyes adjusting to the darkness. Soft slitherings. Wetness moving across the floor towards her.

Zombie-breath.

That room is covered, wall to ceiling, with the half-dead. Fat bubblings. The dark children of Manchester. They explode from the nostrils, a raining shiver of snot.

'Jesus!' Belinda's breath.

Wanita's voice: 'Gumbo makes a home for the lost.'

'Please . . . please save us,' says a deep Zombie voice. It makes Belinda think about Bonanza, the Zombie who helped her escape from Country Joe's Motel in Limbo.

1.30 p.m.

Stirring slowly at the deep centre of his web of roads, Columbus the Kingcab is waiting, waiting, waiting . . .

On Deansgate and Cross Street, the Oxford Road and Wilmslow, on Rochdale Road and Princess, Moss Lane East and Blackfriars, the people are gathered in their thousands, listening to the music coming from shop doorways and the scrolled down windows of stationary cars. Roberman is somewhere in that tangle, his cabwave tuned to fuck, tuned instead into the song, the universal song.

1.45 p.m.

Belinda Jones is now dangling her bare feet into the swimming pool that laps gently around the basement of Gumbo's Palace. Blush the Vurt-child is with her, also with bare feet dangled, and she's telling Belinda that all things will come to pass if the correct path is taken and stuck to. 'You're very special, Belinda,' she says, making a wave. 'You're very much like Coyote. Crazy and naive. But strong and fiery. Good drivers, the both of you and well suited. Never to be consummated now, of course, but what else can you hope for than some kind of revenge?'

'I'm feeling weak, Blush,' says Belinda, letting water play around her ankles like cold hands grabbing her to pull her under. 'I don't know if I can make this trip. I'm scared of the Vurt.'

'I'm scared, you're scared, the whole of crazy Manchester is scared. You got a choice, really? I think not. You're one of the good few, Belinda, you just don't know it yet. You, me, Gumbo and Black Mercury feather; if you can envision a better way to visit Columbus, please tell me about it.'

Silence. Only the slow wave of deep shadows through the basement of the Palace and a lapping of water at the ankles of a not-so-good hero.

1.50 p.m.

Gumbo is playing *Riders on the Storm* by The Doors, and the dark, brooding melody rises from the collected radios and public address systems to form a cloud of music over the city.

Gumbo and Boda; twin riders of the dream.

Who else could save the city?

Stop-time and the sun hangs suspended. The world of Manchester turning on a pirate feather, waiting for a cure.

1.52 p.m.

Zero Clegg gets a call on his telephone. It makes him angry to be drawn from the waiting, but there's only one person he knows who still uses the phone.

'Smokey, that you?' he asks.

'It's me,' Sibyl replies.

'What you after?'

'Can you find Tom Dove?'

'He's right beside me.'

'Bring him over.'

'Sibyl, you okay?'

'Let's do the trip, Zero.'

Inside the secret Palace of Gumbo, the hippy pirate has the Black Mercury feather in his hand. Its flights are sparking off flames from the slew of electrical equipment. Belinda wants to run from the sparks, and also run to them. Her Shadow is split. The time is 1.56 p.m. 'Okay everybody,' Gumbo cries. 'Let's get ready to ride.' His eyes are addicted to the Black Mercury feather. Even through the layers of tears and snot, there's a secret vice in his look. It speaks volumes the lost years from the 1960s, when free love was a viable proposition. 'This feather is so lovely. I want to have sex with this feather.'

'I'm scared, Gumbo,' Belinda says. 'I'm a Dodo.'

'That's right. But the young kid . . .' He patted Blush on the head. 'She *is* the feathers. Your Shadow will be travelling with her. Good driver and feather-rider, riding together through the Vurt. What a sweet combo you are. Hey come on, driver, you've ridden roughshod before now. I'll be following you all the way. Also, the people of Manchester. I'll be your sweet narrator. Just remember Hobart's Law: if you take anything from Vurt, then Vurt will take something from you.' Gumbo sneezes. 'Okay, let's find the man behind this fever, people. Wanita?' Wanita kisses Gumbo as she takes the feather from his hand. He throws some switches, takes another good dose of Cherry Stoner for reason's pathway and then leans into a bakelite microphone . . .

'People of Manchester! Are you all gathered? Are you hungry for love? That was The Doors singing *Riders on the Storm*. The time is dead on two and this is Doctor Gumbo with a cure for *all* of your ills. Hallelujah! I've got a good crew with me. I've got Wanita-Wanita on tech back-up. I've got a Vurtkid called Blush. I've got the rogue driver, Belinda Jones. I've got your own good listening selves. We are gonna ride this storm down!'

Wanita feeds Black Mercury into one of the sockets on the messed-up bank of equipment, surges it with Gumbo Juice, and then holds the feather out towards Blush. Belinda sends her Shadow into Blush, at the same time as the young girl takes the black feather to her deep throat.

A burst of roadness, then, and a new world opening . . .

The trip spreading over the city. The good citizens listening in via the Gumbo. 'This is the YaYa talking. I'm taking you all on a voyage of discovery, into that strange world called Planet Xcab. This is a radio first. This is a happening, my friends. A real cool, dead and gone trip. And what better soundtrack for our adventure than the main cat himself. Purple Haze! Take us there, Mr Jimi.'

Tom Dove moved his hand towards me. Surges of revulsion. Pulses in the Smoke. My Shadow almost *leaving* my body, so terrified it was. The whole room swaying from the madness. The *dream* was in the room.

'This won't harm you, Sibyl,' Tom Dove said. 'There is absolutely no way you will catch the fever from this. Understood?'

'I don't give a shit about catching the fever.'

'Don't be scared, Sibyl—'

'I'm not fucking scared!'

Inside I was wilting from the nerves. My Shadow felt shredded. Gumbo YaYa was still broadcasting from the radio. That pirate had taken my daughter into the Vurt world. He was calling it a monumental trip, the first case of a Dodo visiting the dream world. He was comparing it to a moon landing, a journey into the remotest climes. 'One small step for a girl, one giant leap for Dodokind.'

'You're not really going into the Vurt,' Dove was saying. 'You will send your Shadow into mine. I will then transport my body to the Vurt. Your mind will be inside my body. If all goes according to plan, we will visit the Vurt together. Juniper Suction. But the hole's got some kind of one-way lock on it; it's letting the pollen out, but nothing can go in. I made an attempt. It repulsed me. It hurt. I'm telling you this now, Sibyl, so that you're warned. I think I can sneak your Shadow through. I think you just might be ... well ... smoky enough. Nebulous. Do you understand?'

'Please, I'm scared ...'

'I'll be right beside you.'

'There won't be any problems, will there?' Zero said this to Tom Dove. 'You sure? This is a Heaven Feather, for fuck's sake. She won't die in there? You've done this before, haven't you ... this Shadow-swap shit? Because if anything ...'

I was only catching this through mist, my Shadow struggling with fear. 'We'll be monitoring the whole trip on viewing feathers, don't worry.' It took a while to realise that Zero was talking to me now. 'Any problems ... we bail you right out of there. Okay? We won't feel less of you.'

Some kind of life, and visions of Belinda and Jewel in my mind. My two children ...

'Let's do it.' And then I was reaching into Tom Dove's mind, letting my fingers of Smoke play there, searching for a good hold.

He came back at me with a firm grip, and then I was swirling through broken colours; knife-sharp flashes of yellow and red stinging at my Shadow. It was like digging my teeth into glass. I was trying to bail out already, making for comfort, but the Dove-cop had me by the throat. 'Sibyl, keep cool,' he said. 'We're doing fine. We're travelling. Keep a good hold.' His feathery hands were gripping mine, and then I was swooping down with him towards the realm of stories . . .

My very first dream.

My wings.

Tom Dove floating me gently through the colours, and then down into darkness. Easing the flight with his words: 'Stay calm. I'm here. I'm here for you. Keep travelling. Nearly there. Stay cool. No worries. Nearly there. Nearly there.'

I had no time to think . . . this darkness was . . . did not lend itself to . . . other, stranger creatures were moving . . . through the darkness . . . my thoughts were . . . faces of pain and loss reaching for . . . too fast to be caught . . . my world and theirs . . . all becoming one . . .

I raised my hand to my face, but could feel nothing. I had no hands, no arms, no shoulders, no body, no head, no face, no voice; only the insistence that I was still living, somewhere. A door opens. A door *opens*. A hole. The hole is breathing. This door is slippery. Inside the door, another door, and Tom Dove is dragging me down towards this hole in sky. 'This is where the fever is creeping through,' Tom Dove tells me. 'This is Juniper Suction.' I can feel music. It feels like a purple haze. I no longer know where or what or why I am, only the sensation of falling . . . keeping . . . falling . . . keeping . . . falling me . . . keeping me . . . something. But . . . *Christ!* The hole was small, too small for even a worm to squeeze through. At first I thought this was a trick of perspective, until I realised . . . *shit! I'm right up against the thing!* There was no perspective in Vurt. *Dove!!! What are we—*No time to finish the question. Now my head was being forced through the hole. Yellow grains were drifting through the gap. The pain was burning. Tom's thoughts came into my body of smoke: 'Do I tell you how to travel through the Shadows, Sibyl? All pain is illusory.' Fine, that was good to know, but passing through, between the worlds, was like squeezing through a slit of hot flesh. Like the fear of landing on the moon. My head was popped out into another world.

I could see the garden. The garden . . . I had seen this . . .

Darkness viewing me. The rustling of dry leaves. Pollen clinging to my skin . . .

One almighty push from the Vurtcop and then the pain was dropping away, drips of rain into a bucket . . . into calmness.

First of all Belinda feels revulsion at the intrusion; that feather is going too deep for comfort. Hendrix is running loud through her Shadow. And the map she is travelling is nothing like what she imagined the Hive to be; the roads are green and twisted like the roots of a tree. Belinda is the passenger, and Blush is Mike Mercury, and the Vurtcab called Charrie is dancing through an organic system. So the map is made out of roots, and the city is a flower that grows from the sap of the map. This was new stuff, this was *knowledge*. But in reality Blush is driving the Xcab, and Belinda is just a passenger on that wave. But at least she's back on the map, the Vurtmap even, and she can feel the dreaming leather upholstery of Charrie folding her into pleasure. She can feel the cab shuddering with wonder as the Knowledge comes flooding. WHAT'S HAPPENING, MISTRESS? Charrie says. I THOUGHT I WAS LYING LOW IN LIMBO? Belinda tells him to quit talking and to just ride. SURE THING. WHO'S DRIVING ME? Charrie asks.

'Her name is Blush. You can trust her.'

GRANTED, BUT WHERE ARE WE GOING?

'This is a Vurt trip, Charrie. The centre of the map.'

And then a new voice comes on line: THIS IS GUMBO YAYA

CALLING BELINDA. GUMBO YAYA CALLING BELINDA. THE
WHOLE OF MANCHESTER IS LISTENING IN. YOU READING
ME, BELINDA?

'Reading you, Gumbo.'

YOU WANT TO TELL THE LISTENERS HOW THE TRIP IS
GOING SO FAR?

'The trip is going fine, listeners.'

EXCELLENT NEWS.

WHO'S THAT? Charrie asks. WHAT'S THIS GUMBO
DOING ON MY WAVE?

'Shut up and ride, Chariot.'

I'M RIDING.

But riding where? Because these serious roads are leading
into a dark jungle. The sun has vanished behind a cloud of soil.
Belinda cannot recognise the map any more. Where is she to go to?
These are the roots of the world tree. Pollen is seeping through a
hole in the map. Hot sauce. Sap dripping from bulbous green. Sweltering, black air, closing in. Cab-Christ, we're under the ground,
Belinda thinks. We're underneath Manchester. The back-seat driver
heads the cab towards the map's opening, through the hands of
Blush.

The map of roots unfolding around the centre which has
no centre. A whirling of tendrils and feathers. Blush is laughing
from the driver's seat, 'Crazy! I can't even drive in the real
world.' But Belinda is feeling Vurtsick. Too much dreaming for
one who has never dreamed before. 'Where are we, Charrie?'
she asks.

ERM . . . NOT QUITE SURE, DRIVER-BELINDA. THIS ROAD
IS A MYSTERY TO ME. ALL I'M GETTING IS THE-FORD-WHERE-
OXEN-ARE-DRIVEN-ACROSS-THE-MEDLOCK-RIVER. IS THIS
MANCHESTER?

'This is Vurtchester, Charrie.'

SHIT.

'I think we're on the Oxford Road, Charrie. Scrub that. I think we're underneath the Oxford Road.'

LET ME INPUT THAT. RIGHT...WE'RE HEADING TO-WARDS THE CENTRE OF TOWN. ALBERT SQUARE, OR THEREABOUTS. INFO IS FLUTTERING, DRIVER.

'I know. Stay on course.'

BELINDA, THIS IS GUMBO TALKING. I HATE TO TELL YOU THIS, BUT FROM MY SCREEN-MAP I THINK YOU'RE HEADING TOWARDS THE SOIL BENEATH BOOTLE STREET. YOU KNOW WHAT'S THERE?

'Sure. The cop station.'

YOU WANT ME TO PULL YOU OUT?

'Thanks, but no thanks. We're doing this trip.'

GOOD GUMBO!

And then a cab-ride down into earth. Everything is dark and forbidding, tightly pressed and sorrowful, except for the hole in the soil from which grains of pollen escape. The root-paths are shaky. Blush is sneezing violently from the front seat, and the vehicle is swaying under her spasming fingers. 'Gumbo, I don't think I can hold it,' she cries.

NEARLY THERE. KEEP IT COOL, KID.

Riding the shoot, down to the root.

Belinda can see all the roads of Vurtchester arriving and de-parting from that point in the soil just ahead. Worms are playing through the soil, turning their twistings into words that can be read over the Shadow...

INTRUDER, REVEAL YOURSELF. THIS IS A PRIVATE WORLD. The voice of Columbus.

Belinda sends a tendril of Smoke into Charrie's cab-system, forcing his wheel into a bad position so that he can drive towards danger. The pollen wraps itself around the cab until the vehicle is covered in a fine powder. It gets into the ventilators, clogging the system with botany. Charrie sneezes...

AAAAAAAHHHHHCCCHHHHOOOOOSSSSHHHHHHH!!!!!!
Belinda has never heard a cab sneeze before.

DRIVER-BELINDA . . . he says. I'M GETTING A POLLEN READING OF 1764. I'M SUFFERING.

1766, ACTUALLY, CAB-CHARIOT, the Gumbo YaYa says over the wave. JUST TELL THAT CAB TO KEEP ON RIDING, BELINDA.

DON'T LISTEN TO HIM, Charrie replies. THIS IS A NO-GO ZONE.

'Keep riding, Charrie. Or I might not love you any more.'

The cab stalls then, just for a second, before shifting into ultra-gear, and the dirt and the roots and the worms become a blur.

BELINDA, I'M LOSING YOU! Gumbo cries.

Silence.

And then Belinda is alone, and underground. Jimi Hendrix has fallen away. Gumbo, Wanita, Blush . . . all have fallen. Only Charrie the cab remains faithful to the journey.

This world is tight, dark and damp. Insects crawl through the root-knotted soil that makes up the roads they are travelling. The noise made by flowers as they grow. It reminds Belinda of that crackling message she had heard over the phone when ringing Coyote's pick-up number. Gnarled roots descend towards her taxi, breaking her window, wrapping her, and when she grabs at a tendril to push it aside, her Shadow flashes with vision. She sees all of Manchester stretching away into the mist and the rain, and laid over each road the shimmering lines of the map radiate like the vines of a spreading plant. Thousands of yellow-and-black ants scurry along the netted roots like roads. Along these roads Belinda herself has travelled, and it comes to her then that the ants are the Xcabs. And that each real world cab has its doppelganger down here in the Vurtmap. Charrie's omission from the real map will also entail a missing particle in the dream; this is why Columbus is so desperate to find Belinda's chariot again. The mirror is missing a reflection. In her driving days Belinda had often thought about the true nature of the map, seeing it in her mind as a vast array of pure information. Never for a moment did she consider that the map could be an organic, Vurtual system.

Shadow-cut.

And the cab breaks free suddenly of the root system and the dark earth. Now it travels through to a new sunlight and dazzlement. Belinda riding through the sunlight and the countryside, where all things are peaceful and unbound. Smells like paradise.

Rain dripping onto a deep purple flower. Echoes. Soundings. Tom's voice in there, somewhere. 'Welcome to Juniper Suction, Sibyl. I'm blinded this far. What can you see?'

I can see a world of green under black air. A forest. A blossoming jungle of sex. Flowers twisting around vines. Vines so very black. Dripping wet flowers. Bubbles of golden pollen popping open in the darkness, searching for lovers. Many of the pollen grains were floating through a hole in the forest's floor.

This was the same world I had glimpsed in the last moments of Coyote's life, Zombie's life, D-Frag's life, only changed from emerald to ebony. A demon had spread his hands over paradise, making a dark shroud for the blooms. Let me describe this to you, as best I can: I was hanging upside-down in a black forest, my feet trapped in the tallest reaches of an oak tree, lodged between branches. Above me only a storm-clouded sky, from which a torrent of water fell onto the platform of leaves, bending them earthwards with its force. All around my body lay a tightly knitted web of twigs and branches, a mask of leaves and dark violet blossoms. Sharpened thorns pressing into my skin. My suspended head peeks through the lower branches, surrounded by rotting fruit hanging from the vine. Below, a small clearing in a dense forest. Directly below, the hole in the ground through which the pollen escaped. From that orifice came the music, note for note, pollen for pollen;

the rules of exchange. Day turned into night. The moon shining tearfully onto the glade, where hordes of the *love-lies-bleeding* flower shiver under its light.

Rainfall.

My name is Sibyl Jones. Sibyl Jones. Saying this to myself, over and over, making sure of my identity. This slippery world . . .

I am gazing down into a reversed theatre like an upside-down voyeur. A perverse audience. This is a play, a movement of plots, converging. If I could only work out the scribe of this . . .

A young boy is trapped like me, some few feet away in another tree, tangled into branches. The thorns are pressing into his flesh. His tortured face is familiar. A snake curling around his body. Blood is drawn, dripping down from the blossoms to the forest's floor, red on green. 'Help me, please,' the kid says, his voice muffled by the leaves that creep into his mouth and by the dark snake that squeezes. The boy's cheeks are riddled with maggots. He's crying.

'Who are you?' I ask.

'Brian Swallow . . . Will you not help me please?'

Of course. That picture that Zero had shown me. 'I'm trying to. Did you get swapped?'

'Yes . . . Exchanged.'

'Who by?'

'Persephone . . . Her name is Persephone . . . the flower girl . . . Please help me, lady . . . I want to go home.'

'Where is Persephone now? Do you know?'

The snake is slithering thick coils around the boy's body, and the branches are pulling tighter. Swallow cries out loud. 'Help me lady, please . . . please . . .'

I don't know what to do. Tom Dove's voice has vanished. The hole in the sky that I fell through has now sealed up like a healed wound. I'm alone in a green feather world I know nothing about, with thorns digging into my flesh, and a young kid getting squeezed to death some two feet away. A filthy-looking snake crawling all over the boy's face. Grains of pollen are pushing into my mouth, clinging to my legs, burning holes. The fat snake unties a section just to look at me . . .

It has a human face, that reptile.

The face of a young man, a cloud of flies buzz around his slithering body like symbiotic passengers. A sudden wind shakes the branches. They loosen around Brian Swallow's body, and he drops some ten feet towards the forest floor before the snake darts around to grab the boy around the ankles, and then just lets him dangle there, two inches from the ground. The snake-man is laughing as he swings the boy over the clearing like the pendulum of a human clock. I'm reaching out to the boy, as best I can. My fingers are trying to prise that snake away from his body.

Sibyl!

I can hear Tom screaming over my Shadow, yelling at me that the dream was moving on, the window was closing, but how could I leave that poor boy alone in the devil's garden? 'I'm here for you, Brian,' I cried. 'I'm here! Look at me. I'm a cop . . .'

But I had no hands, no arms, no tongue, no head, no body, no heart to grab hold of him with. I was an overripe fruit hanging on a rain-blasted tree. The soot-black snake held on to Swallow with a knot of hard flesh, and then coiled his head upwards until the human face was staring into mine. 'May I ask what you are doing here?' His voice was as dark as the forest that he had seeped out from.

'My name is Officer Sibyl Jones. I'm a cop. You're under arrest.' Cop rules kicking in, of course, and even as I said the words, the absurdity of it came home to me.

'Really? How splendid.' The snake-man's sharpened teeth were reaching out towards my inverted face, and his split tongue was caressing at my lips. I could not move away.

'Suspected illegal exchange of a human child,' I carried on, my voice weakened by the pollen that tried, unsuccessfully, for my lips. 'Suspected illegal importation of a restricted substance into reality.

Do you wish to say anything? But I must warn you that anything you say now may be used against you later . . . later . . . in a . . . in a . . . in a court of . . .'

The snake's tongue was stroking at my left cheek now, and the bemused look on his face had vanished into a snarl. 'Officer Jones . . . how sweet you are.' His voice was blurred with sibilants. 'You're trying to arrest Sir John Barleycorn, in his own domain! Excellent! You've come so far, but still you haven't got a clue. How ineffectual you are. It really is most beguiling.' As he spoke he enwrapped my exposed neck in his tender coils, and started to squeeze.

The light was dimming over the forest as my brain popped with blood.

Pain.

Pain, and the muscles of soot. This is what it's like to look into the eyes of John Barleycorn. This is all the world comes down to finally. My breath leaving me.

My lonely voice reaching out . . .

Lost. Lost amidst the flowers. The forest closing in around me, caressing, vines wrapping my legs in wires, the man-snake squeezing at my neck with his knot of sinews. The snake whips his head back, pauses for a moment in the rain, and then zooms forward to bite me . . .

Please . . . no . . .

My neck squeezed by the flesh coils, thorns digging into my legs. Fangs. Blood seeping from the fruit.

'Sibyl?'

A voice.

'Sibyl, you still there? I'm trying to pull you out. All pain is illusory.'

Tom's voice, all too distant, all too late, as the jaws of the snake snap shut around my neck.

My head is severed.

Falling . . .

* * *

Belinda drives Charrie along a green lane between endless stretching fields where waves of wheat and corn form billows of breath.
Petals and birds sparkle and sing from hedgerows and bowers. The
sun glistens on each leaf and flower until the world seems made out
of segments of colour. In the distance children are playing around
homesteads and cottages; a pig squeals in delight at being chased.

The cab squeezes through greenery and golden light, Belinda
at the controls, Charrie loving the feel of the latest, hottest road.
Both of them, driver and driven, have lost all trace of troublement.

They are free of all knowledge in a land before the knowledge-
tree was plucked.

On the road ahead, leaning against a tree of abundant leaf,
stands a young man of nineteen years with golden hair and a thumb
that is raised to the road and to Belinda.

A hitcher.

Belinda has never taken a hitcher before this moment, but
now she feels that stopping to make a pick-up is the best-ever
move. Charrie feels the same.

The cab stops and the young traveller gets on board to the
back seat. The cab moves off into a low-leaf-riding fairway between
shadows and sunlight. Belinda asks the passenger his name . . .

'Driver Boda, welcome to the world of Vurt,' the passenger
replies. 'Except, of course, you're calling yourself Belinda these
days?'

'You're Columbus?' Belinda asks.

'So nice to meet you, Belinda,' the passenger says, 'in the flesh
after all these years of caressing. That is what it was, you know?
Animating your chariot was a loving massage, and I very much regret
your mishap. It hurts me to know that you no longer prefer my
chosen cab-name. This is only my human shape I'm showing you.'

'Fuck you, Columbus!' Belinda screams. 'You killed my Coyote.'

A cab drive into the sun.

'This is where I get out, driver,' Columbus says. 'Just here is fine.'

Belinda stops the cab beside a wooden gate that leads into a field. Columbus gets out of the cab and then asks Belinda how much he owes her for the journey. Belinda replies with the life of her lover. Columbus asks the driver to follow him into the fields, where maybe a more fulfilling payment can be made.

Belinda makes the journey.

And in a vast expanse of golden corn, Columbus tells Belinda that this fecund world is a projection of reality once the Vurt has taken over the governance. 'Don't you feel like helping the passage along?' Columbus says to Belinda. 'Doesn't the new world smell good?'

'This is Limbo?' Belinda asks.

'Not at all,' the Xcab King answers. 'This is Manchester in the future. This is where Manchester will live once the Vurt has taken a hold upon the city. Isn't it very beautiful? No more crime or pollution. No more welfare or poverty.'

'Yes, it is very beautiful,' Belinda has to admit. 'But where are the people?' The roots of myriad plants are gathering around her ankles, tightening.

'The people are too busy playing to be seen.' Columbus plucks a flower from the earth. An orchid. He smoothes back the petals. Nothing can have petals that big, six of them, arranged like a unfolding map. The fat stamen is ripe for love. Columbus sticks his tongue into the flower's head. The orchid seems to be reacting to his touches, growing firmer, riper. His tongue comes away covered with pollen, which from there floats upwards through the sunlight towards a tiny hole in the sky's roof. The air is thick and humid, and the globes of pollen give off a glistening light. Belinda can hardly breathe. Her mouth is dry.

'Columbus, you killed Coyote!' she screams. And the roots tighten some more.

Columbus ignores her. 'Isn't it quite beautiful, this flower?' he says. 'Oh, look at those grains dissipate! Do you not see the way that they cover this city with a golden map. Look at them come out of the flower!'

'I want to kill you.'

'There's a new map coming up, driver. A map of pollen. Can you not see it peeling away from the stamen? This is the cock of John Barleycorn. He has been very kind to me. I bet you've never heard of him, have you? You ignorant fool. You are not worthy of the tale. For too long now, the map has followed reality. Now reality will follow the map. This is why I set up the Xcabs, with Barleycorn's help. A way through for the Vurt. Now that journey is almost complete. I'm going to change this city, driver. It will all belong to me.'

The more that Belinda struggles, the more the roots tighten around her ankles. 'I'm not your fucking driver, Columbus!' she cries, finding her purpose once again amidst the flowering.

Columbus laughs at her. 'I must praise you for getting this far, Belinda. But I'm afraid that I cannot allow you to go any further. With the new map, the people of Vurt will find a way through to reality. The stories will come home. It will be very beautiful. What is presently inside the head will shortly be outside the head. The dream! The dream will live! Because what is human life, human flesh? Merely a vessel for the dream. Can you not see the logic of it? Without dreams you humans would still be apes. Please, have some respect for your creations. This is all we are demanding. Is it so very bad? When my new map falls over your saddened streets, you will all get down and worship me. I'm bringing your imagination into flower, and all you do is complain. How pitiful. You make me want to retch. The dream, the dream is good!'

'Why did you kill Coyote?' This is all that Belinda can say.

Columbus's eyes sparkle for a second, and then fall dark. 'What can I say? Some can make the trip, and others cannot. Some will live, and some will die. Am I to blame for evolution? The road goes to the best.' A droplet of saliva falls from Columbus's mouth. It lands on the orchid. 'No, no . . . I am being impolite. Despite your transgressions, Belinda, I have great respect for you. You were always one of my favourite drivers. Why, the very fact that you have managed to sneak back onto the map without my knowledge . . . this is most excellent driving. I must apologize for the death of your friend. This is a pastoral dream, and Persephone can be a little tempestuous at times.'

'Persephone? Coyote's passenger . . .'

'Persephone is Barleycorn's wife. She is the bringer of the new map to the city. Perhaps you should see your black-cabber friend as a deliverer. Why, he's a kind of John the Baptist figure. He will go down in history. That was his role in life. We all have our tasks.' And then Columbus opens his hands to Belinda. On each palm, a ragged hole. Blood flowing from each wound.

'Persephone killed Coyote?' Belinda asks. 'Is that right?' The roots of the field are reaching up to bind her hands to her body, tight in vines.

Columbus looks away. Again, 'Some must die,' is all he says.

'Where can I find Persephone?' Belinda demands.

'Could you find a seed in an acre of ground?'

'You arranged Coyote's death, Columbus, and then tried to blame me for it.'

'You must understand the urgency of the situation.' Columbus looks back at Belinda. 'You must make your decision, Belinda, between the old world and the new; between the dismal and the bright. Which shall it be?'

'I loved Coyote.' Belinda has managed to free one of her hands from the roots' grip.

'Belinda, I'm asking you to come back to the map. It's your home. You're not happy, are you, away from the map? Isn't real life proving rather a struggle?'

Her free hand digs deep into her shoulder bag. 'I gave nine years of my life to the Xcabs, Columbus. You betrayed me.'

'Belinda, I need you.'

Belinda pulls the Colt .45 from her bag and fires without hesitation, repeatedly, until the hammer clicks on empty. Five silver bullets fly from the gun, heading straight towards Columbus.

'Belinda . . .'

My head is severed. Falling . . .

This black world of green revolving as my head tumbles towards the garden. The hole in the sky is sealed, Tom Dove vanishing forever. Even as I fall, I can see the hole in the forest's floor opening wider to greet me, like a wound welcoming a bullet. Another door. My head was popping as the flowers surrounded me. Thorns pricking into my skin . . .

Through the wall of Vurt my head tumbled into darkness . . .

Through a long tangle of roots like a dense underground map of my city.

Into a thick stench of soil, and then from there into a bright yellow light. The sun. The fields of love. The smell of paradise. Grasses and flowers I was stumbling through, my body made out of pure air and a Shadow's breath. Two people standing in the grass in the distance. I reached into their space, finding Columbus the Cab King and my own daughter, Belinda the wayward child.

Closing in on love.

A cloak of roots, a cloud of pollen. The wet tongue of an orchid. My daughter was there, entirely covered with the vines that were also the roads of the city. One of them was wrapped tightly around her neck. Five bullets were travelling from my daughter in dreamy slow-motion towards the young man with the golden hair, name of Columbus on the Shadow. My floating head was moving to the same funereal rhythm.

'Mother . . .'

That word travelling Shadow to Shadow.

'Please help me. He's hurting me.'

The five bullets were moving like listless silver.

'What have we here?' the Cab King asked. 'Another visitor. Columbus *is* popular.' He caught one slow bullet in his left hand, another in his right, and then threw both cartridges away. The bullets vanished into the dense blue sky of this new green world, tunnelling their way towards another story. The third bullet missed the cab-controller's body by some few inches, likewise vanishing into the air. The fourth bullet hit Columbus dead square in the chest, opening a small wound in his skin from which bright orange blood poured. He laughed at the blow and then grimaced, slightly, as though troubled by some minor ailment. The floating pollen grains seemed to waver a little as the bullet struck home, as though they were linked intimately to this controller. 'You'll regret this, Belinda.' He said this slowly, his eyes full of a murderous intent upon my daughter. The fifth and last bullet was still moving towards him, moment by moment. He gathered his strength together and then redirected the bullet through the dreaming air, until it was heading directly towards my face. The bullet moved like a tortoise dream.

'Columbus, leave her alone!' This was Belinda's cry.

Tom Dove's voice came shivering through from nowhere: *'Sibyl, where are you? I'm getting wounds to the Vurt all over.'*

'I'm with Columbus, Dove,' I answered. *'Centre of the map. Paradiseville. Come and get me.'*

'It's difficult.'

'Try it, why don't you.'

The bullet was three inches from my face. Belinda was pleading with Columbus to save me. 'She's nothing to do with this, Columbus. This is between me and you.' Simultaneously, in the Shadow, she sent this message, *'Please, Mother. I'm sorry for this.'*

Oh, my love . . .

The bullet was one inch away from me and I was powerless to move. And then I heard the voice of Gumbo YaYa coming through in roots of Shadow towards Belinda. BELINDA, I'VE GOT YOU

BACK ON LINE AT LAST. I'M GOING TO PULL YOU OUT OF THERE. HANG ON TIGHT. And Tom Dove caressing at me the same time, with winged fingers . . .

(The bullet kissing my skin.)

. . . pulling my head back into reality.

(Bullet still kissing.)

Belinda, you make a harsh landing into Gumbo's Palace. Blush is yelling at you, waving the feather around. 'You've ruined it,' she's screaming. 'You've ruined my Black Mercury! Look what you did to my prize. You *creamed* my Black!' Blush is almost weeping with her anger. And now the black feather is totally cream, and totally dead. Creaming is what happens to Vurt feathers when they are used up, and you can no longer dream with them. Belinda wants to tell her that it was Columbus who had creamed the black feather. It was his way of sealing the clue-door. But what can she say?

There is a flower between your fingers, Belinda. A murderous orchid. Something you have carried from the Black Mercury. It has six petals. Five of them silver like bullets, the other rippled with a portion of the Manchester map. You spread apart the petals, to reveal the stamen and the stigma; the cock and the cunt. The stamen is heavy with pollen, and even as you gaze into the swirl, the grains detach themselves from the anther. They drift into the air, explore your nostrils for a second, find no comfort there, and then head straight for Blush. And for the Gumbo. And for Wanita-Wanita. All the creatures of this room. These players scramble for their masks, screaming as they do so.

Belinda, the flower glowing silver and map-like in your hands. Coyote's death, all for nothing. The murderer still loose. The fever still rampant. A new map of hell. A flower in your serious hand . . .

The realisation bites home just as Gumbo peeks at you from behind his mask, 'Jesus Jagger, girl. You brought something back with you! You plucked a flower from Vurt. You know what that means?'

You know. You can't even remember taking the feather, but you know . . . something has been taken in return. You reach into your shoulder bag for the A–Z map, finding only peanut wrappers and a woollen hat.

Five silver bullets and a Manchester map you have lost to the Vurt.

Bubbles. Bubbles of froth. Words. Splutterings? My own? Somebody's? How could I speak, having no head? Where was I anyway? My house in Victoria Park? Darkness. Greenness. Prickles. Bubbles of words. No head. Just fruit. The black garden. Thorns pricking me. My head. No head. Was I dead? Was I being Shadow-searched? Darkness. Then greenness. Two small glow worms flittering. My eyes, they were. No head, but eyes? What was I growing? Fruity? With a bullet's kiss. Turn those glow worms up to full.

Let me open . . .

Let me open my eyes.

Zero was leaning over me, his mask respirating his words into bubble-talk. 'You do any good in there, Sibyl? Any good at all?' His body was crumpled from the fever, but I could not find the words for him. 'Anything at all, Smokey?' he repeated. 'This a waste of resources?'

I was back now, my hands searching at the creases in my face. Making sure it was there. I was lying on my bed, shaking from the bail-out. 'I . . . I don't know . . .' I was desperate to speak, but my voice was Vurt-lagged.

'Fuck you, Sibyl. You got no news for me? No news about how I'm gonna live forever?'

This is all he wanted? A cure to his ills? Justice had vanished with the bad air he was sucking into his nostrils.

'Play the feather-tapes,' I said.

'Tapes couldn't follow you through the hole, Jones. Tom Dove couldn't get his head around it. Get down and worship his skill, it was all he could do to pull you out. It's up to you, Smokey.'

'Belinda was in there. My daughter, she was . . . and Swallow, Brian Swallow, the swapped boy . . . he was there as well. It's terrible, Zero . . . a terrible place. The cabs are in there as well. Columbus was there. There's a paradise where Manchester used to stand.'

'What are you going on about? Jesus-Dog! What about a cure? Anything?'

'The girl . . . Persephone . . . she's the fever.'

Zero sneezed though his mask, a mighty blast that Jewel echoed from his bedroom. 'What the fuck have you got in that room, Smokey?' Zero's voice. 'Sounds like the whole fucking world is sneezing.'

Later that day, around my dining table. Zero drunk on cheap wine, head slumped. Tom Dove playing with the food I had given him. Myself thinking over and over upon the details of my Vurt journey.

'It's a bad story,' Tom said. 'I'm fearful. I don't think we stand a chance.'

Earlier I had shown them my secret. My secret son. My Zombie. Zero had raised some half-hearted indignation, but really they were okay with it. All three of us were so far from the cop-law now, what did one more illegal Zombie count for?

'It's a serious Vurt case, Sibyl,' Tom Dove was now saying. 'This fever . . .' He placed a morsel of meat into his mouth, chewed on it for a while. 'This fever comes from John Barleycorn. He's one mean demon.'

'Tell me about this John Barleycorn,' I asked. I had already told Zero and Dove everything I could recall from my journey. Zero had retreated into a passive, alcohol-fuelled stupor, Dove into a snot-filled gloom.

'He's the snake that bit you in the garden,' Dove answered. 'He can show himself in many forms. All of them are evil.'

'Let me get this straight. He's just a Vurt creature, right? A character in a story. A story that we, us humans, made up. How can a story harm us?'

'I don't think you understand the true nature of Vurt. The stories are *alive* now, thanks to Miss Hobart.'

'The inventor of Vurt?'

'The *discoverer* of Vurt. Get this right. Vurt was just lying around waiting for us to find it. John Barleycorn is one of the oldest stories, and one of the most popular. One of the best. Because of this he has many names. The green man. Fertility. Swamp Thing. The horned god. Because of his pagan image he was stolen by the Christians, turned into the horned devil, Satan, the serpent, Lucifer. In the old Greek myths, he was called Hades. They banished him to the underworld. Because of this John Barleycorn is angry with us, still.'

'But he's just a Vurt figure, right? He's not real. I can't take this.'

'The Vurt wants to become real. It is a living system. It carries on even when we are not dreaming about it. Miss Hobart made it so. John Barleycorn lives in the feather called Juniper Suction. This is a Heaven Feather. An underworld. A place to store our memories when we die. So we can live beyond death, in the Vurt. Only the dead can visit there.'

'I managed it.'

'Yes. For a few moments. The Shadow is the trace of death in life. Also, you're immune to the flowers. They couldn't harm you in there, Sibyl, and I think they know that now.'

'The pollen is Persephone? Barleycorn's wife? She's the fever?'

'That's right. A goddess called Demeter is Persephone's mother. She's a half-and-half creature: spends her life halfway between the real and the dream. My guess is that she wants Persephone to be allowed to play in the real world, Manchester. She wants her daughter to have a world for herself.'

'Don't we all?'

'Demeter wants an empire for her daughter, and the real world is up for grabs, especially since the world has become so fluid. I believe that John Barleycorn has agreed to this exchange, and now he's using his wife to get through to the real world. He wants a life beyond the story. The new map that Columbus is bringing in, this may be Barleycorn's entry point.'

'This is crazy.'

'Of course it is. But it's happening. The Vurt is breaking through. If they succeed . . .'

'Yes?'

'The dream will take us over.'

'This is the vision that Columbus showed to my daughter?'

'Columbus is also a half-and-half creature. He lives partly in the Vurt, partly in the real world. He's an edge-walker. The nephew of Barleycorn. Columbus is playing the part of Hermes in the old myth. He's the messenger, the god of travel. From what you've told me, I believe him to be the door through which the fever travels.'

'The hayfever is a new map?'

'Each pollen grain is a new road. If this new map succeeds, there will be no freedom in the city. The city will change to suit the map. Reality following the dream, rather than vice versa. We won't know where we are any more. One moment your best friend will live two minutes away. The next moment, twenty miles away. A map of chaos. The dream will come though this new map. The dream will take us over. We will be like lost children.'

'I don't know . . . the new world looked very beautiful.'

'Of course.'

'Belinda shot Columbus. She wounded him. The pollen cloud dispersed a little.'

'Without Columbus the grains would not know where to travel.'

'So if we kill Columbus . . .'

'Yes, that's possible. But he will now be on his mettle. He'll put some mighty defences in place. He'll cream the Black Mercury feather that your daughter used to find him, and then hide himself in the remotest part of the map. Columbus is very elusive; he who makes the map knows best where to hide.'

'Kracker?'

'He's the weak link. I suspect he's made some kind of deal with Columbus. Kracker is power-mad, remember, and sex-mad. He's got too much Casanova inside of him. I think the chief has overshot his mark and he knows it. His job was to guide Persephone into the city, keep her safe. And to take out all witnesses. This is why he wanted you and Belinda taken out. You knew too much. This is why he's now desperate to blame you and Clegg for misconduct. Kracker has failed, and he's fearful of Persephone getting back at him.'

'Where do you think Persephone is?'

'I don't know. Somewhere safe. Kracker would make sure of that.'

'I can't follow this, Tom. It's all too much. The myth is breaking through? What sense does it make?'

'Vurt people don't talk about sense. They're dream creatures, remember? They talk about movement. It's action over words.'

'They want to kill my daughter . . . oh God!'

'She's become the main threat to them. Especially now she's broken through to the new map.'

'We have to find her, Dove . . . Clegg . . . you listening? We have to find Belinda before the Vurt creatures do. We have to find out where Gumbo YaYa's keeping her.'

Clegg raised his head at last and looked at me with bleary eyes. 'I don't think I can carry on with this, Smokey. I'm getting mighty sick.'

'Zero, you can do anything now. Kracker's no longer in control.' Clegg fell silent as I said this. His eyes dropped to the wine glass in front of him.

In those moments I saw all the failure of his last few days come home to him. He had spent his life following the master, even to the point of almost killing innocent people. His subsequent attempt to go against Kracker's back, only to result in one more failure, had really taken away his spirit. And now that he was alone, Zero no longer knew how to act.

'What about your investigations into Gumbo?' I asked him. 'Didn't you get anything?'

'Nothing.'

'Oh come on! Aren't you a cop any more?'

'Was I ever?'

'Zero?'

'Okay; okay. I applied for special dispensation.'

'To do what?'

'To go into Strangeways.'

'Who's there?'

'You remember Benny Veil?'

'Remind me.'

'He was floated into Strangeways two years ago, on a charge of murder. Four life sentences, to run consecutively. We always knew that Benny was a former associate of the Gumbo YaYa, but he had this heavy condom-veil in place all through the trial. We put on all the legal pressure we could muster for a truth-feather trip, but you know what the Authorities are like about that torture?'

'Nothing, huh?'

'Absolutely.'

'But now you're hoping to go back in?'

'Not any more. I talked to the Authorities.'

'No response?'

'Less than that.'

Once a person was feathered into a Strangeways dream, there was no access allowed to the imprisoned mind. It was a big civil liberties case from a few years before; given that Vurt prisons were only set up to relieve overcrowding and violence, which was stated

to be a direct result of Government underfunding, it was decreed
that all prisoners were to be allowed a peaceful, even pleasant stay
in His Majesty's Vurt. 'No dream cruel or unusual,' ran the statute,
'shall be allowed to roam a prisoner's imagination during his sentence of sleep.' It was further decreed that no access was to be
allowed into a prisoner's mind during this sentence, 'even for the
purposes of law-enforcement or national security.'

'There's no way through,' Zero said. 'We'd have to break into
Strangeways.'

Moments passed, none of us speaking.

Zero came up from his wine. 'What chance do we have, Tom?'
he drawled. 'How can we stop this fever? This new map?'

'I don't think we can. We would have to visit John Barleycorn.'

'How would we do that?' I asked.

'We can't. He's got strong locks on Juniper Suction. You have
to die to go into a Heaven Feather, fully. It's like the old Mummer
plays, Sibyl. Like Saint George of England. You have to die, and then
be reborn inside the Vurt.'

'You're telling us we've failed?' Zero asked.

'More than that. I fear for Manchester, for the world. For
reality. I fear that reality is doomed.'

'What?' Zero's voice.

'I can't see a way in. The door is closed.'

At 4.00 p.m. we got a call from Jay Ligule over at Manchester
University. He had something that we might like to see. I was up for
it, so was Tom Dove. Zero, however, said he had more important
matters to settle.

So it was Tom and I who drove over to meet Ligule at the
University. Vurt and Shadow. The journey was easy; the people had
now left the streets once again, after the failure of Gumbo and
Belinda to destroy the source of the fever. Ligule was agitated. He
paced back and forth in the botany department, totally masked-up.
Strangely twisted blooms sprouted all around his feet.

'What have you found?' I asked.

'Let me take you on a journey.'

My second flight that day, this time in a helicopter that belonged to the department. Its cockpit was filled with electrical equipment. Ligule was the pilot. Tom and I were pressed tight in the passenger seat. His Vurt-presence no longer bothered me as we rose above the city. Maybe I'd been cured of something.

'The best way to study global plant change is to get above the jungle,' Ligule was saying. 'We use this equipment to monitor the progress of species. Take a look down there. What do you see?'

I looked over the copter's lip. The city of Manchester was laid out below me in patchwork. The clouds of pollen were now clearly visible as they raced through moments of change. 'It looks like chaos,' I said.

Ligule laughed. 'So it should. Pollen is dispersed by the wind, and the wind, of course, is a chaotic system. Take a closer look.' He handed Tom and me pairs of goggles, which were plugged into the copter's analysis banks. Through these glasses the pollen solidified into strict patterns of movement.

'Jesus-Vurt!' Tom breathed.

'Exactly,' Ligule said. 'This new pollen isn't governed by the wind.'

Through the goggles I could plainly see that the clouds of golden pollen were following very precise lines, each line corresponding to a Mancunian road.

Here was the new map unfolding itself.

At 4.37 that same afternoon, Zero Clegg reported back at the cop station. He walked into Kracker's office without knocking, handed in his resignation, without saying a single word to his former master. By 4.40 he was back outside, walking across the car-park to his vehicle. The duty-officer would later recall how slowly the famous dogcop was moving, compared to his usual swagger. He put it down to the effects of the fever.

Just before Clegg got into his car, the duty-officer saw him
take off his mask.

5.30 p.m. I was back in my flat, alone. Ligule had brought us back
down to earth, and Tom had gone home from there. There wasn't
much we could say to each other. This case was well beyond our
means.

Another ten Dodos had been killed by vigilantes in the last day
or so.

I attended to Jewel as best I could, drank some more wine,
and then collapsed into a deep sleep on the lounger. I had dreams
then, filled with green. No, not dreams as such, because how can I
do them? It was the last vestiges of my flight into Vurt wearing off. I
could not stop my Shadow from revisiting those hot, wet, dark
climes. My daughter was trapped in the forest; thick, snake-like
tendrils wrapping themselves around her. I could do nothing to save
her. Patterns of pollen grains moved over the dream, images I had
captured from Ligule's specimens and from the flight over the city.
A bell was clanging Belinda's death knell in the darkness. It was my
phone ringing, calling me from slumber. The clock moved into and
out of my focus. Jewel was calling from his room. The clock also
was calling, a blurry-eyed 7.42. Was this still the same Saturday?
What else could happen during one day? I picked up the telephone.
It was Dove's voice . . .

'Clegg is down.'

Jesus!

Over to Manchester Royal Infirmary. Fiery Comet burning the
roads into smoke, not even wanting to think about it.

Zero was lying in a neat bed, his mouth covered by an oxygen
mask. He looked so beautiful, just sleeping, his eyes totally gone
from this world. A doctor and a vet were in attendance.

'What are you doing for him?' I demanded of them both.

They could only remain silent.

'Sibyl . . .'

Dove was trying to talk to me. He looked like cop-shit.

'What went wrong?' I asked.

'He took his mask off.'

'And . . .'

'The street-dogs got him.'

Oh shit. Total shit. Why did he have to go out like that? This was Zero Clegg. He was the best dogcop ever. Okay, so the street-dogs hated him for the treachery. Did they have to take it this far?

'He reported into the station at 4.37,' Dove said.

'And?'

'He said he was going home to his kennel.'

'Zero wouldn't call his home a kennel.'

'Sibyl, Clegg handed in his resignation.'

'What?'

'Just before he left, he ripped his mask off.'

'Nobody did anything?'

'Sibyl . . . what could they do? It's not a crime to take a pollen mask off.'

'It should be.'

'We found him at seven o'clock. Somebody rang in. Unknown caller. What could we do, Sibyl? He was asking for it.'

'Sure thing.'

'Jones!'

'You let him get caught.'

'We did not. He chose to get caught. He headed straight for Bottletown. He knew where the street-dogs were living. Who knew more than Clegg? Nobody. We think he waited for a pack to take him. You know how much they hate him. They got him down on the ground. They sneezed into his nostrils. We think he wanted to die.'

'He's not dead yet,' I answered, turning to Zero's bed.

He was just lying there, breathing in second-hand air.

'Skinner did a lung pump, Sibyl,' Dove said. 'They've tried everything.'

I looked over to where the doctor and the vet were standing. And Skinner there as well, his robotic grimace playing on me. 'You did fuck all, Dove,' I said. 'You let this happen.'

'Officer Jones . . .'

I was about to tell Dove all the bad things, but then a small sound from the bed made me bend down low over Zero.

'Smokey . . .' His low growl.

'That's me,' I answered. 'Smokey's here.'

But his voice and his bark and his fur and his eyes, they had all drifted off into nothingness.

No! Please, no . . .

He collapsed in my arms.

And then I was going deep, Shadow-searching. Desperate and swimming, down into Zero's final thoughts, through layers of fur and bone, molecules and genes, hoping for consolation.

Searching . . .

Shadow-falling.

. . . Floating inside a dog's body . . . down here . . . this far down . . . Zero is all dog . . . total dog . . . a world of growling fur . . . a meadow of fur . . . I am stepping through the meadow . . . up ahead, a dog is digging the ground up . . . his front paws working like blades . . . I come up close to him, calling his name . . . Zero looks up at me . . .

'Smokey? What are you doing here?'

'I thought you'd like to talk, Zero.'

Zero goes back to his digging, ignoring me . . . no trace of the human in him now . . . just the old voice inside the body of a dog . . . 'Where is it? I buried it here, somewhere . . .'

He gives up on the hole . . . moves to the side . . . starts digging again . . .

'What have you got to tell me, Zero?'

'Where is it? Where?'

'What're you after, Zero?'

'My bone. I buried it here...years ago...where is it? I can't find it any more.'

'Zero?'

'Leave me alone. Let me find it.'

'You're dying, Zero.'

He gives up on the latest hole...moves over...starts again... digging...and then stops...he looks up at me...'What's that, Smokey?'

How can I do this to him? My eyes are blurred.

'You're dying, Zero. I'm doing a Shadow-search. These are your last moments...'

'My...last...my last moments?' His eyes are darting from me, to the meadow of fur, to the places he has already dug, to the places he will dig, and then back to me. 'That's not true. I'm looking for my buried bone. Where is it?' He starts digging again. 'Let me find it.'

'Who did this?'

He looks up at me.

'We haven't got much time, Zero.'

'That's not my name,' he answers.

'Okay. Zulu.'

He barks a laugh at me, and then his voice drifts into emptiness. His eyes locked on to mine. I could see that old Zero magic in there, hidden behind deep layers of dog.

'Is it really all over, Smokey?'

'Very nearly.'

'That's sad, I guess.'

'You want to tell me who attacked you?'

'The pack was filled with cop-hatred. But it wasn't their fault.'

'Go on.'

'It was my fault. I wanted it to happen. Now, where was that bone I buried? It's around here somewhere.' His eyes stretched out over the meadow of fur. 'Oh well, I guess I'll never find it now...'

'I guess not, Z. Clegg. Why did you do it? You wanna tell me?'

'It was for you, Jones. And for Dove and Belinda, and the whole damn crew of Manchester. I thought I was on a good ride back there. Thought I had the answer...'

'What happened?'

'It was something that Dove had said, about having to die to visit the Heaven Feather. So I just took off the mask, headed over to Bottletown, where I knew a good dealer. No names, okay? He was one of my pigeons. He sold me a copy of Juniper Suction. I paid a fortune for it. I came out of the house, stuck the feather in my mouth, dog-throat deep. Nearby a pack of boy-canines were tormenting my cop-car. I went over to them, pretended to arrest them, put up some struggle. You know me, Jones, I wanted to die in action.'

'It didn't work?'

'It worked enough for me to know that Juniper Suction doesn't want me there. I couldn't even kill myself, not properly. Shit, I'm sorry, Sib. I'm sorry...'

'It's okay, Zulu. Really. I'll get you back, I promise...'

'I feel tired, all of a sudden. I feel like I want to lie down in the meadow for a while. That okay with you, Smokey?'

'No, it's not.' I made a deep search of his soul, found the bone resting deep under layers, and the exact place where he'd buried it. 'The bone's over there, Clegg.' I pointed, and Clegg started to dig in that place, and he came up with a big, juicy bone in his paws, and he was smiling again.

'I've found it, Smokey! I've found the bone!'

'Well done, Clegg. You want to eat it now?'

He clamps his jaws around the bone, breaking it open for the jelly within with his sharpened teeth. He sucks deep of the marrow, it smears across his lips. I see the glint coming back to his eyes. I tell him I'm going back to the surface now, but I'll be waiting for him up there.

'Smokey, I love you,' he says.

He kisses me then, bone-jelly smeared all over my lips, and it sends shivers through me.

'If I ever get out of here alive, Smokey, I'll maybe be wanting to marry you.'

Of course I ran from the feeling.

Shadow-rising.

Leaving the dogman to wander.

But still, after leaving that field of buried bones and finding myself back in the hospital ward, I can't help carrying the message back with me. Was that a message of love from Zero?

What was the world coming to?

I told the doctors to keep the mask on Clegg, and to keep a good eye on him. He remained in his coma and Dove wanted to know what was happening. I told him that Dogcop Zulu Clegg was fighting for his life.

Then I walked out of that ward, down corridors into dark skies, praying for the good bones of Zero, and all who give up their life for a dream. The dream of others. The good dream of maybe giving up your everything for the sake of friends and strangers.

Oh shit. I think Clegg asked me to marry him back there in the Shadow.

The night air was graphed with pollen, each grain following a secret road through the city. The drifting lines were blurred by the tears in my eyes. Zero Clegg, you stupid man. Why did you leave it so late?

The cop station. Saturday. Midnight. A lone cop punching the security code on the door that leads to the morgue. As always he feels a new lease of blood coming into his penis, as he senses the rich emanation coming from the bodies stored in there. He tries hard not to want it. He'd taken his solitary pleasure there last night and that had been an overwhelming experience, followed by a severe bout of physical guilt. And now the cab-riding shadowbitch calling herself Belinda had worked her way into the map. She had found out about Columbus. She had told the secret to Gumbo YaYa, and that hippy bastard was broadcasting it to the whole of the city. And this cop has been so careful. Covering his traces. Oh shit, what is he going to do? Especially when his new mistress finds out. There were no secrets to be kept from the girl of flowers. If only he hadn't made this deal. Still, the need was strong, and the blood was flowing towards his penis already.

The morgue door slides open with a whisper of breath.

The cop steps into the room.

Robo-Skinner is working on the body of a new fever victim. His camera eyes whirl up at the sound of the door opening. 'Chief Kracker, what are you doing here?'

'I . . . I was just . . .' Kracker doesn't know what to say. Skinner's presence is an irritant to his lust-driven system.

'Yes?' Skinner asks.

'I was following up some clues about the fever.'

'Same here. This boy is the latest to go down.' Skinner pushes a scalpel through firm flesh. 'There are some fascinating anomalies.'

'Aren't there just?'

'Look at this, Kracker. The pollen grains are growing in his testicles. Come closer, take a look.'

Kracker comes close to the slab. He picks up a scalpel from the steel tray.

'The pollen is fusing with his sperm,' Skinner says. 'It's like some new—'

Kracker jabs the scalpel into Skinner's plastic stomach. Lenses whir like crazy, like a camera dying from lack of light.

'Kracker? What are you . . .' Skinner's voice slows to a metallic drawl.

Kracker moves the blade back and forth until wires and robo-juice are spilling out into the open. He cuts through the under-growth until he reaches deep enough to sever Skinner's nerve centre.

'I never did like you, Skinner,' says Kracker. 'Fucking bunch of plastic.'

Skinner falls to the floor beside the slab, a tumble of flesh and equipment.

Kracker wipes the scalpel clean on his trousers and then lets his eyes move over to the locked cabinet, number 257, the one that contains his mistress. He feels an almighty urge to join his lust to hers, to make the same pleasure as last night. Every night it is the same: the guilt, the pain, and then the giving in to sick desire.

Already Skinner is forgotten.

Pollen is drifting through the rotten air of the morgue.

The cop sneezes then, and curses the god he had bargained with. Columbus had promised him immunity. All the time his watery eyes are gazing towards the cabinet. He can feel the heat coming from the soil in there. For one last sad time he spits denial at the urge, and then puts his hand on the cabinet door, punching the security combination that only he knows. Fat bees are buzzing around the morgue, eager for what this cop can reveal. This is nothing to do with me, he says to himself, as he watches the cabinet slide open. He sneezes one more time. This is just nature calling. How can I deny nature her blessing?

Petals opening.

Kracker looks down at the young girl who is sleeping there in a bed of soil . . .

Petals opening. Her name is Persephone. Her body is buried underneath layers of dark earth. Only her face is visible, breaking through the top soil. Flowers are growing out of her mouth, her nostrils; every soft curve of her naked flesh is a garden. She is planted in rich soil but really her body is everywhere amongst the vegetation of Manchester. She is the elegant arrangement of roses in Sibyl Jones's Victoria Park garden. She is the succulent orchid that Belinda has brought back from her home world. She is journeying through the lichen that clings to the walls of Gumbo YaYa's secret palace. She is at home in the flowers that cling to Coyote's gravestone, which are fed by death even whilst they make some trembling attempt at life. Her whole consciousness is at one with the greenery of the city; she has made for herself a map of flowers, and she is every street, every root, every road and every branch of this tangled map. Really, she should be at her happiest now. She is free from her mother and her husband. Persephone is adrift from the tug of the feathery seasons at last. So far she has travelled from her own world, to Manchester, to Alexandra Park, and from there to this dark, wet home. And from this nurtured darkness she has established herself and burst like a floral fire through all the ways of the green. But this new world only fills her with the floral blues. At the edges of her map of leaves she can feel a disease gaining hold. A rottenness at the outskirts like the mildew is setting in. This world is turning against her. No, not the world, nature is turning. Ordinary nature fighting back. Reality. She is dying here, slowly dying by degrees. Now her darkened world is opening. Now she feels the gaze of her lover upon her flesh. Persephone lets her petals open to this visitor. She puts on a good show of petals.

The way the heat comes to her body, the way she caresses her own petals, fingers sticky with sap. The way the petals are ruby red, glistening with dew. The precise way in which the petals interlock, six in number. Child Persephone lets one of them float free from the flower head. She sends it through the air towards her mouth. The petal rests on her long purple tongue for a second. Then her sweet, wet mouth closes over it. She can feel her lover watching her.

A young girl eating the petals of a shining flower.

She feels like the sun is sliding down, inside her throat. Her fingers are reaching down between her legs to where the lips are parted below her soft belly, like petals, and the dew has formed on them. The way her lips are wet with seed, and the way her lover gazes at the wetness there.

Petals opening and closing . . .

Now Persephone's slippery tongue is licking at a thick juicy stamen. Specks of gold drifting in the air of the morgue. Her long tongue comes up, the tip coated with pollen, and keeps rising until it dabs at the spot between her eyes, and then away.

Eyes of green flowers.

The tongue leaves a stain of yellow on her forehead which, like the eating of pomegranate seeds, is the sign of marriage. Her husband, John Barleycorn, had given her pomegranate seeds to swallow, nine in number. 'These seeds bind you to me,' he had said. 'Once and forever.' He had spoken to her in a dark English, and he could be very angry with her sometimes, if she didn't follow the rules closely enough. But still, despite the anger and the fear, she felt that she loved her husband more than her mother, which was only proper.

She is only eleven years old now, lying in Kracker's bed of soil, but sometimes she feels that she is ancient, an old woman growing older, a willing participant in many lives, many cycles. Planted as she is in the earth of Manchester, tuning into all the flowers of the city, gathering messages of love from all the petals and buds, her legs break through the top soil, so they can stretch apart. Her lips are ready for the insects again. Both lips, the upper and the lower, smeared with nectar. The bees are crawling all over her body, sick and slow-paced from the scent. Now they are lapping their tongues into her crevices, and gathering pollen on their limbs from her vulva of petals. They tickle. They tickle and play, sucking. Feeding. She is dizzy from their wanderings, over her skin, over her sex. Persephone is drifting through the feelings, making a meal of the gathering; nectar for pollen, pollen for nectar. All of these sweet exchanges, wet with a young girl's juices.

Let them buzz and fly, away into the map of flowers.

Having supped at the root, eaten of the berries, sucked at the stalk . . . she was ready. Having felt the sap leaking from her lips, and the dew on her petals . . . she was ready. Having spread herself like a flower, secreting nectar from her womb, and having bees with it; having coated her tongue in pollen, made in the garden of her body . . . the young girl was ready. Her mother and her husband had deemed it so.

And now the lover calling himself Kracker is staring down at her wetness. Persephone waves her petals ever so temptingly, and like a bee that man comes buzzing. The cop is sweating and sneezing. Drops of moisture are landing on Persephone's exposed face. She receives them gratefully, letting her petals taste the perspiring rain. She is feeding off him, making a meal of the man. He has a look of concern on his wet and sadly human face, but she can feel his excitement growing; Persephone is revelling in his discomfort. She forms her petals into words his small brain can understand.

'What's worrying you, my darling?' Persephone asks. The cop's thin, dry face is creased with doubt, but all he can do is shake his head, back and forth, back and forth, as though denying his own worth. How pathetic these creatures of flesh are, Persephone thinks. What a pity she has to keep this one happy. She has some need of his skills. 'You can tell me. I'm your prize.' Persephone lets her petals fall into these shapes. 'You know you can't resist me. Tell your sweetheart everything. Maybe I'll be nice to you then.'

She hates to speak like this. How it reduces her.

'They're on to us, my precious,' Kracker replies.

'I know this already. Tell me something new.'

'Her name is Belinda,' Kracker continues. 'She was asking about Coyote, the black-cab driver. Columbus told her that you killed him.'

'Can't you handle it?'

'I'm trying to, Persephone.' The cop sneezes. 'You promised me I would never sneeze.'

'You must not be weak. You're not going to deny me, are you?'

'No. Of course not.'

'Remember the pact you made with Columbus. You wouldn't want to make him angry?' It is a simple question, and she lets her petals ask it firmly. She has to stop them from shaking. She doesn't want the cop to know her fears. Because for the first time during her visit to this world, Persephone is worried. She has sensed the girl called Belinda in the map. She has tried to push her green fuse into the girl, searching for identity. Finding only a barrier to her growth. Persephone could not grow in that visitor. The girl was a dark nodule on the map of flowers, a tightly clenched bud that would not open. The girl was immune.

'I'm not making him angry,' Kracker is saying. 'I'm just telling you my fears. Somebody has found us out. Persephone, I'm so scared. I fear that Belinda knows about us . . . about our . . .'

'I want you to take care of her, my darling.'

'Me? Take care of her? I . . . What do you mean?'

'Uproot her.'

'No more of that, please. I tried it once already. Failed. Then I employed a good officer to do it. Even that loyal dog made a mess.'

'Come to me, my darling. Let me comfort you. Soon I will show this sad town my power.'

'What do you mean?'

'Keep watching, my gardener. I will make the people explode with pleasure. Tomorrow I will bring my new home into existence. The people of this city will feel the shock of their little lives. The dream will take them over. This Belinda girl will soon be no more, believe me. I will find her with my flowers. And then you will do what you must, for she is beyond my touch. And also her mother, Sibyl Jones. You must kill them both. I will not allow another mistake, do you hear me?'

'I hear you.'

'Tell me what you hear, my sweet?'

'You will not allow another mistake.'

'What must you do?'

'I must kill Sibyl and Belinda.'

'You must finish their story.'

'I must finish their story.'

'And then we will be safe once more . . . to enjoy each other. Come closer now, taste my need for you.'

Petals opening and closing . . .

Kracker is clambering into the cabinet. He can't stop himself. His fragrant lover is opening up to him. Her midriff pushes up through the soil. A flower is growing from her vagina. Its petals are pink and moist, opening and closing. Her stigma is splitting apart for him. Kracker lowers his thin body onto hers, letting his penis enter the tight orifice. Persephone's petals are clutching at his cock, opening and closing, opening and closing . . . an earthy, natural rhythm that teases out the sap from the stem. Kracker is in heaven.

Heaven is sweaty, and blossoming.

Southern Cemetery. Saturday. Midnight. Coyote's grave. Darkness breathing through the trees. The dog driver's stone memorial completely covered with flowers. They are taking over the image, these flowers, moulding it with petals. The dirt is rich in nutrients from a decomposing body.

Belinda's gift of an orchid placed there.

A new stalk breaks through the grave's soil. It blooms in an instant into a brilliant flower. Petals of creamy white with the darkest brown spots.

Call it Dalmatian Flower.

May the road rise with you.

Sunday
7 May

Shivers of dark light floating over water, shining from a cellar's pavement-level window, and then reflected from pillars of marble that are rooted in the pale water. Shadows shimmer around the floating shapes of a young woman whose naked, street-lined body takes on the glimmers of light and turns them into a movement of glittering feathers. As though from underground wings.

The underground swimming pool at Slavery House, the Gumbo's Palace, cleaned up and renovated by the illegal residents. Early, early morning, Sunday, all the house still sleeping except for one lonely drifter.

Shadows shimmer, and Belinda floating there.

The birthday girl.

3.50 a.m. Sunday morning. I'm woken up from fitful slumber by the telephone. Dove's voice on the other end . . .

'Come to the cop station, Sibyl.'

'You know I'm not allowed there. What's happening?'

'Kracker's vanished. Just get over here.'

I see to Jewel's needs and then head on down to the Comet.

Kracker is parked outside Sibyl Jones' house, drinking down some small measures of Boomer just to get his edge running. He needs all that he can get, having failed in his previous attempts to please Persephone.

How far have I got to go? he asks himself. All the way, Biscuit Boy, is the answer. He pulls his gun loose from the cop-holster.

The pollen drifting through the darkness, golden and global.

A light comes on in Sibyl's house.

'Uh huh.'

The front door opens, and Sibyl Jones walks down the drive towards her car. Kracker watches all of this from the other side of the street. 'Shit. Where's she going now?' he murmurs. 'This time of the morning?' He raises his gun and listens to the gentle whirr it makes as the auto-aim focuses on the woman, the good cop. Kracker's finger starts to squeeze at the trigger, and then relaxes.

'Shit!'

He can't do it. Not yet anyway. He can't stop seeing her as a cop, and a woman he's known for years.

It's easier to kill strangers.

Kracker decides to take the other route first, the one that leads towards Belinda.

Tom Dove led me down into the cop morgue, where robo-Skinner was piled like a heap of dead trash.

'What happened to him?'

'Somebody took a blade to his circuits,' Dove told me.

'Kracker?'

'That's a good guess.'

'Why?'

'Maybe something that he saw. You following me?'

'I'm trying to.'

'Skinner kept his head going way past bedtime. That was one good robocop.'

'It's still in there?'

'Let's take a look.'

So we opened up Skinner's head and found the film and the recording there. The video image came up negative but the soundtrack produced the goods. The quality was bad and only muffled fragments could be heard amidst the static of Skinner's dying head.

Kracker's voice was in there but it was like he was talking to himself. Kracker called the other person Persephone at one point.

'He met the flower girl in here?'

'Maybe she came visiting,' replied Dove. 'Keep listening.'

It was obvious now that Skinner was reaching the end of his tape loops. Kracker's voice was growing misty and distant as the robo-circuits spluttered into final sparks. The last thing we heard him say was this: 'I must kill Sibyl and Belinda.' Kracker said it like an automaton following orders.

I didn't know what to say.

'I think the girl has told him where Gumbo lives.'

'How can she know that?'

'I believe she's moving through the flowers of Manchester.'

Skinner's final information died to a crackling of wires.

'What can I do, Tom?'

'Find Belinda before Kracker does.'

We drove over to the Strangeways Feather Prison. There was a lone warden on the graveyard shift, a low-down-the-ladder robopensioner name of Bob Clutch. 'What's going on?' he asked with a mouth full of bacon and eggs. I told him the cop-code for the day and introduced Tom Dove as Tommy Veil, long-lost brother of one Benny Veil, currently serving the full pillow. The full pillow was the street name for a life sentence in the Vurt prison. 'There ain't no visiting hours.' Clutch spat this out around slivers of meat. I then explained about the request that had come from the Town Hall Authorities, regarding the urgent need to override the usual rights in the Veil case. Clutch stopped chewing the fat whilst his piggy eyes darted from me to Tom Dove. 'I'll have to check that,' he said, reaching for his cop-feather. I then did something I hadn't done since childhood; I sent my Shadow out to the warden's and made him believe me. I made him believe; I forced the overruling into his brain. This was totally against the Shadow Laws but even a good cop must sometimes step out of line. Clutch's face took on a crumpled look for a second. 'Yes, that's fine,' he spluttered. 'Let me show you the way.'

Down through banks of sealed cabinets we walked, Tom and Clutch and myself, moving through a cold air that raged against the outside heat, each cabinet containing a sleeping prisoner. The pillow cases were kept in the deepest part of the prison and Bob Clutch led us there along a wall of controls that the wardens used to regulate the prisoners' life-support systems. These were the mechanisms that kept the inmates alive, even whilst they were feather-dreaming. Finally he found the cabinet marked Benjamin Veil, and pulled it open to reveal a sleeping near-corpse with a crease of pain etched across his features. A black feather protruded from his mouth. I pulled it loose from the prisoner's lips and then turned on the warden. 'What's the game here?' Clutch's face moved in waves of flesh before he managed to get control again.

'I don't know,' he mumbled.

'This is a black feather.'

'Never seen that feather before. Don't know who put it there.'

It was a well-known fact that wardens sometimes changed the feathers in prisoners' mouths, from the official blue and gentle flights into dark and deadly ones. They did this with child molesters, cop-murderers, anti-authoritarian figures and any other serious reprobates. They swapped the blue for a black, which meant that the inmates would be suffering eternal nightmares in their prison-sleep. Tom Dove put on a suitable look of familial concern, and I added to that my best show of senior cop-knowledge.

Clutch went scuttling off in search of a pleasant blue to replace the black, and whilst he was gone I asked Tom Dove if he was up to it, the feather-search. But he was already letting his eyes glaze, as though he was making that Vurt trip already. 'Hang on, Tom,' I said to him. 'Let's make this as legal as possible.' So he came back down, and then waited until Clutch came running back with a sweet blue feather and many apologies for this mishap. Clutch handed the feather to 'Tommy Veil' who sucked it into his mouth and then out again, so that the warden could lodge it in the prisoner's mouth. Benny Veil's face melted into a smile as the new feather took hold, and by then Tom Dove himself was already floating down and dreaming the same dream as the prisoner. I was by then a seasoned expert in sharing my Smoke with the dream, so we went down into that cell together, Tom and I, Vurt and Shadow, searching for clues...

...falling into bliss and numbers...numbers and bliss...the numbers overriding the bliss so that the whole world seemed like a mathematical formula...the bliss was the new feather recently lodged...full of a slow ecstasy it was, a long, drawn-out parade of tenderness...the numbers were a mask over certain parts of the dream's terrain...locks on feathery doors...Tom dragging me down into the numbers, trying for a breakthrough...the numbers ganging up on us like a street tribe, blocking our flight...a veil of numbers that we couldn't travel through... Tom Dove was finding the going hard, but I shoved my Shadow into the formula, stroking smoke through the symbols...I used everything I had ...all my resources...I felt weak and abused, until a small gap appeared between a number one and a number seven, and through that gap I darted my fingers of smoke...Benny Veil's face came up lumbering and cursing...Who the fuck are you?...

It's the cops...

Fuck, this is against the law...

So is murder, Benny...

Get the fuck off my dream...

You enjoying this dream just now, Benny?

Sure is better than that last sentence. That was one black downer. Jesus! Felt like I was being prised apart and stitched back up again. That shit was gonna last until eternity. Sure is kind of you cops to sort that warden out for me. Hey, this blue feather is nice...

You can have the bad dream back, Benny...any time...

Lady cop, please...

Listen close, we're here after the address of Gumbo YaYa...

He'd kill me if I gave that away...

What can he do to you now?...

It was at his word that I killed, you know, and then he put this condom rose of numbers all around me, so that I couldn't name him...

What can he do now? You're safe from him here. Think about it...

Silence then from Benny Veil as he considered his options...

Okay, I'm up for it, only if you guarantee my freedom from that black feather. Let me sleep in peace...

Peace is yours...

Okay, here it is. Slavery House, Strawberry Fields.

That's it?

All I know.

I could feel Tom Dove making for a pull-out.

Wait a second, Tom. I can still feel something.

Sibyl, we've got what we want.

Not yet. He's still got some secrets.

Diving back into Benny Veil's numbers, following the curves down to the root. Kracker's name listed there, amongst the algebra. A catalogue of crimes that Benny had committed for the Chief of Cops, and then covered up with black meshes.

Sad fucker.

Tom and I came back down to the Strangeways with the whereabouts of Gumbo, and with Kracker's guilt confirmed. We told Bob Clutch that he should keep that official blue feather in Benny's mouth forever, or else we'd be notifying the Authorities. Clutch gathered all of his small options together, found them all wanting, and then broke into a rain of tears and snot as the fever took him over.

Once we were back in the Comet, Tom Dove plugged into the Xcab map and got a no-no answer regarding Strawberry Fields. No such street known.

'Now what?' I asked.

Ahead of us a cop-car was cruising. Tom asked me to activate the siren. The cop-car pulled over to the kerb. Tom got out of the Comet and walked over to the cop-car. He flashed his cop-code. 'What's your name, constable?'

'PC Brethington,' the driver answered.

'Let me borrow your feather.'

'Sure thing, Officer Dove,' the road-cop answered. 'What you doing out on the street? The Vurt world wearing you down?' He laughed.

Tom ignored him. He shoved the cop-feather into his throat and called up Columbus over the map-wave.

WHAT THE FUCK DO YOU WANT?

Columbus sounded pissed off about something and this made Tom smile. 'Erm... real sorry for disturbing you, Columbus,' he said, coding his voice deep.

WHAT DO YOU WANT, PC... PC BRETHINGTON, ISN'T IT?

'It surely is, Columbus. I was hoping for some locationing.'

YOU'RE STILL TALKING TO ME?

'Sure I am. You're the King of the Cabs.'

YOU'RE NOT LISTENING TO GUMBO YAYA?

'I don't tune in to no pirate shit.'

HE'S SPREADING SOME TERRIBLE RUMOURS ABOUT ME.

'He's swallowing his own piss. Columbus, baby, you got a location for me? Strawberry Fields? There's some shit going down over there and I can't recall whether to turn left or right.'

THERE AIN'T NO SUCH ROAD AS STRAWBERRY FIELDS.

'Hot dog, must be another crank call.'

HANG ON, PC BRETHINGTON. RINGS A DISTANT BELL. LET ME ACCESS THE MAP... GOT IT. STRAWBERRY FIELDS IS A NEW ROAD.

'How new?'

NINE YEARS NEW.

'Nine years. That's not very new.'

IT ISN'T, IS IT? There was a wavering tone in Columbus's voice, a quiver of doubt.

'Is there a Slavery House on Strawberry Fields?'

LET ME ACCESS . . . NO, NOT AT ALL. NO SUCH HOUSE.

'What exactly is on Strawberry Fields?'

LET ME ACCESS . . . THERE ARE NO BUILDINGS ON STRAWBERRY FIELDS.

'Anything on Slavery House?'

LET ME . . . YES, I'VE GOT A SLAVERY HOUSE REGISTERED IN ARDWICK INDUSTRIAL ESTATE . . . NOTHING TO DO WITH STRAWBERRY FIELDS, AND NOBODY REGISTERED AS LIVING THERE. WHAT'S THE GAME HERE, PC BRETHINGTON?

'I guess we bought a bad clue, Columbus. Maybe some juicer's got a hard-on for my ticket.'

Tom closed the wave down and then walked back to my car. 'Let's go, Jones. Ardwick Estate.'

'You think that was wise, Tom?'

'I reckon we've got a few minutes.'

I started up the Fiery Comet.

Belinda is floating on underground water, her naked flesh entirely covered with tattooed streets. Only her face is free from the map. She's just finished shaving her head and her pudendum back to their former pristine states. A tube of Shaving Vaz and a Jillette Ladyblade lie on the pool's side. Beside them a glass she has carried from Gumbo's kitchen specially, recently filled with Orange Chrism, now empty, and her shoulder bag; within its folds the bottle of Boomer taken from Country Joe. Belinda is a swimming map now, as she drifts herself into ever deeper waves of despair. Last night, Wanita-Wanita had driven her over to Alderley Edge in the Magic Bus. There she had picked up Charrie, looking a little scratched and ragged from his Black Mercury adventure. Belinda had felt numb at the wheel, driving him back over the boundary, but Gumbo's downloading of the Shaky Path had proved good; Belinda was totally ignored by the numerous Xcabs that she had driven past. They didn't even register her presence. She was a hidden rider. Gumbo was angry with her for the firing of the gun at Columbus. He said that those bullets could one day prove costly. At the same time he was in a state of amazement at Belinda's story of the paradise in the Vurt. 'Science discovers Eden!' he had shouted. Belinda is due to make her next broadcast at 7.00 a.m. How can she resist? She's not a captive of the Gumbo; Belinda is a captive of herself. And she is tired. Tired of wondering and wandering; tired of never getting anywhere. She had found out Coyote's killer, but there was nothing she could do about it. Gumbo had searched all the various waves of the city for a trace of some young girl called Persephone, found nothing. And even bullets had proved impotent in the face of the Vurt. How can a young good-for-nothing Dodo girl possibly fight the dream? The thought of floating on the edge came to Belinda then. The idea of actually floating off the edge, of falling into a dream from which there was no awakening.

Kracker is driving towards the secret home of the Gumbo Hippy. Persephone has found it through the flower map, drawing him along streets of green. He's got his mission now. Persephone has named Belinda Jones as a victim. This girl he must uproot. He failed at the first attempt, but now his orders are written in bright flowers. This girl he must kill.

Spasmodically the fingers of his left hand play at the handle of the cop-gun nestling inside his jacket pocket, his right hand controlling the steering.

5.30 a.m. Somewhere along the Hyde Road.

Kracker turns right onto a greasy, overgrown path towards the Ardwick Industrial Estate. He parks his car on some place called Wigley Street. In front of him a deserted web of railway sidings rusting under a blood-red morning sun. Beyond the tracks lie the packed-tight buildings of Ardwick Estate. An air of loneliness drifts over the ruined factories and the ghostly warehouses. His shoes are sticking to the pavement. One of his prize flowers is pinned to his lapel. He has plucked this bloom from Persephone's skin, and he imagines that its scent is drawing him forth; Persephone is in the flower, she is directing him. The cop-gun in his pocket, his mind blasting itself to pieces on the imagined bullet. The vast bulk of Slavery House stands in front of him, its walls and windows entirely covered by the queen of all flowers in her infinite beauty. There are no ways into this building, every door is super-sealed. He can hear noises from beyond the alleyway he is standing in. He walks the length of the building towards a courtyard at the front. In this open space a tribal camp of dog-gypsies are gathered, predator-like. Kracker gets the distinct impression that they won't take kindly to visiting cops. This job is turning out to be a monster. He feels the pull, then, of Persephone in his soul; one part of the Chief of the Cops was always open to the petal-girl's caresses. The flower on his lapel is dripping with moisture, leading him on. Persephone brings him by this method to a locked-tight door in the alleyway.

Here Kracker waits.

Columbus has the city spread out all around him, radiating from the centre of his brain. This is the Hive of Manchester, but these last few hours Columbus has been having problems. First of all there was that reality bullet from Belinda lodged in his heart. It was just an irritant, nothing more, but he didn't need the distraction just now. Anything that weakened him, weakened the map. And also, because of that Gumbo bastard the whole of the city seemed to be turning against him. Of course the Xcabbers had remained loyal to the last, it's just that people didn't seem to want to travel any more. Well, all that would change when the new map came through; they would be forced to travel then, and Columbus would make a killing.

Scanning the map, he can see Kracker the Chief of Cops moving through Ardwick, his cop-wave turned to mask-mode. What was that loser up to now? He was supposed to be in charge of Persephone. He was supposed to be bringing the rogue cab back on line. Columbus can't act until that cab is back. He can also see on the map the Vurtcop calling himself Tom Dove. He is accompanied by the Shadowcop Jones, the woman who poked her head into his business yesterday. What was wrong with Kracker, couldn't he control his players? Was the chief being unfaithful to the vision? Jones and Dove are sharing the same vehicle, driving towards Ardwick. What was going on over there? Columbus computes the combined trajectories of Kracker and Dove, and comes up with their mutual destination: Slavery House. That cop, what was his name now, PC Brethington, he'd been asking about Slavery House some minutes earlier. And that new road called Strawberry Fields. Why should the Council build a new street into the system nine years ago, and then leave it empty? No houses on there, no utilities, no nothing. Because of these doubts, Columbus is now making a zooming run over the Strawberry Fields. Nothing comes up; that street is a desert. Columbus calls up the Authorities over the wave, gets put through to one David Gledders in the Town Planning section. Gledders is hesitant to acknowledge Columbus at first, moaning about all the bad stuff he has been hearing. Columbus sends a scorching wave down the feather towards the Town Hall.

'Shit! What are you doing?' Gledders screams. 'That hurt.'

IT CAN ONLY GET WORSE, MY DEAR.

'What do you want?'

Columbus asks David to check on a new street built nine years ago, name of Strawberry Fields.

'Like in the Beatles, you mean? I *love* the Beatles!'

WHAT'S THE FUCKING PICTURE, MOPHEAD?

Dave comes back with a no-no on the picture; no such street ever listed. Columbus thanks him and then zooms into Strawberry

Fields again. Something is nagging at the edges of the map. He can't make it out. He calls up all the new streets developed since Strawberry, gets back that all of them are by now clustered with housing and businesses. The only other one still free was Shaky Path, declared only yesterday. Then he goes back to Strawberry and makes for a super close-up zoom; it takes some memory away from the Xcab system, but the drivers will just have to put up with this. Strawberry Fields comes up close to his Hive-mind. Columbus is now living inside the very numbers that make up the street. There is a shadow falling over him, a cold dawning at the edges of the formulae. He can travel the whole of that empty street in his mind, but a small portion of numbers has a slight fuzziness around it. Columbus goes in closer, again drawing power from the Xcab system, and finds a minuscule area of darkness on the map. He zooms in even closer, but the nodule refuses to give itself up to him; there appears to be some kind of condom barrier around the darkness. Columbus cannot break through to the Knowledge. This unnerves him dearly; previous to this moment he had thought the entire map his own. He tries again to break the barrier. Nothing. Emptiness. Darkness. Meanwhile the cabs are screaming at him for more power. The Switch tells them to keep on steady hold for a while as he tries to work it out. He zooms back into Strawberry again. He chooses the nearest free cab, which was registered under the name Golden Hind, and sends it on an imaginary pick-up in Strawberry Fields. It takes fifteen seconds for the cab to get there, and to report back, 'There's nothing here, Switch. It's just fields around here. There ain't no such road. What you sending me on?' Columbus tells the driver to stay put, as he zooms in once more. Strawberry Fields is registered on the map as an offshoot of Moor Road, which is in Ramsbottom, a godforsaken village on the Northern limits. Columbus gives the driver the exact co-ordinates for Strawberry Fields, and then tells him to drive along there. 'It's just grass, I'm telling you,' the driver replies. 'You're expecting me to drive on *grass?*' JUST DO IT, Columbus replies, and then watches the map as the Xcab makes a slow path onto the non-existent street called Strawberry Fields. The cab goes so far, reaches the dark shadow where the numbers start to go fuzzy, and then vanishes. Columbus panics, calls up the driver over the wave, gets no answer. Columbus is still wondering what to do, when the cab appears again, the other side of the fuzziness, with the driver's voice bristling over the system: 'Jesus, Switch! What happened then? Everything went black. I was calling you up, but you weren't there. The whole fucking map wasn't there!' Columbus tells the driver to stay calm, and then to reverse into the darkness again. The driver complains about this, but the Switch reminds him of the Xcabs' Code of Faith: to journey wherever the map shall take them. AND THIS TIME, Columbus says, FIRE ALL GUNS. 'What?' JUST DO IT. The cab backs into the dark area on the map again, and Columbus can only wait for nervous seconds, until flames start to emerge from the dark nodule. The Switch starts to compute each trajectory as it emerges, and each of them is diverted slightly from its true path. Columbus moves through the formulae, feeding back the true path into the false one. The numbers start to break up. GOT YOU! Columbus asks for the name of the Xcab at that location, and gets back this message, GOMALDGICEN HIBUNDS. Columbus puts a filter on the name, takes out the words Golden Hind, comes up with what's left. Magic Bus. Jesus-Cab! That was the name of Gumbo YaYa's vehicle, the one he often mentioned over the air. And the Magic Bus was eating the Switch's Knowledge, he could feel it now. Waves of the Hive-system were seeping into the trespasser's shapes. Columbus selects the empty street and presses the Erase button in his head. To his amazement the street doesn't vanish, it actually starts to move over the map until it reaches the Ardwick Industrial Estate. Once there, the road settles down beside the very-popular-all-of-a-sudden Slavery House, and then vanishes. The Magic Bus is now parked outside Slavery House, the very house that the cops had asked about earlier.

THIS IS WHERE GUMBO YAYA LIVES. The Switch then travels
through the map until he finds Shaky Path, the latest addition to the
network. He finds another dark nodule there. Columbus calls up
David at the Town Hall, gets a 'no-such down-load' answer, and
then goes in search of whatever he can find behind this illegal
condom. It takes him only five seconds, this time, to bring the
name Chariot onto the system. He does the same Select-and-Erase
motion he did on Strawberry, and then watches as the Shaky Path
wanders over the map until it drops down beside Slavery House.
Chariot is parked beside the Magic Bus. I HAVE YOU NOW,
ROGUE CAB!

The circuit is complete.

6.19 a.m.

The pollen count reaches 2000.

Columbus brings up a button called BARLEYCORN'S
FLOWER MAP into his Hive-head and then presses it.

Activation . . .

All over the streets as we passed people were taking the pollen into
their noses, and then spreading out messages of joy. I saw lovers
kissing. No one had kissed in the last few days, fearing the worst; a
gentle rubbing together of masks was all that could be expressed.
Now the youngsters were sharing their breath again, making a pas-
sion out of defiance. The filthy palaces of deadened industry were
passing by on our left as I turned into Ashton Old Road. People
were dancing on the tops of the abandoned blocks, amidst the
flowers that grew there. Sneezing gleefuliy. The early morning rays
of the sun rainbowed by a hail of snot descending . . .

Aaaaaahhhhh . . .

Aaaaaaaaaaaahhhhhh . . .

Aaaaaaaaaaaaaaaaahhhhhhhhhhh . . .

The air was contracting into a tight second of waiting. Wet
and slippery it was, that moment, and the sun seemed to grow fuzzy

at the edges, as though spiked. Like an immense globe of golden pollen it hung there, suspended above the horizon.

The calm before the . . .

And as Tom Dove and I rode down the Old Road towards Ardwick and the Gumbo's secret palace, I heard the sound of a million intakes of breath. And then the explosion. The storm of mucus.

The storm . . .

The time on my dash was 6.19 a.m. Pollen count at 1999. One more click as the display moved on, and then a sudden and vicious blast. The sun pulsed. The Comet was sent careening.

'What the fuck . . . ?' Tom's voice.

Sneeze bomb.

Aaaaaaaaaaaaaachhhhhoooooooooooshhhhhhhhhhhhhhh!!!!!!

Five and ten and fifty fold.

Coyote hears the big sneeze. He is six feet beneath the soil, but still it gets to him, waking him from green and black slumbers. A shower of mucus falling heavily onto his grave and his stone. The muffled explosion causes tremors in the worms and the roots all around him. Coyote is the root. It must be that time of year again, that season of fruit. Now he is rising. The sneeze activates his passages. He makes his brain out of a ganglion of hard roots, twisting together, passing sap to each other, making synapse jumps with the juice.

It's not just the sneeze that gets him going. Some other presence is there, forcing him awake. Some hidden presence.

He doesn't know what he is, or where he is, or even *why* he is. Just that he has to get out of this wooden box somehow.

It's easy.

He joins his cells to that of the coffin, making the elm unfold like a flower. He *is* a flower. He must get to the air, to the sunlight. He must have growth.

Coyote's stalk pushes through the soil until it breaks the surface. Only the glimmers of the sun coming up slowly to greet him,
misted, and the spray of snot from the city. This will do. He drinks
deep, feeling his spotted petals unfold into the light. Coyote has the
strangest desire he has ever felt: the need for a bee. Somebody to
scrape some pollen from his fur, from his petals. Petals? Fur? He
doesn't know what he is. Petals and fur. This will do.

More and more of his stalks escape the ground. They form
themselves into green legs. Flowers sprout from the stalks, black
and white petals, locking together into the shape of Coyote's old
body. He has the pattern lodged in his floral mind somewhere; he's
forming the petals into a perfect copy of what he once was. His
body is a compound of flora and fauna; flowers and dog-flesh. And
humanity. Somewhere in that bouquet, a tiny trace of the human.
He fixes all of his attention upon that vestige. This is what he must
become.

The flowers are dragging at him. *Dancing ... dancing.* He remembers, vaguely, the tongue of a passenger, one last fare. How
she had taken him down into this world of green. Now he is free
again, but still he can feel her fingers inside his mind. He's made
from the same stuff as her. She wants him for her own.

No, not her. Somebody very like her.

Coyote fights against the flower. Realises that he can't.

He doesn't know what he's doing, or why he's doing it. Or
even *how* he's doing it. Just that he must do it. He is a dog, a plant,
a human. He is everything he has ever known, and a map of what
he must become.

The force in the root grips him. He digs down deep within
himself, comes back with the words *Little Sir John.*

Who the fuck is that?

Save my wife.

These words coming from the deepest root.

Fuck off.

Coyote uproots himself; a black-and-white-spotted plant-dog,

stalking the shaky pathways of a graveyard. Now he sees where he
is; his map clicks into action. Southern Cemetery. The map is changing even as he grows. That's okay, he can change with it. He moves
his flower head slightly to the left side, seeking out on the new map
where he must journey to. Central Manchester. Why is that?

Boda.

It comes to him in petals on the wind. Boda? Who was that?
His last . . . last what? Last bumblebee? Last furry bitch? Last cab-
fare girlfriend? He will set out on a urine-posted path. He needs the
sunlight; it is his meat and his fare. He has the knowledge that he is
scary, the first of his kind. A new way of being. For now just
travelling will do.

Growth patterns.

Dalmatian petals.

This Boda fare is the sunlight.

BELINDA, I'M BEING DRAGGED BACK. These words on the
Shadow coming to Belinda as she floats in the marbled pool.

Charrie's words.

BELINDA, I'M BEING DRAGGED BACK. COLUMBUS HAS
ME. BELINDA, I LOVE YOU.

Charrie's words, his last words.

This is when the sneeze bomb explodes. 6.19. The flower she
has brought back from the Vurt is drifting in the water between her
legs, where she has placed it. The water shivers into waves suddenly
that pulse up towards her thighs, and then ride back mixing in
with their slower followers. Belinda watches the resulting chaotic
patterns with interest, thinking them not unlike the recordings of
earthquakes she has seen on television. But this is Manchester, not
TokyoCo or San FrancisCo. She looks around nervously, but the
rest of that underground temple is perfectly still. Then she hears
the sound of the explosion, a far-off discharge of soft cannonballs.
The snot hits the pavement-level window.

Thud! Thud! Thud!

Impactions . . .

Squelch . . . slither . . . slither . . .

Those packages make a mighty racket against the glass, and Belinda makes her own fearful waves in the water as she reacts to the noise. She looks toward the window to see what all the commotion is, but then more snot hits the target and she's scared now, suddenly. Plaster falls from the ceiling. She has to get out of this pool. The window is covered with mucus; the pool is smothered in a furry darkness. There are muted screams from outside. Belinda feels so lonely in that darkness. What was going wrong?

Belinda sinks back into the pool. She closes her eyes, drifting back slowly until her mind is drowning again. It feels so good to be falling into watery sleep. The stolen orchid is nudging at her thighs, and she lets it make a gentle, petally kiss there.

That flower is watching you, Belinda.

Drifting thoughts . . .

Maverick tendencies . . .

I won't shed no tears. Come the morning, Joe, I'll be running clear.

Her sweet voice echoes around the marbled chamber. This song of cattle and grass and flowers and air. Sirens whistling through the morning. Emergency procedures. The city is dying. Does she want it saved? Does she care any more? Isn't Coyote Dog dead and buried? She can't bring him back. She can't even avenge his death.

It creeps up on her . . .

What good is her life without Coyote's promise?

Belinda, you never even *knew* the guy . . .

She doesn't listen.

Poison dripping. Thinking backwards, Belinda walking through the Wonderwall . . . how the taking of that step was an acceptance of her deathly side . . .

Backwards . . .

Kitchen scene. Pre-cabian. Belinda listening from the top of the stairs . . .

Her father and her mother arguing at the table. Her father

calling her mother a bad word, a Zombie word, a bitch from Hell. Cursing her for bringing only corpses into this world. Her mother names him as flesh, only flesh, pure flesh. 'All you pure boys want is more purity. You can't stand confusion.' Her mother's words.

'That girl is death.' Her father's words.

That girl, meaning herself... Belinda. Belinda is death. And this is too much to take. Down the stairs she walks. She punches her father square in the face. The slow passage of time as her father collapses onto the floor tiles.

The irascibility of that moment. The day she had started to not belong. Not to belong to a family. A time to escape, to run, to walk along the edges of life. For nine years Xcabs had been her family. Now that was gone as well. There was no place for her any more.

Poison dripping...

Maybe it's time. The edge beckoning. Because, after all, isn't the Shadow only the trace of death in life? Maybe it's time to complete that circuit.

Belinda's eyes glance at the shoulder bag lying at the pool-side, and then away. And then back again. Finally she reaches over to undo the clasp. Opening the bag. Tangled darkness. Taking out the bottle of juice, that gift stolen from Country Joe.

Boomer.

Belinda, my daughter...

You're opening up the small canister. You're pouring one measure into the dirty glass, and then closing the lid on the bottle, replacing it back in the bag. *One measure for a good time, two for a blast.* You open the bag again, pour another measure. Close the bottle, back into the bag. *One measure for a good time, two for a blast. Three for a clean and sexy death.* Open the bag, unscrew the canister, pour a third measure. Close the bag. Open it. Pour a fourth, and then a fifth measure. And then hold the bottle over the glass until the bottle is empty. That should do it.

It creeps up on you, like things always have done.

A clean and sexy death.

Is this what you desire?

Your body is so beautiful, my daughter. Pale white skin covered with a tangled map of Manchester. All of the streets and their names are written there on your curves. You slide deeper into the water. Manchester, sliding deeper into the water. Luxuriate in that warm pool for a few minutes and then pick up the glass. 'I guess I'm coming to find you, Coyote.' You say this aloud to the shadows and the mists that rise from the water.

And then put the glass to your lips, Belinda. Take a drink . . .

The time on my dash was 6.19 a.m. Pollen count at 1999. One more click as the display moved on, and then a sudden and vicious blast. The Comet was sent careening.

'What the fuck . . . ?' Tom's voice.

Sneeze bomb.

Aaaaaaaaaaaaaachhhhhooooooooooshhhhhhhhhhhhhhhh!!!!!!!

Five and ten and fifty fold.

The kingdom of snot blowing itself into existence. A nasal Hiroshima. All of the citizens of that city exploding the mess from their nostrils. Unmasked and unforgiving. Snot rained down on my windows. Ashton Old Road. The car was pushed forward by the blast, adding miles per hour to my meter, until I was unlawfully speeding.

Thump! Thump! Thump!

The Fiery Comet was covered in nose-shit. I couldn't see ahead of me.

'Where the fuck are we?' I shouted.

'It's happening,' Tom Dove said.

'What is this?'

'The new map.'

'But we're nearly there. Ardwick is just to the right here.'

'I don't think we can . . .'

I jammed the car into a vicious right turn.

And ended up in Namchester, Fortress One.

'What?'

'Shit.'

'What are we *doing* here?'

'It's happening, Sibyl. The new map is coming through.'

Ahead of us two cars were engaged in a head-to-head collision of metal and flesh. People were screaming and falling from their vehicles.

'I can hear Columbus laughing,' said Tom, as I swerved the Comet away from the pile-up.

One second passing.

And then we were back at my house in Victoria Park.

I spun the wheel around in a daze, desperate to find a way back to Ardwick.

One second . . .

And then we were in Whalley Range, my daughter's house. Some more cars were mangled up together there. Some street-cops were running to help the passengers.

'It's no good, Tom,' I said. 'We've failed.'

'No. There's a way,' he answered. 'There's got to be a way. We're in the Vurt map now. This is all a story. Keep driving.'

'Tom? I don't like this.'

'Just drive.'

And then we were in Bottletown, and the glass was splintering under our wheels, making a rainbow of fragments. I stopped the car. I could hear people crying out loud from the glittering houses. 'We're not getting anywhere, Tom.'

'We're in a dream, that's all. We're in a story.'

'What story is it?'

'Forget about distance and direction. We've got to find the narrative connection.'

'I'm not up for this.'

'You are. Just use your Shadow.'

'My Shadow feels like a maze.'

'It's John Barleycorn's story, Sibyl. Can't you see? What's the last thing that Barleycorn wants to happen?

'Tom, you're talking crazy.'

'What's the one thing he fears in this whole world? Think about it. He's a man who only lives in a story.'

'The immune . . .'

'The Dodos. They're the only people he can't infect. The only ones he can't be *alive* in. Above all things, Barleycorn wants to be alive. The Dodos are his greatest fear. This is why he built into the fever's symptoms the urge to kill the Dodos. The last thing he wants in this story he has prepared for us is that the Dodos get together. He's actually trying to stop you and your daughter from getting together.'

'Which means . . .'

'There's something in your meeting . . . You and your daughter . . . I don't know . . . Barleycorn's recognised a potential threat. Sibyl, I think we're on to him now.'

'But what can we do, Tom? He's controlling the story. There's no way through.'

Through the snot-blackened windscreen I could see a lonesome car crashing into a wall. The driver stumbled from the vehicle, holding her head in her hands.

'Christ-Vurt!' Tom banged his hand against the dash.

'What is it?' I asked.

'God, I'm so stupid! Barleycorn can't touch *you*, Sibyl. It's me he's working through.' And with that, Tom Dove opened the Comet's door and stepped out.

'Tom? Where are you going?'

'It's up to you now, Sibyl.'

'Tom?'

'Keep driving.'

I watched him as he went in aid of the injured woman, and then I shut down my mind to let the Shadow have full play. Immediately a tiny light flickered into life in my smoke. Like the smoke was an ever-changing map and the light was my love. You must always follow the fire. And I had a vision then, of all the Dodos of Manchester being motivated by some hidden design. A time to fight back. Even my daughter . . . at last, a role to play . . .

I started up the Comet and then took the third turning on the left.

One second passing . . .

And then I arrived in Ardwick Industrial Estate.

Kracker experiences the nasal blast as a welcome sign. Demon snot fills the alleyway, and the building shakes with the vibration. He can hear screams from the inside and the outside. Persephone has shown him the true and faithful route. She has warned him about the explosion. 6.19 a.m. The new map. 2000, the pollen count. Hot and painful was the flowery route, but this is the way he would take, clinging onto that young girl's petals whenever she let him. Persephone has been so sweet to him, so tempting for a man whose veins ran with Fecundity 10 rather than normal blood, how can he resist her pleasures?

Petals to petals, opening and closing; his long ride to success.

He steps forward to view the outrage at the front of Gumbo's building. The camp is in a shambles; dogmen and bitchgirls of various mixes are running around the area, some of them trying to help the injured on the ground, others just running for cover. Screams and curses rise through the sweltering heat. A black woman with an afro hairstyle is bending down to comfort one of the victims. A man with long, straggly hair and flared trousers is wandering through the chaos, his arms flung to each side, and a mad peal of laughter springing from his lips. Kracker imagines that this must be the old Hippy Gumbo himself, purging his soul because of the breakdown.

Kracker steps back into the alleyway, guided by Persephone's flower.

The side door is now split asunder by the snot blast. Kracker wrenches the partition aside. Now he is stepping down lightly into a vast underground room, stippled with shadows, and filled with water amidst marble walls.

A young woman is floating in the water, a cut flower of a quite delicious hue nudging between her legs. Persephone herself is floating between Belinda's legs, which is how she has led him this far, this close.

Belinda . . .

The target of this day. The good target. This time he will finish it.

Kracker steps down into the shadows . . .

Belinda, that glass of poison to her lips. Two-fifths of the Boomer swallowed down by now. Absolutely blasted, good and strong. The high carries you over into wanting to finish the job, to suck down the whole trip.

Death is very patient. He doesn't mind the few extra seconds taken to make the decision. The glass tips against your mouth. Some drops touch your tongue. They tingle.

Tingle and burn.

A noise from the far end of the pool . . .

Shit!

Belinda listens, willing these visitors to go away, whoever they are. Is it Gumbo or Wanita? Can't they see this girl is trying to kill herself? Do they think this is easy?

'Who is it?' Belinda shouts.

'It's the cops,' a voice answers. 'Come easy now.'

Belinda waits for five seconds. And then . . .

'What do you want?' Peering through the shadows to where a thin, dry shape trembles . . .

'Don't worry, Belinda. We know who killed your doggy friend. We know it wasn't you.'

Seven seconds. The voice is kind of familiar.

'I already know who killed him,' Belinda says. 'Persephone did, with Columbus's help.'

'You're a very clever girl,' replies the voice. 'I'm going to have to kill you.'

Our various lives moving closer. My daughter is floating naked and mapped out in the pool. Kracker, the Chief of Cops, moves forward into the light, sweating like a wound. He sits on the edge of the pool, his shoes dangling into the water. Persephone's flower is stroking her petals between Belinda's thighs. The half-finished glass of Boomer is back on the pool-side. The cop-gun hidden in Kracker's pocket. All the elements in place now. Myself working towards the scene. Columbus also, revelling in his new map. That underground swimming hole, that shimmering hole, my daughter at the centre, magnetic in the shadows and the marble. A compass of strange desires all around her, closing in like the far-apart streets that rest on top of each other as a map is folded.

The outside world still green-darkened by droplets of mucus. Inside, a stuttering of ghosts from the snot-covered window, the only light.

'It's you again,' my daughter says. 'Your name is passenger Deville.'

'No longer, no longer.' Kracker smiles. 'A mere disguise. My name is Kracker, the Chief of Cops.' His target looks so tender with her map of skin shivering under the water; she's making the Casanova unfurl in his groin. He can't keep his eyes off the floating flower between the girl's legs, the one that has led him this far. He feels jealous of the flower taking its pleasure elsewhere, and he can feel Persephone's eyes crawling all over his skin from the patterns of lichen that cover the ancient marble walls of this dungeon. All he has to do to please his lover is plunge a bullet straight into the target's body. But he's afraid of death, his own and anybody else's. He has killed criminals before now, gleefully taking them out, but an innocent, a fellow sufferer? How can he manage this task?

'What do you have to do?' Belinda asks.

'I have to kill you.'

Belinda stares at him.

'I'd like you to,' she says.

'What?'

'It's simple. I want you to kill me.'

'But why?' His glands are dripping in the heat.

'It feels right.' Belinda's mind is clear now, cold.

Kracker is taken aback by this. It really gets to him. A simple man, simple needs. He pulls the gun out of his pocket, snagging it on the cloth, so that he has to reach around with his other hand to free it. Then he has some trouble releasing the hammer. 'Please . . . I'm sorry,' he mumbles. 'I'm sorry . . . I can't seem to . . . There! I have it now.' The gun is cocked, at last. This clumsiness makes him feel so normal. It gives him courage, the normality. He's no longer trying to prove himself. Maybe he can really pleasure Persephone this time. He holds the weapon out in front of him, as far from his body as he can reach. The barrel is trembling, catching tiny glints of light from the shrouded window.

Belinda smiles. 'Can you do it?' she asks.

'I . . . I can try.'

'Go on then. Make it a good one.'

Be a man. Be a man at last. This is what the girl is saying to him. Despite all the Fecundity surging through his blood, be a man at last. And he cannot take it. His gun-hand is shaking. He brings his left hand up to hold the right hand steady around the butt. Still it shakes.

'You're laughing at me,' he says.

'No. I'm working this out with you. That's what we both want, isn't it?'

Belinda has picked up the glass of Boomer from the pool's edge. She holds the glass up in front of her face. 'This is Boomer. You know Boomer?' Kracker nods his head. 'You've taken it?' Kracker tells her that he has. 'You know the ruling then?' Kracker does, but she tells him anyway: 'One for the money, two for the show. Three to get ready for a clean and sexy death.'

'Are you going to kill yourself?'

'If you won't do it.'

'Please...'

'There are over five measures in this glass, and I've taken two already. I'm feeling very good at the moment, very sexy. Don't you want me?'

The gun is moving through the gloom, trying to fix upon her. Kracker cannot find his target. This girl is spooking him. 'Please... I...' he says. He fumbles at the gun. 'I don't think you should...'

Belinda dips her tongue into the poison. She lets the Boomer burn her nerve-endings for the tiniest part of a second.

'Don't...'

Belindia tilts the glass until the Boomer is edging against the lip. 'This is what you want?'

'No!' The cop's voice crying. He stands up from the pool-side. 'No... yes... I... shit! Please... it's all going wrong. I just wanted to... nobody should die. Nobody...' Kracker can hear Persephone screaming inside his head. 'Please,' he says. 'Don't do this.'

'It's what we both want.' Belinda's Shadow has never been so fluid.

Kracker sweating. Sneezing. But the aim is firm now, he is motivated. The gun steady and true in his clenched fingers. If he could only break this circuit—his fingers and the handle and the trigger and the young skin of this girl. Maybe then he would be free of all this worry. Persephone's perfume is yelling at him. The stench of her is filling the cellar. All he has to do is pull the trigger, complete this story. Belinda tips the rim of the glass. Kracker jumps into the water, making a fat splash, and then pushes through heaviness to get at Belinda.

'Please, Belinda . . . don't kill yourself!'

I drove my Comet into this tangled story. 6.22 a.m. Even time was becoming fluid under the new map. None of the old rules applied. The map was filled with broken roads. Twenty-five car crashes occurred that day, drawn together by the newly tangled roots of the city. But I was free of that structure now; I was driving on Shadows.

A dirt track running between factories. Everything was still and silent at the edges, ghost-ridden and abandoned, but as I rode closer to the centre of that lost industrial city, it was like entering into Babylon. A screaming woman ran towards the Comet, her clothing in rags and her face covered with mucus. I worked the wheel to avoid impact, and she glanced off the left-hand side of the bonnet. She was down on the track for a few seconds, but I didn't stop the car. Let's think about the daughter, this was my only vision. The poor woman staggered to her feet. I kept on driving until I manoeuvred the Comet into a wide open space between a square of warehouses and depots. A Gypsy-dog camp was set down in the arena, a chaotic mess of bone-piles, iron sculptures and tepee kennels. The whole place was covered in a glaze of nose-juice and bodies were covering the ground, some writhing around, many others lying as still as death. A black woman sporting an over-funded afro was administering to some of the victims of the quake. That would be Wanita-Wanita. I parked the Ford Comet and walked over to where Wanita was offering a glass of something to a sufferer. The dog man refused the drink, so Wanita drank it herself, and lowered her head to kiss the dog, passing the healing mixture from her mouth to his. I'd loosed my gun from its holster, but it seemed rather heavy in my fingers now, seeing that act of kindness. 'Wanita-Wanita?' I asked. She looked up at me, her eyes heavy with resignation. She saw the gun in my hands and knew me for what I was: a bastard cop, everything her whole life had raged against. I could see the deviance dying in her eyes. She looked over to a warehouse, where an Xcab and a painted van named Magic Bus were parked. Above the door the words *Slavery House* were partly obscured by flowers, so that the sign seemed to read *S ave y ou*. The whole building was covered in a verdant net of blooms. An aerial feather fluttered from the roof, and I could feel Belinda's Shadow from within the warehouse, struggling against temptation.

The time was pushing on towards fullness, and the morning air was inch-thick with yellow heat and pollen and snot.

I pressed a finger on the door's intercom system. A metallic doggy voice answered me. 'Who that?'

'It's the cops,' I said. 'Open up.' The main entrance spread its two doors like a slow lover, a reluctant sigh, and then I was through to the lounge area of Slavery House. I was pulled along by anger, feeling Belinda's Shadow from below my feet. Something was happening to her. The desk clerk was a balding masked-up robodog cowering behind his counter, clutching a copy of *Nude Bitch Digest*. 'What want?' the dog growled.

'Key to the cellar, please,' I responded, flashing the badge.

'We no cellar.'

I pushed my gun Into the dog's face: 'Shall we dig one together, mutt?' The doggy clerk was lolling his long pink tongue out of his jaws, searching for good air. He looked over to a door beneath the stairwell. His left paw was reaching to a key that hung on a numbered board behind him. 'This you want,' he growled. As soon as the gun was off-target, that robohound was running out of the door on all fours. I felt his fetid breath pass by me on the furry wind as I worked the key into a door under the stairs, following the scent of Belinda.

A voice from below, soft and sweaty: 'Who's at the door?'

'Nobody,' I shouted. 'Just your worst ever fear.'

'Oh yeah? Like who?'

'A Shadowcop called Sibyl Jones.'

'Shit!'

'That enough for you?'

'Fuck!'

Panic from below.

I take the dark steps two at a time, three at a time.

Radio waves . . .

Colours in the black air as messages were sent. Febrile scents on the wing. Scrapings and breaths. Glimmers of blue transmitter lights. Iridescent purple feathers floating through the waves of panic. Dark aromas. Sweetness. Sweetness and fear. I was falling into those colours. Wires and sparks. A Sixties beat from the radio. My vision seeping away into the gloom, and the Gumbo Hippy himself rising up from the feathers.

'You're under arrest, Gumbo,' I said to him.

'Who's taking me?' he answered, 'You're all done, cop lady.'

'Where's Belinda?'

'Who knows?' Then he was stepping towards me, his long, raggedy hair swinging from side to side. 'Who cares any more? Don't you realise the whole fucking world is ruined now. What you cops gonna do, uh? Arrest a dream?' Gumbo started to laugh. 'Reality is fucked.'

'I don't care about the world right now. I want my daughter back.'

'I can't allow that.'

'What's your problem, Gumbo? If it's really all over, what are you fighting against?'

'I'm a lover, not a fighter, and this new world will still need a guaranteed shit-detector.'

'I'm still a cop and you're still breaking the laws of broadcast.'

'I'm taking you into static.' He had an electronic knife in his hands, wired into his equipment. Fire was shivering from the blade. I brought my gun up tight on his forehead but that pirate never even wavered. Belinda was screaming at me over the Shadow, and I was trying to make a homing signal. Gumbo thrust forwards.

A burning sensation in my stomach.

I made a swinging motion with the gun, glancing against the hippy's head. It just made the blade turn slightly in the wound; I could feel feather waves entering me from the implement. It felt like I was being spoken to, deep down. Like I was full of feathery voices. The edge of chaos. I shot a cop-bullet into the heart of Gumbo's equipment, which brought a lessening of the pain. Gumbo ran to his circuits, shrieking at the dying of the lights. He was working the switches like a madman, even as the feathers creamed at his touch. Gumbo was shouting over the dying waves, telling the world he was still fighting, still willing to give everything for the people of the dream. 'This is the Gumbo calling the world. The cops are at my tail. Don't believe the hype. We can still find ourselves in the map. This old hippy will always believe in you . . .'

I slipped a pair of cuffs onto Gumbo and fixed him to a steel bracket on the floor. Then I was slipping away along underground corridors, clutching the wound in my stomach, chasing the Shadow of my daughter, and the glimmer of water reflected on a marble wall.

Around a labyrinth of stone until a locked door came up close. I found Belinda's Shadow in there, rippled with pain, and then the stranger's—shiny red it was, coloured with anger and fear. Male Smoke. And the intent: his troubled need to kill. And then the name of that Shadow: Kracker. I brought out my tube of DoorVaz, poured some into the lock, and then tried my cop-key. The lock slipped a little, the tumblers complaining. More Vaz, that slick releaser, and then one well-aimed kick. The door banged open.

Steps leading down. Shouting out: 'Police! Don't do anything!' The Shadows of love breaking. Fury. Screams. *Please . . .* Swearing. *Christ!* A sudden thrust in Kracker's Shadow as he reached towards his climax. My feet falling on the pathway.

That picture I dropped into: my daughter taking a full drink of

wine, her body naked and floating in a pool of shivering water, the
Chief of Cops paddling towards her, cop-gun outstretched. The
Shadows were dancing in fear and delight. I was feeling my daughter's pleasure for a second, before the pain came to me. Not knowing what to do except to shout out, 'Hold it right there!' I was
acting like some kind of soap-cop. That useful. Kracker was moving
slow through the water, towards Belinda. Shadows dripping all over
his thin body. That gun was going to make a big hole . . .

I did it. I managed the job. My one and only cop-job. I shot my
chief.

The rules kicked in at the last second, causing me to aim wide.
His gun arm folded up into a wing-like shape and then collapsed
under him, blood-rich as he plunged into the water. My daughter's
head was disappearing under the surface. The glass was bobbing on
the surface, loading with water, and then following her down. I
jumped into the pool, to grasp Belinda's body to mine, up to the
surface, her body of maps . . .

'Belinda . . .'

No answer. Her eyes were glazed with joy, far-off and wandering. Kracker was making sad noises from the side of the pool, his
legs thrashing the water into waves, his arm painting the water red.

I turned my head quickly. 'Shut the fuck up!' I shouted. 'You're
under arrest, Kracker.' Kracker's eyes full of panic, his Shadow
jumping with fire. He couldn't stop twitching, moving the water into
scarlet waves, words from his slack mouth . . .

'It was Boomer,' he breathed. 'Boomer. She took some
Boomer. Too much Boomer. I was trying to . . .'

'Is this true?' I had turned back to Belinda now, taking in the
sinking glass.

'I was trying to stop her,' Kracker said. 'That was all. I'm
sorry, Jones. I'm really sorry. Columbus made me do it. He was
blackmailing me . . . my crimes . . . my petty crimes . . . what could
I do?'

Everything was cool and slow, like a bad memory that was only just happening. Everything was struggling towards life. Everything was losing.

Losing it . . .

My daughter in my arms as I clung to her tightly, willing the breath back into her quiet flesh. Her eyes flickering for a second and then closing. And then the very Shadow of her drifting away into the water, into blood-reddened water. I lifted her up lightly, just like when she was a kid and had taken a fall in the back garden. Kracker was struggling towards the surface, clutching his mess of an arm with one good hand, shouting at me . . .

'What about me! What about me!'

I carried Belinda out of that cellar, away from that sad noise, out of that warehouse. Her body . . . the breath of a ghost. My daughter's life floating away in slow waves.

Coyote's long legs are loping along the Princess Road towards Manchester Central. He no longer feels troubled by the fever. The map is changing constantly as he runs, but that's no problem to his flowering soul. He feels like a road himself, like a part of this new world. Coyote is a flower; the road opens up to him with parted petals. This is the travelling he has always dreamt about. But still something is missing, some vehicle for his desires. The scent of blossoms from Platt Fields Park makes his hind-stalks grip the pavement. The flowers are growing out towards him. Coyote is walking through their perfumes, adding his own sweet message to their throats. It is only then that he realises. *It doesn't have to be like this; I can travel freely. The flower in me is still growing, still learning. It's easy. So easy. No one need see me. I can just . . . you know . . . just grow . . .*

So then, Coyote just *folds* himself into the new flower map of Manchester, moving his patterns from stem to stem. He is living in the vegetation, remaking himself again and again like the seasons changing, from the flora that he meets upon the way. This is the coolest route he has ever travelled. Coyote Flower Dog is conjuring himself out of the petals and the leaves and the thorns, turning that greenery into a black-and-white Dalmatian plant. The Little Sir John seed is still growing inside his body, running with the sap; he can sense him there. All along his long and growing journey, the man in the root is trying to redirect Coyote. Coyote shrugs him off, or tries to; in fact all he can manage is to send him spinning back down into the deepest stem.

Now the city is opening up to Coyote's patterns.

How it has changed. He remembers it as a dark place of wet desires; now the world is floral and choking. Coyote can journey anywhere through the green veins of Manchester. Flowers are cascading from every building, vines are clinging to lamp posts. A pink rain of blossoms is falling on Albert Square, brightly lit by lasers from the top of the Town Hall. The city is deserted, as though in quarantine. There are cop-cars on the streets but they seem to move like lost souls, screaming through the morning, making embroideries of noise with their sirens. A few Xcabs here and there; only these vehicles seem to be making any kind of progress. Coyote is blooming his shapes into a small bush growing to one side of the square. From there he pushes himself through lichens clinging to the pavement, through mosses growing on walls, through the very pollen that is breezing through the air above Manchester. By these routes he makes his way towards the back of Bootle Street cop station, where the impounded cars sit like fossils behind criss-cross wire.

Here Coyote finds his first lost love. His Yang.

The black cab.

Everything comes home to him: where he has come from, and where he must go.

Coyote sees a light shining from a room in the back of the station, a lone cop sitting at a desk. He works his essence through the sap-streams of a willow tree that hangs over the locked gate to the car pound, drops down onto concrete, working his stalks into strong, fast legs that take him towards the office. He knows by now that he can change his appearance at will; he can make a mask out of flowers. He knows he must make himself look like a cop. Coyote extends an eye on a green stalk until it can see over the window's rim. From this vantage he watches the cop for a few moments, and then realises who he must become. He taps on the glass with a branch from his body. The cop looks up from his paperback novel. He has plugs up his nostrils, but his pollen mask is lying on the desk. It takes less than two seconds for Coyote's face to regrow itself into a new shape. Then he lets one of his branches bang against the office door, making it sound like an urgent call. The cop puts down his book with a sigh, gets up from the desk, walks over to the door, opens it. 'What you after?' he says to the cop standing in the shadows of his doorway. 'You need a car? What is it? Somebody paid a parking fine?' The cop at the door doesn't answer. His face is obscured. 'Spill it out, buddy. There's trouble exploding all over town and I'm halfway through a sex scene.' The figure at the door moves forward into the light, bringing his face into the picture. 'Christ Almighty!' says the car pound cop. 'No, no! Jesus, no!' Then he falls silent, his breath caught in his throat. He is reaching for the gun in his holster . . .

Coyote steps into the office.

The car pound cop feels like he is falling into a bad mirror. He screams, his gun slipping from his fingers, slick with sudden sweat. 'Who are you?' he manages to ask.

Coyote answers, 'I'm you, of course.'

Coyote has formed his petals into a perfect replica of the cop's face.

The cop cannot take the sight.

'Shit!' His only response. 'Leave me alone!'

Falling back . . .

Coyote shoots out a strong branch-like arm, knocks the cop

some times in the face until he falls to the floor, unconscious. Taxi-flower-dog lets his cop-shape drop away. Now he is just drifting, growing. His twig-like claws reach over to where a bunch of keys are hooked on a steel pin. This is what he wants. He makes his loping way back to the gates, tries each of the keys until he finds the opener. He releases the wire gates from their tight coupling. Now he is strutting back to where his black cab lies waiting.

Black cab!

He lets his leaves brush along the cab's scratched paintwork, making a soft music from the contact. It feels like foreplay. And then Coyote forms a twig into the remembered shape of his cab key, twists the lock, opens the door, slips inside.

He is home.

He shapes the twig into the exact pattern of the ignition key, works the clutch, turns the engine. He's full of juice. Petrol. The cab is humming with life. He guns it down until the city is swirling all around in flowers. Coyote is howling now, turning the road into liquid so he can glide down its throat. Towards Boda, wherever she may be. His last known chance at love. His Yin. He would find her if it took the rest of his life, his second life.

Work it good, taxi-flower.

I was hugging my Belinda child ever so tightly, as though I could force her into a new life. I was carrying her through from darkness to light, fluid smoke dripping away, gaps between my fingers. Hospital starkness. Manchester Royal Infirmary. The journey over to the hospital had been a nightmare ride surrounded by crashed cars and twisting streets. Only my Shadow-hold on the story unfolding had managed to bring me this far. Somebody in white took my daughter away from me. My second child . . . was I to be doomed with wayward offspring? Was I always to be the mother of death? I was holding my heart back from the losing of my daughter once again. A pain was resting in my stomach. I watched until Belinda disappeared into whiteness, and then I collapsed to the hospital floor. Darkness falling in ribbons of smoke . . .

Waking. Another room, another world . . .

Belinda. A bed. Instruments. But there was very little of her left. So very little.

A doctor was searching deep inside Belinda's flesh for messages; some small, hidden moment of life. He had already sealed the slit in my stomach taken from Gumbo YaYa. It was a superficial wound anyway, in the sense that nothing else mattered now except my daughter's life.

Nothing to say or do, but to hold my daughter's folding body so tightly that the flesh was squeezed into a semblance of breath. Only an illusion. Belinda was dying; I could no longer feel her Shadow. Everything was at a loss; myself, the world, my case. Instruments sending out a sad, slow wave.

My child . . .

Pulling back the sheets from her coma . . .

'Help her! Help her, please!'

'We're doing all we can, Officer Jones.' A cold doctor's voice. I ripped the sheets from my daughter's bed . . .

Hugging her.

Hugging her to death.

Daughter . . . daughter . . .

'Save her!' I had turned my face towards the doctor, who was busying himself with instruments. 'Save her, please.'

'Officer Jones . . .'

Shaking her. Shaking Belinda.

'I killed her. It was my fault. I misread the Shadow. That's . . . oh God . . . it's never happened before . . . Please. Please save her.'

The doctor looked on impassive.

Shaking and cursing.

No response. Holding on to Belinda. Holding on to air.

Instruments pulsing into silence. My daughter dying...

'She's gone.' The doctor's words.

Please, no...

I went deep. Deepest ever.

Sailing...

Belinda... Belinda... Belinda...

My Shadow was breaking into Belinda's body, searching for the root. I was travelling through a dead part of town. Her unmapped body. Shadowless. I saw a clutch of Boomer snakes wrapping themselves around her heart.

Belinda... Belinda...

This is the moment... the worst moment of my story...

I will not have this!

I sent my own Shadow into her, forcing it deep into the veins, the heart, the brain, the skin. All of her.

Come on. Do this! Show me some fucking love for once...

A small movement... her chest...

Please...

I was drifting down through layers of muscle, hoping for one last lingering trace of smoke. Finding only dead meat, a stopped heart, a shrivelling brain. Belinda's mind was giving room to the ghost. No hope. No hope...

I pushed myself even deeper into her, giving my Shadow to her, cutting the last knot with my love. My Shadow was leaving me, leaving me with a hole inside.

This is for you, ungrateful slut! Happy fucking birthday!

Belinda breathed again...

Shadow Fall.

A young girl died in my arms that day.

But then breathed again. It was a small breath, but the best I have ever felt. She breathed again. *Belinda, take this gift to your soul. Please live! Please live, you stupid fucked-up warrior.* Her eyes opened. I felt them open from within. I was emptied now of smokiness, having given everything, but Belinda opened her eyes again. This was worth it. I knew it was worth it.

My body was drained, unshadowed; I felt like hollow flesh. Belinda pushed away from me, newly born. 'Mother!' she cried.

That was my name. Her name.

My Shadow had gone into her body, replacing what she had lost. I was my own daughter now, living like a ghost inside her skin. Belinda didn't know who to talk to—herself, or her mother. They were one and the same, and talking was redundant.

In the real world Belinda had reached up from her coma, screamed once, called out my name, and then had fallen back onto the bed with a hard thump.

The real world? What was that any more? My cold body sitting in a hard plastic chair? A hospital somewhere in Manchester? My daughter struggling towards a second life? Is that real? I was too far gone to care. I saw all this through parched eyes, a troubled stomach, my brain registering the patient's reaction as the aftermath of the body's system being forced back into life. My own body was hard and ritualized now, lacking any kind of emotional response to the sensual input. The doctor had left the ward, believing this to be a hopeless case. Maybe it was. I was really drifting in thin smoke somewhere through my daughter's warmed-up interior.

'Oh shit,' Belinda said, direct through the flesh. 'You're inside me.'

I'm inside you, daughter. Her memories came flooding into my Shadow; I took them as my own. Her suicide bath . . . Christ, it sickened me. How could she possibly want to take her own life? Weren't my genes good enough for her? Was I that bad a mother?

'What are you doing?' Belinda screamed, trying to push me away, out of her body.

Saving your life, stupid bitch. What's this with the Boomer dose? You like to die, is that it?

'Get the fuck out of my body.'

We're both here together. No more secrets . . .

'Why have you done this?' I could feel my daughter's body trying to reject me with muscle pushes. But I was clinging on tight. Clinging to . . .

Love? Maybe love. I can't tell. Is that an answer?

Belinda's body was like frost around my Shadow. 'I don't want this,' she said. 'I don't want love.'

You think there's a choice?

I was looking at the world through my daughter's eyes. It was the picture of a small hospital room. A lonely woman sat beside her daughter's bed, her eyes filled with a terrible emptiness. Belinda was telling me all about her lost love for the taxi-dog over the Shadow, and all about her doomed overtures, and about the loss of her Xcab Chariot. And about how it had all gotten too much, her life too bitter. I gave in return all of my own secrets and how I had tried my best to make her whole. No secrets between us any more. Well, still the one. *I'm not proud of losing you, you know?* I said to her.

'I should hope not. But I'm proud of losing you.'

Why are you doing this to me?

'Why not?' She shrugged her shoulders. I *felt* her shoulders shrug, from within.

You'd be dead if I wasn't here.

'I wanted to die,' Belinda replied, cold as death. 'I am dead anyway. You think this is life?'

Jesus!

'What are you going to do now, Sibyl? What use is a Shadowcop without a Shadow. I think you're finished.'

I saved your life . . .

'Thanks a fuck, parasite.'

Shall we call it symbiosis?

'Fuck off.'

Do you have to swear so much?

'Oh Sibyl, how motherly you are. I'm sure you could stop me.

You're my soul now, aren't you? You think I want to live with somebody else's soul? Even my mother's?'

I'm giving you everything.

'You've got a screen up.'

I don't think we should . . .

'You're not showing me the full story.'

I don't want to hurt you.

'You can do worse than this? Tell me about it.'

It's not the time.

'Help me, please, mother.'

That call weakened me. A black curtain ripping.

The truth was I had kept Jewel and his story from Belinda for so long, why should I reveal that pain to her now? She knew nothing of her older brother. Revelation would only be a pain. Maybe my daughter wanted pain? She pushed some feelings into my Shadow then, and I got inklings of love in there, like we were one and the same now, and Belinda was ready to accept everything. Belinda was a taxi that would die without her latest passenger.

So I let the screens melt away. The thoughts ran sluggish for a second, and then sparkled into knowledge.

Our feelings merged.

It is the Jewel in the box, Belinda.

Belinda's mind pounced on the story. 'Tell me about the Jewel.'

The Jewel is the name of my son. It was the brightest name I could find.

'I'm your only child.'

Not so. There is another.

'What?'

His name is Jewel. He is one year older than you. I had him from a solitary lover.

'Why have you kept this from me?'

I was ashamed. Jewel's father was a sailor on the New Manchester Ship Canal. He rode the false waves of the river, and the false waves of me. My body. I was anchorage for him. The sailor was my first lover. I did not know how to respond, except to get pregnant. My belly was cheating on my Shadow.

'What was the . . . the baby . . . what was it like?'

He was hideous. He was a monster, a half-dead creature.

'A Zombie?'

Yes. Call him that. But he could dream! How could I throw that child away? I have him lodged in your old bedroom.

'Wasn't he ejected by the Authorities?'

He was. But he came back to me. He's very cunning, very loving. He hitched a lift. Found me again.

'I hate you.'

Jewel is a beauty, if only to my eyes, and I love him dearly. He's only two feet tall.

'Christ! How sickening.'

One foot wide. Fully grown.

'Fuck.'

He came from my insides, Belinda. He's mine. No one will take him from me. He's dying now . . . from the fever. If anything should happen to me . . . you would have to look after Jewel. He's your brother. You under-stand this?

'What are you going to do, Sibyl? Now your Shadow's gone?'

My Shadow is yours now, my love.

'Shit!'

Belinda! Will you please stop swearing! Please . . . I'm sorry. It's just that . . .

'Sure. You're my mother.'

Yes. Oh God, it's been so long . . .

'Leave me alone.'

That is no longer an option, my child.

The manifold paths we have crossed to get to this moment: myself splitting in two, one part to Belinda, her dead body animated by my Shadow, the other part to my hollowed-out bag of flesh. It felt like an auction, my body going to the highest bidder. And this is why I know so much about my child's story. Because I took over her memories. I made them my own.

So it was that I came out of my daughter's form, leaving my whispers there to give life to her. It was not life after death; it was just death clinging on to life. Is that such a crime? My other self, my underself, was leaning over Belinda's body, seeing the breath come back into her. I called in the doctor. He looked like he'd just seen God in his instruments; waves of light were floating back into the screens. Tom was right behind him. 'Sibyl, you okay?' he asked.

'Tom, you made it through the map.' I was grateful to see him, but more important matters were pressing upon me.

'I took a cab. They can still journey the city. But the drivers are well pissed off, Sibyl. It was Roberman that brought me here. He's willing to—'

'Tom, I'm busy.' I pushed past him through the door.

'Sibyl, I was worried. They told me that Belinda had died.'

Let them all wonder.

I wasn't proud of what I had done. I wasn't happy, or anything. I was dead. I had done what Belinda had wanted to do. I had killed myself. More or less. Did it matter? Distinctions between moments? My Shadow had left me. What was I now? A vacuum inside a bag of dry skin. I could feel nothing good, only the gentle caress of my Shadow keeping Belinda alive.

I was moving like a cold robowoman. My body was drifting through the walkways of the hospital, a passenger of whatever dream would have me. Tom Dove followed me into Zero's ward. Zero's slumbering body was locked into apparatus, mere machinery keeping him alive. I knew that feeling now. I touched his forehead with my ghostly hand, whispering that I would love him forever.

'Roberman took me to Gumbo's Palace,' Tom said. 'We collected him and Kracker. They're both under arrest. You want to see the boss?' Then a cold journey into Kracker's room, where the

Chief lay bandaged and sedated. I gleefully spat into his floury face. 'Kracker spilled the goods, Jones,' Tom Dove continued. 'He made a bad deal with John Barleycorn, through Columbus. The boss has a secret history of crime. Columbus knew about this. In exchange for silence, Kracker agreed to give a home to Barleycorn's wife. Her name is Persephone, right? She's the seed of the fever. Kracker picked her up in a cop-wagon at Alexandra Park, this is after she's killed Coyote. Kracker takes her home to, guess where? The fucking cop station. The flower girl is lodged in the morgue, cabinet 257. Apparently she brought this bag of soil with her, from the Heaven Feather. Kracker reckons she can't live without it, not for too long, so there's a weakness to the plan.'

I needed clean air. Tom Dove was behind me all the time as I headed for the outside, again asking me if I was all right. I didn't answer. I got into the Comet. 'I've already sent word to the station, Sibyl,' Tom said as he climbed into the passenger seat. 'It's maybe too late.' Christ, it was always too late. But then, as we drove down Oxford Road, I saw a black cab passing us. Behind the wheel I caught a glimpse of a black-and-white-spotted dog driver. I saw a ghost. Tom was messing about with his gun so he missed the apparition. I never said anything to him, but inside I was tracing the glimpses of a plan. I was driving on auto-pilot, my hands moving around the wheel like a pair of gloves, whilst my true self, my Shadow, was resting inside Belinda as she rested in her bed. But, seeing that apparition of Coyote pass, I was motivated now, fired. If I could just get the details in place, we maybe had a real chance to fight back against the Vurt. I could keep my Jewel alive.

Cops were bunched up around the morgue's door, all of them fully loaded and striking various macho poses, but I could see the creases on their brows above their pollen masks, the sweat of nerves. The corridor was bristling with fear. This business with the new map had them all on edge. Reports were coming in all the time of car crashes. A dozen people had died already that we knew of, victims

of car crashes. The Xcabs were still running but nobody cared to
journey any more. Columbus was not answering to the cab-wave.
The cops no longer knew how to act. Some of them had given up
the badge. Tom Dove took control, and I was glad for that; my body
was too empty for physical battle. He adjusted the tightness on his
mask and then punched the security lock on the morgue's door,
and I followed him into the room, the other cops alongside me. The
room was thick with pollen, globular organisms that swam around
as though they owned the air. Wet lichens crept over the walls.
Water dripped from the ceiling. Dove walked up towards cabinet
257. There was a smell of fecundity in the space around its door.

'This is Kracker's hole, Dove,' I said. 'We need the code
number.'

'Rest easy, Jones, I can do this.'

'Some kind of Vurt trick?'

'Easier than that. I tortured it out of him.' Tom Dove smiled
at me then, and then punched in the code. He stepped back.

Two seconds . . .

The cabinet slid open with a soft breath, shoulder height, and
from out of its maw came the stench of Eden turned rancid. The
fleshcops fell back from the aroma. Tom activated his gun and
moved towards the cabinet.

'Be careful, Tom,' I said.

'Hey, come on, Sib,' he answered. 'I'm Tom Dove, okay? The
best Vurtcop in town. You cops backing me up?'

Nods of assent from a parade of masks. Cop-gun clutched in
both hands, Tom Dove peered over the lid of the cabinet.

There was a scream then.

Tom! Back away!

There was a scream like all the flowers of the world were
being uprooted one by one, and a long, thick shoot of vegetable
matter surged from the cabinet, twisted in space for a second, and
then daggered its sharpened point deep into Tom Dove's left eye.

I let off six bullets into the thick stem, the other cops firing as well. The room filled with smoke and the stench of powder. The stem burst into splinters and a thousand black petals floated through the exaggerated silence as the guns fell quiet. Confetti at a funeral. Tom Dove lay on the floor, his face covered in blood. A cop screamed from behind me. Another was calling for a doctor as I knelt down next to Tom. I cradled his head in my arms. 'Tom . . . I'm here . . . talk to me . . .'

He mumbled something in return.

'What? Tom? What was that?'

'Roberman . . .'

'What?'

'Roberman . . . Xcabber . . . he's willing to help us find Columbus . . . the map . . .'

'Tom, a doctor's coming.'

'Find Columbus . . . kill him . . . close the map . . .'

'I'm going deeper than that, Tom. To the source.'

'Your daughter . . .'

'Belinda's fine, Tom. Just fine. We're together now. We're everything that Barleycorn fears. Remember?'

'Do it for me . . .' With that he closed his eyes. His body felt suddenly heavier in my arms.

'Nice working with you, Tom Dove.'

I stood up. The doctor had now arrived, two seconds too late. I walked over to the cabinet. There was a girl-shaped depression in the soil. The fleshcops were just hanging around looking shocked and scared. One of them was vomiting. Another one asked me if the flower girl was dead now. I dragged him close so that his head was lodged over the rim of the cabinet. 'I want every bad fucking chemical poured over that soil. Fucking weedkiller!' He squealed some. 'You got me?' He squealed some more.

Outside.

Faithful old Ford Comet was waiting for my caress. It had started to rain, soft droplets of water falling over the car's windows

as I started the engine. I guess Persephone was watching and laughing from the heights of her flowering vines, as her seeds dispersed
through the roads. I was putting an end to that laughter. A long drift
of bright colours parting before me as I rode the Shadow through
the map. One second passing and then I was pulling up outside a
hotel in Manchester Central called the Olympia. It was twenty-
seven stories high. I booked into a room on the twenty-first, calling
myself Jane Smith in the register. I ordered a bottle of Bombay Ruby
gin from room service. And a five-fold measure of legal Boomer. I
told the clerk that it wasn't all for me, don't worry, I was expecting
guests. A surly robobitch brought the stuff up to me. I gave her my
cop-gun as a tip. Its power and its presence were too overbearing.
What was I going to do, kill somebody? 'Go kill someone evil,' I told
her. She left with a wicked smile. Alone now, I drank three measures
of the Bombay neat from a hotel tumbler. Then I opened the window to look out over the city. My dying city. Manchester. Millions
of flowers grew there, a garden in the sky. A thick, yellow mist
moved through the air.

I lay down on the soiled bed and fell into a deep sleep. I would
need all of my strength for this battle.

Dreamless.

When I awoke it was to a blue 11.09 p.m. on the hotel clock.
I had finished everything that I could finish here on Earth. My life
was Belinda's now. She would have to watch over Jewel. I poured a
fistful of gin into the glass, and then added the five measures of
Boomer, finding Belinda's poem in her faraway mind: *One measure
for a good time, two for a blast. Three for a clean and sexy death. Five
for a total emigration.*

I drank that Bombay Boomer cocktail in one.

A sudden punch to the head, and then the feelings settling
down into fingers of bliss. I was getting stroked at. My vagina was
wet. Now *that* had been a long time. *Hey, I'm kind of enjoying this.*
And the sudden black thought of what I had done. *What you playing*

at, sexy, copying your daughter like this? You ain't got your own way to go? Shame on you.

The Boomer was pulling me down with caresses.

I guess you're right about that.

Stepping out like a dancer, through the open window onto the ledge of dreams. I got a feeling then, looking out into the abyss: a bad, crazy feeling I could hardly suppress. The need to leap. Manchester foreplaying my soul. I kicked off.

Flowers on the wall as I descended, through the night's air. Blurs of colours. The journey was thick with pollen, and I felt it tugging at my gravity. It was a long and slow fall into goldness. The pavement was rising to greet me, this sad and sweet hotel tumbler.

Falling over and over, like a rotten fruit from a branch. The pavement, soft with flowers. But not quite soft enough, thankfully.

Death welcoming me.

This is a story told by a dead woman. Not life after death; just death clinging on to life. So it was that I awoke from my physical death inside Belinda's body. Belinda awoke with me. I could feel her fingers clinging to the hot, wet sheets. Her voice was screaming my Shadow down: 'What are you doing?'

May 7 creeping into 8.

Ssshh. Ssshh. Be still, my child . . .

'Where's your body gone?'

Boomer took it.

'Shit! Why?'

It was good enough for you . . .

'That was ages ago. I was weak then.'

Now you're strong. I'm inside you.

'I don't want you here. I told you—'

Your choices are dead, daughter. I'm your mother now.

'Fuck off.'

We've got work to do, Belinda. We've got to fight John Barleycorn.

*Only we can do it. Don't ask how, because I don't know, not yet. I just
know that we have to be together. You up to it?*

'I don't want to be together!' Belinda shouted. A night nurse
came into the room then, and I thought she was going to ask what
was wrong. Instead she told us that a taxi was waiting for Belinda
Jones, down in the carpark. Belinda looked at me; I looked at her. It
was a mirror looking into a mirror; a puzzled look of affinities.
'Maybe it's Roberman?' Belinda asked me.

Maybe it is.

But I knew it wasn't.

The nurse didn't hear anything of this smoky conversation, of
course. She couldn't see me living inside the patient. 'Did he give a
name?' Belinda asked the nurse. The nurse replied that no, no name
was given, just the admonishment that Belinda should 'get her arse
down to this taxi, or else feel the heat of a fat and furry palm.'

'It's Roberman,' Belinda said.

'Of course you are allowed to leave,' the nurse added. 'Just
the papers to sign. The instruments say that you are perfectly well.'
That was my doing, and wasn't I proud?

'Let's do it!' Belinda said to the nurse and then followed her
down to the ground floor, where my daughter signed the required
papers and then stepped the two of us into the pollen-rich air.
Clouds of golden grains were floating against our vision, trying our
nostrils for pleasure, finding only a cold bed there. 'There's no Xcab
here,' my daughter said to me, but I merely *allowed* her eyes to
move slightly to the left where a dark shape was waiting under
the shade of an elm. Waves of disbelief were coming through our
joined-up Shadow. An old-style black cab was parked under the
tree. A black-and-white paw was waving from the window. I felt
Belinda take in a deep breath. 'Mother, it's Coyote! How can that
be? Coyote's dead.'

So am I, remember.

'You knew? You knew he'd come back for me?'

I was hoping he would.

Coyote had now climbed out of the black cab. He smiled. It was a radiant display.

Are you gonna kiss him, or what, Belinda? He's waiting.

Belinda ran over to the black cab, where Coyote lifted her up into a swirling dance of joy. Belinda called him a bitch's son. Coyote called her a no-good player at a dogman's heart, and the two of them were laughing then. I could not but let my Shadow join in with their convulsions. They kissed. I felt the kiss from within. It lasted a minute and a half.

'Coyote! Shit!' Belinda screamed. 'How come you're back?'

'Like Lassie, Boda, you know that?' the taxi-dog said.

'The name's Belinda now. Who's Lassie?'

'You've not done Lassie Vurt, girl? Course you haven't. Lassie is one fine Vurtdog heroine, one crime-solving dog. Time passes. The original star dies. And gets replaced. No trouble. They clone a Vurt-twin. Magical. I'm the same. What you're seeing, Belinda ... Coyote Two. The sequel. That's your new name now? Belinda? Guess you made a change. Coyote's the same. He's a plant-dog now. And boy, can I grow, or what?'

'You're talking good these days, Coy.'

'Sure thing. I'm plant-eloquent. You want to ride some?'

'Yes please,' Belinda replied.

'Down to Bottletown to visit my seedling.'

'Karletta? Sure, but then I want you to take me up to the Limbo moors a while. Erm ... to Blackstone Edge.' I could feel Belinda's discomfort at saying these words, because it was I, her mother, speaking *through* her body. 'Where you picked up Persephone, Coy? Erm ... can you do that?'

'Coyote can do any journey now, but what's the purpose?'

'I want to take in the moonlight, Coyote. I want you to make love to me on the moors.' Now that really did shock Belinda, and even Coyote was taken aback by her directness.

'Oh yeah!' Coyote howled. 'Wanna make that ride. Feels well good.'

I was getting the sense of my story coming together. If Coyote really was a part of the plant world now, I had the feeling that he could maybe take us to Barleycorn in his new state. But I had to play it cool as yet, keeping up the dialogue, just in case Belinda started out doubtful.

Let's do it, Belinda. Urging.

'I'm doing it. Erm . . . I've got some luggage, Coyote.' Again, these were my words, not hers; she was just saying them.

'Give luggage to the boot, Belinda. No trouble.'

'Erm . . . luggage isn't here. Not yet. We've got to pick it up.' Belinda's voice was shaking.

'Sure thing. Where from?'

'Victoria Park.' My voice in my daughter's mouth.

'No trouble. One dog-breath from here on the new map.'

Belinda climbed into the back seat of Coyote's black cab, dragging my Shadow with her. She settled into the leather, telling Coyote to burn the juice some.

Midnight.

'Sweet doll, let's ride!' Coyote howled, before taking his cab into a juicy Oxford Road exodus. 'Awooohhhhh! Like Lassie, babe! You dig this?'

We dug.

Monday
8 May

irst fare, Victoria Park. Coyote rode the new map like a natural, no help from me, like he had his own story up and running. One that, fortunately, involved bringing Belinda home at last. I pushed her up the stairs to her old bedroom. The old cot in the centre of the old room. *This is Jewel's home. Your brother. Go on. Open it up.* Belinda wanted to run a million miles, but I forced her eyes to look closely. *Look at your half-brother.* Belinda drew in harsh breath, stepped back from the image. I stepped back within her, but then forced her to look again, and more closely this time. I could see Jewel pulsing weakly in his sheets, desperate for food. Belinda gasped.

One of Jewel's eyes was glued over by thick skin. His nose was bent to the left. His mouth was a small hole in his broken face. He had a swollen tongue. His arms ended in overlong fingers, like talons. His legs were two stumps. His back was hunched, his stomach bulged, his chest was a package of cracked ribs. His head was whispered with two or three silver hairs, and his neck was a roll of fat.

It's not that bad. You get used to it.

'I know you do. I've talked with Zombies. It's not that . . .

I know. This is your brother. Jewel . . . meet your sister.

'Why are we taking him?' Belinda asked me.

Because he's one of us. The half-dead. I'll explain when we're on the moors.

Travelling . . .

Second, down into Bottletown. It was a time of gatherings. Coyote parked on a crush of glass, told us to hold tight, and then went sailing into the trees.

Where's he going?

'To see his daughter, stupid.'

Oh.

After that we waited in silence, myself nestled deep inside Belinda, until Coyote flowed back into the cab.

'How did you get on, babe?' Belinda asked.

'I did fine,' Coyote answered. 'I tapped on the window with a branch. She came up to greet me.'

'Karletta?'

'Sure thing. A sweet kid. I gave her my best smile of petals. There was a bad sneeze living inside her.'

'I'm sorry for her.'

'We're riding to love, babe.'

'I hope so.'

The cab was shimmering with joy. We rode the slickness through till morning, catching up with the sun as it rose above the trees. It was like hitching a good lift, the very best; clean driver, fine car, mutual destination. The customs house at the northern gate was deserted; all of those Guardsmen had long since vanished now that the new map was in place.

Third fare.

Out into Limboland. Blackstone Edge. Myself riding the Shadow inside of Belinda. Belinda riding the black cab of Coyote dog. Jewel in his box on the seat next to us. Extra luggage. Passengers within passengers. Life after death. This day was unfurling, the colours of dawn flagging us down for a ride home to daylight. The moors were panting with mist, ghostly breath.

'How come you knew where we were, Coyote?' Belinda asked. I just loved that use of the plural.

'I went visiting the Xcab rank. There was a plastic and fur boy there. One of the last still working the road. He delivered your pick-up.'

'Right. His name's Roberman.'

'Good dog, that driver.'

Coyote pushed his black cab into hyper-mode, making a glaze of the passing trees. We were speeding along, breaking the rules, and I was loving it. It felt so right being inside my daughter. Like I should have done this years ago. And with a smooth-dog lover up front, driving us to bliss, and with Jewel there as well. With this team on board, how could I lose? John Barleycorn was going to regret his intrusion into my family and my city. I was just clinging to the insides of Belinda's body, praising Coyote for giving Belinda the hope. And for making her accept me. I could feel her mind glowing. This love was too good to miss, and I was the mechanism taking her there. Listen, I didn't mind being a mechanism. I was painting *dreams* into her. But I had to be careful; I didn't want them running scared from what I was about to ask.

Coyote was speaking: 'Coyote and the flower-world. There's no difference between us now. I'm a dog. I'm a plant. I'm a human. Not so much dog. Not so much human. But there's plenty of the plant on board. Can't you feel me growing?'

'I feel it,' Belinda answered.

'Good rutting, babe.'

Coyote drove us to a bleak outcrop, beyond a pub and a farm, where a lonely telephone line fed its way into the earth. The whispering corpse of an oak tree. Zombies could be heard, dribbling through the morning weeds. We could hear those creatures hissing and croaking. There was a smear of dawn above the tree-line. Coyote got out of the cab, opened the door for us. Let us loose. An oiled-up Half-aliver came shambling over the dead ground towards us, talons gleaming. Coyote put his paw into that alien claw, he shook it tight. The Zombie smiled at him and then fell, flopping-like, into the soil. And the earth all around us was littered with twenty or more of these soft and bulbous creatures. Zombies. They moved and breathed very slowly, their feelers weaving elaborate patterns, like language.

And then Coyote came up close, his big brown eyes staring deep into ours. 'I've brought you here for a reason, Belinda,' he whispered. 'That's all to do with love, sure. But something else . . . somebody else is making me choose this place.' His spotted fur was a constantly changing array of leaves and flowers. He sure was beautiful just then. 'This is where I first picked up Persephone.' Coyote held his hand out in front of Belinda's face. I could only gaze through my daughter's eyes as Coyote turned his fingers into stems, into stalks. A yellow rose sprang from each of his fingertips. He cracked each bloom off with his other hand and then pressed the bouquet into Belinda's hand. Then he spread his roots all around and under this parched earth, until a bed of soft grasses and flowers blossomed there. A private garden amidst the Limbo. Coyote smiled and then asked, 'You want some love now, girl?'

I squeezed at Belinda's Shadow until she gave in easily to the invite. It didn't need much squeezing.

Down amongst the leaves and the petals, down amongst the flowers and the weeds, we made love to him. Coyote pushed us up the shaky path we craved, and then pulled us down into the waving grass, to drown. He was a dog-lover and a half, that Coyote, his penis-stem making itself into the exact shape to please us. I was well pleased with the lengths he could go to. Belinda the same. Each of us crying out. My daughter's naked atlas of skin. Manchester was trembling with delight. Maybe this was the only map now existing of the old ways. Coyote was moving his branches along our streets. The morning's soft, early lamp was playing over us. Zombies were squelching through the grass, rubbing their soft tendrils over our naked bodies. We hadn't told Coyote that I was living inside Belinda, but maybe he guessed. Maybe there was a look in Belinda's eyes as she came. I felt that I was plant-like myself for a moment there, a tiny moment, when Coyote carefully fed one of his yellow roses into Belinda's mouth. A thorn dug into her lower lip; a dribble of blood flowed down her cheek. Coyote removed the flower, licked up the blood, and then started to cry. I wanted to ask him what all those tears were for, but then he came, that lover, came inside of us, feeding pollen and sperm to our womb.

Seed tossing.

Receiving it gratefully. Sucking it down. Sweating under the sun. Flowers in our skin, our brain. We clutched that dog to our wet breasts. Time was dripping and slipping. Coyote broke off a piece of fruit from his body, fed it into Belinda's mouth. It tasted like paradise, ripe and wet, a splash of ebony and green. It brought a taste to Belinda's tongue, and a picture to her mind. The same world I had half-glimpsed inside the victims, and in the feathery arms of Tom Dove. I knew then that Coyote was to be our deliverer to the world of the dream.

Let us take this.

We were lying naked, exhausted, in the dew-lined garden. Below us and faraway to the South, Manchester was sweltering in a haze of light.

'We've lost our city,' Belinda said.

'It's changed,' Coyote answered. 'We are the lucky ones.'

'Lucky in love?'

'Lucky in death. Not many will find their way through the new roads.'

'I feel sad for them.'

'Sadness is right.'

The time had come. I used Belinda's voice to explain the plan. She gave me easy access. 'Coyote, this is Sibyl Jones speaking.' I began. 'I'm Belinda's mother. I'm living inside my daughter's body. I will not explain that to you, except to say that, like you, I died and was then reborn. Our enemy is called John Barleycorn. He lives in a Vurt world called Juniper Suction. From this realm comes the fever. Juniper Suction is a Heaven Feather. To visit a Heaven Feather you have to die and then be reborn. Like you have, and like I have. And also, like Belinda has. The luggage we are carrying is called Jewel. He's my first child, a Zombie. The presence of death is very strong within him. What I'm saying is this: we have all been touched by death, and survived. I believe that we can now visit John Barleycorn in Juniper Suction. You will take us there, Coyote, in your black cab, because you are part of Barleycorn's world now, the plant world. Can you do this for me?'

Coyote nodded. 'I think so.'

'I will give no false hopes,' I continued. 'Barleycorn is a power-ful creature of the dream. He will not take lightly to our struggle. But Belinda and I are Dodos. Barleycorn fears Dodos because he cannot control us with his stories. Now we are doubly strong. Nevertheless, he will make a fearsome opponent. Can I be sure of your commitment?'

I thought that Belinda would've been the more doubtful of the two, but, although I could feel her fear over the Shadow, she assented to the journey and I blessed her for that. Coyote, however, was worried by something. 'Sibyl Jones,' he whis-pered, 'this John Barleycorn . . . it was he that raised me from the earth.'

'What?'

'I have driven here not only for you, but also for Barleycorn. He also has a task for me.'

'What is it?'

'I don't know. Only that I should come here. Maybe something to do with his—'

Coyote stopped speaking. He was looking scared. The grass and the flowers of our loving bed were shivering in a sudden breeze all around us. 'What is it, Coyote?' I asked.

'His wife . . .' Coyote started. The grasses and the flowers around us rose in a wave of knowledge and then spun themselves around us, tightly, until we were powerless to move.

Belinda screamed.

*   *   *

Persephone is dying. She clings on tightly with vines and sticky creepers, but in her green heart she is growing bad with reality's weeds. She no longer likes being here, she doesn't like this world. Earlier she had barely managed to escape the noise and the fire of the cops bursting into the palace of the cop gardener. She had sucked her body into the lichens clinging to the damp walls of the house of death where her sweet bed had lain. And, by that desperate route, she had pulled herself free. And now these people have destroyed her dreaming soil. Where is she to go now?

Into the network of flowers.

She had been then a thousand, million sparkles in the blossoming net. Petal messages had spoken to her, leaves coated with decay. Each fluttering a plea: *please save me, please save me.* Reality was fighting back. Persephone had spoken to all of her flowers, all at the same time, telling them to keep the faith, this world shall be ours, one day soon. Keep on growing.

But the seed-girl is worried. Count Pollen has lodged tight at 2010. Maybe the world is saturated? Is this the point of mutual play-off, when opposing species agree to step down from competition? Is nature turning against her? Persephone is angry and the weeds are clutching at her skin. She feels stunted. A horrible tightening around the roots. The hands of the immune. The Dodos. Maybe this world has finished with her? The soil was dying . . .

She finds the bad seeds at play in the fields of love. The taxi-flower is doing that crude animal thing, that penetration. The immune girl, Belinda her name, oh isn't she enjoying his ministrations? And Sibyl, the Mooner-cop, she's in there as well, somewhere. An unseen presence. Persephone has gathered herself into the grasses they are defiling under their fleshy bodies. She closes the grass over them, smothering them to death, but then another seed comes to her. *Let them loose, Persephone.* It was her husband's voice. *I want them to come to me. Let them come. I will deal with them in my realm of power.* Shall I come back with them, Sir John, Persephone enquires of her roots. *Yes. It's time. Come back to me* . . .

And doesn't she feel like going home anyway, now? Isn't this world altogether too much to take, so very parched and sapless? So very immune? She would do nothing to stop these travellers from finding the black garden of her mother and husband. In fact she would guide them there, easing the passage. To this end she releases her grip on the creatures and joins her changing shape to the lichens that grow under the nearby vehicle. She has come into this world by the black cab; she will leave it in the same way.

The creepers unwrapped themselves from our bodies as quickly as they had grown there. 'What the fuck was that?' Coyote asked.

'Some kind of warning, maybe. Come, let us do this.'

Belinda refused to put her clothes back on, saying she wanted to ride it down naked, so when Coyote ushered us back into the black cab, I could feel my daughter's wet flesh sliding against the hot leather. Coyote told us to hang on tight, this ride was going to be liquid.

A rain started to fall.

A black rain.

The ground turned into mud and the black cab started to sink into the soil.

Belinda Jones's eyes were damp with tears; this greasy trip was too much for her. Pupils widening. The black mud covered our windows as we slid into deep earth. Coyote was steering us towards the black garden. Sibyl Jones, myself, hanging on tight to the reins. Jewel's small, weak Shadow crying from his box.

I will save you, my firstborn. Don't you worry.

The world was dissolving and the new day bled away.

Coyote dug away from the fingers, away from time and loneliness, away from care and woe, safety, the rules, cartography, instruction, shit fares and meta-cops; all the bad things were peeling away. Black cab was sinking towards a small green glimmer in the night-dark soil. 'Just like breaking through quarantine,' Coyote said to us. And then we were . . .

We were . . .

We were cabbing it down.

We were . . .

And then we were . . .

We were descending . . . the roots growing over our journey.

We were . . .

We were pushing through to another world. A deeper world. Falling asleep. Dreaming. At last, *dreaming*. Waking up to another time, a different garden. An underworld garden. Myself inside of Belinda.

We were . . .

This garden was as deep as night. Flowers of pitch, petals of slow flame. Dark seeds glowing. We were digging into that soil.

Dreaming . . . dreaming . . . floating . . . floating and falling . . .

Through to pictures. Lilac shadows opening. The cab snarling like a dog, pushing apart the damp tangle of roots, penetrating, coming to rest at last. The thick roots of an oak tree. Stunted and braked. Blurs of seeds slowing down into gardens.

The black garden.

And at that precise moment, 8 May, 4.16 a.m., a young boy named Brian Swallow finds himself released from constricting snakes and vines. He finds himself swapped back into a small bed in the suburb of Wilmslow.

His parents, John and Mavis, are roused from sleep by their son's cries.

Everything was all together: the plants and the earth and the dog and the moment; all of them fading into motion, and then bursting into stillness. I could feel deep ebony roots drilling through soft soil.

I looked through Belinda's eyes, out of the cab window, into a forest of darkness. It was night-time once again. Time was speeding up into a blur of motion. Where had the last day gone? A bleak moon whispered through the branches. A few fireflies flitted here and there, making thin maps of light between the purple flowers. Coyote got out of the cab, forcing the driver's door open against the crush of branches. He pushed away a bunch of wild hyacinths to get a good grip on the passenger door. We stumbled out, as you do from a taxi after a long night of cheap barley wine. The two of us, one inside the other, making like a drunkard. I was trying to get a grip on Belinda's body, but she was too excited, too weak from the journey. She was sniffing at the black-petalled flowers, breaking them up, pushing their dark colours into her mouth, tasting at fecund sweetness. Her naked mapped-out body was rolling around on the ground, pushing down beds of violets. Belinda was suffering from cab-lag, Vurt-style; the shock of moving between worlds. It took all of my Shadow to get even the smallest purchase in her flesh. Getting her to stand up was like lifting a heavy, heavy weight. Coyote helped me, curling a strong branch around our waist. We pulled Jewel's box free. I let Belinda slump against the taxi's side, turning her head so I could see where we were.

It was a different part of the garden than I had seen with Tom Dove's help, but still the overall feeling of despondency prevailed. The air was very thick and grainy, and I could feel it pushing at Belinda's skin. Heavy globules of black pollen. Moving slowly they were, on the slight breeze. So dense, and the night garden so dark that I could hardly see in front of me. The cab was lodged against the trunk of a large, overbearing oak tree. Beyond this the ground was thickly carpeted with violets, before they gave way to a tight cluster of elms. There were faint glimmers from the darkness, and as Belinda's eyes grew accustomed to the gloom I could see that two ornamental pillars stood amidst the trees.

Vines crept around them and at the top of each a carved angel, the left-hand statue representing a young boy, the right a dog. Pale ghosts of stillness. Between their winged sleep a faintness existed in the foliage, a slight easing of the sombre mood, as though a path might be lying there. Or more closely, the remains of a garden path long since overgrown.

'I've got luggage for the fare,' Coyote said to us. He was holding Jewel's case in his arms. We told him to put it down on the ground and then to open it up. He did so, working the locks with his leafy claws. 'Cab-shit!' he barked. 'First time a Zombie pull one on the black cab.'

Belinda looked at him. 'He's my brother,' she said alone. Alone, she said it, and I was so happy then, I wanted to hug her. Which is difficult from the inside, but I tried it. I could feel her receiving my inner glow.

Jewel crawled out of the box and up the length of Belinda's body until he was clinging to her breast. Maybe he saw me inside of her. Whatever. Belinda shifted him in to a better position and then turned to Coyote. 'Shall we explore?' she said.

I said the same, the same time. Exploring together.

And between the stoned angels we walked, along a thin path through the swaying trees. Coyote was leading the way, his black-and-white Dalmatian flowers flickering ahead of us. Myself inside Belinda following.

Belinda's black-and-white map of old Manchester was moving through the harsh thorns. They cut into her skin, digging up new roads. Jewel was clinging to Belinda's chest. Her arms were tight around him. My son seemed at home in this world, this forest, and his fever had let up a little.

Initially it was hard-going. The trees locked fingers above our heads, making a dismal, ink-black tunnel for our trip. Branches swung back at us, prickles stung us, roots caught at our ankles. But eventually the forest started to clear; the trees grew more spacious, the path wider, more pronounced. It was like the path was leading

us on, wanting us to travel. A yellow moon was visible now, inter-
mittently, between the branches. It cast a pale shimmer on the
leaves. A pack of dogs were howling at the moon; we could hear
the terrible baying of them through the trees. Belinda wanted to
hang back on account of Jewel, but Coyote was already parting the
tangled, ebony fronds of a fern and then stepping through into a
luminous glade. We could only but follow.

The pack of dogs were there for us, waiting. At our sight they
rushed towards each other, forming their various shapes into one
terrible body, which licked and snarled at the air. Each of its mighty
jaws dribbled black venom. Snakes slithered through its steely fur.
Dog shit covered the ground in a smoking carpet. Beyond the jaws
of this beast lay an ornamental wrought-iron gate embedded in a
thick growth of pine trees. The fifty-headed dog growled at us, and
then lunged forward, foam dripping from its array of teeth.

'Jesus!' Belinda fell back, taking Jewel with her.

'What want, dog-head?' Coyote asked.

'My name is Cerberus. I'm the guardian of the forest.' One of
the many heads came close up to Coyote's face, spat some juice at
him, and then said, 'Flour. Flour and honey. Honey and flour. Cakes
of honey and flour? Got any?'

Coyote turned to us: 'Anybody got cakes of flour and honey?'

We shook our head.

'Got anything?' the beast growled.

'Naked totality, dog-head,' Coyote answered.

Dog-head snarled viciously, whipping his faces around like a
fairground ride.

Coyote growled back at Cerberus. 'I've got a set of teeth
made out of Manchester's maps. You want to take a chance?'

'We'll take anything.'

Coyote snapped forward and dug his teeth into the leader
dog's neck.

Cerberus howled like a dog from Hell. And then composed

himself into a puppified picture of calm. 'That will do.' Whimpering.
'Pass through to the next gate.' And then the mighty creature dis-
solved into its separate parts: a humiliated pack of wolves that
slinked off into the darkness, leaving the glade clear for moonlight
and travellers.

Coyote opened the iron gates at the far side of the clearing
and we entered a bleak pine forest. The air was sharp with the tang
of resin, hard needles crunching under our feet. We were walking a
well-defined path between the tree trunks. The path curved like a
snake, so that we lost all sense of direction. But still, the sense of
being led.

We could hear the sound of water slowly lapping ahead of us,
and eventually the tree-line gave way to an immense lake of purple
water. Fronds of violet mist were playing in half-human shapes over
the surface. We were standing on the lake's blackened shore,
watching the moon reflecting in gold on the ripples. At the centre of
the lake a small island held a creamy bandstand. Amidst its flowered
columns a brass band was playing a deathly, mutated version of the
national anthem, *Ferry Across the Mersey*. This is the land that I love,
and here I'll stay, until my dying day. Shards of brassy light were
catching on the trombones and the trumpets as they blew. Beyond
the bandstand, over on the other side of the lake, glimmers of light
could be seen in the sky, as though shining from distant eyes. In
front of us a rowing boat was knocking gently against the boards of
a weed-covered jetty. In its bow stood a black-cowled figure, as
long and as thin as the boat itself. 'Good evening, my deathly travellers,' this figure announced in a cracked voice. 'Welcome to Juniper
Suction. Lost your way in the dark, have you? Well, well, never
mind. Quite understandable in these parts.'

Coyote asked him his name.

'My name is Charon,' he replied. 'I am the ferryman of Lake
Acheron. Presumably you are seeking passage?' Coyote said that we
were. 'Oh splendid, I do love a good passage! Have you your obo-

lus?' Coyote looked at us, we looked back. Coyote asked the ferryman what an obolus was. 'What's an obolus!?' His voice was
spluttering now. 'An obolus! Don't tell me they didn't . . . you mean
to say . . . they didn't put an obolus in your mouth . . . when you
died? Your relatives? Oh dear, that is most unfortunate. Most unfortunate. How in hell's name did you get past Cerberus?' Coyote told
him that Cerberus the many-headed dog had wanted hardly anything for the passage. 'Hardly anything! Outrageous. I shall have to
have words. Really, this is against all the rules.' Coyote asked
Charon if an obolus was like a cab-fare. Charon looked puzzled, so
Coyote explained to him what a cab-fare was. 'Yes! That's it! Exactly. A cab-fare. An obolus is a fare. Now we are finally getting
somewhere. So, have you a fare, an obolus? Really, they should have
placed one in your mouths. One silver coin worth exactly one sixth
of a drachma. Any luck?' Coyote shook his head. 'Anything at all
then? Anything to give as a . . . as a cab-fare? Anything?'

Jewel slithered down Belinda's body and then clambered between Charon's legs into the body of the boat.

'Hang on a second,' Charon squealed. 'What's that lump doing
in my vessel?'

'He's hitching a ride,' Coyote answered.

'Well get him out of there!'

'Do it yourself.'

Charon made a move towards Jewel, but that zombified son
of mine had melted his shape into the boat's shape. He could not
be removed. The boat rocked like crazy. Charon nearly fell into the
water. 'This episode is getting on my nerves,' he squealed.

'Get rid of the hitcher,' Coyote said. 'Or else take all of us.'

Charon looked up and down the shore, as though nervous,
and then said, 'Oh, very well then. Hop in! Quickly, quickly! Before
somebody sees. Really, it's too much, giving passage for no payment.
No flaming cab-fare! Do you think I can run a business like this?
Well, do you?!'

So it was that we came to be, the four of us, passengers on board a thin blade of a boat that threaded its way through thick, sluggish water. The moon was the only light, an orb of pollen shaded by the mist that danced around our journey. The twin oars of Charon made the only sound, apart from the muted ballad that crawled from the central island. The band played the same song over and over, slowed down to a dirge, as though playing that tune was some kind of dire punishment. Charon was sitting in the stern, skeletal hands peeking out from his cowl, each clenched around an oar. He worked the water effortlessly, despite his evident lack of strength. Coyote was in the bow, Belinda in the middle of the boat, myself inside Belinda, and Jewel peering over the edge of the vessel, looking down into the water. He made a sneeze, just a slight one. He was definitely feeling better, that was obvious. But what would he be like when we got back to the real world? Wouldn't his fever come back then? And maybe even the worse for this journey? And where was the real world anyway? I had only dim memories of what I had been. The Vurt was working on my Shadow, erasing the feelings. Everything was very calm, very still and timeless. The moon, the lake, the darkness, the sound of the oars, the sad-hearted tune of brass. The wraiths in the mist. Belinda's hand was trailing in the water . . .

'Please!' Charon cried. 'No touching the lake. Thank you.'

'Why not?' Belinda asked.

'Because it might eat you.'

Belinda's hand moved back to safety, and it wasn't until we were over halfway across, and the brass band was just a soft trail of whispers in the past, that she spoke again. 'Coyote?' she said. 'Any idea what's going on here?'

'This is a story riding,' Coyote answered. 'The story of dog-many-head. The story of water-cab-driver. The garden will be black and deep-rivered. Little Sir John is waiting. I can feel him waiting for us.'

The ferryman pulled us to shore. 'This is the drop-off point, Belinda,' Coyote said. 'Are you staying cool?' I made Belinda affirm her coolness, and then we clambered out of the boat. Jewel climbed back into Belinda's arms. Coyote turned to Charon: 'You'll keep the clock running?' he asked. The ferryman spat into the lake and then replied, as though he knew exactly what Coyote was saying, 'Nobody comes back, buddy. There ain't no return trips.' The boatman laughed, and then pushed off from the quay.

Quietness falling over us.

Only the faint gasp of each oar entering and then leaving the water, entering and leaving, until the waves died down into stillness. The brass band a frosty shimmer in the air, and then fading to silence. The moon sliding behind a cloud.

Darkness. Darkness was a breathing flower.

In front of us the high wall of a hedgerow. It grew to twice our combined heights and above its tall ramparts we could see pale light shining in the air. Belinda told Coyote to grow himself taller than the tallest plant, and to just *peer* over that wall of flowers. He snarled at her for a second and then tried it. Even before he was halfway to the top, the plants closed in, forcing his body downwards. After the fifth attempt he gave up and told Belinda that the story didn't want him to see above the trees.

'You're pissing me off, Coyote.' Belinda said. 'I really thought you could take us through.'

Coyote was silent for just a moment, as his nose petals worked the scent-paths. Then he set off walking, choosing the left-hand route, skirting the hedge. The three of us followed him, all bungled up together. Ages, we travelled, or so it seemed. Time was malleable. It could have been merely seconds. Eventually we came to an opening in the wall. Or the wall opened up for us. Or we opened up for the wall.

Whatever. Something happened. Something happened slowly, too slow for thought. A dark space between two worlds. A night path between hedgerows. We looked down into black mirrors; paths bled off from paths, like wayward sentences in a convoluted tale. Fireflies flickered through the gaps between words, between leaves.

'Needing the A–Z of maze-map, Belinda,' Coyote said.

Belinda told him that we should just keep moving: 'Like, what the fuck? Let's chance it.'

Wandering lost through the knot garden of a thousand flowers, a thousand cuttings and corners. Every blind alley ending in darkness, studded with the warm blur of fireflies. The moon came back, peeking out from behind a ragged cloud, showing us just how lost we were.

'Don't you know about labyrinths?' Belinda asked. Coyote shook his petals. 'Well, you know, I thought you would. Jesus, aren't you supposed to the best-ever cab-driver. What's wrong with you?'

'Belinda, you're starting to get on my nerves,' Coyote petal-growled.

'I mean, aren't we supposed to take every left turn, or something? Or maybe pick up a thread of gold. Follow a trail of bits of bread or something. Something like that? Or maybe we just wander around in circles forever? Is that the key? Well?'

Coyote had no answers for us. Twice we arrived back at the entrance way. Each time we set off again, this time hoping for a new route. You have to picture this clearly: a nude girl with a map tattooed on her body, a dog-plant whose very bones were roads, a Shadowcop passenger with infinite knowledge of the bad routes to take, a Limbo-child who had found a forbidden way back to life. And all of us lost in a simple garden maze. And when the moon tucked itself back behind a new cloud, and the garden was tainted with fog, and the hedgerows were closing in tighter around us, what could we do but fall despondent? Belinda was starting to protest now, about how Jewel was weighing heavy on her shoulders. But just then, one more turning to the left, a light could be seen. There was an opening in the hedge some few feet away, and the pale wavery light was shining through the gap. We rushed towards it, hoping for a . . .

The lake stretched out in front of us. A third time. The moon, the same moon. The same lake. The same old tune from the bandstand. Not heard, just felt; dust motes in the air. We turned back to the maze. The same dark-breathed mouth was waiting there.

'Cab-Dung!' was Coyote's cry.

'I thought we were part of this story?' Belinda said.

'The green-road keeps changing, is what.' Coyote's eyes were hooded with leaves. 'The map is too fluid, it keeps changing every step we make. There's no clear way through . . .'

A firefly glittered, zooming from petal to petal, and then set off in a lantern flight into the knot garden. 'Catch that fly, Coyote,' I made Belinda say. Coyote sent out a nimble-twigged branch, caught the fly in his soft petals. His Dalmatian flower was illuminated.

'Maybe we're following the wrong flower,' I said through my daughter's voice. Inside I had drawn the connection between that firefly's flight and the way in which my Shadow had worked in the new Manchester map. You must always follow the fire. Coyote let loose the shining insect. It flickered away into the hedgerow. We set off at a pretty pace after the darting flame. Corner to corner we ran, curve to curve. Following. The hot path of small wings, a fiery map. Jewel was struggling to keep a hold of Belinda's neck, so quickly we were moving now. Left, and then left again. And then left. And then left. Left again, tracing the fire through the darkness. And again left. And left once more. Left from there. Left at the next turning. Left again. Left. And then left. Left, left, left. Turning and twisting. Left, and then right, just the once. And then once more, to the left, a final left, and then . . .

Cupid pissing.

A stone baby perched on an ornamental fountain, dribbling

into a pool of green stagnant water. Small willy in tiny fingers. Thin trickle of water from the carved penis. Small, stubby wings sprouting from his bleached shoulder blades.

The centre of the labyrinth. A common or garden fountain in a circle of flowers. No grand palace. No John Barleycorn. No way through. Only the soft trickle of water flowing over stone, over lunar shadows, over faint gaspings for breath. The wind playing, gentle at the pool.

The firefly headed directly for the cupid's flow, got drenched there, and then fell, wings sodden, into the algae.

'What now, Big Dog?' asked Belinda.

'We follow.'

It was simple. We follow. We take a drink from that fountain. We follow Coyote who was already dipping his face into the piss stream. Drinking. Jewel jumped from Belinda's shoulders, straight into the pool, and then opened a wound in his soft flesh, so that the urine could find a river.

'You're all still here,' Belinda said.

'Maybe waiting,' Coyote answered, his petals bright under moonshine. 'Maybe Barleycorn is still waiting. Let all passengers drink.'

It took some doing, Belinda so reluctant, but eventually I forced her along the Shadow, to step into the water. Our naked feet cold from the bath. Pushing her mouth into the urine. Drinking deep, drinking. And then the tiny sculptured penis growing to a monstrous size. Hands of stone. Two strong hands, one on each shoulder, forcing Belinda's mouth towards the fat bulb of the cock, which was now turning into soft and purple longings . . .

Belinda falling head first into the pool of darkness, her lips quenched by piss.

Golden showers . . .

Tuesday
9 May

olden showers . . . rain dripping onto a plate of meat. Belinda was sitting at a large, square table laden with fruit and flesh. She was pushing a fork into a thick, barely cooked steak. The meat was alive with pink worms. In Belinda's other hand a knife, with which she sliced off a portion. And as that meat touched her tongue I came alive to her insides from my fountain-fall, feeling the juices flowing, and the worms moving over her lips. It took all my Shadow-power to force my daughter's hand away from her mouth. *Don't touch the meat, my sweet. Don't eat.*

It was raining inside.

I looked through my daughter's eyes.

Where were we? This room . . .

Its walls faded into the distance, patterned with mist. A slight drizzle fell from the ceiling. Yellow droplets. Clouds were partly obscuring the chandelier. The light was buzzing with static, electric blue. The noise of flies, hungry for flesh. Lichen grew on the wet surface of the table. Maggots were scrambling through the blue cheese, and worms were in the meat. Pewter mugs of heavy wine were set beside each plate. I was resting my Shadow inside Belinda, who was sitting at one side of the table. She was dressed now in a velvet gown. Coyote was sitting at our left-hand side, digging in with slack jaws to a plate of raw pork. Jewel was perched on the table itself, lapping with a fat tongue at a bowl of sour-creamed rice. How sad it made me to see them eating, and how useless. To eat in the Underworld, didn't that mean staying there, forever? Wasn't that the story? Persephone the flower girl was sitting cross-legged on the table, leafing through a stolen A–Z map of Manchester. Its pages were sodden, rain-dappled. To my right, an empty chair. Opposite Belinda and myself, across the vast reaches of the table, sat a young man with shining midnight blue hair and skin the colour of soot.

'Good day to you, Madam Jones,' he pronounced in a velvet voice. 'Welcome to the feast.'

'I can't move. Why can't I move?'

'I trust you had a pleasant journey? I took the liberty of covering your daughter's nakedness. After all, it is your own nakedness now.'

I tried to get Belinda to her feet. Her body felt like lead.

'You are here at my bequest, and you will leave when I have finished with you. I cannot guarantee the state you will be in. Welcome to Juniper Suction, my travellers.'

Neither Coyote nor Belinda seemed to respond to his overtures, and I realised then that the man was speaking only to me; his voice of soot was drifting over the Shadow. 'Quite right, Madam Jones,' he responded. 'How astute. The others are helplessly in my control now. There remains only your good self. But I see that your given name is Sibyl. Yes. Splendid! I like that. A nice touch.'

'You're John Barleycorn?' I asked. 'I saw your face on that snake in the forest.'

'I must thank you for the safe return of my wife.' He smiled at the young girl on the table.

'We didn't bring her.'

'My dear Persephone can be very resourceful. But, how rude of me. You were enquiring about my name. I think, in your country, they call me Fiery Jack? Is that correct? Or else Jack O'Lantern. Or else the devil himself, Satan, the serpent. Hades. Ah, the endless bounty of the human imagination; it finally comes to rest in a few chosen words. Sir John Barleycorn.' He savoured each syllable as though each was a piece of fine meat. 'John Barleycorn. Yes, that is my favoured name. I am your very own god of fermentation, the spirit of death and rebirth in the soil. I am your wine. Really, the stories you people come up with. But does it matter? Names are for small humans. Does a flower know its name?'

Once again I tried to make Belinda stand up from the table, but some darker, stronger force was hindering me.

'Where the fuck do you think you're going?' Barleycorn's eyes burned into my daughter's flesh.

'You have no right to keep me from . . .'

'Please. Don't . . . try . . . to do . . . anything. You will only cause me to . . .'

His gaze was hurting me.

'I must apologize, madam . . .' A little light returned to his eyes. '. . . for my previous remark. It is most ungentlemanly to swear at the dinner table.'

'You have a powerful Shadow, Mr. Barleycorn . . .' I was trying to please him, to gain time.

'I thank you for the compliment. Unfortunately, you will never please me, Sibyl, and you will never gain time. Yes, I know every little thought, every pathetic, human emotion that travels through your skull. But really . . . I am whatever you want me to be. To Coyote I'm a dog-flower king. To Jewel I'm a good father. To Belinda, a good lover. For all their wilfulness, they make rather easy targets, I'm afraid. Look at them. Can you not see how easily controlled they are? Helpless within my grasp. Finally, after long years of struggle, I get some real living, breathing *humans* to converse with, and they turn out to be mere playthings. Perhaps you will prove yourself a worthier guest. My dear Sibyl, whatever shall I be for you? I was quite fascinated, you know, by your presence in the forest some days ago. I've always wanted to talk to a . . . erm . . . to a *Dodo*. This is the correct phrase, I believe? Or maybe you would prefer Unbeknownst?'

'I haven't come here to talk.'

'*You* haven't come here for anything. You are here because I deemed it so. Now please, stop struggling, and pay me some re-spect. After all, I'm one your greatest creations.'

'You have to stop the fever, Barleycorn. People are dying.'

'Sibyl, I do believe you're lying to me. You no longer have any interest in the outside world, in *reality*. People!' He breathed the word as though it were a curse. 'It is your son—this ugly, little swine who now dines at my expense—it is he that you want to save.'

'Yes . . .'

'Louder, please, and more pronounced.'

'Yes. Please don't let my Jewel die.'

Barleycorn smiled. 'It is quite remarkable, your journey. No, really. To save your daughter like that. To give yourself up to her. Such a long fall it must have been. Belinda was quite ready to meet her death.'

'What gives you the right to interfere with human life?'

'Did you not enjoy the entertainments, Sibyl? The fifty-headed dog? The boatman? The brass band? The knot garden? Of course you did. You had fun working your way through the puzzles. This is an unexpected pleasure for me, you must realise that. I ordered Coyote to bring my wife back, and he brings along some . . . 'extra luggage' I believe he calls it? Well, I'm glad. It gets very lonely sometimes. I just want to entertain you, Sibyl, as best I can, in the tradition to which you are accustomed. After all, isn't that why you invented me? Now eat. Enjoy the repast.'

He scooped up a portion of meat with his bare hands and placed it against his tongue. I could feel the hunger in Belinda's mind, but she was in my control now; my daughter would go hungry for a while yet. She was captured here, as were Jewel and Coyote. I was the only one still resisting Barleycorn's charm. I could not even speak to my daughter any more. I took the opportunity to study John Barleycorn. He really was very beautiful . . .

Tight, dark skin revealing perfect bones. Eyes of night, filled with a silken weariness. A thin blade of a nose. Pinched nostrils. Thick, glistening hair which he now pushed a grease-stained hand through. A carefully trimmed goatee beard. A tailored jacket the colour of ink. Crisp white shirt. A bootlace tie knotted with a skull and crossbones amulet. Late twenties, early thirties. He had the look of a predator, but I knew this was only Belinda's projection. Full, sullen lips, perfect for love, a bruised love.

'Shall we now praise that mysterious process,' Barleycorn announced, 'whereby the fruit of the vine is changed into wine, which, in turn, transports the human mind to a more exciting realm. Let us drink.' He raised his glass and we all followed suit, even young Jewel and Persephone; I could feel the blood-red wine dripping down my daughter's throat. Too late, too late . . . I was too late to stop her from swallowing. How strong was this wine? How could I escape its river of warmth and comfort?

Coyote slobbered into his plate. Jewel sneezed into his bowl, and then laughed, delighted. Belinda guzzled down the wine.

John Barleycorn had a hold on us. A spell had been cast.

'Yes, a spell *has* been cast,' he said, reaching deep into my Shadow for knowledge. 'I'm so glad you could make it this far, my dear Sibyl. You cannot believe how lonely it gets, inside these feathers. These stories . . . they are like dungeons. And to have *human* company, if only of a tepid kind. Really . . . it is most delightful.'

Coyote and Jewel were fighting over a piece of steak, and Belinda was just in love with the party. I felt I was the last voice of reason. The rain was falling over Belinda's mapped-out skull.

'I would like to be free, of course,' Barleycorn continued. 'Free from the tale. This is why I sent Persephone and her fever to you. You think I enjoy this? You think I like being trapped here? You really believe I like being just a part of one of your petty tales?'

'Persephone is a murderer.'

'Is that the word? Murderer? Of course you mortals hold such store by it. Life, I mean. And the clinging on to it. Oh dear, how you love to cling. Really, it gets quite tiresome. Have you ever heard a plant complaining about death?'

Persephone slithered over the table towards Barleycorn's lap. Once settled there, she ran her fingers through his hair. Shining blue like dark lanterns, his hair seemed to be *moving*. A thick glistening strand of it rose into the air, and then settled on the pink steak in front of him. It was feeding, his hair was feeding! Barleycorn's hands were wandering over Persephone's body, the left to the budding breasts, the right hand reaching down between her legs. Persephone was giggling.

I pushed Belinda's plate aside: 'I don't know how you can eat this. It's rotten.'

The man's eyes were catching black fire: 'Oh I am sorry. I like my meat well hung and raw. Sibyl, my dear, I assumed you would have the same tastes . . .'

I didn't answer. No smile, no laughter.

'Coyote certainly seems to be enjoying his meal,' Barleycorn continued, looking over to where the dog was guzzling down another pink lump of pork. 'Yes, your friend would make a fine guardian. I mean, old Cerberus, well he's a little . . . a little *creaky* these days. You noticed? But I want to tell you about my penetration. I've got the wanderlust, you see, the need to infect. The need to be the teller, not the tale. There is a slight problem. If I should ever leave this Vurt-story of Juniper Suction, this tale shall fade into a sad ending. Miss Hobart herself wrote this into the feather's workings. She wanted to make sure that every story had its centre. My great desire for your world will be eternally unrequited. I mean, who would invite the devil to dinner? So, I had this idea that I could send something into your world, and who better to travel than my own dear, sweet wife, Persephone? And from her seed would a thousand, million tales grow forth, and all of them my children.'

'You're scared of me, aren't you, Sir John?'

He paused in his breath for a moment. For the first time he

actually seemed to be considering something that I had said. I wasn't going to let this go. 'You're scared of me because I'm a Dodo,' I said to him. 'You can't infect me with your stories. You can't harm me.'

'Your life's story will end in your death.' He smiled then, before continuing: 'Whereas, the more stories that you tell, the longer that we of the dream world shall live. And whilst your sorry flesh decays and dies, we of the dream shall never die. There will always be another mouth to feed. A story is like food, is it not? Food for the tongue. And a tongue should be well hung. What are you planning to do, Sibyl? What is your purpose in coming here?'

'I want to destroy you.'

'And how would you do that?'

'I want to destroy you for the pain you've brought to my world, my friends . . .'

'How would you kill a dream? It would be like killing your own head. There's no way out, Sibyl. I am a tasty story that your ancestors once dreamt. The story of the world under the world. Of your fear of death. Out of that fear you made me. Oh, it was quite simple in the early days. Stories were told, and then they vanished. Into breath.' He took another drink of wine before continuing. 'I do believe this blood-hued elixir to be the very first example of Vurt. Only through its transformations could your ancestors imagine another world beyond the everyday. From the gulp of wine flowed the books and the pictures, the cinema, the television—all the ways of capture. And with Miss Hobart, and the feathers, the Vurt, and the shared dream of it all, now we live on. The tale has turned. The stories keep growing, even when you're not telling them. We no longer need to be told. And one day we will tell ourselves. The dream will live. This is why I brought the fever to your world. I want a grip on the world. I want to *infect* you with my love.'

Something very strange happened then, if I can use the word *strange* in such a context. Four bullets appeared out of nowhere at the far end of the dining room. They travelled slowly along the line of the table, missing each of us. They crept through the air above the fourth and empty chair, and then vanished into the mist. John Barleycorn watched their passage with disgust. 'You know, it really angers me when people do that,' he said. 'Firing bullets in the Vurt. Don't people realise that those bullets are just going to travel through every tale until they find a worthwhile target? Nothing is lost in a story, only exchanged. That was Columbus's seat. He was invited to the feast. What can I do? Such rudeness.'

The slow drift of the bullets brought me back to task. 'Please . . . you have seduced my children and my city with your love . . . but can you not save my son?'

Barleycorn sighed. 'Here we are, inside my golden palace. Which lies inside the garden. Which lies within the dream, the story. The story inside the Heaven Feathers. Inside the Vurt world, which is contained by reality. We are nestled within story within story, and all you can squeal about is the life and death of your firstborn. Really, Sibyl, I expected more from you.'

'There isn't any more. That's my story. Give me back my child.'

Barleycorn waved my words aside. 'Having succeeded in releasing the dream from the body, Miss Hobart realised that the body was mere vessel. Dreams could live on in the Vurt; the body could die. *Et voila!* Heaven Feathers. If you have the resources, these days . . . well then, death is no longer the end for mere humans. Your dreams can live on in a choice of settings, worlds, religions. A choice of stories. This is where Miss Hobart herself lives now, having died many years ago. She lives on in the heavenly Vurt. Nobody knows where, of course. She has chosen her own safe and secret story.'

'Please . . . cure this fever.' I was becoming desperate. 'Cure my Jewel.'

Barleycorn swept aside his mug of wine and brought his fist down onto the table. 'Will you not have done with your pathetic desperation?!' His voice was scalding, and the look in his eyes burned deep. 'Is this all you can desire? Is it? A life for your death-riddled child? What's wrong with you? Please...show me some strength.'

'This is what humans want, Barleycorn.' I said it coldly. 'They live on in their children. Your stories are children. Our children are *our* stories.'

Barleycorn breathed harshly, bringing himself back down from anger. He looked deep into Belinda's eyes. 'My father was called Cronus, Sibyl,' he said. 'He was the clockmaker, the maker of Time. He did not want me born. This is where *my* particular story begins. A fortune teller had told Cronus that his children would kill him one day. My, how seriously he took that cheap trick. He killed off my older brothers and sisters at birth. He swallowed them. Myself also, he swallowed. It was only by sheer cunning that I managed to live on inside my father's stomach. That stomach of soft tickings and tockings, the days measured out in drips. Juice was flowing down into darkness, marking off each moment. It was very like dying, I suppose, but I managed my escape from death. I was reborn. Can I be blamed because you humans have not yet managed that task?'

'Some of us are doing it,' I answered.

Barleycorn's eyes turned onto some distant scene, far off through the rain.

'This story of yours,' I continued. 'It sounds like—'

'This story of *mine!* How dare you?' He had turned on me suddenly, his face twisted with pain. 'You think I make this up? *You* make it up. This is your story, Sibyl, and all of your sorry kind. What puny stories you tell, at the same time insisting that we be happy with our lives within their confines.'

'We created you.'

'Yes. Oh yes. And one day we will leave you behind. Can you blame us, can you really, if we desire to carry on? To be better than you?'

'All I want is a cure for my son.'

Barleycorn looked at me for a second, and then away, his eyes flooding into sadness again. 'Miss Hobart is so disappointed. She really is. Now there is a human being worthy of the name. A true creator.'

John Barleycorn fell silent. He sighed and then looked at me again. And when next he spoke, it was with a heavy, saddened voice: 'Wandering for all those years alone, inside my father's dark stomach, what could I do but think about escape? And having made my escape, what else could I do but plunge myself into the dark earth? I made my life below the earth, feeding off the roots. Lonely, so very lonely. Until I heard a young girl's feet scampering over my ceiling of grass. I reached up towards her, overcome with desire. I made her my own. My flowering bride. I fed her with pomegranate seeds, in order to keep her faithful. Isn't that so, my sweetness?'

Persephone's long, purple tongue was licking at John Barleycorn's neck. His hair shifted slightly, of its own accord, buzzing hair, in order to give her access. The young man smiled, his eyes closed in pleasure. Time moved slowly whilst the girl lapped at the dark skin. Thin rain was falling onto the table, making pools of water between the dishes of food. Worms were moving through wet meat that Coyote, lost to the spell, shovelled into his jaws. Jewel crunched on a wriggling beetle he had found in his creamed rice, the moisture running off his greasy skin. Belinda's head: I could feel the rain flowing through the streets of Central Manchester, and then running down her neck, along her body under the robe. I tried once again to make her body stand but the weight was overbearing. Belinda shivered, and with the shivering John Barleycorn's eyes opened again, this time fuelled with dark hatred. 'Persephone's mother was very angry, of course,' he said. 'Very angry. Her precious daughter, and all that shit. Pardon my language, Sibyl, but Demeter deserves the cruellest words. She wanted her prize back. Demeter was so angry that she sent a deadly flower to your world, making the ground as dry and as cold as her own heart. Of course, you've met Persephone's mother, Demeter?'

I told him that we hadn't.

'You have, you have! Keep listening. That poisonous flower she sent to you, you called it Thanatos, I believe.'

'Thanatos came from the Vurt?' I asked.

'A good name, if I may be allowed? *Thanatos.* The god of death. Of course you are quite *au fait* with Death, am I right, Sibyl? Oh yes. Quite enamoured. Your mother, for instance. That putrid corpse. Your father's cock, stinking from a graveyard fuck. The Shadow inside you, which is the soft kiss of death. This half-dead son of yours. Your daughter's suicide, which was a love affair. Your own long fall from that hotel window. And look at you now, pretending at life, inside a dead puppet you still dare to call by the name of daughter. How else have I allowed you access this far into the Vurt? Thanatos and Sibyl, I now pronounce you man and wife . . .'

He laughed. It made me angry. Also, the feeling of having journeyed so far and all for nothing; the frustration of being totally controlled by that which you foolishly believed you could one day destroy. 'I don't want my son to die,' I cried. 'There has been too much suffering.'

'Ah yes, of course. I was forgetting—the mother's love for her children. The suffering. The urge towards resurrection. They will do anything, anything . . .'

Persephone had climbed from his lap, back onto the table. She was now stroking at Jewel's puckered skin, whispering tendrils falling over damp hide. Barleycorn was gazing sweetly at his wife, his voice speaking over the soft drizzle of indoor rain. 'Her mother wanted her back, of course,' he said. 'And the plague that Demeter sent to England . . . well, to be honest . . . it quite pleased me. I was never a lover of life, as such, for how could I love that which had served me so barbarously? It was Miss Hobart that changed me. Yes, she came to visit. It was first time I had ever seen her. Of course one had heard stories, rumours: she was the original creator, the maker of the feathers, the bringer of joy. The first dreamer. To meet her in the flesh, so to speak, well it was altogether too much. What could I do but give in? The strangest thing, she thought I was more powerful than her. Imagine, if you can, God saying that Adam was more powerful, you will understand my feelings. I allowed Miss Hobart access to pluck a green feather from one of the birds that flew in Demeter's forest. Fecundity 10 you called that solution. A terrible name, may I be so bold? But the wonders it created. And so we agreed, according to the story, my wife would spend two-thirds of the year with her mother, only one-third with me. And so the seasons were made. Isn't that more than fair?' Barleycorn laughed then, briefly, his hair rising from his head into a smiling wave of deep blue smoke. He stood up from his seat and walked around the table to stand behind me. I could feel his hands resting on Belinda's shoulders from behind, the fingers gently massaging my despair. I could neither move nor speak just then; the devil had my soul in his grasp. I could smell burning. I could hear the buzzing of the flies. I could sense his voice penetrating my Shadow . . .

'Because I was tired,' he sighed to me. 'This is why the pollen came to visit. Because I was tired of being only *told*. I want to live, Sibyl. Like yourself. I want a flesh and blood life. A life of surprises, a life of pain. A life ending in death. I am jealous, yes, I admit it. Death means so much to your species. Without it where would you be? Death is your fuel, the parent of your desires, your art. I want to feel that hunger, but Miss Hobart has deemed it so that I must remain forever in the dream. I must never die.' His hands were now stroking at Belinda's skull-map. 'Persephone was my attempt at death-after-life. There will be other attempts, and from more powerful demons. The Vurt will one day make an entrance. Come, let me show you the future . . .'

Barleycorn curled his fingers around my daughter's neck, squeezed, hard and gently, and then brought his wine-red lips down to brush tenderly against her neck.

And then he bit me.

The bite travelled right through Belinda's flesh until it had a hold on my Shadow's breath. Barleycorn tugged at my smoke with his mind so harshly that I actually bled away from Belinda's flesh. My amorphous Shadow danced around the room at the bequest of John Barleycorn. I felt dissipated and homeless. Blown apart. Barleycorn played with my shapes for a few seconds, displaying his effortless power, until finally letting me coalesce into a perfect, imagined sculpture of smoke; a younger woman's body I now became, ripe and lovely in her curves but composed only from the grey swirling wisps of my unleashed Shadow. I looked down at my daughter's empty flesh. 'Don't worry about her,' Barleycorn said to me. 'She will be looked after until we return.' And with a single wave of Barleycorn's hands the dining room vanished into hot, shimmering air. I was transported by his wishes to a small clearing amidst the tangled entrails of a jungle.

'This is *my* vision of the new world, Sibyl,' John Barleycorn said, now moving through the verdant growth like a slow, cool warrior. 'Columbus has got the future totally wrong. This is *my* Manchester, my picture of what it will be. Regard it well.'

All around us, as I struggled to keep up with the dream-creature, a myriad of strange characters were fighting and dancing and kissing amidst the trees and the flowers. The Grendel was there, Achilles was there, Robin Hood was there, Gargantua and Pantagruel were there, Vladimir and Estragon were there, Tom Jones was there, Humbert Humbert was there, Popeye the Sailor Man was there, the Spiderman was there, Jane Eyre was there, Dave Bowman was there, Eleanor Rigby was there, Jesus Christ and the Tin Man were there, Leopold Bloom and Rupert the Bear were there; all the fictional characters of human endeavour were planted in that green world, and all of them were tumbling and loving and cussing in a story-go-round of intimate chaos.

Whilst being clutched at by various rampant dreams including Sherlock Holmes and the Famous Five and King Lear and Mickey

Mouse and Joseph K and the Venus de Milo and Dick Dastardly and
Mutley and Holly Golightly, I was also aware of the John Barleycorn
figure turning around to ease my Shadow-flesh through the clutches
of a network of story-blades.

'This is the world I am struggling to bring forth,' Barleycorn
said to me. 'A globe of stories infecting reality. In these stories my
children will live forever and, who knows, perhaps one day they
shall die in peace, at last . . . at last . . . like normal.' He paused then
for a moment as the elaborate jungle-narrative spun a covering of
flowers around us. And then off he stepped towards a glimmer of
light in the distance. 'Come quickly, my dear Sibyl,' he urged. 'The
gates to the city are just ahead. Quickly, quickly. There's somebody
I want you to meet. Can you not be more nimble, Sibyl?'

He took hold of my hand.

The story took hold of reality's hand, imagine.

I tried my best against the weight of the engulfing stories, and
eventually we came to the vine-wrapped iron gates. It was only then
that I placed myself, these being the very gates to Alexandra Park
where first I had seen Coyote's body. I followed Barleycorn through
the gates out onto the streets of Moss Side. But the jungle en-
croached all over the streets, making a dense canopy for the deserted shops and houses. Here and there a few humans could be
seen, a few dogs and robos, but mostly the tree-roads were occu-
pied by characters from fiction. It was as though Manchester had
transformed itself into a tropical paradise in which the usual exotic
birds and animals had been replaced by figments from the human
mind. What was the nature of this world? Was I moving through
Barleycorn's mind, visiting through the Shadow the dream of a
dream? Can a dream really dream? And whilst walking along these
dreamt-about streets I took the chance to examine this body of
smoke that Barleycorn had fashioned for me. I was a random map
of shadows formed into grey shapes: hips and breasts, neckline and
stomach worlds. And in the pit of my stomach there rested a

glistening black beetle of carefully folded wings, waving legs and antennae, crunching jaws: the Dodo insect. The dream-eater. That presence within me that stopped the dream from entering my system. Never before had I seen the Dodo in my flesh, and I felt that I could almost reach inside myself to pluck out that offending creature.

Barleycorn was now kneeling down into a patch of street-flowers. He plucked a crimson specimen free from the ragged pavement-bouquet and then came back up to face me, holding the flower aloft. 'Of course I didn't pause to consider the Dodos,' he said. 'The non-dreamers. Take a look at this future-flower.'

I saw a flower that was being eaten away at the roots by a viral worm of great appetite; the worm's name was Black Dodo. I realised then that the Dodo insect in my stomach—once upon a time, my curse—could now be my saviour.

'I *am* scared of you, Sibyl,' Barleycorn whispered with sad breath, as though confirming my thoughts, 'and all of your closed-up kind. I never believed that so few could have such an effect upon the dream. I imagined the real world opening up to me quite easily, but then I got word of your struggle, and Belinda's struggle. And then my sweet wife became ill from your world. I had to call her back home. That's fine, no problem, her job is completed; the seed is planted and Columbus is still making a way through for the pollen, but the dream cannot yet make a life in reality, not truly. Not completely. Maybe one day . . .' He sighed then, again, and again, and breathily. 'It saddens me, you know? This whole thing . . . do you really believe I wanted to cause you harm? No, I wanted us to work together. The dream and the real. As you can witness all around you now, a new world, a good and fruitful world is to be made out of the joining. This is my vision, Sibyl. What can I do? You Dodos are like the sting of a wasp. Moments of blindness in the stories. I would have to kill you all to make my vision complete. I would have to kill the dreamless ones.'

And whilst he was saying this to me, I leached a tiny portion of my Shadow into my internal Dodo beetle. There a small part of my soul now rested, hopefully cut off from Barleycorn's province. Now I was further split; in the Shadow and the Dodo I now lived.

'I think your story is very sad, Sir John,' I said with my Shadow whilst, at the same time, with my Dodo-self I told him that his precious wife was nothing more than a cheap, nasty, murderous slut.

'Truly, truly sad,' Barleycorn answered my Shadow. 'Just a sad story told by a sad human one day, far ago, in the face of death. But still, a glimpse has been given. We may yet find paradise.'

So the Dodo-barrier seemed to be holding. I tried again to insult his wife from the folds of my stomach beetle. Nothing. No response to my bile.

'Whatever can you hold against paradise?' he asked, instead.

'The fact that people must die for its birth.' Knowing inside that now I had a dark place of my own that Barleycorn could never reach.

'But the human race *invented* this concept,' he snarled. 'Your history is grave-pitted with the bodies of those who gave their lives for the greater good. Nearly all of your stories are based upon this moment of sacrifice . . . and yet how you complain when the stories themselves want to employ the same narrative. Why, you yourself, Sibyl . . . didn't you make the same story of death for life out of your love for your children? Really, it's all too much to bear. The injustice of it all. But come quickly, there is much I want to show you . . .'

Barleycorn threw down the diseased flower and set off along the newly fecund Claremont Road until eventually we reached Broadfield Road. This was the road in which Belinda had paused in her flight from myself and Zero Clegg after the Vurtball match. Maybe Barleycorn had planned for me a trip through the real-world story as pictured in the dream. I was now containing most of my thoughts with the Dodo beetle, which was my secret haven within this dreamland. Barleycorn was now ringing the bell on one of the flower-wrapped houses in Broadfield. 'I do hope he's in,' he said. 'In this house lives one Octave Dodgson, the eighth cousin, eight times removed, of Charles Lutwidge Dodgson, one of your finer creators. I'm presuming you know of his talent?'

'I know of it,' I answered through the Shadow.

The door was opened by a white rabbit fully the same size as myself, who led us through to a living room where a young man was sitting cross-legged on a pile of cushions. I can only presume this was Octave Dodgson himself, twenty-seven and three-quarters old. He was heavily enraptured by the smoky kiss of the bubbling drugs that he sucked, with expert embouchure, through the mouthpiece of a raspberry-jam-stained hookah pipe. He made no comment as Barleycorn led me to the foot of a flight of stairs.

We ascended together to the landing where three different doors waited. From behind one of them came a sad song called *The Walrus and the Carpenter*. Of shoes and ships and sealing wax, sung in a young girl's voice but one so heavy with pain that the notes seemed to crack in the air. Barleycorn gently knocked upon the bedroom door and then opened it wide when the singing stopped. He stepped into the room and my Shadowy shape followed him through. The trapped air smelt of decay and sick breath.

'Yes? What is it?' Sad, brittle voice . . .

A young girl of sickly pale aspect, of lank blond hair and vomit-stained pinafore dress, of seven and a half years; she was lying on the bed playing feebly with a wind-up tortoise that had long since wound down. 'Barleycorn, what do you want now?' she whispered with cracked breath.

'I have brought a real person to see you,' Barleycorn answered. 'Her name is Sibyl Jones, and most desiring she is to converse with you.'

'Is that you, Alice?' I asked.

Alice could only cough and whimper. I'm sure she said something like Do-Do-Dodgson but there was a noise behind me then and when I turned to look, the white rabbit was standing on the threshold. He walked past me to the side of the bed, where, taking out a watch from his waistcoat-pocket, he picked up Alice's wrist and started to count out aloud her pulse-rate. 'How is she?' Barley-corn asked.

'Barely here at all, really,' the white rabbit answered. 'I'll say she's got a few days left . . .' The rabbit looked very sad to be saying this, and Barleycorn was equally worried.

'What's happening here?' I asked.

'Alice is dying,' John Barleycorn answered.

'Alice in Wonderland? But surely . . .'

'This is what happens when the dream withers.'

'You told me that the dream couldn't die.'

'A dream undreamt is a dying fantasy and nobody, it seems, these days, wants to dream about dear, sweet Alice. So you see, Sibyl Jones, this is a two-way mirror; the only way I can keep Alice alive is by transporting her to reality through the new map. Do you see now? You call the fever a disease, whereas, in reality, the fever is a salvation.'

Alice laughed, rather rudely, and then said, 'The way is cork-screwed.'

'The way is certainly troubled, dear Alice,' Barleycorn agreed, 'but can you not see now,' and with this he turned to face me once again, 'just how desperate my situation is, Sibyl?'

I myself, in my body of smoke, was at a loss as to how to respond. I saw before me a beloved *imaginary* companion of my early years dying for the lack of a dreaming pathway, and the poten-tial of this loss made me consider the times in my youth when I had been desperate for the dream to come into my body.

Barleycorn came up close to me, put his hands upon my shoul-ders, spoke to me very softly: 'You have shown great fortitude, Sibyl, for a human girl.' Now his hands were stroking at my shadowy breasts, trailing down to my stomach, and all the time his warm breath was close to my neck. 'You have excited a sad old boy in his weariness, but now, I'm afraid, the party draws to a close.' And the soft words were lulling, lulling. 'You must give yourself up to my caress . . .'

'You can't harm me,' I said, sleepily. 'I'm a Dodo in the Vurt. All pain is illusory.'

'Your daughter, also . . . must finally die.' Lulling, lulling . . . 'It's very simple. All Dodos must die. For the dream to live.'

'You can't touch me, Sir John. I'm a . . .'

His fingers played gently at my belly of smoke and then plunged through into the pit of the stomach where they closed around the black beetle of my Dodoness. He plucked the wriggling insect free from the stomach and brought it back through the Shadow-skin into the light. 'Is this your protection, my dear?' He waved the beetle in front of my face, laughing at me. 'I do believe, Sibyl . . . that you can now dream the infinite dream. Your daughter also.'

'No . . .'

'And therefore you are both open to my desire. Which is to bring death to you.'

'Leave her alone!' I was pleading for my daughter's life, of course, all of which had no effect upon Barleycorn. He stepped away from my body, holding the black insect by the tip of one leg, as though it could damage his dream-flesh. Part of myself still rested within the amputated beetle, and I gathered some small hope from the fact until the bad dreams started, as Barleycorn invaded my newly opened Shadow with his evil imaginings.

Dreams . . . I was dreaming dreams . . . real dreams . . .

I was swallowed by pain and blood and knives of thorn. I was riding a blond-carpeted horse through a thick patch of sharpened fog-pianos. I was falling into octopuses, invaded by umbrellas, skewered by trouser-glue, stretched to the edge of my skin's clock by stinging bicycles and the weather of fish.

So this is what it's like to dream. Barleycorn was killing me with strange fables, the very worst of all nightmares, and my Shadow started to shrivel from the intrusion. I wanted no more of it, and in the distance somewhere, somewhere distant, I could feel my Belinda protesting the same.

I was dwindling. Going out. Darkening. Dying . . .

You can't do this, Barleycorn, I called over what little remained of my Shadow. To which dismissal he merely laughed and waved the Dodo beetle some more to taunt me for my weakness. And to my small and fading Shadow I pledged then to harm the dream-master, if I could. I sent out a sliver of tight smoke that still rested in the beetle; a sliver of smoke that wrapped itself around Barleycorn's arm and then made a darting move to pluck the beetle from his grasp.

All the while the bad dreams were gathering in my soul, threatening to drag me under into a moth-coloured sea of chicken-magnets and the laughter of lobsterized Tuesdays.

I had the black beetle free now. My tendril of smoke curled around Barleycorn's body until it reached Alice on her sickbed. With no time for thinking I plunged my smoke deep into Alice's mouth, carrying the Dodo insect with me. She struggled a little. Just a little, almost like she was welcoming the end of her story.

Barleycorn gasped, and it was lovely to hear. A gasp from a dream.

The white rabbit cursed the very same story that had brought him this close to danger. He vanished through the doorway saying only this well-remembered saying: 'Oh dear! Oh dear! I shall be too late!'

Barleycorn closed on me. 'What are you doing?' His voice was edged with doubt.

'What does it look like?' I answered. 'I'm killing Alice in Wonderland, no less.' I shoved the beetle deeper, against Alice's weak protests, down through the tightness of her throat muscles until it was lodged in her stomach. 'Isn't this how you killed Coyote? Now your dear, sweet Alice will feel the same choking breath. With this Mooner's darkness inside of her, this dream will die. Isn't that what you want?'

'You can't do this,' Barleycorn swore, trying to get a grip of my Shadow with his fingers. My Shadow was stronger than dream-flesh now, aided by the Dodoness, and his fingers clutched around a mere trembling mist. All of his evil dreams were flittering inside my head like lost birds, scared by sudden weakness, failing to nest...

'All of this is unreal,' I said to him. 'This isn't Wonderland, and this isn't Alice. This world is just the dregs of your pathetic mind scrambling for sustenance.'

'No... Don't kill her.'

'Take me back, Barleycorn. Show me who she really is.'

Barleycorn waved his hands through the air and in half of a dreaming second we were back in the dining room. Rain was still falling. Barleycorn was back in his chair and I was sucked deep back into Belinda's body. Coyote was still enraptured with the meat in his mouth and Jewel was playing fisherman's knots with a rice-worm. Persephone was flattened on the table under my daughter's grasp. This girl of the flowers had played the part of Alice in Barleycorn's imagined Wonderland. Belinda had the girl by the throat with one hand, from the other hand streamed a river of Shadow-smoke that poured into Persephone's mouth.

Unbeknownst insect, pressed deep into the body of Persephone.

'Please...' John Barleycorn's voice; the first ever pleading.

'For the sake of your wife, Barleycorn.'

'Please... don't undream my love. She will die with that black creature...'

'For the sake of my child,' I said, quite coldly. 'For the sake of Coyote's child. For the sake of my city and my friends. For Zero

Clegg and for Karletta the puppygirl, and for the remembrance of
Tom Dove. I came here to battle against you, John Barleycorn, but
now I realise . . . I have come here to ask you to save us.'

A lifetime passing. And then, eventually . . .

'Do you know the saddest thing, Sibyl?' In a blue voice, tinged
with sorrow, Barleycorn was now resigned to the passing moment.

'Tell me the saddest thing,' I answered.

'I don't know if I'm alive or not.'

'I think that you are.'

'Of all the creatures around this table, you are the most alive.
You have proved that fact. Sometimes it gets so difficult . . .'

'I know.'

'To be only told.'

'I know.'

'To be a trail of smoke in the mind only.'

'Yes . . .'

'So this is human life, at its best? I wonder . . .'

I pushed the beetle even deeper into Persephone's stomach.
She struggled weakly against the planting. 'I could kill your wife with
this Dodo,' I said to Barleycorn. 'Isn't that right?'

Barleycorn came up to attack my Belinda's body, but Coyote
and the Jewel were now released from the trance. Barleycorn had
grown weak from the battle; with too much confusion and too
many stories to recollect, the dream-master was now letting loose
his prisoners. Coyote easily took a hold of the Barleycorn's body,
squeezing him between giant paws.

'Please . . . be gentle,' Barleycorn pleaded from his capture.
'What else can I offer?'

Persephone fell into slumber under the influence of the Dodo
beetle.

'A cure for Jewel?' I said.

'And for all the fellow sufferers, no doubt, you little worm?'

'You could do that?' I asked.

'Don't insult me.' His eyes blazing. 'I know when a story is complete. Please . . . give me that insect. I am tired, very tired of the waiting, and the dream grows cold around me. Let my wife go free.'

'You'll let me return? You'll stop the fever?'

'You would have to face Columbus. The King of Cabs won't be keen to give up his new map.'

'We'll do what is necessary.'

'It would mean keeping my wife from the real world.'

'She can't survive there, anyway, Barleycorn. You know that now.'

'I know that now. The Dodos are too strong.' He gazed longingly at Persephone. 'Of course, her mother will be very angry. Demeter . . . well, she wouldn't like her sweet Persephone to stay rooted in the mere dream. Demeter is very powerful, but also very stupid; she has a rather limited vision, I'm afraid. She likes the idea of her daughter making flowers in reality, despite the fact that reality will damage her daughter. That was the latest deal we made, you see. One-third of the year in Vurt, two-thirds in reality. You would have to fight Demeter as well as Columbus. You would have to persuade them both. Be prepared . . . there is only one way through the wood, and you have already taken it. I made your incoming trip rather easy, but returning . . . I wouldn't relish that battle myself. Without my help you would be stranded. Perhaps a deal can be struck?'

'Where is this Demeter?' I asked him. Persephone had fallen quite still under the Dodo's lingering presence.

'You make up the stories . . . and yet you don't know the stories,' Barleycorn continued. 'Demeter is everywhere, in all things green and cultivated; she lives in the dream and the dreamer. The Vurt and the real, both provide her with nourishment. She is stronger than I am. She is the Goddess of Corn. Why, even your dim-witted Christians still make hay for her, every harvest; tiny models they fashion. Quite, quite pathetic.'

'You would really cure Jewel?'

There's only one way that can happen. In reality he will die in two days' time.'

'Please, not that.'

'You would have to lose him, anyway. He has eaten, Coyote also. They are mine now. Really, my good woman, I do believe that we have reached stalemate in the game. In order for Jewel to survive, it would mean him staying here with me. Only in the dream could I cure such an advanced fever-case. And that would involve exchange rates.'

'Anything.' I pulled the black beetle of my Unbeknownst world free from Persephone's body. She stirred a little, and then more than a little. 'I will always reside within this insect, this virus,' I said. 'And you will never reach me there. Never. And whenever I need to fight against you, this beetle will always be willing to close you down.'

Barleycorn sighed, like the moon was blinding its eye. 'I was desiring of the real world.' His voice was a breathing whisper. 'Now I find myself as entrapped as always. Reality closes down around my struggle. I have lost the present game. The Dodo is too deep for my kiss. But, perhaps there is another way to make my entrance? A more and surer way? I am suddenly full of a certain desire. Can you believe that?'

'Go on.'

'May I fuck your daughter?'

'What?'

'Then I will grant you passage, as best I can. I'm sorry. Did I offend you, Sibyl? Please, give me that beetle.'

I handed the Dodo beetle to Barleycorn, who then opened his trousers, producing a sooty prick. A story being told, unfolding. John Barleycorn was bending Belinda over the table. His hands were reaching towards Jewel . . . digging deep. His cock was digging deep. Jewel was bursting his flesh into long tendrils of deep red blooms: Amaranthus Caudatus. A tropical flower. Barleycorn's dark voice:

'If I should take Jewel to my heart, I would have to give an item in return.'

'What would you give?'

'Oh, I would think of something.'

His cock entering me, entering Belinda, entering...

Saying good-bye to Jewel.

The bloom that never fades.

Barleycorn coming inside me, inside Belinda. Scorching time. We were being pushed through a cock of stone into a pool of stagnant green. Cupid pissing. The palace melting. John Barleycorn's hair rising in a swarm of blue. A dark passage; trees whispering words all around us as we ran along passages of fruit. The woods were alive. Pictures...

Lost in the knot garden. The moon was deadened by clouds. Darkness and sweat. Dripping shadows. The hedges were growing in strength around us, closing in like the hole between a woman's legs. The moon hidden. Darkness creeping. Coyote vanishing into the leaves.

'Coyote!' My voice. 'Don't get lost, Coyote.'

Fireflies and glow worms were leading the way through a lover's knot. A woman's anger was whispering at me from all corners and curves; the maze enclosing. My Shadow flexing. My daughter's map convulsing into new shapes, changing with each moment...

Barleycorn was...

...a way through the knot...

The map of Manchester on my daughter's head was turning into the map of the maze.

Barleycorn was helping us. I was reading the tangled passages as they filtered down through Belinda's body. 'This way, Coyote!' I called. 'Keep tight.'

And the hedges rushing by then, as I steered the party. Until ...until...

A gap in the wall. Through...

The black lake shimmering before our eyes. No sign of the boat or the boatman. Behind us the sound of branches thrashing the wind. The brass band striking up, far off, with a slow, stunted rendition of *Michael, Row Your Boat Ashore*.

'What now, Belinda?' Coyote asked.

I made my daughter walk a few steps, down into the cold, cold water.

'I think we swim it.'

'You don't say.'

'You got a choice, Coyote?'

A wicked grin on his teeth.

What a day it has been. What a day! Charon shivered. He was feeling well put upon. Standing as tall and as rake-like as he could manage, which wasn't easy in a softly lapping boat. Did people think this was an easy job or something? Ferryman on the Lake of Death ... maybe they should try it one day! He rattled the few coins he had managed to collect in the last week. He kept them in a pouch under his cowl. They made a tinny rattle. Pathetic! What was a poor Ferryman on the Lake of Death supposed to *live* on, these days? And yesterday he had ... No, he couldn't even *think* about it. That strange party. I mean, he'd had strange parties before. I mean, if they pay for this feather, well they were *entitled* to be strange. But not an obolus between them! Not a speck. That big spotty dog character. That naked girl with the maps and everything. That lump of ... of ... that lump of *stuff*! Clinging to the girl's shoulder it had been. And then clinging to the boat. Ughhh! Horrible. He had promptly commenced to tell them to go to Hell. No obolus, indeed. Hadn't even *heard* of the word. Disgraceful. And then ... and then ... that word from John Barleycorn ...

Behind Charon the band started to play.

What?

Charon turned, awkwardly, almost upsetting the boat. *Yes! At last. Somebody new arriving. Some passengers.* Because the band only struck up when visitors were expected. And what was that they were playing? Some new shit. Horrible racket. One of these days, he would row out to that island and . . . and . . . well, never mind that now. He turned back to the forest. Yes! He could hear Cerberus howling for his various doggy parts to come together. Somebody was expected. Lots of oboli, Charon hoped. Not like yesterday, when he had received word through from John Barleycorn himself: the next party go free. Free! Free passage! It was unheard of. This time that was *not* going to happen. This time Charon would be paid. He stood up, extra tall, extra thin. Menacing grimace. Cowl arranged just so. Perfect!

Oh please, oh please, oh please . . . let them get past Cerberus. Let them have cakes of flour and honey . . .

A noise from his back. Sounded like . . .

No!

He twisted around again, this time just a little too quickly. The boat rocked. What was this? Something on the water there, through the mist, something like a . . . sounded like a . . . his neck twisted this way and that, trying to get a better look. It looked like a boat out there. Like a fucking canoe, or something. 'Hey!' he shouted. 'This is my fucking Lake of Death. I have complete and utter exclusive rights to sailing this lake. Get the fuck off my lake!'

The boat just kept on coming. He could see it was a boat now, a fucking canoe. Black and white it was painted. Black dots on a white ground. And somebody in there, rowing towards his jetty. *His* jetty, mind. 'No way are you landing here!' he shouted. And then he saw who the solitary rower was. That girl! From yesterday morning. The one all naked and tattooed with maps. This was all too much. Altogether too much. A return trip she was making? Nobody made a . . .

'Hello, Charon,' the girl said, as she drew her boat up to the other side of his jetty. 'Give me a hand here.'

What? No way was he going to give her a hand. Let her fall in, for all he cared. But she had already jumped on to the boards, and now the . . .

Death-shit!

The boat was *climbing* out of the water. The two oars had clattered against the jetty. Charon watched in amazement as those oars sprouted woody fingers, like twigs, like claws! Big, strong hands of timber sprouting from the deck, clutching at the boards, lifting a heavy-trunked body out on to dry land. The body of that fucking dog from this morning, breaking itself free from the boat's shape. This really was altogether too much, and the ferryman stepped back as Coyote's grinning, spotted face came up close. 'Nice lake, Charon,' the dog said. 'A good ride.' And then a good push from a spotted paw, and the boatman was tumbling over, over the side into the water.

A small cache of oboli sinking into mud . . .

Time moving through a pine forest.

And then Cerberus was crouching in his glade of dung, howling back at the laughing moon, and then reaching down to bark at the party that stood just outside his clearing.

'This is my drop-off, Belinda,' Coyote said to us.

'What?'

'The ride's over.'

'Coyote?'

Cerberus snapped and growled at the air, plagued by a swirl-ing, tightening madness in each of his heads. But Coyote wasn't bothered by that show of dripping teeth. 'The time has come, sweetheart.' His rich breath was hot on Belinda's face. 'This spotty dog is dead already. I'm gonna *replace* this monster.'

'But . . .'

'No buts. No ifs. Just the road unwinding. You're taking it now? Picking up the fare?'

'I've got it,' Belinda answered. 'Picking up . . .'

A kiss then, from the flowery hound. Open-mouthed and longing, full of the taste of mint and flame. And Coyote was stepping forwards into the glade. Cerberus was coming down at him with fiery jaws. Coyote told that dog-head to go fuck his own dung. I could not bear to look, Belinda neither. The sound of claws digging into flesh as we slipped away into the forest.

Away. Streaming . . .

Into the forest, the black sheen of Coyote's cab seen through gaps between trees. The moon shining good for the map, pollen-bright. Finding the path now. Easy moving, keeping the Shadow cool in Belinda's body. A vicious barking from behind us. *Don't mess this up, daughter. Please. Keep walking.* A cool breeze was blowing through the leaves. Nice. Tender it was, that breath. Black cab was just ahead now. I could see a wing-mirror gleaming, the moon caught tight in its glassy embrace. Smooth. No problems. Just a few easy steps through this undergrowth, and then . . .

The pollen moon in the mirror was eclipsed.

Darkness, suddenly. Eyes blinded. *Please, no . . .*

The forest twisting root and branch around us, making a solid mesh. The cab was shut off from sight. The trees were closing above our heads. The moon dying away into sadness, and the world was only a tight clearing in the middle of a lowering wood. The leaves were wet and sulking, as though drenched by rain. But there was no rain in the forest, so that wetness must have been tears. The weeping wood. And I knew that pain, then, for what it was. A mother's pain. This forest was Persephone's mother. Demeter . . .

And then she spoke to me, that forest, in words made out of leaves: 'I will not allow this. Persephone is my only child. She is my life. She must have air. She must breathe again, the breath of earth. Do you hear me? Do you care to? You call yourself a mother, and yet you allow your children to die. What nature is this?'

The world growing smaller as the trees crept inwards until they were pressing sharp thorns into Belinda's flesh. Pain shooting into the Shadow.

This was no good. This was not what I wanted to happen.

'Belinda?'

A voice. A young voice of flowers. And some small pink buds growing on one of the branches, just over there, towards where the cab was waiting. Persephone's voice, it was. 'Belinda, this way, please,' the voice was saying. And then, 'Mummy, please.' Like she wanted to please everybody. The pink buds bursting open, accelerated; ruby red flowers growing amidst the tangled branches of Demeter. Love lies bleeding. 'Mummy, please, do this for me. I'll die if I go back to the real world.' Why was Persephone helping me? Why? Demeter's leaves were crackling in the wind, turning as golden as the moon, as though Autumn had come early, and then drifting down to the forest floor, the undergrowth. A mother's sad voice in the falling. A mother giving in to a daughter's wishes. Was that the sacrifice? Vibrant red flowers were opening until they filled Belinda's eyes with grains, and Belinda was just *blossoming* through that halo of petals, into the black cab, landing. I was not asking the why or the wherefore, I was just turning the key that Coyote had left in the ignition. A cold-hearted turn from the engine, spluttering into nothing. The key, again. *The key, the key.* The cab's innards as slow as death. There was no fire down there in the black bowels. No way home. Turning the key, turning . . .

Cold shivering. One dead engine. Through the windscreen I could see that the bonnet was all cracked open against the trunk of an oak tree. Busted. No deal from the black cab, no way through. My fists were banging against the steering wheel, as though by that method I could work the cab into life. Jesus, I had animated a dead daughter, couldn't I start a dead cab?

'Here, let me.' A voice from the seat beside me. And when I turned . . .

John Barleycorn was sitting in the passenger seat, holding the black Dodo beetle in one hand, his other working the car key with sooty fingers. 'I think I can manage it,' he said. His hair was dancing, slithering through the cab, touching at my face with soft whisperings.

I saw now clearly that his hair was made out of a thick swarm of flies, but their touch did not repulse me; I found in those soft wings a caress of saddened love.

'Why are you helping us?' I asked. 'You made Persephone and Coyote find a way through for us. Why? You wanted to kill me a few moments ago.'

The why and the wherefore of a nearly missed death.

'You'll find out,' Barleycorn replied. 'Exchange rates, Sibyl. The old road is closed to my sperm. This is my new way through to your world.'

'You've taken Jewel,' I said. 'What are you giving in return?'

'There is a feather-story told in ancient Africa, of how a young warrior wanted to take the chieftain's daughter for his bride. The chieftain told the warrior that first he must kill a lion bare-handed, only then could he take the daughter for his own.'

'What are you telling me?'

'The fever is the lion. You'll find out.' That same dumb answer. 'You've proven yourself worthy. Keep driving.'

'What?'

'Here you go . . .'

The black cab engine was stammering back to life as John Barleycorn leaned over to kiss me. That kiss had a thousand flavours. Death and life and green feathers, all mingled up together.

A noise then, from the passenger compartment of the cab. 'What the fuck is going on here, Barleycorn?'

Barleycorn broke off from the kiss, and then twisted around to view the new passenger. 'You're rather late for the party, my friend,' he said.

I also twisted around to see who was there.

Columbus . . .

'You promised me a new map, Barleycorn,' Columbus said. 'Now you're wanting to stop the fever.'

'Columbus, don't be angry.' Barleycorn's reply.

'Don't be angry? I've worked all of my life for this moment, and you're telling me not to be angry. I've not finished the new map yet. Maybe you're forgetting my power, Barleycorn. I control the ways between the worlds. And no way is this girl getting back to reality.'

'I need this woman to help me make the new world happen.'

Columbus laughed. 'This road is closed.' And then: 'What's that noise?'

I heard it too, a soft slithering through the air from all directions.

'Barleycorn, no!' screamed Columbus. 'Don't do this to me.'

And then all the windows of the black cab were broken as four bullets flew together towards a single target, high speed. All four of them pounded their way into Columbus's skull, the North, South, East and West of him. He screamed again, and then his head exploded. A crown of thorns. The black cab was blood-map-splattered.

'There you go, Columbus,' John Barleycorn whispered. 'Bullets coming home to roost. That's the end of your story. Excellent ending!'

'Did you make that happen, Barleycorn?' I asked.

'Why, it would take a very powerful creature to make that happen. What do you take me for?' He laughed then and leaned closer to me. 'Come visit me, Sibyl.'

'What about Jewel? And Coyote? How will they survive?'

'They'll survive. And when you're ready, so will you. Free passage. A taste of wine. You hear?'

'Give me back the insect.'

John Barleycorn fed the Dodo beetle back to my lips. I swallowed it whole.

Dreamless I was, once again. The fluttering in my stomach. Thankful for that.

The fight over.

And then the cab was moving into free space, under my Belinda's command. John Barleycorn vanished from the passenger seat. Only the hot breath of his dark-lipped mouth remained. I looked over to the forest one last time. The moon was a glistening droplet of pollen, and the black-hearted leaves were shaking against the edge of the garden, marked by the stone columns with their twinned angels, the boy and the dog. *Oh God!* I was receiving the message at last: exchange rates.

Of course . . . Belinda had taken *two* lovers.

Christ! How would I cope with it? How would Belinda cope?

I noticed a pack of Napalms on the dash. I stuck one in my mouth, lit it, read the pack message: SMOKING IS NOT GOOD FOR PREGNANT WOMEN, REPEAT, *NOT* GOOD—HIS MAJESTY'S MUTANT DAUGHTER.

Oh well, one last drag. Black cab gliding away towards home . . .

Home. Manchester. The new map turning into the old as I travelled backwards. The fever coming to rest against the edges of love. The black cab travelling into St Ann's Square where the people were already dancing on air at the lessening of the fever. Roberman was parked there, almost as though he was waiting for our return.

I climbed out of the cab inside Belinda's body and fell into the arms of the robodog driver.

'Belinda, you made it!' Roberman barked over the Shadow.

'Yeah,' Belinda sighed. 'We made it.'

Monday
28 August

Rise and fucking shine, prisoners! That's right, you guessed it. This is Radio Strangeways YaYa. In the living world it's 4.00 a.m. on a bleak, August morning, and the whole of Manchester is sleeping. Unfortunately, for us outlaws, it's time to leave our clotted beds. Wakey, wakey! This is Doctor Gumbo himself, at the feathery controls. Exercise time. Down to the yard-feather, you lot. Double quick. Boy, am I loving this! Wanita-Wanita, come close to me. Oh please, stop whining, you prisoners. We're here in the Vurt. All together and forever, in the feather. Pollen count is down to a sad 29, and still falling. This first record goes out to Chief Inspector Kracker over in dream-cell number nine. It's by The Move, and it's called *I Can Hear the Grass Grow*. Keep stretching, Vurtbirds. May the flowers of love come visit you. On visiting day. There ain't no such fucking day. Hah, hah, hah, hah, hah!

Autumn came early that year. By the end of August most of the trees had shed their leaves and the ground was hard and brittle with frost. Inspector Zulu Clegg left his desk at the Bottle Street cop station at 12.30, deciding to take an early lunch. He walked out into the cold air, bought a beef sandwich and a paper, and then went to sit at one of the benches in Albert Square.

He was the only person there, it being too cold for the usual lunchtime crowd.

Halfway through the sandwich, his mind nodding off in the middle of a story about how the new Safecabs were proving such a success, he heard footsteps approaching, cracking against the frost. The person sat down on the bench, some feet away from him, and, when he looked round, Clegg saw that it was a young woman.

She's looking back at him, smiling.

Clegg ignores her, returning to his paper.

'You're Inspector Clegg, aren't you?' the woman asks.

Clegg puts down his paper. 'Do I know you?' he asks, without looking round.

'I should hope so,' the woman replies. 'You tried to kill me once.'

'Did I?' Clegg had pointed a gun at many people in his time, and remembering every one of them was difficult, especially since his fever. 'What went wrong? Did I miss you?'

'No. I shot you first.'

'Oh.'

'In the shoulder.'

Clegg turns then to study the woman. 'Sibyl . . .'

'Her daughter.'

'Of course . . . erm . . .'

'Belinda.'

'That's right. Belinda. The memory's not up to much. I'm sorry.'

'Don't be. We only met once. And I had a shaved head then.'

'No, no. I don't mean that . . .'

'Oh, for trying to kill me? That was your job.'

'I'm sorry about Sibyl, I mean. Your mother . . . she . . .'

'Yes.'

'She was a good woman . . . I mean . . . a good cop.'

'She was both.'

'I was very sad to learn of her . . .'

'Suicide.'

'Yes. I was suffering from the fever at the time. I just wish I could have done something.'

'My mother was happy with her life. She'd done all that she could. I guess she wanted to leave it at that.'

Clegg looks away from the woman. One of the new Safecabs moves slowly along the road, its dull grey sheen smeared with ice.

The woman asks him how he's doing, and he replies that he's doing fine, fine, a desk job, which is, well, boring to be honest, but, otherwise, fine, fine . . .

'I'm pregnant,' the woman says. 'Twins.'

Clegg is suddenly embarrassed and he's not sure why. He looks back at the woman. He looks closely at her face, searching for traces of her mother in her features. He finds very little resemblance, except for . . .

'You have your mother's eyes,' he says, finally, which makes Belinda smile.

'You loved her, didn't you?' she asks. 'You loved my mother.'

It takes an age to answer. 'Yes. Yes, I did. Very much.'

'Thank you.'

'You're thanking me?'

'Well, I mustn't keep you.' Belinda stands up.

'You're right.' Clegg stands up. 'I should be getting back. The desk . . . beckons.'

Embarrassed once again, especially by the way he towers above her, Clegg wants to run for cover, but feels also the need to reach out for this woman.

Belinda saves him the trouble by touching him, gently, on the shoulder. His right shoulder. Where she had wounded him all those months ago.

Clegg turns away and then starts to walk back towards the station. Halfway across the square the woman calls out to him. At least, he assumes she had called out; it sounded like the word just *came* into his mind. 'Zero . . .'

Zero? Nobody had called him Zero, not since . . . not since Sibyl Jones . . .

He stops, turns around. The young woman is still standing by the bench, smiling. 'Take care,' she says. Clegg can't see her lips move, but maybe that's just a lingering symptom of his fever.

He turns once again, to shuffle over the frost back to his desk, his paper in one hand, a half-eaten sandwich in the other.